EVIDENCE

OTHER BOOKS AND AUDIO BOOKS
BY CLAIR M. POULSON:

I'll Find You

Relentless

Lost and Found

Conflict of Interest

Runaway

Coverup

Mirror Image

Blind Side

EVIDENCE

a novel

Clair M. Poulson

Covenant Communications, Inc.

Covenant

Cover image © Jupiter Images, Image Farm 22993368

Cover design copyrighted 2007 by Covenant Communications, Inc.

Published by Covenant Communications, Inc.
American Fork, Utah

Printed in Canada
First Printing: March 2007

11 10 09 08 07   10 9 8 7 6 5 4 3 2 1

ISBN 978-1-59811-252-8

To Wade, Ben, and Tyler.

My daughters are lucky they
found the three of you.

PROLOGUE

The door closed softly behind Bridget. For a moment Cody stood on her porch, savoring the lingering fragrance of her perfume. His hand still felt warm from holding hers the past few minutes. His face involuntarily creased into a smile as he turned to leave.

Before he had taken two steps, a heavy, metallic click abruptly turned him back.

"Are you still here?"

"Just leaving," Cody said sheepishly to the attractive face that peeked through the slightly open door. Bridget had gentle features framed by wavy, shoulder-length, light red hair.

She grinned, revealing a slight dimple at each corner of her mouth. "Thanks again, Cody. I had a great time tonight."

"Yeah, me too," he agreed wistfully. "But I better get going. I'm a little late tonight, and Dad will be wondering where I am."

"I'm sorry. It's my fault you're late. I talk too much," she declared with an apologetic smile.

"Not really. But hey, maybe we can go out again in a week or two. I'll give you a call."

"I'd like that," Bridget replied. The light from the porch lamp reflected magically off her grayish blue eyes as she smiled. Then, as the soft hair and pretty face withdrew, the door gently clicked shut.

Lifting a hand in farewell, Cody walked quickly down the long sidewalk, glancing at his watch. It was already twelve thirty. He would be late again, and his father didn't like that. It was several miles to the cattle ranch west of town where he lived with his widowed father and three younger sisters. His dad would be waiting up for him and wanting to know why he was late. The same thing had happened the last time he'd had a date with Bridget. But tonight he was even later than before.

Oh well, I'll do better next time, he promised himself as he hopped into his late mother's light green Buick, a grin plastered on his face. *What a girl! What a date!* This was actually his third with her, and he knew it wouldn't be the last. Not only was Bridget pretty as a summer sunrise, but she was smart, too, and as much fun as the Harrisville Days community carnival.

Still smiling, Cody slipped the key into the ignition. At that moment, something cold and hard touched the back of his neck, startling him out of his reverie.

"Don't look back or you die," a muffled voice said, sending chills racing down Cody's spine. "Just start it up and drive. I'll tell you where to go."

A tremor shook Cody's athletic body. *Is this a joke?* he wondered. The voice, though disguised, sounded vaguely familiar. His voice cracked when he asked, "What do you want?"

"Just shut up and drive."

Cody drove, and the cold steel gradually warmed as it remained pressed authoritatively against the back of his neck.

CHAPTER 1

Bridget Harrison awoke to the persistent ringing of the telephone. Someone else in the house apparently answered the phone, and during the ensuing silence she drifted into that strange world between wakefulness and sound sleep. Her father's voice called her back from her trancelike state.

"Bridget, you're wanted on the phone. It's Kyle Lind," he said.

An unexpected chill raised bumps on her bare arms as she slipped from bed and pulled her slippers on. Kyle Lind was Cody's father, a well-to-do cattle rancher. *What could he want?* Bridget wondered, squinting at the bright sunlight streaming through her window. A glance at the luminous green numbers on her alarm clock told her groggy mind that it was nearly six o'clock, almost six hours since she had reluctantly closed the door on Cody's handsome face.

Her father pressed the phone into her hand. He made no move to leave. Bridget's hands shook as she nervously brushed back her rumpled hair and pressed the receiver to her ear.

"Hello?" she said in a weak voice.

"Bridget?" Mr. Lind's voice seemed unusually strained.

"Yes?" Not as strained as hers! She could scarcely speak.

"I'm sorry to disturb you, but I'm trying to locate Cody. He didn't come home last night. He's never done anything like this before. You were with him last night, weren't you?"

For a moment, Bridget thought her heart had stopped. Her voice squeaked as she tried to speak. "Y-yes. Yes, but he brought me home just after midnight," she finally stammered. "I . . . I thought he was going straight home," she added after a slight hesitation, wondering where he could possibly have gone. "That's what he said he was doing."

"Well, he's not here, Bridget. I've driven all over town looking for him. I couldn't see the Buick anywhere."

Bridget's mother had joined her father in their daughter's bedroom. They both watched her with a questioning look. She clamped a trembling hand over the phone and explained. "Cody isn't home yet."

"But he brought you home just after midnight, didn't he?" Bridget's mother asked. "That was nearly six hours ago. He's a good boy. Surely he went straight home from here."

Bridget shook her head as the worried voice on the phone questioned, "Bridget, are you still there?"

"Yes. But . . . I . . . I don't understand. I don't know where he could be," Bridget mumbled helplessly, both to Mr. Lind and to her parents.

"Did he say anything about going somewhere after his date with you?" Mr. Lind asked.

"No, no, of course not." Now fully awake, she began thinking more clearly. "Like I said, he told me he was going home. He just said you expected him there by twelve thirty. He knew he was a little late, but not *that* late."

"Was he upset or angry or anything like that when he left you?"

"Oh, no, not at all," Bridget said, remembering Cody's smile as he stood watching her through the crack in the door just before she shut it for the second time.

"Were any of his friends around last night? Could he have gone somewhere with some of them after he dropped you off?"

"I guess he could have, but I don't remember seeing any of them after the movie. In fact, now I remember that Cody said something about having to be to work by eight this morning, that he didn't want to be late, and that you needed help with something before he went."

"That's right. He was going to help me sort some cattle at six. And he and that Enders fellow, Gil, were both supposed to be to work early to stock shelves before they opened the store at nine," Mr. Lind explained.

The mention of Gil Enders made Bridget bristle. In his midtwenties and still single, he had asked Bridget out at least a half dozen times, and each time she had politely refused. It was not just that he was a lot older than she was, but he was just, well . . . different. He always seemed to be watching her—no, more like *spying* on her—when he was around. Gil, whose given name was a mouthful—Gilbert Washington Enders—had been angry when Cody had asked her out and she'd accepted the first time. Cody had told her about the argument they'd had at the store over it. He'd explained to Gil that he, at seventeen, was only a year older than Bridget, while Gil was almost ten years older. But that hadn't fazed Gil. He'd raged that she had no right to turn him down and then go out with Cody.

That had been several weeks ago, and Cody said that the already tense working relationship between the two of them had steadily deteriorated since. It was no secret that Gil was conceited, and he seemed to resent the way customers at the hardware store walked right past him, flocking instead to Cody for assistance. Bridget figured that a lot of Gil's problems stemmed from his brusque manner with customers. It contrasted greatly with Cody's ready smile as he offered help. Bridget knew she wasn't alone in enjoying Cody's company. His winsome personality drew people to him.

"Well, thanks, Bridget," Mr. Lind was saying. "If you hear anything . . ."

"I'll let you know right away," she offered lamely when his voice trailed off.

Bridget stood holding the receiver long after the connection was broken. Her father finally took it gently from her hand. "You might as well try to sleep a little longer, Bridget," he suggested. "There's nothing you can do. Anyway, Cody probably ran into some of his buddies and—"

"He's not like that, Dad," she interrupted, speaking a little louder than she had planned, even as doubts began to gather in her mind. After all, she didn't know Cody that well, since he was a year ahead of her in school and lived in a different ward. Then again, his sister Candi was Bridget's best friend. And if anybody could point out his faults, surely it would be his own sister, and she had mostly good to say about her brother.

Bridget's mother took her hand and said, "Don't worry, sweetheart. He'll be home soon. He probably met some of his friends after he left you here and then the time just got away from them."

"No, he was going straight home, Mom. I know he was. He was already a little late and he was nervous about it." Then, as her uncertainty increased, she said in a small voice, "Dad, would you mind . . . I mean, could we go out and just look around a little?"

"I don't think that would help," he said.

"Please."

"Why don't you, Houston?" her mother asked, coming to Bridget's aid. "It can't hurt."

"Well, all right," he replied gruffly. "We're wide awake now anyway, and it's Saturday, so I don't have to go to work this morning."

Bridget's concern escalated after several minutes of driving around town. Even though it was Saturday, the town was already emerging from its weekend drowsiness, and several cars were on the streets. After a few minutes, they passed Kyle Lind. Then they saw Police Chief Ron Worthlin, who waved at Bridget and her father as they drove by him. A few minutes later, even Sheriff Vince Hanks appeared. Bridget had a feeling they were all looking for Cody, and it frightened her.

It was a warm morning, humid after the previous day's late-May rainstorm. After an hour, Houston pulled into the parking lot of Harry's Hardware, where several cars had gathered. Bridget stood wringing her hands while her father spoke with Cody's father, the police chief, and the county sheriff.

"This is not like Cody, Sheriff," Bridget heard Kyle Lind say. "He's never done anything like this before. Something is wrong . . . very wrong."

"We'll keep looking, Kyle. You go on home. Your girls need you. We'll keep you informed," the sheriff said.

"Maybe in a few minutes. The girls are all right for a little while," Kyle said. "They were still asleep when I left the house."

"But what if Cody shows up at home?" the sheriff asked. "We wouldn't know it."

"I left a note on the front door," Kyle replied. "I told him to call my cell phone the moment he got in. And he'll do that if—" His voice choked and he couldn't go on.

Watching and listening to him caused fresh tears to sting Bridget's eyes and roll down her cheeks. The more Cody's dad worried, the more she did. She looked away from Mr. Lind's stricken face when a couple of highway patrol troopers pulled into the parking lot, followed closely by one of Chief Worthlin's officers. A minute later, a tan GMC pickup with the sheriff's star on the door parked next to the sheriff. Bridget recognized the county's only female deputy, Kara Smith, a tall brunette in her midtwenties.

Bridget's father talked to the officers for a few more minutes while Bridget remained velcroed to the side of the car. As the gravity of the situation became more and more apparent, she found herself wiping her eyes frequently. She couldn't believe this terrible thing was happening in her peaceful little town.

Kara Smith suddenly left the group of officers and walked over to Bridget. "Your dad said you had a date with Cody last night?"

Bridget nodded, trying to smile but failing miserably.

"Lucky girl. He's a cute guy. I've often thought it was too bad that I'm too old for him," Kara said, her eyes twinkling in a teasing way.

That finally brought a tiny smile to Bridget's face. But it didn't last long. "Do you think he's okay?" she asked.

"I'm sure he is. There's a logical explanation to this. We just don't know what it is yet. But we will," Kara assured her.

The confidence in her voice gave Bridget more hope, and she said, "Yeah, I'm sure he's okay."

But as soon as Kara rejoined the other adults, that confidence faded, and Bridget closed her eyes and offered a short prayer, praying with all her heart that Cody was okay. A moment later, her father rejoined her. As they climbed back into the car, he sighed. "I wish we could do something," he said. "Poor Kyle's beside himself with worry. After losing his wife six months ago, I just don't know if he can cope with another tragedy."

Bridget trembled at the word *tragedy*. Ice seemed to have replaced the blood in her hands and face. Surely there wouldn't be another tragedy. It was unthinkable that something bad might have happened to Cody. It just wasn't possible! Things like that didn't happen in their town.

But as Bridget thought about Cody's mother, she had to admit that it was possible. Ellen Lind had been very active in both the community and the Church before her untimely death at the age of forty. Ellen had been serving as the stake Young Women president at the time of her death, and every girl in the stake had not only looked up to her, but also mourned deeply at her passing. She'd been especially close to Bridget because of Bridget's friendship with her daughter Candi. It had come as a total shock to both Bridget and the community when Ellen was diagnosed with cancer a week before Halloween. And it had been an even bigger shock when she died just a few weeks later, the day before Thanksgiving. Sister Lind's death had been a blow to everyone who knew her.

But it had been hardest on Kyle, who'd been left to raise Cody and his three younger sisters alone. Candice, better known as Candi, was the oldest of the girls. She and Bridget were only a few weeks apart in age, both sixteen. Candi had assumed much of the responsibility for the two little girls, and Kyle paid a woman to come in and clean three days a week. He had also been grateful for the help of his only nephew, Jake Garrett, who had taken time off from his job in Arizona to help out for a few weeks. Candi had mentioned what a big help Jake had been during those first difficult weeks. She'd also told Bridget that Jake had refused to let Kyle pay him a dime for the time he'd spent helping the devastated little family.

"We might as well go home," Houston said after driving up Main Street in one more fruitless search. "I'm sure he'll show up soon."

But he didn't, and Bridget—as well as most of the community— grew more distraught with each passing hour.

CHAPTER 2

Saturday was heartbreaking for all of Harrisville, Utah, and the surrounding area. There seemed to be little doubt that something tragic had happened to young Cody Lind.

Sheriff Vince Hanks called out his search-and-rescue team late that morning, and they were joined by hundreds of community volunteers in a massive hunt for Cody and the light green Buick that had been his mother's. Neighboring counties were alerted and joined the search. When no sign of the car or the young man was found by early afternoon, an all-points bulletin was issued statewide and even in the surrounding states.

All the effort was in vain. It appeared that Cody Lind and the car he was driving had simply vanished. Emotions ran high in the community, and theories about what had happened to Cody were abundant. The sheriff patiently listened to many of the ideas, absurd though some of them were.

The most recent theory had come in the late afternoon from a man Sheriff Hanks knew as one of the least reliable sources in town— Sammy Shirts. Sammy considered himself an expert in many areas. In the sheriff's mind, however, Sammy was an expert at very little, especially anything that even remotely resembled work. Various things could be said about Sammy's skills, none of which was complimentary. One was that he was an expert at milking the system. He was also very good at letting other people know what they were doing wrong, although rarely adding any useful suggestions as to how things might be done better. Many, including the sheriff himself, suspected that Sammy was a thief. If he was, he did indeed have one area of expertise, because he'd never been caught.

"Sheriff," Sammy began in his slow, exaggerated drawl, "I talked to Chief Worthlin, but he said I'd better come see you."

Sheriff Hanks nodded, knowing he had more pressing issues to face and wondering how to politely get rid of Sammy as quickly as possible. "Well, if you've talked to the chief, that's probably sufficient," he replied.

Sammy's face darkened. "The chief says yer in charge 'cause the Lind kid lives out of town, out in the county. So I gotta talk to you."

"Yes, I suppose that's right, but Chief Worthlin and I work very closely on things like this. He'll let me know if there's something I need to—"

"I gotta tell you, Sheriff," Sammy interrupted. "Yer wasting yer time looking for him."

Listen to you, the sheriff thought wryly. *Wasting time is another thing at which you are skilled, Sammy Shirts.* But Sheriff Hanks simply said, "I am?"

"Yup. The kid's not in the county no more. Yer rescue people and everybody else just as well go home, and all them cops that's floatin' 'round out there too."

"Sammy, we can't do that. We're covering every possibility we can think of. We're still in the early stages of this investigation. We've got to keep trying."

"I tell you he's not around here no more," Sammy insisted.

The sheriff wiped the perspiration from his forehead. Sammy sounded serious. Perhaps he knew something after all. "What makes you say that, Sammy?" he asked, showing more interest now.

"Well, that kid's not worth a sack of wet salt. Shifty, that's what he is. He just up and run off, that's all. He's out of state by now, spendin' his ole man's money and havin' a great time," Sammy said confidently.

Perhaps he didn't know anything after all, Sheriff Hanks decided. "Now, Mr. Shirts, you're just guessing, and we can do that ourselves. Thanks for coming in, just the same."

"You better listen to me," Sammy insisted. "The kid has a lot of people fooled, but not me. He's plain no good."

"Now listen here," the sheriff said, growing impatient. "I know that boy very well, and his dad, too. There's not a more reliable young man in the county. I just can't see him running off like you say, especially with his mother having so recently died and three little sisters to help with. Cody's just not that type."

Sammy snorted, his ruddy face darkening even more. "He's just a twerp—a spoiled kid. Ain't nothin' happened to him. You just as well forget about him. He'll come home when he runs outta money." Sammy stood up.

"Sit down!" the sheriff ordered, the law officer in him suddenly on alert. It was not so much what Sammy had said but more the way he'd said it. Sammy was the first person to have said anything derogatory about Cody to the sheriff, and his eyes burned with what appeared to be intense dislike—or worse. Sheriff Hanks's instincts told him this was something he shouldn't ignore.

Sammy smirked and sat. "Whatever you say, Vince, old pal."

Sheriff Hanks bristled inwardly. The way Sammy said his first name was offensive. Many people called him Vince, but Sammy made it sound demeaning—like an insult. The sheriff swallowed hard, wiped his brow again, and leaned forward. "Why don't you like Cody Lind, Mr. Shirts?" he asked in a hard voice. "Surely you must have a reason."

Sammy hesitated just long enough to make the sheriff's unease swell. "Nothing, 'cept what I've heard, Vince. And of course, there's that shifty look in his eyes."

The sheriff leaned still farther across his desk. Emphasizing each word, he said, "That's not good enough, Sammy. If you expect me to take you seriously, you better come clean."

"What's that mean?" Sammy thundered, rising to his feet again.

The sheriff rose too. "Calm down," he said, thinking quickly. "I just figured the kid must have done something to you, or said something—something he shouldn't have."

There was a distinct hesitation again, and then Sammy declared, "Nope, he's just no good, Sheriff, that's all. I gotta go now." He turned toward the door.

Sheriff Hanks moved quickly around his desk and stepped in front of Sammy. "Hold on, Sammy. Let's talk about this. If I've misjudged the boy, I need to know it, but I need more to go on than 'shifty eyes.' If I don't know Cody as well as I thought I did, then maybe I need to redirect my efforts."

Sammy smirked again. "You just pay attention, Sheriff. He's run away, and that's all there is to it."

"You mentioned something about the kid running out of money and coming home. I don't suppose he'd have had a lot on him, do you? I'm sure he doesn't make much at Harry's Hardware after school and on Saturdays."

"His old man's got a bunch, and you know it, Sheriff. The kid don't need to work. Kyle just makes him, probably to keep him out of his hair. He knows his kid ain't good for much."

The sheriff swallowed hard, working to control his anger. He was certain he detected jealousy in Sammy's voice, but why? It was true that Kyle Lind was well off. At least the townsfolk figured he was, although Ellen's medical bills must have cost him quite a bit. Kyle himself had told the sheriff that Cody wanted to work more for the experience than for the money. He was that kind of young man. But the sheriff said none of that to Sammy.

Sammy went on. "That ranch of Kyle's is a nice one. And I hear tell he's got the best herd of cows in the county. Always driving new cars and trucks."

Definitely envy. Just how deep does it run? the sheriff wondered with mounting suspicion. "Sit down, Sammy," he invited, waving at the chair Sammy had vacated. "You may be on to something here." Although the sheriff knew better, he also knew it wouldn't hurt to try to draw out more information from Sammy.

"I gotta get," Sammy responded, turning away again. "I said all I gotta say."

"Before you go, I have a couple more questions, Sammy. When was the last time you saw Cody?" he asked.

Sammy glowered at him. "Don't remember," he said, and he stormed from the office.

Sheriff Hanks sat down, and with his head resting on his hand, he considered Sammy Shirts. His surname was actually Shurtliff, at least originally. Rumor had it that Sammy's father couldn't spell the name and changed it to something he could spell—Shirts. Whether or not it was a legal change was debatable.

Sammy came from a long line of good, strong pioneer stock. Haskill Shurtliff, an ancestor, settled in Harrisville in 1851. He was followed a short time later by the hardworking Luman Shurtliff and his son Noah, who made red brick by hand in the early days of the community. Somewhere along the line of progeny, hard work was eschewed in favor of hard living. Sammy fit into the latter category.

As the sheriff let his mind run with his thoughts for a moment, he realized there was more to Sammy's dislike for Cody than just Kyle's money. The question was, what was it? He reached for the phone. "Sheriff Hanks here," he announced when the call went through. "I need to chat with Chief Worthlin."

"I'm sorry, Sheriff. He's not in. Would you like me to have him call you when he gets back? Or I could radio him and have him swing by when he can."

Obviously the chief's secretary is getting some weekend overtime, Sheriff Hanks thought grimly as he heard her voice.

"Please do. Either one. Or better yet, does he have his cell phone with him?"

"Probably. He usually does. Do you have the number?"

"I do. Thanks, I'll give him a call."

The sheriff replaced the receiver just as his receptionist's voice came over the telephone intercom. "Sheriff, Gil Enders would like to see you."

"First Sammy, then Gil. And this is Saturday," the sheriff mumbled to himself. Then he instructed her to send Gil back.

A moment later Gil stepped through the office door, wearing a blue shirt that read *Harry's Hardware* in bright gold lettering over the left pocket.

The sheriff stood, stepped around his desk, and extended his right hand. "Hello, Gil. What can I do for you?"

"Keep your deputies away from me!" Gil demanded loudly, ignoring the sheriff's outstretched hand.

Taken aback, the sheriff began, "What are you—"

"I don't know anything about where Cody Lind is! And I don't care, either. He's nothing but a spoiled, bratty kid anyway. And I don't like having some hotshot cop coming around asking a lot of nosy questions."

"Now Gil, you've got to understand, this is serious business, and Chief Worthlin and I have assigned officers to speak to anyone who is associated with Cody in any way. We're just searching for clues. We've got to find him," Sheriff Hanks explained slowly, hoping his calm would rub off on Gil.

It didn't. After only a moment's hesitation, Gil snapped, "If I knew something, I'd say so, but I don't. And I don't appreciate your sending people around asking insulting questions!"

The sheriff took a deep breath and then exhaled slowly. "They weren't meant to be insulting. And I'm sorry you're offended, Gil, but we must check with anyone who could possibly shed any light on this situation. You work with Cody, and because of that, I hoped you could tell us something. You know, something he might have said, or someone who might have been in the store and talked to him that seemed unusual. Anything, really, that might help point us in the right direction."

"Work with him?" Gil exploded. "He's been trying to get me fired ever since Harry hired him. I wouldn't call that working with him. We have the same employer, but that's where it ends."

"He tried to get you fired?" the sheriff asked, careful to mask his sudden suspicion. "Sit down, Gil, and tell me more."

Gil's face turned purple and he shouted, "I had nothing to do with his disappearance if that's what you're thinking! Just leave me alone, and keep your people out of my face!" He turned and stomped out the door.

Sheriff Hanks sat down with a sigh. *And I thought the kid couldn't possibly have any enemies,* he reflected. Gil Enders had not said a single word at a reasonable decibel. That worried him, and he thought for a minute about Gil Enders. It was quite clear that Gil disliked Cody. As with Sammy, he suspected that Gil was jealous. Even more, he couldn't help but wonder if Gil's irrational behavior could have been partially provoked by guilt. One thing he did know was that both Sammy and Gil worried him a lot.

The sheriff reached for the phone again. But before he'd punched in the chief's cell phone number, Deputy Kara Smith walked in. The sheriff held no romantic notions about her—after all, he was a very happily married man—but he had noticed that Kara was unusually graceful. How anyone, especially a young single fellow like Gil Enders, could be offended by Kara was beyond him. She possessed a self-confident manner that helped put others at ease, and she was polite and genuine almost to a fault. Tall and willowy, with shoulder-length brown hair framing her face, she was an attractive young woman. Kara was also the youngest daughter of the previous sheriff, Sheriff Hanks's former boss, and as she'd told him when he had interviewed her for the job, law enforcement was in her blood. She was an excellent officer, as her father had been.

"Thought I'd see what else you needed me to do," she said.

"Have a seat, Kara. Anything of interest turn up yet?" he asked as she lowered herself gracefully into a chair. Even in a gray and black uniform with a 9mm handgun and handcuffs on her hips, she looked deceptively meek. In reality, Kara Smith was as tough as rawhide when she needed to be. When on duty, she was thoroughly professional.

"Not really," she answered. "I'm sorry, Sheriff. People are concerned, though. I just haven't found anyone who saw anything relating to Cody's disappearance." She paused, blinked, and then said hesitantly, "Actually, not everyone's been real nice."

The sheriff leaned back in his chair and asked, anticipating her answer, "Like Gil Enders?"

"I'm sure it doesn't mean anything, but he seemed real nervous when I spoke with him. In fact, he got quite angry with me."

A smile creased the sheriff's tired, leathery face. "I know."

"Did he complain?" she asked, instantly angry. "I was polite with him, but—"

Sheriff Hanks raised a hand, and Kara stopped. "Seems a little strange, I know, but yes, he came in. He doesn't like young Cody at all. Also doesn't like being questioned. And he seemed unusually nervous to me, too. That only raises more questions, wouldn't you agree?"

"I guess so, but he surely wouldn't have had anything to do with—"

The sheriff cut her off again. "In our business, we should never assume what someone would or would not do, Deputy," he said sternly. "Something happened to Cody Lind last night. We can't rule anything out at this point—or anyone."

"Of course," Kara said softly.

"Where was Gil last night?" the sheriff asked.

"At his apartment, I guess. He really wasn't very cooperative when I tried to talk with him, and he didn't exactly say that was where he was all night, but I guess . . . well, I assumed . . . She cut herself off, smiling sheepishly as the sheriff frowned. "I know I should never assume," she said. "Dad always told me that."

"And your father was right. Find out, would you please? And while you're at it, speak with Harry and see if Cody has ever tried to get Gil fired."

"Gil said that?"

"He did."

"Wow, I didn't think anyone had hard feelings against Cody. He's so polite whenever you go into Harry's Hardware," she said, genuinely surprised.

"I didn't either, Kara, but I've had my eyes opened. Sammy Shirts came in, too."

"What did he want? I'm surprised he had the ambition to bother, even if he'd seen anything or knew something," Kara said.

"Seems he doesn't care for our missing boy either."

"What?" Kara exclaimed, her face stiffening. "Maybe something bad—you know, something terrible—has happened to Cody."

"I hope not, Kara, but we can't rule out the possibility. I'll see what the chief knows about Sammy's dislike for Cody. Maybe Cody caught Sammy trying to steal something in the store."

"Sammy must do *something* for a living," Kara said in disgust. "He doesn't work, that's for sure. Must be on welfare. But I'll bet he has other sources of revenue as well."

"We all suspect Sammy of dishonesty," the sheriff replied. "But we can't prove it. And right now, we have more important things to do."

"You're right, Sheriff. I'll get back to work then—unless you need me to do something else, maybe in another part of the county or something."

"No, I have some of the other deputies out talking to people all over the county. I need you to stay around here and keep an eye on things. Just make sure you check up on Gil for me and let me know what you find out about his whereabouts last night," Sheriff Hanks said. "In the meantime, I need to speak with Chief Worthlin. Then I'm going to run over and talk to that little Harrison gal. Maybe she's remembered something by now that might help us. Poor kid. She's sure upset."

CHAPTER 3

"That was as close as I've ever come to arresting Sammy Shirts," the police chief said pensively as he and Chief Worthlin discussed the case at the police office. "Cody almost had him dead to rights, but when Sammy denied it so emphatically, Harry backed down and told me to forget it. It was a fairly minor loss, just a set of drill bits. It should have been recorded, but the camera that would have picked it up had malfunctioned. Harry decided that it wasn't worth pursuing, that he didn't want any trouble. You know how vindictive Sammy can be. Anyway, Harry said he would keep a closer eye on Sammy when he came into the store in the future."

Sheriff Hanks sat back, a grim look on his face. "Would a man, especially a lazy one like Sammy Shirts, hurt or even kill someone— and I think we can't afford to rule out that possibility in this case— over being accused of stealing a thirty-dollar set of drill bits?" he asked.

"Who knows, Vince? To a rational person, that seems absurd, but you and I have both met enough irrational, warped people to know that anything is possible," Chief Worthlin responded.

"Harry believed Cody, didn't he, Ron?"

"Oh, yeah, for sure. He thinks the world of Cody," the chief answered. "Harry just decided Sammy might be more trouble if he prosecuted him. And when it came down to Sammy's word against Cody's, he decided it wasn't worth a court battle over some drill bits. He said he was thinking as much about what it might put Cody through as anything else. I talked to Cody later. He said he'd only told Harry about seeing Sammy commit the theft because Harry had made a big deal out of watching him whenever he came in the store."

"I see, so Harry had previously suspected Sammy?" the sheriff asked.

"That's right."

"I think we'd better keep an eye on Sammy until we find Cody. I know it stretches the imagination to consider him a suspect in something this serious, but he definitely dislikes the boy," the sheriff said as he rose to his feet. "Who knows what might be going on in the dimness of Sammy's mind."

* * *

Sheriff Hanks parked his unmarked car in front of the Harrison residence right where Bridget had told him Cody had parked when he brought her home. He examined the sidewalk and street in the vicinity of his car, looking for anything out of place, anything unusual—any kind of clue. The normal street detritus was present—small pebbles and rocks, flattened coins, bits and pieces of paper, tree pollen, pop-can pull tabs, a few cigarette butts, and particles of different kinds of food. An average assortment. He walked up the long walk that Cody had walked down a few minutes past midnight after leaving Bridget at the door. From the porch he could not see the front end of his car, which was hidden by a hedge of tall lilac bushes. He stared thoughtfully at the bushes for a moment before ringing the doorbell.

Bridget answered it. "Sheriff Hanks, come in. Have you found Cody?" she asked anxiously.

"No, I'm afraid not, Bridget. A few things have come up, and I just need to ask you some questions," he said gently.

Her face paled, but she said, "Please sit down. I'll try to answer your questions. I . . . I just don't know much. I wish he'd come home and be okay," she went on, her gray-blue eyes clouding over as she spoke.

The sheriff waited until Bridget sank onto the sofa before pulling up a hard-backed chair and facing her. He wasted no time on meaningless small talk. "How well do you know Gil Enders, Bridget?"

In his years as a lawman the sheriff had learned to watch people's faces when he questioned them. Many times, more could be learned from their expressions than from their answers. "Not very well," she said in a shaky voice, but her face told him there was something bothering her.

"Bridget, have you ever talked to him?" he pressed.

"Yes, but not very often. I've run into him at the store a few times," she said evasively.

"What have you talked with him about?"

"Nothing much. He's . . . you know, asked me out and stuff," she explained with lowered eyes.

That sparked the sheriff's interest. "Did you ever go out with him?"

"Oh, no," she said quickly.

"Why not?"

"He's a lot older than me."

"Is that the only reason?"

"Well . . . no, I guess not. He's really not the kind of guy I want to go out with." She looked up. "Why are you asking about Gil, Sheriff?"

Now it was his turn to be evasive. "We're trying to learn all we can about people Cody was around a lot."

Although it was a poor answer, it seemed to satisfy Bridget. "Oh, I see. What else did you want to know?" she asked. She was looking him in the eye now, and he was saddened to see how red her eyes were.

"Bridget, what is it about Gil that makes him the kind of person you don't want to date?" the sheriff asked. "I mean, is there something specific about him that really bothers you?"

"I don't like to say anything bad about people," she responded, lowering her eyes again and brushing absently at her light red hair.

"All I want are your reasons, Bridget. If they cast a bad light on Gil, then that's just the way it goes. Remember, the object here is to find Cody."

"I know. Well, Gil seems kind of strange. I don't like the way he always stares at me. And it bothers me that he treats Cody like dirt."

"What do you mean by that?" the sheriff asked. Now he was getting somewhere.

"For one thing, he got really mad the first time Cody asked me out and I accepted. Sheriff, Gil wouldn't do anything to Cody, would he?" Bridget questioned anxiously.

"I don't know. I hope not, but it appears that he didn't like Cody. Bridget, how many times did Gil ask you out?"

"I don't know. Six or seven, at least. Maybe more."

"Had you ever turned Cody down before you went out with him the first time?"

"Oh, no, I'd never turn Cody down," she answered, and her face went scarlet at the admission.

"I don't blame you. He's a fine boy," Vince said, trying to soothe her embarrassment. "So it made Gil mad. Did he threaten Cody in any way?"

Bridget thought for a minute. "No, I don't think so. Cody said Gil just swore at him and stuff. That's another reason I don't want to date him—his language."

"And I don't blame you. Now let me get this straight. Do you believe that Gil seemed to feel he should be able to go out with you but that Cody shouldn't?" Sheriff Hanks asked.

"Yes, I guess so. He told Cody he had no right to ask me out when he knew Gil . . . well, you know, liked me," she said, and again she turned red.

"Was there anything else that you can think of that might have made Gil angry with Cody, Bridget?"

She shook her head. "No. We didn't talk about Gil except for what I've told you."

"All right. Have you been able to think of anything else that might explain why Cody didn't come home last night?" the sheriff asked.

Again she shook her head, and Sheriff Hanks got to his feet. "Well, I guess that's about it. I'll let myself out, Bridget. Thank you, and remember, if you think of anything, call me. I don't care what time of the day or night it is," he said.

"All right," she answered, her eyes downcast again.

"And Bridget, it would be best if you don't talk about what you and I have discussed concerning Gil. Fair enough?"

"Okay," she said, and he walked out the front door.

As he strolled down the long walk, Sheriff Hanks thought about what he had just learned. For Gil to have been turned down time after time by Bridget and continue to ask her out anyway indicated that he must have a very strong attraction to her—maybe even an obsession. And knowing of Gil's inflated ego, he thought that it must have been a serious blow to his self-esteem when Cody succeeded with Bridget where he'd failed. Perhaps, the sheriff thought, the fact that Cody had disappeared after his date with Bridget elevated Gil to the top of his list of persons of interest in the case. He would have to dig deeper into Gil's past and keep a very close eye on him.

* * *

Sheriff Hanks's young deputy, Kara Smith, was also having a conversation about Gil Enders. Harry Reynolds, the owner of Harry's Hardware, had closed up shop before she arrived back at the store, and she found him a few minutes later at his home.

At first, Harry had been reluctant to talk about Gil Enders and had kept trying to steer the conversation back to Cody. It was readily apparent that he thought very highly of Cody and that he was deeply concerned about Cody's disappearance.

Finally, after Kara had spoken frankly, informing Harry of Gil's intense dislike for Cody, Harry had consented to discuss Gil. Kara also told Harry how angry Gil had been when she'd questioned him earlier that afternoon.

"That sounds like Gil," Harry agreed.

"He also voiced a particular dislike for Cody when he talked to the sheriff," Kara disclosed.

"Yes, I guess there are some bad feelings there."

"Tell me about it," she urged.

"Not much to tell, Deputy. Gil's efficient and works fairly hard, but he's a little brusque with the public. When Cody started working after school, people just naturally sought him out, it seems. He's such a pleasant young man. I think Gil resents that."

"Is that all?"

"Just about."

Kara shifted in her seat to prevent her sidearm from digging into her hip. After she had found a comfortable position again, she asked, "Mr. Reynolds, did Cody ever try to get you to fire Gil?"

"Good heavens, young lady, of course not. Cody was not . . . is not . . . that kind of person. Anyway, I don't believe Gil ever did anything to warrant me doing such a thing," Harry said.

His surprise seemed genuine, but Kara pursued the matter further. "Did Gil ever say anything to you that might have indicated that he thought Cody wanted him fired?"

"I can't imagine what. Why do you ask, Deputy Smith?"

"Gil accused Cody of that when he spoke to the sheriff."

"Oh, my goodness. I can't imagine that. Maybe I'd better talk to Gil and straighten it out."

"Don't talk to him on my account," Kara said quickly.

"I won't, but I will on my own account. Maybe I don't know Gil as well as I thought I did. You don't think he could have had anything to do with Cody's disappearance, do you?" Harry asked incredulously.

"We're just trying to learn anything—even something that might seem insignificant—that could shed some light on what has happened to Cody," Kara explained, avoiding a direct answer. "But I think it would be best if you didn't mention our conversation to Gil at all. We're quite interested in his recent activities. Not that we necessarily suspect him of anything, but we also can't rule anything out at this point."

"Well, I really would be shocked if Gil did anything to Cody. I honestly don't believe Gil is capable of violence. I think you're wasting your time worrying about him, but I do wish you luck in finding young Cody. I feel so bad for his family," Harry said, shaking his head sadly. "Poor Kyle. What a blow this must be after losing his Ellen just last fall."

* * *

A long, fruitless weekend passed. The general mood in Harrisville was one of sadness and concern. Special prayers were offered in every ward in town, and many people fasted for Cody and his family. Kyle Lind made it to church, but he didn't stay for all the meetings. After returning home, he was ill with worry. When the girls got home, Candi was so worried about her father that she called Dr. Odell at home. He agreed to come right out and take a look at Kyle.

Dr. Marshal Odell was just three years older than Kyle, and they'd known each other all their lives. For several months the doctor had even dated Ellen, the woman Kyle later married. Dr. Odell eventually married a beautiful woman he met in medical school, but the marriage had ended in divorce not many years after he set up his practice in Harrisville. His wife, a big city girl, had taken their one child and walked out on him when their daughter was only four. Apparently, her dislike of small towns and Marshal's refusal to move his practice to someplace like Salt Lake City finally became the straw that broke the camel's back. It was rumored that his wife, after the divorce, had gone back to medical school. However, it was pure speculation, as no one in town ever actually heard from her, since she had made no close friends while she lived in the community.

The nearest hospital was forty miles from Harrisville, and Dr. Odell had to drive there to care for patients he hospitalized, but he still kept his practice in Harrisville. Dr. Odell still made occasional house calls, although they were considered by most in the medical profession to be a thing of the past. He made one that Sunday afternoon to the Lind home, as he had done in the early days of Ellen Lind's illness the previous fall.

Dr. Odell examined Kyle and noted that his blood pressure was a little high, but other than that he was perfectly healthy. His biggest problem, the doctor concluded, was that Kyle was both grieving and worrying. He prescribed a sedative, told Kyle to get some rest, and then left, promising to come back if he was needed. Kyle did try to follow his advice by lying down for a while, but he didn't improve much. He was in a deep state of mourning, the memories of his wife's recent illness and death made all the more bleak by Cody's disappearance. His girls rallied around him, but they weren't of much help as they too were sad and worried. Needless to say, it was a very rough weekend at the Lind home.

* * *

On Monday morning, Sheriff Hanks was no closer to solving the mystery of Cody's disappearance than he'd been on Saturday night. The sheriff sat in his office with his chief deputy, Shawn Fullman,

Deputy Kara Smith, and Chief Worthlin. After thanking them all for coming, he got down to business. "As you know, Shawn, Hal's still down from his surgery, so I've asked Kara here to help with some of the duties that would normally have been his. So you'll need to spread the other guys around however you need to in order to keep things covered. And I may need more help from you and perhaps from Phil, since he's close." Phil Simmons had been a deputy sheriff for the county for as long as Sheriff Hanks could remember.

"Yeah, we could sure use Hal about now," Shawn lamented. Hal was the small department's only detective, but there was no way he could work on this case for several more weeks. "But Kara will do a good job," Shawn added, giving her a smile of confidence.

"I agree," the sheriff said. "I've been on the phone with the other deputies from across the county, and several other officers as well. No one's learned a thing about Cody, even though a lot of man-hours were spent over the weekend trying to develop leads. Anyway, I thought maybe the four of us should go over everything we've covered so far in our investigation. We're missing something vital, and maybe if we brainstorm we can figure out what it is. To start with, Kara, tell us about Harry Reynolds and Gil Enders."

She recited everything she knew about Cody's boss and coworker. Even though officers had made several attempts to speak with Gil again on Sunday, they hadn't been able to find him. So they still didn't know where he had been when Cody disappeared, and they had no idea if he had an alibi. Kara had talked to some of Gil's neighbors, but they knew nothing and had become increasingly curious about why she wanted to know.

"What did you tell them?" the sheriff asked.

"I did like you suggested and told them we were trying to talk with anyone who was close to Cody in any way, to see if Cody might have said something that would give us a lead to his current whereabouts. They all accepted that as being logical. I'm sure none of them came to the conclusion that we might suspect Gil of having something to do with Cody's disappearance."

"What about Sammy Shirts, Chief?" Sheriff Hanks asked.

"A couple of my men and I have dug into his past, Sheriff. We've found nothing of interest. Other than a few vagrancy and intoxication arrests, he's clean. He does manage to get welfare occasionally. Where the bulk of his money comes from, we haven't been able to figure out. Of course, he doesn't spend much. Never goes to see Dr. Odell or a dentist, buys a few groceries with food stamps, but seldom has anything to wear except the same old rags, so he doesn't buy clothes," the chief reported.

"Where was he when Cody disappeared?" the sheriff questioned.

"He claims he was at home. We can't find anyone who can say differently. Of course, not many people are up and about in this town late at night, so that's no surprise. No question that he dislikes the Lind boy though. When I questioned him about the drill bit business again, he cussed Cody long and loud. Still maintains the kid just ran away."

"Yes, and I spoke with Kyle Lind about that," Shawn interjected. "I asked him how much money he thought Cody might have had with him. He said he couldn't have had much because he puts almost all of his money in the bank as soon as he's paid. Kyle says the boy's been saving for a mission, and he's really serious about it. I also asked Bridget Harrison about that yesterday. She said she didn't have any idea how much money Cody had with him when they went out. All she knew was that when he paid for their dinner, it was with a twenty-dollar bill."

"What about credit cards?" Kara asked.

"He doesn't have any," Shawn reported. "He uses cash and occasionally writes a check but he keeps a balance of only a couple hundred dollars in his checking account. Everything else goes into his savings. I looked at his checking account just before the sheriff asked me to come in here. Cody hasn't written any checks for over two weeks."

"I believe Sammy's theory is way off track," Sheriff Hanks said. "But it's Sammy's attitude that worries me. It's the way he talks about Cody. He despises the boy."

The sheriff's secretary called him on the intercom. "A Mr. Norman is here to see you," she reported.

"Is it about the Lind case?" he asked hopefully.

"No, but he sure is anxious to see you."

"All right, tell him to have a seat. We're about to wrap up here. I'll let you know as soon as I can see him," the sheriff said.

"Norman. Isn't he a farmer from over in the west side of the county?" Kara asked. "Isn't his farm several miles past the Lind ranch?"

"That's right. And just FYI, Roscoe Norman is Dr. Odell's cousin, although the doctor doesn't like to admit it," Vince said with a smile. "Not that I blame the good doctor. The two of them are about as different as night and day. Norman's a farmer only if you use the term loosely. His wife sits in the house and does nothing most of the time. I've heard Dr. Odell say that she's in poor health but won't do anything about it. Roscoe, on the other hand, is healthy as a horse—just lazy. Half his place has gone to weeds and sagebrush. I wonder what he wants . . . The last time he was in, it was over boys from here in town hunting rabbits out on his place. Probably that again," the sheriff guessed. He turned to his deputies. "We've got to talk to Gil again. Kara, why don't you go see if you can find him. Shawn, I'd like you to stay while Roscoe comes in. I may need you to run out to his place."

They both groaned, and Kara said, "All right, Sheriff, but even if I find Gil, I don't think he'll give me the time of day."

"Let me talk to him, Sheriff," Chief Worthlin suggested. "Maybe I can get somewhere. If I can find him, that is."

"If you wouldn't mind, Ron, that would be helpful. Well, is there anything else?"

"Yes," Kara said slowly.

"What is it, Deputy?" the sheriff asked, leaning forward as was his habit when something caught his interest. The tone of her voice hinted at something important.

"It's probably nothing, but I heard that one of the teachers at the high school had words with Cody the day before he disappeared. Nothing really serious, but I thought I should mention it," she explained.

"Which teacher?"

"Miss Taylor."

"Mariah Taylor?" Chief Worthlin asked, his eyes growing wide.

"Yes, the English teacher."

"She's a nice woman," the chief said.

"That's what I think," Shawn added. "She's single, my kids tell me, and good looking. That part is from my boy. Divorced before she came here. I'm not sure where she came from. Two of my kids have classes from her. They both like her."

"I've heard nothing but good about her as well," Chief Worthlin added.

"And my kids are all grown and gone. What did she and Cody have words over, Kara?" the sheriff pressed, leaning still farther forward and looking intently into Kara's clear brown eyes.

"Kyle Lind. I guess she's been seeing Kyle for the past month or so, and Cody said something to her about it. It apparently made her angry, and she told him off."

"Is that all?" Sheriff Hanks queried.

"All that I know about."

"Find out more, Kara. Find out all you can. We can't afford to overlook even the most inconsequential clue right now. Find out where she comes from, her background, and so forth. And get back with me as soon as you can. She's new here, isn't she?"

"It's her first year teaching here," Chief Worthlin affirmed.

"How old is she?" the sheriff asked. "Do any of you know?"

"She's probably about five years younger than me," Shawn answered. "I've talked to her several times in parent–teacher conferences, and she seems like a good woman. Anyway, I'd say she's thirty or so. So she's at least eight or ten years younger than Kyle."

"Not that a difference of age like that matters," Kara added quickly. "I've never met her, only heard about her. I'll see what I can find out if you'd like me to."

"Thanks—to all of you. Shawn, let's see what Norman wants," the sheriff said reluctantly, letting out a big sigh.

Roscoe Norman seemed extremely agitated when he came through the sheriff's office door. "I'm a busy man, Sheriff," he complained loudly. "I don't have time to be kept waiting."

Nice opening, Sheriff Hanks thought. Roscoe's self-importance rubbed him wrong, but he tried to conceal his annoyance. From the looks of Roscoe's rundown farm the last time the sheriff had driven by, the man couldn't be all that busy. But the sheriff shook the old farmer's hand and said, "I'm sorry, Roscoe, but I'm rather busy myself. Investigating the disappearance of Kyle Lind's boy is wearing me right out. I've hardly slept or eaten in the past two days. What can I do for you?"

"Trespassers again," Roscoe said. "Thought you told those kids to stay off my property the last time."

"Same kids?" Sheriff Hanks asked, suppressing a sigh.

"I don't know. Ain't seen 'em."

"Are they driving the same truck?"

"Ain't seen it neither."

"What have you seen?" the sheriff asked, his patience wearing thin. "Have you seen their tracks, or can you just hear them shooting?"

"Ain't seen no tracks. Ain't looked. Ain't heard no shooting, either."

"Then what have you seen?" the sheriff questioned sharply.

"A light. A kind of rigid light," was the perplexing response. "It shines straight into the sky."

"A rigid light?" Shawn spoke up in amazement. "Shining into the sky? I've never heard of a rigid light before."

"You heard me right, Deputy. It was about midnight when I seen it, Sheriff. Last night."

"I see," the sheriff said, but he really didn't. So he asked, "What do you mean by a rigid light? And exactly where did you see it?"

"Down in the field by my granddad's old homestead. It was just a beam of light shining straight up into the sky. I only seen it for a few seconds, then it was gone. Had to have been them kids from here in town again," Roscoe insisted.

"Was it car lights?" the sheriff pressed wearily. *Why can't you just come out with the whole story and get it over with?* he wondered.

"Nope. Just a small light," he said and snapped his mouth shut.

"Small light. Flashlight, maybe?" Shawn asked.

"Probably, but like I said, it shined straight up. It didn't wiggle or nothin'."

"How many times did you see it?"

"Just once. Had to've been them kids. Need to have you get after 'em again. Don't need no kids around spookin' my stock with their guns."

"But you didn't hear any shooting," Vince reminded him.

"Nope, no shots, but they probably didn't see nothin' to shoot at," Roscoe said reasonably.

"Probably not," Sheriff Hanks agreed indulgingly. "Did you go down to see if anyone was there?"

"Yup, but like I said, I didn't see nobody. Didn't hear nobody. Nothing but that light. Well, gotta go, Sheriff. You talk to them two kids you caught last time. Tell 'em if they don't stay off my place, I'll shoot their tires out, and I mean it."

"If you see their truck," Sheriff Hanks added, and then wished he hadn't. Roscoe scowled at him. "Don't be shooting. Call me if you see something strange again."

"You better believe I will. I'm goin' now," the old farmer said, and the sheriff was more than happy to let him leave.

"*Rigid light*," he said with a chuckle to his chief deputy after Roscoe had left. "Crazy old coot." But he picked up the phone and dialed the parents of one of the boys he'd caught shooting rabbits on Roscoe's farm the previous summer.

As the sheriff expected, the first boy's mother said it couldn't have been her son, since he'd been at home the previous night. "In fact, we keep a pretty tight rein on him now," his mother said.

"Well, thanks," Sheriff Hanks responded. "Just make sure he continues to stay away. Old Roscoe's a bit off, I'm afraid, and he could be dangerous."

A call to the other boy's mother netted the same results. "Well, must be someone else," the sheriff said. "I was pretty sure it wasn't your boy, but I thought I'd better call just in case. Old Roscoe is upset enough to be talking about shooting tires, and I'd hate to see anyone get hurt."

"Tim wasn't there, and he won't be, Sheriff. But thanks for your call. Frank and I do appreciate the way you handled things last summer. If we'd had any idea that was where the boys were hunting, we'd have put a stop to it. Mr. Norman is a scary man," the boy's mother said. "We don't trust him at all. Don't know of anybody in town that does, except maybe the doctor, but then, they're related and all."

CHAPTER 4

Hay lay yellowing in Kyle Lind's fields. He'd begun cutting his hay a couple days before Cody disappeared. He'd planned to bale on Friday, but the rain had hit that morning. It had been warm and windy since then, and the hay was dry enough to bale now, but Kyle just couldn't get to it. He was sick with worry and grief, and the pills Dr. Odell had given him kept him sedated. So he sat in the house, devoid of energy, staring at the TV but seeing nothing. It wasn't even turned on.

Kyle felt guilty for neglecting the girls, but he couldn't seem to find enough incentive to do anything about it. Agnes Arndt was cleaning the house, and he was vaguely aware of her each time she passed, but until she spoke to him, he hadn't really paid any attention to her.

"Mr. Kyle," she started.

Agnes always called him that. Never just Kyle or Mr. Lind, always Mr. Kyle. He looked up. "I'm sorry, Agnes," he said, pulling himself together as much as possible and forcing a sluggish smile.

"My old heart's just a-breaking for you, Mr. Kyle," she explained with emotion in her voice.

He looked at her more closely. Tears were streaming down her face. She wasn't all that old, but she always called herself old. Actually, she was not yet sixty. She was not a pretty woman—never had been—but she was a good woman, and he could find no fault with her housekeeping. He liked and respected her, and it hurt him deeply to see her so upset because of his problems.

"Agnes," he said gently, "don't you worry about me. I'll get by somehow."

"Sure you will, Mr. Kyle," Agnes agreed. "But them girls of yours, what can I do for them?"

Trying to concentrate on the immediate future, Kyle asked, "Would you have time to help Candi fix dinner tonight?" He knew how hard it was for the girls. The loss of their mother had been a terrible blow, and only recently had they seemed to be adjusting. But Cody's disappearance was just too much for the girls as well as for himself. They were all overwhelmed. He'd had a hard time getting them off to school that morning, but he'd insisted, and they had finally, tearfully, started up the lane toward the school-bus stop.

"Course I will, Mr. Kyle. I'll give Candi a break and it won't cost you no extra. I'd just love to cook for you and the girls. Fact is, I'd like to cook for you every day until that boy of yours comes home," she said.

He knew she meant it, but he didn't want charity. "I'll pay you, Agnes, or I won't let you cook," he said with another forced smile.

"You don't need to do that, Mr. Kyle," she stated sincerely.

"I know, but I want to."

"In that case, I better be deciding what to fix," she said. With the new responsibility came renewed energy as she bustled off in the direction of the kitchen.

"Use whatever you can find," Kyle called after her as he pulled himself to his feet and walked to the front door, glancing at his watch. It was after three. The girls would soon be home from school. He put on his hat and stepped out onto the large porch that stretched across the entire front of the house. He was surprised to hear a tractor and looked up the road to see Milt Soward's big John Deere pulling a hay baler. Within minutes another tractor and baler appeared, followed by a couple of hay wagons. His neighbors had come to help.

That proved to be all the motivation Kyle needed, and he started for his own tractor. He and the other men worked until dusk. "We'll be back and help you finish up tomorrow," Milt promised.

"That won't be necessary," Kyle protested weakly.

"Course not, but we'll do it anyway," Milt said with a hearty chuckle. With a cheerful smile and wave, Milt started up the lane on his tractor, raising a cloud of dust that drifted slowly over the fields to the west.

Kyle turned back to the house. In the diminishing light, the structure looked especially impressive. Times had been good for Ellen and him, and he'd built her this new house just four years ago.

A long porch roof, supported by tall, white pillars, gave the house a distinguished Southern look. The white house stood two stories tall, its bluish gray shingles contrasting appealingly with the light red brick of the chimneys at either end. The burgundy shutters on all the front-facing windows seemed to catch the eye and beckon one to come closer. Ellen had called it her Fourth of July house. Not only did it have a semblance of patriotic colors, but the Lind family had moved into their new home in early July.

It had been far bigger than they'd needed, but Ellen had wanted it, so Kyle had had it built. He and the kids rattled around in it now like mice in a barn. Without Agnes's help, it would be impossible to keep up the large house, even though there were rooms they didn't even use.

"Think of when the kids are grown and they all come home with families of their own," Ellen had reasoned when they had discussed the size of the house. "There'll be room for everyone."

Now Ellen was gone. Cody was gone too, but Kyle prayed that he would return. With sagging spirits, he stepped onto the porch. The aroma of his overdue supper reached him through the open windows of the large family room. He had forgotten that he had asked Agnes to prepare supper. He'd kept her waiting, he realized, and quickened his step.

"Think nothing of it, Mr. Kyle," Agnes replied, when he apologized for being late. "I fed the girls and kept your potion warm. I'll have it on the table before you're washed up," she promised.

His daughters greeted him when he entered the kitchen a few minutes later. They looked at him hopefully, Candi speaking first. "Dad, have you heard any more about Cody?" she asked in a voice that lacked its normal sparkle.

"Not a thing, Candi, but the sheriff and his deputies are working hard. He'll turn up."

"Are you sure, Daddy?" six-year-old Lori asked. She was his youngest, and Kyle could scarcely bear the innocent hopefulness in her voice.

He couldn't respond to that, because he wasn't sure. He could only place Cody's well-being in the hands of the Lord. To his daughters he simply said, "Remember to pray for him, girls."

Several hours of hard work had worn Kyle out, so he didn't take the sedative Dr. Odell had given him. He was not quite finished with his meal when the phone rang. Candi answered it and called, "It's for you, Dad. It's Jake."

Kyle rose from the table and crossed the room to where the phone hung on the wall near the door to the living room. "Hello, Jake," he said.

"Hi Kyle. I was sorry to hear about your troubles. I thought you'd had more than your share when Ellen died."

"Jake, it's nice of you to call. I sure appreciated all your help last fall."

"It was nothing. You're the only family I have left, and I was devastated when I read an Associated Press article in the newspaper about Cody. Surely it's exaggerated."

"I don't know what you heard, but it's serious, Jake. Cody just disappeared. The sheriff hasn't been able to turn up anything to indicate where he might have gone. I've got to admit that I'm mighty worried."

"I'm on my way to help, if I can," Jake stated.

"Oh, Jake, you did more than you should have when Ellen died," Kyle protested.

"Kyle, I'm a good architect and I make good money. I've already arranged for a few weeks off. It's no problem at all. I want to do it."

"Thanks, but you really don't—"

"I'm calling from Salt Lake, Kyle," Jake cut in firmly. "I drove here last night, attended to a few details that have to do with my work, and I was just getting ready to drive to your place. I'll be in later, but whatever you need done in the morning, and until this matter with Cody is settled, I'll be there to do it."

"Jake, that's real nice of you. I don't know what to say," Kyle responded gratefully. First his neighbors, now his nephew. He marveled at the goodness people showed when others were in trouble.

Jake Garrett, Kyle's sister's only son, had been a lifesaver after Ellen's death. Jake's parents had died in a car accident several years before, and since then Jake had visited Kyle's family at least annually for several days at a time. He took the kids out on the hor? ice cream for them in town, and brought them presents. The кιиs were always delighted when he came. But besides spending time with his young cousins, Jake always pitched in and helped with the work on the ranch.

Grateful for Jake's offer now, Kyle finally said, "You're welcome here, as always, Jake. I'll be waiting up for you."

"I'll be there, Kyle. And I'll plan on staying until Cody shows up, which will probably be soon. I just can't understand this whole business. He's such a good kid."

"He's the best, Jake. I can't imagine what could have happened to him, but he'll be back, I'm sure," Kyle agreed, trying to override his growing uncertainty.

"Of course, he will, Kyle. Never doubt it for a minute. In the meantime, I'll help out the best I can. I'll see you later then."

"Is Jake coming again, Dad?" Candi asked when Kyle hung up the phone.

"He'll be here tonight. He wants to help, at least until Cody's back. It's real generous of him."

The phone interrupted any further conversation. "It's Miss Taylor," Candi groaned as she held the receiver toward her father.

He didn't miss the roll of his eldest daughter's eyes as he took the receiver. "Hi, Mariah," he said. "Nice of you to call."

"I had to, Kyle. I would have called earlier, but I just didn't know what to say. I'm so sorry about Cody. Could I come out and see you tonight?"

"Why, uh, sure, Mariah, if you'd like," he answered. He knew the kids didn't like her out of loyalty to their mother. First Cody, and now Candi. *She only wants to comfort me,* he thought, *and she's very pleasant company.*

"I won't stay long," she promised, and promptly hung up.

"What did *she* want?" Candi asked. Kyle couldn't mistake the emphasis and distinct dislike in her voice.

"She's coming out to see us for a few minutes," he sighed.

"To see *you*. I'm going to my room. Come on, Lori and Shanna. Dad's *girlfriend* is coming." They were all gone from the room before Kyle could think of a response.

Mariah stayed late that evening, more a result of Kyle's encouragement than her own desires. He found her company very comforting. She hadn't talked much to him about her past in the few weeks he'd been seeing her. Not that it mattered one way or the other. He liked her more than he cared to admit. He did know she'd been through a divorce not many years back, and that she'd taught school in Wyoming before coming to Utah, but that was about the extent of it.

Mariah seemed genuinely concerned about Cody, and Kyle appreciated that. She seemed like a kind person, and he couldn't imagine why his kids didn't like her. Even before he'd asked her out just a couple of weeks earlier, he'd heard what a good teacher she was. He was certain that Candi and Cody had liked her at first. *Oh well, whatever it is about her that bothers them, I guess they'll overcome it in time,* he reasoned. *If Mariah and I . . . oh, I shouldn't be thinking ahead so much. Why, Ellen has only been gone for six months!* But he was very lonely, and Mariah had begun to fill the dark emptiness in his heart.

Kyle was sitting close to Mariah on the family room sofa, holding her hand tightly. Her long, blonde hair had fallen across his shoulder, and she was watching his face intently.

"Are you thinking about Cody?" she asked when their eyes met.

"Well, to be honest, I was thinking about you just now," he admitted quietly.

"I hope they were good thoughts," she said softly.

The doorbell rang.

"Oh, my goodness, that must be Jake! I forgot all about him!" Kyle exclaimed as he untangled his fingers from hers and stood up.

"Who's Jake?"

"My nephew. The only close family I have left. He helped out here when my wife died. He just drove up from Arizona to help us until we get Cody back," he explained as Mariah trailed him through the large house to the front door.

"Kyle, I'm sure sorry about Cody," Jake said the moment Kyle opened the door.

"Thanks, Jake. Come on in." They first shook hands, then embraced.

Jake, a lean thirty-two-year-old well over six feet tall, was lugging a suitcase with his other hand. "Bring it right this way, Jake," Kyle instructed as he shut the door. Then Kyle smacked himself in the forehead, exclaiming, "Oh my, aren't I the thoughtful one? Jake, meet a friend of mine, Mariah Taylor. Mariah, this is my nephew, Jake Garrett."

They exchanged greetings as Jake's dark brown eyes surveyed Mariah with a look of open admiration. Jake nodded his handsome head. "You didn't tell me you had a pretty lady friend, Kyle," he murmured with a smile, offering an outstretched hand.

Mariah grasped Kyle's hand as the younger, darker man stared at her with sparkling eyes. Then she declared, "I really must be going. I've overstayed my welcome, I'm afraid."

"You'll never do that," Kyle said, his feelings running deeper than he would ever have imagined just a few short weeks ago.

"I'll find my way back to the kitchen. I need a drink of water. You two can say your fond good-byes," Jake said with a grin and a wink.

He picked up the suitcase he'd temporarily placed on the floor and left the room.

Mariah turned to Kyle. "He seems nice."

"Yeah, tall, dark, and handsome—and more your age," Kyle retorted sourly.

"Hey, Kyle, none of that. Yes, he's handsome, but I . . . well, I like older men," Mariah clarified with a smile that eased Kyle's aching heart.

She came around, her head close to his, her eyes turned up. Almost instinctively, his arms went around her and their lips came together for just a brief moment. "I'm . . . I'm sorry," she mumbled as she jerked away.

"Don't be, Mariah," Kyle said. "I wanted that. Thanks for coming tonight. And please, come again soon."

"If you insist," she managed. "Now, I really have to go. You need to see to your nephew. I'll call in the morning."

"Thanks," Kyle replied as he opened the front door for her. He watched her as she walked toward her car. She was not just attractive, he decided; she was really quite beautiful. If only Cody would come home now, he thought with a painful wrench of his heart, everything would be all right again—as right as it could be without his beloved Ellen.

* * *

Bridget was glad this was the last week of school. She felt awkward as she walked down the main hallway of Harrisville High School. Kids she hardly knew flocked around her as if it were somehow fashionable to be friends with someone who was connected to a tragedy. Bridget said a few words to some of the girls walking with her, then stopped at her locker and fussed with the combination.

Another group of girls approached and Bridget saw her friend Candi Lind in the center. Apparently, Cody's sister was now just as popular as the girl he'd been dating when he disappeared.

Candi forced her way from the middle of the pack, her arms full of books. "Hi, Bridget," she said, looking relieved to see her friend.

"Hi, Candi," Bridget said in return just as the bell rang. The flock of students surrounding them began to disperse.

"Isn't it awful?" Candi sighed after the crowd had moved away, hurrying to their classes. Tears suddenly filled her dark brown eyes. Her face was drawn and haggard, and Bridget could tell she hadn't slept much lately.

"What do you mean?" Bridget asked worriedly.

"You know, the way everybody acts. I guess they just think it's cool to be with me because I'm Cody's sister. And they want to be with you because he was your . . . your friend," Candi said.

Bridget forced a smile. "Yeah, it's weird, but I know they don't mean to make us feel bad, especially you. Are you okay? I know this must be really hard on you."

"It's hard all right, but I don't know if you realize how much Cody liked . . . likes you," Candi stated. "He's wanted to ask you out forever, but he didn't because of that creepy Gil Enders. Now that Cody's missing, I can't think of Gil without my skin crawling. I wonder if he had anything to do with—" she said, stopping suddenly as a pained look crossed her pale face. "I almost accused Gil of doing something awful, and I don't know anything, really. But it worries me, Bridget. I don't trust him." Candi shuddered and dabbed at one eye.

"You know how he creeps me out," Bridget replied, wishing she could share with Candi the conversation she'd had with the sheriff. But he'd asked her not to tell anyone, and she had promised.

"Come on, let's go to class before we're late," Candi said, wrinkling her nose. "I hope we're not too late to get a seat on the back row."

"The back row?" Bridget asked in surprise.

"Yeah, the back row. I don't want to be any closer to that . . . that teacher than I have to!" Candi said with a frown.

"Miss Taylor isn't so bad, is she?"

"She is to me. She's after my dad!" Candi declared, fire flashing in her eyes.

"What?" Bridget exclaimed. "I know you said they'd gone out a few times, but you didn't think it was serious."

"I was wrong. It is serious, and I don't like it. Neither did Cody. She's after my dad! You know about what she said to Cody, don't you?"

Bridget was stumped. "No, he never mentioned it."

"Wow, I thought everybody in the school knew."

"Knew what?" Bridget asked earnestly, stopping and turning to face her friend.

Candi was pep-club pretty—the perky, happy type. Her hair was dark like Cody's, and her eyes reminded Bridget of his so much that a sharp pain stabbed at her heart. But Candi's brown eyes were spitting flames right then. "Lately she's been with my dad, like, all the time. She comes out to the house a lot . . . even last night!" She virtually hurled the words from her mouth, as if they were bitter on her tongue.

"Last night?" Bridget couldn't believe it.

"Yeah, but I'll tell you about that later. Let's walk. I don't want to be late. Anyway, Cody asked her one day in the hallway why she kept calling Dad. He said that Dad should be the one to call her if he wanted to, that it didn't look good, her calling him all the time and stuff. Miss Taylor snapped at Cody something awful. Said something about it being an adult matter. I don't know exactly what else they said, but Cody wasn't very happy. He said he felt bad about getting mad, but that didn't stop him from telling her that Mom's grave wasn't even settled yet, and that Dad ought to wait a bit before he started dating. That's what I think, too, but anyway, that really made Miss Taylor angry and she said to him, 'Well, I'm sorry,' and stormed off. That was on Thursday, I think—or Wednesday. Anyway, it makes me really mad."

"You said something about last night," Bridget pressed curiously.

"She called and wanted to come out to our place. It was quite late. She and Dad were talking, and I don't know what else, for a long time. I thought she'd gone when the doorbell rang. We were expecting my cousin Jake."

"Cool. I think he's hot, even if he is old," Bridget said. She'd met Jake several times and really liked him.

"Yeah, I guess he is. Anyway, he's come to help us again until Cody comes back," Candi mumbled.

"That's great." Bridget touched Candi's arm tenderly as they turned into Miss Taylor's room. They found seats side by side at the very back and sat down. Miss Taylor looked up from her desk and eyed them for a moment with what Bridget called her evil glare. Then Candi leaned over and whispered, "Anyway, it was Jake all right, but Miss—her—she was still there. Jake came into the kitchen grinning. After he hugged me and Shanna he said, 'Looks like your dad has a lady friend.'

"'I hope not,' I told him, but then Shanna and I snuck back to see if she was leaving, and you won't believe what we saw!"

"What?" Bridget exclaimed, her wide eyes glued to the angry face of her friend.

"They kissed!"

"You saw that?" Miss Taylor asked in an angry whisper.

Bridget and Candi both jumped. They hadn't seen the teacher walk to the back of the room. Miss Taylor continued in a lecturing undertone, "It's not good manners to spy on people, Candi. Your dad would not be happy about that."

"I . . . I know," Candi stammered, her face turning almost purple.

Miss Taylor turned on her heel, and as Bridget watched her march back to the front of the classroom, she thought she noticed something sinister in her walk. A chill went through Bridget, and she turned to Candi in time to see her friend shiver too.

"What am I going to do?" Candi wondered quietly, so close to tears that she could scarcely speak. "I don't know how much more I can stand."

"I don't know what you can do. This is awful."

The bell rang and the class began. It was the longest class period Bridget could ever remember. She'd always enjoyed English, but now she found it unbearable. And to think they still had a couple more days of it before school let out for the summer!

After class, Candi and Bridget walked from the room together. "Bridget," Candi began with a shudder, leaning close so the other kids wouldn't hear. "With Cody gone, it seems like people who used to just seem different actually seem scary now—like maybe they're evil or something, you know?"

Bridget knew exactly what Candi meant. First Gil Enders and now Mariah Taylor. She nodded in grim agreement, and then she said, "Tell me about your cousin. What's he doing here?"

"Like I said before, he came to help out on the farm. He's the only cousin I have on Dad's side of the family. He comes to visit at least once every year, and he always brings things for us kids. He must have lots of money. He's a neat guy. He stayed for a month after Mom died. He says he wants to help again until Cody is home. Nice, huh?"

"I'll say. He doesn't have a wife, does he?"

"Seems crazy that he's never gotten married, he's so good-looking and all. That's probably one of the reasons why he can come whenever he wants. It's nice to know there are nice people like him around. Hey, this is terrible to say, but maybe Miss Taylor and Jake . . . Oh, I shouldn't even think that! But he's more her age than Dad is. Dad's really happy that he came." Candi grinned halfheartedly.

"He wouldn't be if Miss Taylor got interested in Jake, though," Bridget pointed out.

Candi's grin faded. "I just wish she would keep her hands off Dad!"

"And I wish Cody would show up," Bridget murmured despondently.

"Yeah, especially that. I really miss him, Bridget. I miss him so much." Candi tried to stifle a sob. "And I'm so afraid for him."

Bridget understood. She missed Cody, too. More than she would have ever imagined.

CHAPTER 5

Late that Tuesday night, Roscoe Norman stepped out of his house and peered across his unkempt fields, a shotgun cradled in his arm. He didn't trust the sheriff or his deputies to protect his property. Those kids would probably come back again, and when they did, he'd be ready. When he got through with them, they'd need the services of his cousin Marshal. It was still hard for Roscoe to believe that Marshal had become a doctor. He was Roscoe's father's younger sister's son, and a sniveling brat of a kid he'd been. Roscoe had never cared much for him—Marshal was too sissified for him, even if he was a doctor.

Roscoe tried to quit thinking about his cousin. They'd never been close, and although he'd taken his wife to see Marshal when she became ill, it was because he was the only doctor in town. Roscoe found it hard to admit that Marshal's care had actually helped.

For a long time Roscoe looked over toward the old homestead where his father and Marshal's mother had grown up. He was about to go back in his house when he saw it again.

A very small light was shining straight into the air. It stayed rigidly in place as if anchored somehow. It was there for no longer than a second or two, and then it disappeared. If he'd blinked, he might have missed it. *Those boys are back again!* he thought angrily.

Roscoe stormed off to his over-the-hill pickup truck. It belched a cloud of dark gray smoke, bucked like a young colt when he let out the clutch, and then charged up the road with a clamor.

The light had come from across the fields near the old homestead, just as it had the other time. When the light shot into the sky, Roscoe had noticed the stark outline of the old hay derrick his grandfather and his father had used for stacking hay. He raced to the highway, drove west a few hundred yards, and then crossed the rusty cattle guard and raced south, his old truck rattling like a logging chain on the hard, bumpy road. Roscoe stopped beside the obsolete hay derrick and jumped out of his pickup, dragging his shotgun with him. He looked around in frustration, fully expecting to see a car and catch the kids in the act, but he could tell immediately that there was not another soul in the bleak landscape.

Roscoe was quite certain that this was where the light had been. The old pole derrick stood in the moonlight like the skeleton of some huge prehistoric creature, its highest point a good thirty feet or more in the air. He couldn't go any farther in his truck, because a ditch full of water ran through the road and past the derrick. Shining his flashlight across the ditch, he could see nothing except weeds, old farm equipment parts, and the ancient rock foundation of the cabin his grandfather had built many decades before.

The logs that had made up the cabin walls had long since fallen and now lay rotting among the weeds and brush. Looking to the right, Roscoe quickly scanned the remains of an old shed and corral, the lid to a rock cistern that hadn't been used for years, a few yards of stone walkway, and what was left of the old icehouse, cellar, and outhouse. This place hadn't been used for over seventy years.

Once again he looked around carefully as far as the flashlight beam would reach. There were no rabbit hunters that he could see, or any rabbits, for that matter. It didn't make sense. He had seen a manmade light, and there were always a few jackrabbits and cottontails around. He'd call the sheriff again tomorrow. The kids might have crawled away while he was driving around. It was the sheriff's job to figure that out.

* * *

The next morning, Edgar Stevens, controlling owner and president of the Harrisville Community Bank—and grandson of its founder— arrived at work very early. He wanted time to think before his vice president and the other employees came in. In truth, he wanted time to scheme. Edgar was without a doubt the wealthiest person in or around Harrisville. Not satisfied with that status, however, he was always looking for ways to increase his wealth, even if it meant a little exploitation on the side, or inflicting some suffering—whatever might work to his advantage.

Edgar knew the financial status of his customers intimately. In fact, his early-morning "thinking" sessions, if he were honest about them, could definitely be construed as "snooping" time. One of his customers had huge gambling debts and was constantly coming to him, groveling for yet another loan. Another customer, also in deep financial trouble, had a large note coming due, and if it wasn't paid in two weeks, Edgar would hastily foreclose at a profit of more than two million dollars. And most of that would wind up in his own already healthy account. He was prepared. The paperwork was almost completed. All he needed now was to have the sheriff serve the papers, and his bank would own one of the nicest ranches in the county. With Edgar's financial skills, he would personally own the ranch in no time at all.

After retrieving the appropriate file, Edgar sat down behind his large oak desk. A twisted, greedy smile crossed his face as he stared at the name on the folder: KYLE LIND.

Unbeknownst to the rest of the community, Ellen Lind's illness had been a terrible financial burden for Kyle. Of course, Kyle could eventually get back on his feet again, but for the present, he was quite strapped for cash. He had inherited the ranch from his late parents and had owned it outright until Ellen's illness, when he had to mortgage it to pay her medical bills—and that was on top of the loan for the new house, taken out just four years previously.

The Lind ranch was an excellent piece of property with some of the best cattle in the state, so Edgar needed to foreclose as soon as the note came due. He knew that Kyle couldn't make the payment without doing some refinancing, and Edgar knew better than to allow that to happen.

Edgar wanted Kyle's ranch, and he knew how to get it.

* * *

Hiding deep in the early-morning grayish light, a shadowy figure watched Edgar Stevens enter the bank that Wednesday just before the sun rose. That person dreamed of other men's wealth—the wealth that he shared only when he obtained it illegally, and then only enough to carve out a meager living. If he could have just a fraction of what Stevens had, he would be satisfied. In fact, even half of what Kyle Lind had would do. Then he could stop sneaking around in the night, always watching behind him, stealing whatever he could find and then trying to hide the evidence. All he really wanted was to be able to sleep every night without worrying about where his next meal would come from. It wasn't fair that others had what they needed— and more—while he was always living on the edge.

Sammy Shirts, with stealth that came from years of practice, slipped through the shadows after Edgar had disappeared inside the bank. He stole up the alley toward where he'd left his old Dodge truck—unnoticed, he was sure, like he always was. Sometimes he thought of himself as the invisible man.

* * *

Sammy was wrong this time. He was being watched by a very interested set of dark brown, penetrating eyes. Later that morning, Deputy Kara Smith entered the office of her boss, Sheriff Vince Hanks, to report on her work. Sammy was very much on her mind as she sat down and faced the sheriff.

Sheriff Hanks's face was grim, and he looked as if he hadn't slept in a month. When he spoke, his voice reflected his fatigue. "I just can't believe it, Kara. I had hoped that something—a letter, a card, a phone call, anything from Cody—would tell us that he's all right. I know that would more or less prove Sammy Shirts right—that Cody left of his own volition. But that is so far-fetched. And I'm thinking more than ever that he really didn't run away. But who would hurt him? And why? It just doesn't make sense." He stopped his rambling, rubbed his eyes, and smiled wanly at Kara.

She was tired too. She'd spent many hours on the job the past few days—she'd had to in order to cover for Hal, the detective, during his recovery. But she was angry at herself for not having spent even more time, and she said to the sheriff, "If I'd just been out earlier this morning, I might have caught Sammy at something."

"Sammy? What makes you say that?" the sheriff asked.

"I saw him this morning at dawn. He was watching Mr. Stevens enter the bank and—" she began.

Sheriff Hanks interrupted with a frown. "Stevens? Why in the world would he be going to work at that hour? He usually doesn't show up there until at least nine."

"I don't know, but he was there, and Sammy was watching him, or at least he seemed to be. Anyway, he headed for his pickup right after the banker went inside. What I wish is that I'd been out early enough to see where Sammy had been and what he was up to."

"He was probably stealing parts to keep that old rattletrap truck of his going," the sheriff said. "We don't have the manpower to watch Sammy around the clock, especially with this Lind situation and Hal being sick. That kid is somewhere, and we're not making one bit of headway in finding out where. With each day that passes our job gets more difficult, and the prospects for a happy ending get more remote. Anyway, what have you learned about Mariah Taylor?"

"Something that may be of interest, I'm afraid. She taught school in Cody, Wyoming, before coming down here. She was married for a while but had no children. Then she got divorced. The divorce was several years ago," Kara reported.

"Any criminal record?"

"Not that I could find, but her ex-husband is in prison in Montana."

The sheriff leaned forward, his eyes suddenly alert. "For doing what?"

"Kidnapping," Kara answered, and she almost smiled at the look that word brought to the sheriff's face.

"You're sure he's in prison?"

"Oh yeah, I'm positive. He and a younger brother held a woman captive for a couple of days. They were trying to get money from the woman's husband."

"Did they get it?"

"No. The police got to them first."

"My goodness," the sheriff said, leaning back and lacing his fingers behind his head. "This is becoming interesting . . . very interesting. It could be important."

"I know," Kara responded.

"What about the younger brother? Is he still in prison too?"

"He's out now. He was paroled a couple of months ago."

The sheriff leaned forward again, his eyes intent, his face grim. "Where is he now, Kara?"

"I have no idea, Sheriff. He seems to have disappeared."

"What about his parole officer? He should know where the guy is."

"He hasn't reported to him in over a month," Kara said.

"What's his name?"

"The ex-husband is Roger Griggs. The little brother's name is Ashton—Buster Ashton. He's actually a half brother."

The sheriff absorbed that information for a moment before asking, "Did you think to ask when Roger, Mariah's ex, has his next parole hearing?"

"I did, and I learned that he already had it. He's scheduled to be released the first of July," she responded.

"The first of July of this year?"

"Yes, sir. Just a month from now. That's what the warden told me."

"Has Mariah written to him since he's been in prison?" the sheriff asked after another period of thoughtful silence.

"I'm sorry. I didn't think to ask that," Kara admitted, embarrassed that she had overlooked something so important and obvious. "But I have the warden's phone number," she added, opening the folder on her lap.

"Let's have it," the sheriff ordered. "I'll find out right now."

Kara read it off to him, and he dialed the number. While he talked, waited, talked, waited, and talked some more, she stood and paced around the room. When he hung up, she quickly returned to her seat. "Well?" she asked anxiously.

"Mariah didn't write to her ex-husband when he was first imprisoned, but she has written. The warden said they don't read inmates' mail without cause, but every letter is logged. The first letter came about the time his brother Buster was released. The most recent letter from Mariah was the first of last week. And that's not all. Buster has also written to Roger. His last letter was about the same time as Mariah's," Sheriff Hanks explained, leaning forward again and looking more grim than ever. "We haven't had any ransom demands on Cody . . . yet. At least, if there have been any, Kyle hasn't reported them. And he might choose not to, depending on what kind of threats he's received. Kara, I think Mariah Taylor just moved to the top of our list of people of interest in this case."

"What about Gil Enders and Sammy Shirts?"

"We can't forget them. Either one or both could still be involved somehow, I suppose. But right now, our priority has to be Mariah Taylor. We've got to learn more about her and this Buster Ashton. In fact, I think I've got enough to bring her in for questioning. Not to accuse her of anything, just to get some background."

"Should I find her?" Kara asked.

"That shouldn't be hard. She'll be at the school. I hate to create a stir, but on the other hand, this is definitely important. I'll get on the phone and see what else I can learn about Ashton while you pick Mariah Taylor up," Sheriff Hanks stated decisively. "She's certainly got some explaining to do."

* * *

First period was almost over when the high school principal walked into Miss Taylor's classroom, accompanied by Deputy Kara Smith in full uniform, sidearm and all. Bridget almost fell out of her seat, and Candi's brown eyes grew as wide as saucers. A hush fell over the class as the principal whispered something to Miss Taylor, who nodded and then followed the deputy out. As soon as the door closed behind them, the hush was replaced by an eruption of excited whispering.

"Class, be quiet, please. Miss Taylor has had an emergency of some sort. The bell should be ringing any moment. Please stay in your seats until it does," the principal commanded. Then he left and the whispering erupted again.

"They got her!" Candi whispered fiercely. "She must have had something to do with whatever happened to Cody. Oh, Bridget, what if she's hurt him or something?"

"We don't know that she's involved. The principal said it was an emergency," Bridget cautioned quietly.

"He had to say something, Bridget, and you know he wouldn't say she was wanted for kidnapping. I just know it's about Cody. I just know it," Candi insisted. "If she's hurt him . . ."

* * *

Mariah Taylor did not speak as Kara drove her to the sheriff's office, but Kara sneaked a peak at her periodically. Mariah's face might have been carved from granite, considering her lack of motion and emotion. She looked straight ahead and said nothing, even when Kara opened the door for her and escorted her into the building.

Sheriff Hanks came around his desk as Kara ushered Mariah into his office. "I'm Sheriff Hanks," he said, extending a hand. Mariah Taylor shook his hand, mumbling something that must have been meant to pass for a greeting. She then sat where she was told, her eyes in her lap, watching her folded hands. Kara stood behind her, near the door. The sheriff sat down and gazed at Mariah for a moment before clearing his throat.

Mariah looked up then, and the sheriff said gently, "Thanks for coming in, Mariah. I'm sorry to have bothered you during school hours, but this is important."

The English teacher finally spoke, and when she did her voice sounded soft and cultured. "I would have come in on my own if you'd called," she declared in mild rebuke.

"I'm sure you would have," the sheriff said in a neutral tone.

"I know what this is about," Mariah said. "I've been expecting it."

"Tell me what it's about," Sheriff Hanks invited politely.

"My ex-husband. You've learned he's in prison for kidnapping."

"That's right. Can you enlighten us more?"

"You and Deputy Smith appear to be intelligent people. You've probably already learned about all there is to know by now," the schoolteacher responded coolly.

"Maybe, but we'd like to hear it from you."

They heard it, and it was accurate as far as Kara could tell. She even mentioned her ex-husband's half brother, Buster Ashton.

When she'd finished, Mariah asked, "Is that all you wanted to know?"

Sheriff Hanks slowly shook his head. "No, I have a few questions."

"About my divorce?"

"We'll start with that."

"It wasn't pretty, Sheriff. When Roger and I were first married, we got along very well. But then things began to go downhill. He'd never told me he'd been in trouble before. When I found out, we fought about it. He abused me—you know, shoved me around, blackened my eye, and occasionally bloodied my nose. I took the abuse as long as I could, and then I left him. We'd been married a couple of years. That was all a few years ago. My life has changed a lot since then. It's hard for me to look back and realize that I actually married the guy in the first place."

That was a rather tidy explanation, Kara thought when it became clear that Mariah was finished.

The sheriff asked, "That's all there was to it?"

"That's about it. If you're thinking I may have had something to do with the disappearance of Cody Lind, you couldn't be more wrong, Sheriff. I know he resented me a little, and so do his sisters. I understand that, but Kyle Lind is the kindest, sweetest man I've ever met. I wouldn't hurt him or his kids for anything."

"Do you love him?" the sheriff asked bluntly.

"We haven't seen that much of each other. So no, I can't say I love him, but I've grown very fond of him over the past few weeks," she admitted, and for the first time she seemed to lose her self-assurance.

"I see. When did you last talk to your ex-husband?"

"I haven't talked to him since before he went to prison."

"I see. Have you written to him?"

Kara couldn't see Mariah's face, but she was sure the woman smiled briefly when she responded, "You know I have, and you want to know why. Well, I'll tell you why."

She went on to explain that after Buster was released from prison, he located her and started asking for money. Despite repeated attempts to get him to leave her alone, he wouldn't. Finally, she wrote to Roger and asked him to help. When Roger wrote back, it was to explain to her that he probably couldn't do anything about his brother but that he would try.

It turned out that he eventually sided with Buster, telling Mariah that Buster was broke and really needed help. In one letter Roger told her that if she would give Buster five hundred dollars, he wouldn't bother her again.

After listening to the account, Sheriff Hanks asked, "Did you give Buster the money?"

Mariah nodded her head. "Yes, but after a few weeks, he wanted more. I wrote Roger again. That was the first of last week. I haven't heard back."

Kara had to admit that Mariah Taylor sounded believable, but the worst crooks, her father had always said, were often the smoothest talkers. Maybe she was just smooth.

"Where is Buster now?" Sheriff Hanks continued.

"I have no idea. Every letter is postmarked from a different place. I just hope I never hear from him again. Please, Sheriff, you've got to believe me. I have had nothing to do with Cody's situation. I'll . . . I'll not see his father again if that's what I have to do to convince you and this town," she pleaded, pulling a tissue from her purse and wiping at her eyes.

The sheriff didn't acknowledge Mariah's remark about Cody's father. Instead, he asked, "May I see the letters?"

"The letters?" Mariah sounded confused.

"Yes, the letters you received from Roger. That would be a great help."

"Oh, I see. It would make me more believable," she retorted with a note of sarcasm in her soft voice.

"That's right, Mariah."

"I don't have them. I threw them away," she said. "I hated them. I had no reason to keep them."

The sheriff nodded slowly, then stood. "Thank you for your time, Mariah. Deputy Smith will take you back to the school."

"Thank you," she murmured as she arose.

Sheriff Hanks stopped her at the door as she stepped past Kara. "And, Mariah, I'd appreciate it if you'd let me know if you hear from Buster again."

"Of course."

"And please, don't leave the area. I know school is almost out, but we may need your help."

Kara wondered about that statement all the way to the school and back. As soon as she returned to the sheriff's office, she asked, "What did you mean when you told Mariah that you might need her help?"

"Just that. If this Buster character is hard up for money, and if he knows that Mariah Taylor is soft on Kyle Lind and that Kyle Lind is well off, then maybe, just maybe, he is the one responsible for Cody's disappearance. Mariah may be a victim as well," he reasoned.

"Do you really think that's possible?" Kara asked. In some obscure way it did make sense to her, because she couldn't help but like and feel sorry for Mariah.

"Of course, it's possible, but I honestly don't know what to think," Sheriff Hanks answered with a frown. "It would help if she'd kept the letters from Roger. She could most definitely be a victim. On the other hand, it's possible that she's involved in a kidnapping up to her pretty neck. Now, let's see if we can get some officers around the country looking for one Buster Ashton."

CHAPTER 6

Kara had just fixed herself some dinner when the phone rang. It was Sheriff Hanks. "I know you've had a long day," he said, "but I wanted to run out to Kyle Lind's place this evening. I wondered if you'd like to go along."

"Sure. Can you give me twenty minutes?" Kara wondered what the sheriff planned to accomplish with this visit.

She met him at the office and they headed out of town. "What's up?" she asked after waiting impatiently for several minutes for the sheriff to tell her something.

He shook his head. "Not much, really. I just wanted to speak to Kyle again. He's probably furious over the way you and I brought Mariah in today. I think he needs to hear firsthand why we did it."

"Okay. I suppose you're right."

"And then I thought we'd take a swing over a little farther west. Roscoe Norman was in again," the sheriff continued.

"Another spotting of rigid lights?" Kara queried snidely.

"It seems so."

"That's all we need right now," she moaned.

Vince nodded, but he said nothing else until they pulled into Kyle Lind's large farmyard. "Nice place, isn't it?" he commented.

"I'll say!" Kara responded as she looked at Kyle's house in awe. She'd only seen the house from the highway, and that was a good half-mile away. It was huge and very attractive, and the yards were gorgeous—or at least had the possibility of being stunningly beautiful.

"I wonder who owns that car," the sheriff wondered as he parked beside a sporty green Mustang with Arizona plates.

"Family?" Kara suggested.

"Yeah, that's probably it. It could be his nephew. You know, the fellow who came out when Kyle's wife died. Let's see if anyone's in the house," he said as she stepped out and led the way up a long sidewalk. "I don't see anyone out at the corrals or in the fields."

Flowers bloomed in slight disarray; snapdragons from the previous year's planting had germinated in unexpected places. The lawn was well overdue for mowing. Each was mute evidence, Kara surmised, of Kyle's personal tragedies—his wife's death and his son's disappearance. As Kara rang the doorbell, her heart ached for Kyle Lind. Despite his apparent wealth, he certainly had more sorrows than any man should have to bear simultaneously.

A minute later the door was opened by a stranger. Kara stared as the sheriff made the introductions. The man who invited them in was not only handsome, but also seemed capable and self-assured. He gave his name as Jake Garrett. Well over six feet tall, Jake had deeply tanned skin, dark wavy hair, and brown eyes. He shut the door behind them as he explained, "Kyle's a little tired tonight. This has been really rough on him. Dr. Odell came out and checked him again. Kyle's blood pressure is through the roof. If he isn't careful, he could have a stroke. The doctor gave him a few samples of some blood pressure medication and a prescription for more. Other than that, there's not much he can do, I guess."

As Jake spoke, his dark eyes fell on Kara, and a brief smile lit his face. He opened his mouth to speak again, but the sheriff cut him off.

"You must be from Arizona," Sheriff Hanks stated.

The stranger's eyes lingered for a moment on Kara's blushing face before they turned to the sheriff. "Sure am," he affirmed. "How did you know?"

"Arizona plates."

"Oh, yeah, of course," Jake chuckled. "I'm from Phoenix."

"You must be Kyle's nephew. I've seen you around town in the past. I remember hearing that you drew up the blueprints for this house. Impressive." Sheriff Hanks could be very good with small talk when he tried.

"I work for a large architectural firm in Arizona. It's a good job, but it's pressure packed. Every year I come up for a few days to help out here and to get away from the office. Kyle's ranch, even when I'm working on it, is usually a relaxing place. Of course, when I came shortly after Ellen got sick, it wasn't so relaxing. It seemed like all I did that time was help take her to the doctor. That was when I met Dr. Odell for the first time. For a small-town doctor, he seems very competent."

"Yeah, he's good," the sheriff agreed.

Jake went on. "I was here again for a month after Ellen's death, helping Kyle with the ranch. I came to see if I could help out again. Like the last two times I've come, it's been in a time of crisis for Kyle, and I want to do what I can."

"Yeah, tough thing here. But it's nice to see you, Jake. I'm sure Kyle's grateful for the help," the sheriff said. "Now, if you could find Kyle for me."

"Sure. He's with the girls," Jake said. "Have a seat." He waved to a sofa near the door.

Kara said nothing, but her eyes trailed the trim, well-dressed figure as he left the room.

"Didn't expect *him,* did you?" Vince asked, his voice betraying his amusement.

"No," Kara said softly. She'd never been so struck by the sight of a man in her life. *He's amazing,* she thought.

"I wonder if his wife's here, too," Sheriff Hanks continued.

A sharp pang pierced her at his words, and she fought sternly to control her feelings. Of course he would have a wife, she told herself. It was just that . . . well, it didn't matter. They were here on business.

"Hey, don't look so taken aback," the sheriff teased with a twinkle in his eye. "There's no reason I can think of why you shouldn't be rendered speechless by a guy like Jake Garrett. Anyway, if I'm not mistaken, I think I remember hearing that he's single."

Kara blushed deeply, but before she could think of a reply, Kyle Lind appeared from the same door Jake had exited a moment before. "Sheriff," he greeted, extending a hand. "Good to see you. And you too, Deputy."

It is? Kara wondered. *Hasn't Mariah Taylor talked to you since our visit with her this morning? She's had plenty of time.*

"Won't you sit down?" Kyle invited, pointing to the sofa Jake had previously indicated.

"Sure. Thanks, Kyle," the sheriff answered.

As Kara sank into the plush sofa beside the sheriff, Jake Garrett reentered the room. As if drawn by a huge magnet, her eyes went immediately to his tanned face. He smiled and sat on a hard-backed chair opposite them. He was dressed in blue jeans, a dark yellow western shirt, and what looked like very expensive cowboy boots.

"Sheriff, Deputy, I guess you've already met my late sister's son. Jake drove up from Arizona to help me out for a few days," Kyle said. "Maybe you remember when he was here a few months ago."

"Actually, I'm here for as long as he needs me," Jake corrected.

"One bachelor helping another," Kyle added.

Kara's heart skipped a beat. *So he is single,* she thought, and then tried to force her mind back to the purpose of the visit. That thought sobered her, and she tore her eyes from the dark face of Jake Garrett and looked at Sheriff Hanks's stern profile as Kyle asked, "What brings you out here, Sheriff? Do you have some news?"

Sheriff Hanks cleared his throat, and Kara was glad that he had volunteered to explain about Mariah. The sheriff was not enjoying this. "Sort of," he replied in answer to Kyle's question. "But I have a question first."

"What's that?" Kyle asked.

"Have you had any kind of demand for ransom? You know, a letter, a phone call, an e-mail?" the sheriff asked.

"No. I'd have told you if I had," Kyle said. "But honestly, I've been expecting something of that sort. It's the only thing that makes sense."

"I have to ask you something else," the sheriff said.

"That's fine."

"Have you heard from Mariah Taylor?"

"Not since yesterday," Kyle answered, shifting nervously in his chair. "Why do you ask that?"

"I just thought she'd call you. Deputy Smith and I had a talk with her this morning. We upset her a bit, I'm afraid."

"Oh?" Kyle's eyes narrowed suspiciously. "Why did you need to talk to her?"

"How well do you know Mariah, Kyle?" the sheriff asked, dodging the rancher's question.

Kyle shifted uneasily in his seat again. "We're just friends," he replied. "I guess I don't know a lot about her, but we do enjoy one another's company. I met her at a stake singles event that a friend coerced me into attending. That was about a month ago. Why? Has she done something wrong?"

"I hope not, but there are some things that came up about her ex-husband. I suppose you know about him?" Sheriff Hanks ventured.

"I know she has one, that's all," Kyle retorted sharply. "We've never discussed him. Why the sudden interest in Mariah?"

Kara's eyes kept drifting back to Jake, who was watching the sheriff's face. A faint smile seemed to play about the corners of his mouth, exposing the tips of his exceptionally white teeth. At least it seemed like a smile. Perhaps it was just the way he looked when he was concentrating. He did appear to be very much interested in what the sheriff was saying, and there was nothing to smile about in that.

Sheriff Hanks cleared his throat again. "Please don't take offense, Kyle. I've got to look at every angle of your son's disappearance."

"But why Mariah? She's his schoolteacher, for heaven's sake!" Kyle said adamantly.

"Yes, but there are clearly things about her that she hasn't told you."

"Like what?"

"Like she's the ex-wife of a man who is in prison, convicted of kidnapping," the sheriff responded.

Sheriff Hanks's words had the effect of a hammer blow to Kyle Lind. He sank back in his chair, the blood draining from his face. After a moment, he stammered, "But . . . but . . ." He couldn't go on.

"Like I said, I can't ignore anyone who—" the sheriff began again.

"That's right," Jake chimed in quickly. The faint suggestion of a smile was gone from his face. Kara wasn't sure it had ever been there. "Don't leave any stone unturned, Sheriff. Whoever did this horrible thing must be caught and punished. And we've got to get Cody back."

The sheriff glanced at him, but only for a second. Then he went on. "Kyle, I'm sorry. And I'm not accusing Mariah of anything, but I need to talk to you about it."

"Well, talk then," the rancher sighed with downcast eyes. "I'm listening."

Sheriff Hanks then explained everything he and Kara had learned about Mariah Taylor, her ex-husband, and his half brother. When he'd finished, Kyle said, "It looks bad, Sheriff. But I can't believe Mariah could—"

Jake Garrett interrupted. "Kyle, don't let your emotions get in the way of your common sense. Sounds like the sheriff may be on the right track. This Buster Ashton fellow could well be involved. That's not to say Mariah isn't innocent, but who knows, maybe that's why she's taken such an interest in you."

"You don't even know her, Jake. None of you do," Kyle muttered, but both his voice and his face betrayed a mixture of anger and doubt.

"I'm sorry, Kyle," Jake said. "I didn't mean to upset you. But the sheriff is right, and you know it. He can't afford to overlook anyone. I really hope that Mariah has nothing to do with Cody disappearing. But the cops have to look at every angle."

Kara appreciated Jake's words. She too hoped that Mariah Taylor was innocent. But the situation did seem suspicious, especially since Mariah said she'd destroyed the letters her ex-husband had written to her when she asked him to try to keep Buster from demanding money from her.

Kyle looked defeated. "I'm sorry, Jake. You're right. They can't exclude anyone. I wouldn't want them to. All I want is the safe return of my son."

Jake nodded and said, "I know how you feel, Kyle. Right now, though, the most important thing for us to do is support the sheriff in his efforts, no matter where the evidence points."

Kyle nodded, and Jake turned to the Sheriff. "Do you have any idea where this Buster fellow is now?"

"No. But we're looking."

"Good. When you hear anything about him, keep us posted," Jake said.

Kyle Lind glanced at his nephew as the sheriff and deputy got to their feet. Jake rose quickly, but Kyle remained seated and rested his head in his hands.

"I'm sorry, Kyle," the sheriff said quietly. "This is tough. When you talk to Mariah, see if she can tell you anything at all that might help us find Buster Ashton." The sheriff thought momentarily of Mariah's vow to avoid all contact with Kyle in order to prove her innocence but decided not to mention it. "And please, if you get any demands for ransom in any form, let me know immediately. I don't care what time of day or night it is."

Kyle nodded as Jake interjected, "You can bet we will, Sheriff. And if there's anything I can do to help, you just let me know. I came up here to help in any way I can." He looked at Kara and smiled warmly as he spoke. She returned his smile, and he added, "I love this family. They're all I have, you know."

Later, back on the highway and headed west, Sheriff Hanks pulled the visor down to keep the low-hanging sun from his eyes. "Kara, what do you think now?" he asked.

"Well," she responded, "one thing's clear. Mr. Lind didn't know anything about Mariah's ex-husband being a convict. You caught him totally off guard there. He seems devastated."

"True. But do you think Buster could be our man?" the sheriff asked.

"Right now, I'd say he's our main suspect. I just hope Mariah Taylor is not involved with him in some way."

"I agree with you. What do you think of Jake?" Sheriff Hanks questioned, glancing her way briefly as he spoke. "I mean besides the fact that he's single and good-looking."

Kara felt her face flush, but she replied, "He seems like a decent person. He's certainly got the interest of the family at heart."

"Yes," Vince agreed. "It seems like he does. I just hope he remembers who the law is and lets us do the police work. He seems a little pushy, like he might get overly involved if he thought he could help."

"Is something wrong with that?" Kara asked.

"No, not generally, except when it comes to our line of work. You see, people who like to help out often end up in the way. Without meaning to, they can cause someone to get hurt, or destroy evidence, or even throw us onto the wrong track."

Kara nodded in agreement, but she couldn't help thinking how nice it might be to work with Jake Garrett. She smiled at the thought.

* * *

After the sheriff and his deputy had left, Jake said to his uncle, "Hey, don't be so down, Kyle. You've got to be strong. You know what the doctor said. You just need to stay busy and try to be positive. They'll catch this Ashton character and find your son. Everything will work out just fine."

Kyle shook his head. "Trouble is, I can't shake the idea that Mariah might somehow be involved, and I hate myself for it. She's been nothing but good to me—for me—since the day I met her."

"You have to watch people who try to get close to you, they say. You never know what they're really after. My guess is, there'll be a note or communication of some kind coming soon, demanding money. They must know that you have plenty, and they want a piece of it. And you just can't let that happen," Jake said.

Kyle looked at him for a moment before responding. "Jake, I'd give this whole darn place away to have Cody back."

"Oh, I know that, Kyle. Of course you would. What's money when compared to life, especially of someone we're close to?"

"That's right. Oh, Jake, he's my son, my only son," Kyle managed in a trembling voice. "Trouble is, if it's money they want, it will be hard."

"I'm sure that's true, but Kyle, you must have a pretty good-sized chunk of savings in the bank," Jake said with a frown. "I'll help out too, if it comes to that. After all, you're the only family I have."

"No, you don't need to do that, Jake. I feel guilty the way you're giving your time as it is. Although, I admit that my financial condition isn't as good as many people might think. We sank a lot into this house and then, when Ellen got sick . . . Well, I wasn't prepared for that. I had no insurance and the bills were huge. I'm mortgaged to the hilt, Jake."

"Then you can sell a few cows," Jake suggested.

"They're mortgaged too. And I can't sell without permission from the bank. Of course, I have a fair amount of collateral in them, but Edgar Stevens, the banker, can be difficult."

Jake's surprise was reflected in his voice. "I can't believe this, Kyle. I thought you were in good shape financially. You may have to let me help."

"No, I can't let you do more. I wouldn't feel right about it. And besides, I'm sure it won't come to that. But everyone, like you, believes things are better than they are, except Stevens. He knows the whole story." As Kyle spoke, something important suddenly occurred to him. With all his problems he hadn't given it a thought. He looked at his nephew in alarm and said, "Jake, I just remembered something. There's a huge note due in a few days. I've got to see Stevens, or I could lose everything."

Jake looked alarmed as well, and Kyle felt faint. "Oh," he moaned, "what will I do? If only my boy was here, then it wouldn't matter so much. Nothing would matter."

Kyle sank down on the sofa, his head cradled in his hands. Jake began to pace, and Kyle glanced up at him. His nephew appeared upset—almost as upset as he was. Kyle felt a surge of gratitude. Jake was a strong, intelligent fellow, and Kyle realized that his nephew could prove to be a great help before this nightmare was over. Both a help and a comfort. With Jake around, the load didn't seem quite so overwhelming.

* * *

Roscoe Norman met the sheriff's car in his cluttered yard just as the sun was sinking through gathering clouds in a blaze of color over the low western hills. "About time you got here!" he shouted as Sheriff Hanks pulled up beside Roscoe's old pickup and shut off the engine. The sheriff and Deputy Smith climbed out of the car.

"Sorry, Roscoe, but we've got a missing boy to worry about. We came as soon as we could," the sheriff explained, trying to seem calm but actually feeling more agitated.

"Well, I expect you to stop those boys this time, Sheriff. I ain't tolerating no more trespassing."

"They haven't been around, Roscoe," the sheriff retorted more sharply than he'd intended.

"You saying I ain't been seeing lights?" Roscoe demanded, shoving his whiskery face closer to the sheriff's.

"I didn't say that," Sheriff Hanks responded sternly. "But those two boys haven't been here. They have solid alibis. It couldn't have been them."

Roscoe scowled. "Don't believe you," he mumbled.

The sheriff and deputy exchanged glances. Then the sheriff said, "Show us where you saw the light, Roscoe."

"Foller me," the old man ordered gruffly as he headed for his truck.

Sheriff Hanks and Deputy Smith followed a cloud of foul-smelling blue exhaust back to the highway. By the time they reached the abandoned homestead of Roscoe's grandfather, the color in the cloudy sky was fading and dusk was settling in. However, there was still enough light for the officers to examine the area. It was clear that Roscoe Norman had made more than one trip here in recent days. And the sheriff thought there might have been another car too, but the tracks were not clear enough to know for sure. Just because the boys who'd hunted rabbits here before hadn't been back didn't mean someone else, perhaps some other kids, hadn't been.

In the dimming light, the sheriff and Kara searched for footprints, spent bullet casings, and anything else that might indicate someone had been there hunting rabbits. As darkness closed in, they'd found nothing but normal road litter—cigarettes and cigarette butts, gum wrappers and other assorted bits of paper, pop-can pull tabs. Vince was getting angry. Roscoe was wasting their time. He and Kara needed to leave.

Roscoe sensed Sheriff Hanks's unrest and began to grumble. "You ain't found nothing yet, Sheriff. Keep looking."

The sheriff bristled but reminded himself of his duty to the public. With his mind on the Lind case, he was merely going through the motions here, he admitted reluctantly to himself. He stepped close to Kara and whispered, "If it'll keep the old man off our backs for a while, let's spend a little more time here. I'll get a couple of flashlights from the car."

Kara nodded in agreement and followed him back to the car. They'd worked their way across a ditch and through the weeds and rotting poles and logs that were strewn around. On the way back to the car, they jumped over the ditch again. After securing a couple of flashlights, the sheriff led the way back. Roscoe followed them at a distance, grumbling to himself.

The sheriff crossed the ditch once more and walked several steps beyond it. He was standing on an old stone walk of some sort when Kara called out, "Sheriff, come look at this."

He turned to see the deputy still on the far side of the ditch, shining her light into the clear, slow-moving water, and he walked briskly back. Kara continued to stare into the ditch where her light was shining and pointed with her free hand. "Right there, beneath the surface of the water on your side of the ditch, is a track. Looks like it was made by a cowboy boot."

Sheriff Hanks leaned forward. Kara's light shined steadily into the water, illuminating the bottom of the ditch. A boot track appeared in the mud, as clear as if it had just been made. The sheriff studied it for a moment before flashing his own light at Roscoe's feet.

The old man chuckled. "Ain't never had a pair a them dang pointed things on my feet," he smirked. He wore a pair of badly worn leather lace-up boots with a round toe and flat heel. "Just making sure," Vince said as he straightened up.

"Told you someone's been down here. That proves it, Sheriff. Now what're ya gonna do about it?" Roscoe demanded.

The sheriff ignored him and jumped across the ditch so he could look at the track from Kara's angle. The water was clear, with very little sediment, and it moved very slowly. The track, he reasoned, could have been there for several days. Turning to Roscoe, he asked "When was the water last out of this ditch?"

"Two weeks. Maybe a little more. One of them kids musta stepped in the ditch," he said with a chuckle. "Got his boot full of water, looks like."

"Looks like it," the sheriff agreed. Then he directed his light up and down the ditch but saw no more tracks. "Must have just misjudged as he crossed," he said to Kara.

"But those two boys haven't been back here," she reminded him.

"That's true. And their folks would skin them if they came here anyway. No, it wasn't them, but Roscoe's right. Someone's been here. Let's look around a little more, although I'm afraid it might be a waste of our time. That rain the other night could have washed out any tracks."

"Except the one in the ditch beneath the water," Kara said.

"Yeah, except that one."

The north bank of the ditch was grassy, so no boot track would show there. The south side was the same until a few feet from the edge where it met the old stone walk the sheriff had been standing on earlier. He searched all around it in the weeds and brush, but there weren't any other footprints. He then followed the walk for a short distance, noticing that weeds grew up in the cracks between the flat stones and along the edge. *If anyone has walked here, they wouldn't have left any tracks,* he thought.

He followed the walkway, which forked after a few yards. One branch led to the decaying remains of the old cabin that he'd already inspected, and the other fork led toward the outhouse. Taking the latter path, Sheriff Hanks was amazed that the outhouse still stood, even though the door was gone and the lumber was badly weathered and cracked. The walkway forked again in front of the outhouse.

He followed the right fork of the path and ended up in front of an ancient root cellar. The door was still in place, but like the wood of the outhouse, it was cracked and twisted, and weeds and brush nearly hid it. The sheriff shined his flashlight all around but saw no more tracks. As he turned to leave, a breeze stirred the weeds and brush with a low moan. *Spooky place,* he thought with a wry grin as he walked back to where Kara was now standing.

"What have you found there?" he asked.

"An old cistern," she responded.

"Grandpa used to fill it with water from the ditch every fall," Roscoe said. "That was what him and Grandma used to drink and clean up with. Held enough to last them most of the winter if they was careful."

Sheriff Hanks nodded an acknowledgment and continued to search. There were no more boot tracks. "Let's look closer on the other side of the ditch," he suggested a half hour later.

Suddenly, the wind picked up, and clouds began to fill the sky. Several times the wind moaned like it was in mortal agony. The sheriff mentioned the sound to Kara, who shuddered. "Yes, I can hear it. Reminds me of death. I don't like this place," she admitted as they again approached the ditch.

Finally, after failing to find any additional tracks or other evidence of trespassers, the sheriff said, "Well, I guess we'd better go. Roscoe, let me know if you see a light or anything else. Call me. I'll come out. This thing has me puzzled."

"That light was there, Sheriff," Roscoe grumbled. "I seen it twice."

"I don't doubt you," the sheriff responded. "But it's not here now. And the only sign that anyone has been here is that boot track in the ditch."

A drop of rain struck the sheriff's arm. He looked up to see the night sky black with swollen clouds. "Might get wet if we don't get moving," he said as he stepped toward the car.

He opened the door, then stopped and spoke to Roscoe, who'd followed him past his old truck and was still mumbling beneath his breath. "I'll be back. Can you turn the water out of that ditch?"

"Sure, but I don't want to. I'm irrigating over yonder."

"I don't mean now. But I would like you to when I come back. I'd like to photograph that boot print, and I'll need the water out when I do it so the picture won't be distorted. Until then, the water needs to be left in. It's actually preserving the print."

"Come back in the morning," Roscoe ordered gruffly. "I'll shut the water out just long enough for you to take your picture."

"Well, I'm not sure I can come then. I do have this problem with the missing boy from Harrisville. I'll call before I come," he said. "It will be tomorrow sometime if I can possibly make it."

Sheriff Hanks slid behind the steering wheel, and Kara asked, "Why do you want to take a picture of that boot print? Whoever made it hasn't hurt anything. Mr. Norman even admits that."

"I don't know why, Kara. I just think I'd better," he answered evasively.

She didn't press the issue, and he thought about it as they entered the highway and headed toward Harrisville. He couldn't explain it, even to himself, but something about that lone boot print made him uneasy. Maybe it was just the darkness, his own fatigue, the moaning wind, and the stark desolation of the old homestead that had instilled an eerie feeling in him. But whatever it was, he couldn't shake it.

As they rounded a curve in the road, the sheriff looked in the rearview mirror and caught a glimpse of the old pole derrick as a bolt of lightning lit the sky. The old homestead was almost directly behind them now, not more than a half-mile, he guessed. He looked back a second time, then shook his head and looked again. He could have sworn he had caught a brief glimpse of a light shining into the sky beyond the derrick. But if so, it had only lasted a moment. It couldn't have been, he told himself. Just more lightning, he reasoned, and he dismissed the thought. This place was making him crazy.

CHAPTER 7

The shrill ringing of the phone awoke the sheriff. Glancing at his alarm clock, he wearily rolled out of bed. It was two in the morning. He grabbed the receiver and pressed it to his ear. "Hello," he said groggily.

"Sheriff, I seen it again!"

"Roscoe?"

"Yup, it's me. I seen that light again. It shined longer this time."

"Are you sure?" Vince asked dubiously. He could hear the rain pounding on the roof and saw a flash of lightning through the bedroom window. "Lots of lightning tonight."

"Sheriff, you said you'd come. I seen it. Get out here. If I catch 'em myself I'll rip 'em in two with this old twelve-gauge of mine," Roscoe threatened fiercely.

"I'm coming, Roscoe. Meet me where your lane joins the highway in twenty minutes," he barked.

"Can you be here that soon?" Roscoe asked.

"My car's a little quicker than your old truck," the sheriff responded sharply, and without waiting for a response, he slammed the phone down.

"What is it, Vince?" his wife asked as he began to dress.

"Roscoe Norman is seeing lights again," he moaned. "I promised him I'd come."

"Oh, Vince, you can't. Call one of your deputies. You're going to have a heart attack or a stroke or something if you don't slow down," she complained.

"Sorry, honey," he replied. "I've got to do it. I'll be back as soon as I can."

As Sheriff Hanks sped west to meet Roscoe, he saw only a single car. The driver failed to dim his headlights, and with the added glare caused by the falling rain, the sheriff could tell only that it was a car, not a pickup. Other than this car, which he passed about halfway between Harrisville and Roscoe's farm, the road was deserted.

As he'd agreed, Roscoe was waiting for him. "Yer late, Sheriff," he scolded.

The sheriff glanced at his watch. "Twenty-two minutes. The rain slowed me down a bit more than I'd figured. See anyone come out of there?"

"Nope. Nary a soul. Did see car lights down the road a piece. That was all," Roscoe reported.

This time, Sheriff Hanks led the way to the homestead. The sheriff parked his car in front of the old derrick, stepped out into the pouring rain, and pulled out his flashlight. He saw no one, and nothing suspicious, and if there had been tracks, the heavy rain had destroyed them. After several minutes of tromping through the weeds and brush, the sheriff gave up.

"Mr. Norman," he said wearily, "if anyone was here tonight, they must have been crazy." Vince was soaked to the skin, and so was the old farmer. "Nobody would be after rabbits on a night like this."

Reluctantly, the old man agreed. "But I seen a light, Sheriff," he insisted.

"I'm sure you did," the sheriff stated skeptically as lightning once more tore through the pouring rain. *I was crazy for coming out here tonight,* he thought. To Roscoe, he said, "I'll be back to photograph that boot print."

Despite the storm, the boot print, although distorted by the rain on the surface of the water in the ditch, was still there, undisturbed and intact.

* * *

The phone woke the sheriff again. This time sunshine was streaming through the window; the storm had run its course. A glance at the clock told him he'd overslept—it was nearly seven. Before he could get his hand on the phone, it quit ringing. A moment later his wife entered the bedroom. "It's for you, dear," she said.

The sheriff picked up the receiver and waited until he heard the click that told him his wife had replaced the one in the kitchen. "Hello."

"Sheriff, Kyle Lind here." The rancher sounded very agitated, causing the sheriff's heart to speed up.

"Good morning, Kyle," he mumbled, fighting the sleep that still dragged at his eyelids.

"I got a ransom note!" Kyle exclaimed, driving the sleep from the sheriff's head.

"Are you at home?"

"Yes."

"I'll be right out."

"Vince, are you leaving again?" his wife called from the kitchen as he hurried into the living room, still fastening on his gun belt.

"Yes."

"You've got to have some breakfast first," she called. "I'll have it on in a minute."

"Haven't time, hon, but I love you. See you later."

"Vince!" he heard her call as the door closed behind him. He felt bad as he recognized the worry in her voice. *I'll make it up to her when this thing is over,* he promised himself without looking back.

When he arrived at the Lind ranch, the sheriff found Kyle Lind, Jake Garrett, and Agnes Arndt huddled near Jake's car. The road was covered with puddles from the night's storm, and the sheriff's car was plastered with mud.

Jake held a piece of paper in his hand. He offered it to Sheriff Hanks. "This is it, Sheriff. I figured something like this would be coming. Do you think it's that Buster guy?"

"Probably," the sheriff affirmed as he took the note, holding it gingerly by the edge. "How many of you have touched this?" he asked a little more sharply than he intended.

"We all have, Sheriff," Kyle admitted. "Should we not have?"

As Kyle spoke, the sheriff scanned the note. Unless he was mistaken, it had been produced on a typewriter rather than a computer. It was unsigned, very brief, and so serious in tone that it made the sheriff shiver. After reading it through twice, he looked up. "Where was it? The mail isn't delivered this early out here, is it?" he asked.

"No," Kyle answered. "It comes around ten, usually. Agnes found it when she got here this morning. The note was in the mailbox, but it wasn't even in an envelope. It was folded in half, just like you can see there."

Agnes added, "I had a letter to my son that I'd meant to leave in my own box when I left my place this morning. But I forgot. I remembered when I saw Mr. Kyle's box, so I stopped to put it in there. The note was there when I opened the mailbox."

A rural carrier delivered Kyle Lind's mail. His mailbox was beside the highway at the end of the lane, a half mile from the house. Anyone could have put the note inside unobserved.

Sheriff Hanks questioned, "When was the last time anyone looked in the box?"

"Candi picked up the mail when the kids got off the bus yesterday afternoon."

"So it could have been put in there anytime after that," the sheriff surmised.

Kyle nodded and Jake spoke up. "Might have been there when you were here yesterday for all we know."

"I guess it could have been," the sheriff agreed as he again looked at the note.

An hour later Chief Ron Worthlin, Chief Deputy Shawn Fullman, and Deputy Kara Smith met Sheriff Hanks in his office in Harrisville. "I have a note here," the sheriff said. "I've already dusted it for prints. We'll need to have someone take everyone's prints out at Kyle's place so we can compare, but I don't expect much. They all handled it, all but the girls, that is. I expect all the prints will match one or the other of them."

"What does it say?" Ron Worthlin asked.

Vince picked up a photocopy of the note; the original now lay in his safe. His voice was somber as he read.

The kid's alive. If you want him to stay that way, get your money together. A half million will do. I'll be in touch.

* * *

An early-morning fisherman cast a line. "I got a big one!" he shouted to his buddy as his line suddenly bent and his rod bucked in his hand.

For several minutes, he fought to reel in his catch. Twice the huge fish broke the surface, sparkling in the sun, but eventually it came loose, and he reeled in an empty line. The hook was still there, but it held a small piece of flesh from the fish's mouth. Disappointed, the fisherman cursed and reached for his tackle box. "I'll get him again," he vowed. "That was the biggest fish I ever seen in this lake."

"Forget it," his buddy said. "He won't bite again today. He's hurting. Let's come back in a couple of days and try. Then maybe we can hook him again."

* * *

One-way glass gave Edgar Stevens the luxury of studying customers before they entered his office. Grim satisfaction blanketed his face as he watched the worried, haggard man who stood wringing his hands on the far side of the glass. After making the man wait for a sufficient amount of time, Edgar buzzed his secretary. "Have Mr. Lind come in now," he instructed.

"Good morning, Kyle," Edgar greeted in a friendly voice as the rancher entered his plush office. "What can I do for you?"

Kyle slumped into a chair without being invited, and the act made Edgar's temper rise, but he controlled it. He waited for the rancher to speak. "Edgar, I need help," Kyle started in a low, strained voice.

"That's what I'm here for," Edgar answered, trying to determine the right amount of concern to put in his voice. "What seems to be the matter?"

"You know about my son, I suppose?" Kyle asked. For a moment, Edgar thought the rancher was going to cry, but he didn't, although it was apparent that he was nearly a broken man.

"Yes, and I'm terribly sorry," Edgar offered, adjusting his voice so that it dripped with sympathy.

"Well, it's sort of put me in a tailspin. I should have been in sooner, but I forgot. I need an extension on the note I owe. The bills are still coming in from my wife's illness. I could sell some cattle, if that's okay with you, but I need a little time. It would help if I could also sell some hay, and maybe even some of my range land," Kyle explained.

Edgar settled back into his leather chair, removed his glasses, and peered at Kyle thoughtfully. "Well, well," he said softly. "This is a problem. You really don't want to cut yourself short of land or feed, do you?"

"No, but I'll figure something out, Edgar," Kyle promised. "I just can't think straight right now. With the worries over Cody missing and all, I just don't know what to do. If you could grant me an extension of a few weeks, I will take care of it. I'll be able to sell something, I'm sure."

"I suppose I could let it sort of slide for a few days," Edgar acquiesced, staring at Kyle through narrowed eyes.

"Thank you, Edgar," Kyle said quickly, but the banker could see no real relief on the rancher's weathered face.

"Will that be all then?" Edgar asked, anxious to get Kyle out of his office. It was all he could do to keep from smiling at his good fortune. Kyle hadn't even asked for an agreement in writing! *The poor man must be quite distraught to overlook something as crucial as that. With nothing in writing and Kyle put at ease, the ranch will soon be mine,* Edgar thought joyfully.

Edgar stood, but Kyle did not, so he added, "Well, I'll talk to you later, Kyle. Don't worry about a thing."

"I am worried," Kyle suddenly burst out. "I got a ransom demand for the return of my boy this morning."

"You did?" Edgar asked. "I'm sorry to hear that."

"Yes. I need a half-million dollars in cash."

"Now Kyle, that's not possible! You know that. Why, you'd have to deed over the whole ranch—house and all—to the bank if I were to give you that kind of money. I know how you love the place, but if your boy's life's at stake, I suppose you'd be willing to do that." Edgar was immediately revising his earlier thoughts, thinking how much better it would look to the community if Kyle simply sold the ranch to the bank. Then he wouldn't have to go through the nasty task of foreclosing.

Kyle stood. "That would be a last resort, but thanks anyway, Edgar. And thanks for the extension." He walked out.

After the door closed, fat Edgar danced a jig on the carpet. The best ranch and one of the nicest houses in the county were as good as his! He glanced through the window, surprised to see a young, dark stranger talking earnestly with Kyle. Edgar didn't recognize the man and wondered who he could be. He dressed well and seemed to have a close relationship with Kyle.

As the rancher and the stranger walked away, the stranger looked back. If it weren't for the one-way glass, Edgar believed their eyes would have met. Edgar definitely did not like the look on that man's face. *Will he stir up trouble before the foreclosure is complete?* he wondered. *Well, he'd better not try anything. I'm too close to owning that ranch to lose it now.*

* * *

"I can't believe he wouldn't even consider lending you the money for the ransom, Kyle. That may be the only way to save Cody," Jake declared angrily as he and Kyle left the bank.

"I'm sure the sheriff is doing all he can to find Buster Ashton, but I'm sure Buster is doing just as much to keep from being found. And maybe that's not even who took Cody," Kyle said, fighting to keep his emotions under control.

"That's got to be who it is!" Jake exclaimed. "Everything points that way. Especially with the ransom demand. He's even done it before."

Kyle nodded, in full agreement with Jake, and it frightened him more than he could admit. Mariah hadn't called him, although he'd left several messages on her answering machine. As hard as he fought them, his doubts about her continued to haunt him.

Jake spoke again. "At least he granted you an extension on the loan. I'll bet you had to sign your life away for that."

"No, he didn't make me sign anything. He just said he'd give me a little time."

"Oh," Jake answered, and the doubt in his voice made Kyle look at him sharply. His nephew's face was dark and brooding. "Do you trust him that much, Kyle?"

"I have no reason not to. He's always been good to his word before," Kyle replied.

"I see," Jake replied, but Kyle was not sure Jake meant it. And Jake's doubts planted seeds of worry in Kyle's mind.

"Don't worry about the place, Jake. He won't foreclose now," Kyle stated with growing uncertainty. "He's a greedy man, but he would never do that. He has to live and do business in this town. Let's get back to the ranch. There's work to do."

"Sure," Jake agreed. "We'll just have to leave things up to the sheriff. He seems like a competent man."

"He is."

"And I like the looks of his deputy."

"Which one? He has several."

"I've only met one. And she is . . . well, you know, very appealing," Jake finished lamely. "And she seems really nice."

CHAPTER 8

The very appealing deputy to which Jake referred was just leaving the sheriff's office, and she was worried. The ransom demand had driven home with grim surety the seriousness of the whole Cody Lind affair. She wondered if the boy was even alive. In a way the note gave hope, yet Kara had heard stories about people making ransom demands even after killing their victims. Her heart went out to Kyle and his family.

The sheriff had taken steps to intensify the search for Buster Ashton, and he had assigned several other deputies to take the lead. In the meantime he'd asked Kara to confirm what the other suspects had been up to for the past day. That meant she needed to discover where Gil Enders, Sammy Shirts, and Mariah Taylor had been during the past twenty hours or so.

She'd begin with Gil, Kara decided, since he was probably at work right now. She drove to the hardware store. On the way, she saw Jake Garrett's sporty green Mustang coming down the street, and despite herself, she felt a shiver of delight. As he passed, he seemed to be in earnest conversation with his passenger, Kyle Lind, and he didn't even look her way. Where had they been? She really hadn't expected to see them in town so soon after finding the ransom note—unless they'd been to the bank to arrange for the cash needed to pay the ransom. She hoped that wasn't the case because she knew the sheriff would frown upon the idea of actually paying out the money unless it was a last resort.

Kara put that thought on the back burner as she pulled up to the hardware store. Gil Enders wasn't in, so she asked Harry if he'd taken the day off.

"He went home sick yesterday afternoon, and then he called in this morning and said he was still not feeling well," Harry responded.

"Does he have the flu?" she asked.

"I don't know," Harry replied. "He didn't look very sick to me, but he said he was, so I let him go. Sure leaves me shorthanded."

Kara thanked Harry and left. As she drove to Gil's apartment, she mused over his absence from work. Maybe it didn't mean anything, but then again, maybe it did. Gil finally answered the door after she'd knocked a third time. He looked like he'd been sleeping—his eyes were red, his hair mussed, and his shirt wrinkled and damp.

"Gil, I'm sorry to bother you," she started, "but Harry told me I'd find you here. He said you're ill."

"Yeah, I am. And I got nothing to say to you," he said sharply.

The deputy took a deep breath. "I need to talk to you a minute. May I step in?"

He began to swing the door shut but apparently thought better of the idea and let her enter. "Say what you got to say and get out," he ordered. "If it's about Cody Lind, I don't know anything more now than I did before."

Kara stepped further into the room, looking around as Gil turned to shut the door. Glancing through an open doorway into what was apparently Gil's bedroom, she was surprised to see a fairly large picture of Bridget Harrison on the wall. She only glanced at it, then turned her head. The last thing she wanted to do was let Gil know she'd noticed the picture. She moved quickly to where it was out of her sight.

"Gil," she said, facing him, "the sheriff asked me to come by. There have been some new developments in the case involving Cody."

"I'm sure there have," he responded sarcastically. "And like I told you before, it really doesn't concern me."

Kara felt her skin begin to crawl, and the thought occurred to her that it might not have been too smart to come here alone. Her right hand moved closer to the butt of her pistol as she said bluntly, "I need to know where you were last night."

Gil snorted. "Here, of course! I'm sick, like Harry told you."

"Yes," she replied, repelled by the anger and hatred plainly visible in his face and eyes. *But you don't appear ill to me, just uptight,* Kara reasoned to herself. The thought was unsettling.

She hesitated to ask her final question, but orders were orders. "Do you have a typewriter, Gil?"

Gil glared at her. "What kind of stupid question is that? People don't use typewriters nowadays. And I can't see where it's any of your business if I did have one. Get out!" he ordered, moving to the door and flinging it open so hard it bounced on the doorstop.

Kara left willingly. *Gil Enders is still very high on the suspect list—at least on my list,* she thought as she headed for her patrol car. Yet she admitted to herself that the ransom note didn't seem in character when it came to Gil. If he were involved, the sheriff had noted earlier, his motive would have been his jealousy over Bridget, and that would more likely point to homicide than to kidnapping for ransom. But now, after the way he exploded when she mentioned a typewriter, Kara wondered. He certainly didn't act like an innocent man.

Well, Kara thought, maybe they would have to come back with a search warrant. If Gil had a typewriter, they would need to compare its type to that on the note. If he had typed the note, such a comparison would confirm it.

Kara wished she could speak to the sheriff right away, but he was gone and she didn't want to talk to him about this on their cell phones. She knew Sheriff Hanks was anxious to get the photo of the watery boot print in the ditch, and she knew he'd already left for Roscoe's farm, so she drove to Sammy Shirts's trashy house across from the city trailer park.

Sammy's truck was gone, and Kara received no answer to her persistent knocking at his door. She drove around town but failed to spot him, so she decided that she'd have to try later. That left Mariah Taylor. Reluctantly, the deputy drove to the high school.

Miss Taylor was in class, the principal told Kara. "I'll get her out if you need her right now," he offered. Kara hated to bother her in class again, but now that she was here, she wanted to get this over with.

Mariah looked drawn and tired when she appeared a few minutes later. "You may use my office," the principal suggested.

"Thank you. We won't be long," Kara promised, uncomfortable under the English teacher's sad gaze.

As soon as they were alone, Kara said, "I'm really sorry about this, but there have been some new developments, and we need your help."

"I see," Mariah responded without even looking at Kara.

"Where did you go last night after school?" Kara asked.

"Home," Mariah said shortly.

"And you were at home the whole time—all through the night?"

"Yes, until I came to school this morning."

"Have you talked to Kyle Lind?" Kara asked, hoping to somehow make the interview easier.

"I told you I wouldn't if that's what I had to do to convince you I'm not guilty. And I haven't," was the sharp reply.

Kara had expected that answer. "Have you heard from Buster again?"

"No."

"You haven't seen him?"

"That's right. I would have called if I had," Mariah said firmly, her eyes finally meeting Kara's. Then Mariah took the offensive. "I know you don't believe me—you or your boss—but I had nothing to do with Cody's disappearance. If I could help, I would, but I know nothing."

"We were hoping that . . . well, that you'd heard from Buster," Kara began uncertainly.

"Why?"

"Because we think he may have been around. We now know that Cody was kidnapped for ransom," Kara explained.

The look of surprise and dismay on Mariah's face seemed genuine. "Has Kyle received a ransom demand?" she asked, sounding concerned.

"Yes," Kara said.

"That sounds like Buster," Mariah sighed. "How much did he ask for?"

"A half million dollars."

"Oh!" Mariah gasped, and for a moment Kara thought she would faint. But she quickly regained her composure and asked, "What else did the kidnappers want?"

Kara told her what the note said—that Cody was alive and would stay that way as long as the kidnappers received the ransom money— and once more Mariah seemed almost overcome with emotion. Kara felt like she was riding a roller coaster. One moment she dismissed the very idea of Mariah's involvement, and the next her suspicions resurfaced. They talked for a few more minutes. Mariah promised to do all she could to try to find out if her ex-husband, Roger Griggs, had any idea where Buster was without tipping her hand that her questions were related to Cody's kidnapping.

By the end of the interview, Kara's instincts told her that Miss Taylor was being straight with her. Then, as she went to open the door, Mariah said, "A half million dollars! That's how much Roger and Buster demanded the last time. It must be them. At least Buster. Roger's still in prison."

After leaving the high school, Kara thought about driving out to talk to Kyle and Jake, but she decided to first drive by Sammy Shirts's house again. Seeing his old truck in the driveway, she stopped out front and started up the badly cracked, weed-lined walk.

She knocked several times on the front door before Sammy finally answered. When he did, it was obvious he'd been drinking. The thought occurred to her that she might have been able to arrest him for drunk driving if she'd waited here for him instead of going to the school. With Sammy in jail, he would soon either be eliminated as a suspect or incriminated.

"Whaddaya want?" Sammy demanded in a drunken slur.

"I just need to talk to you for a moment," she responded.

"Well, then, come in, missy," he said, swinging the door wide.

The stench of his filthy little house nearly gagged her. Looking around, Kara saw at least part of the source of the odor: there was clutter everywhere. One corner of the room was filled with empty beer bottles and cans, dishes covered with dried-on food, and stacks of paper, the last of which she thought might have come from various dumpsters. It took her a moment to calm her stomach and remind herself to breathe through her mouth so she wouldn't have to smell the foul odor.

"What can I do for you, miss lady cop?" Sammy pressed.

"The sheriff was wondering where you were last night," she replied.

"Right here," he answered without hesitation.

"All night?"

"Yes. I didn't leave until about nine this mornin', and then I went to the store," he mumbled.

"Could I see your typewriter for a minute?" Kara asked, hoping to catch him off guard.

"Typewriter?" he asked with a slurred laugh. "Now, what would I want one of them for? I don't think hardly anybody has them anymore. And anyway, I couldn't use it if I had one."

"Really?" she asked. "So are you telling me you don't own one?"

"I don't read much, and I write less. I ain't never so much as touched a typewriter since I was a kid in school."

"Really?" she asked again.

"That's right."

"Home all night, huh?"

"Yup."

With sudden inspiration, she asked, "What about the night before? Where were you that night?"

"Home."

"All night?"

"Yup?"

"What time did you leave yesterday morning?"

"Late. Like today," Sammy said confidently.

"I see. Then how do you explain my seeing you over by the bank at dawn?" Kara asked, watching his face carefully.

His mouth dropped open and his red eyes bulged. "You seen me?"

"Yes, I saw you. You were watching Mr. Stevens, Sammy." She paused, staring hard at him, trying to intimidate him.

For a moment he stammered. Then he finally answered, "I was just watchin' him."

"Why, Sammy? Why would you be watching Mr. Stevens?"

Again, he hesitated. He was obviously trying to think, and in his state that was a painfully slow process. Finally, he managed, "I was just trying to help the sheriff."

Now it was Kara's turn to be surprised, but she recovered quickly. "How would watching Mr. Stevens enter his bank help Sheriff Hanks?"

Sammy looked around as if he might discover someone eavesdropping. The action, coming from him, was comical, almost ludicrous. After doing so, he stepped toward her and said in a loud whisper, "I think he took the Lind kid."

"What? Why do you say that? I thought you told the sheriff that Cody ran away on his own," she said, her mind whirling, wondering why Sammy would say such a thing—and if it might possibly be true.

"I think he done it, that's all. You better watch him. You might learn something," he said, squaring his sagging shoulders. "If I could help, do you think there might be a reward or something?"

Quickly deciding to play along with him, Kara gushed, "You might be on to something, Sammy. And there would be a reward, all right—a big one. But can you really help us?"

"Yes," he said. "I sure can." Again he looked around, and Kara found herself doing the same, but all she could see was filth, ragged furniture, empty beer cans, and more filth.

"I was watchin' him again today," Sammy confided.

"You were? I thought you said you were home. Are you being honest with me, Sammy?" she asked doubtfully. "You could get in a lot of trouble, maybe even spend some time in jail, if you lie to me."

"Well, I mighta lied a little," he admitted. "I ain't been to the store. But I didn't go out any earlier than I told you, about sunup, that is. But I went out again later. I was watching the bank. Mr. Lind and some good-looking cowboy-type stranger went in. When they come out, they was plumb mad. If I was you, I'd look into Mr. Big Guy Stevens."

So that was where Jake and Kyle had been. They had to have been trying to raise the ransom money. Kara wondered what had happened at the bank to upset Jake so much, and she remembered the look of agitation on his face when she passed him earlier. If Sammy was right, Kyle had also been angry. They had probably failed to get the money, which was no surprise. Edgar Stevens was a very stingy man.

Kara spent a little more time questioning Sammy, but learned nothing more of any substance and finally left. She had detected both envy and hatred whenever Sammy mentioned the banker, but he had raised some important questions. When the sheriff returned from the Norman farm, she'd see what he thought.

After returning to her car, Kara checked with the dispatcher to ask the sheriff's current whereabouts. When she learned that he was still in the west end of the county, she turned her car toward the highway and drove out to the Lind ranch.

It was just after noon when she pulled into the yard and parked next to Jake's green Mustang beneath a large poplar tree. Kara couldn't see anyone in the corrals or the nearby fields, so she went to the door and rang the bell. Jake answered it and smiled when he saw her. "Well, hello," he said. "Come on in, Deputy Smith. To what do we owe this visit?"

His dark eyes held her speechless. He chuckled. "Don't tell me you don't know."

With a struggle, she found her voice. "I need to speak with Mr. Lind, please."

"Of course. I'll get him. Please sit down," Jake invited, directing her to the same sofa she and the sheriff had occupied the previous evening.

It scarcely seemed possible that Kyle Lind could look worse than he had the night before, but he did. His eyes were sunken, his normally tanned and robust face was waxy, and his shoulders looked so limp it was hard to believe they were supported by bone. When he spoke, it was with a lifeless voice, one that reminded her of impending death. She heard a rattle in his voice, and he frequently had to clear his throat. He was in such bad shape that Kara feared he was going to have a stroke or a heart attack.

"Hello, Deputy," he said.

"Hello, Mr. Lind. Have you got a minute?"

"That's about all I have left," he said as he sank into a chair. "Time, I mean. I've lost about everything else."

"I've been to see Mariah Taylor," Kara said abruptly, shaken by the rancher's deathly appearance and equally thrown off balance by Jake Garrett, who had just sat down right next to her.

"What did she have to say for herself?" Kyle asked bitterly.

"She suspects her former brother-in-law," Kara replied.

"So do we," Jake interrupted.

She glanced at him, and those dark eyes held hers a moment longer than she had intended. Looking back at Mr. Lind, she explained, "Mariah wants to help. I believe she's sincere, and I don't think she's involved in the kidnapping."

Kara didn't think the sheriff would condone her saying that, but she couldn't stand to see the pain in Kyle Lind's eyes. A little good news couldn't hurt him. "I think you should talk to her," she went on. "She's hurting too, you know." When her words seemed to lift Kyle a little, she added, "Why don't you call her as soon as school is out for the day?"

Kyle slumped again. "Don't you think I've been trying? She doesn't answer her phone or return my calls when I leave a message on her machine."

"Then go see her."

"Yes, why don't you do that, Kyle?" Jake suggested, siding with Kara.

"Well, I don't know."

"Please do," Kara urged. "It would help both of you, I'm sure."

"No, I don't think so. I don't think she wants to see me," Kyle said hopelessly.

There was an awkward silence. Then Jake cleared his throat and said, "Kyle, why don't you rest. I'll visit with Deputy Smith for a minute. Then I'll get to moving your wheel lines. We need to get that second-crop hay growing."

Kyle nodded an acknowledgment, pulled himself from his chair, and dragged himself from the room without another word. Jake stood. "Why don't we go outside?" he said to Kara.

He showed her to the door. Once they were on the large porch, he said, "You are a very lovely lady—and I don't just mean you're attractive. But you are that, too. Deputy Smith, you are remarkably kind and understanding with Kyle."

Jake's compliments made Kara blush. He was direct, far more direct than she was used to, but he seemed sincere. "Thank you," she managed to mutter, "on all of the above."

"Kyle has a great place here, don't you think?" he asked.

"Yeah, it's something else," Kara agreed as they strolled down the long walk. "Sheriff Hanks mentioned you drew up the blueprints for the house. It's beautiful."

"It would be terrible if he lost it, and the ranch," Jake declared.

"He won't lose it," Kara said quickly.

"I'm afraid he could. He's deep in debt," Jake answered.

She stopped and looked at him, stunned at what he'd just revealed to her. "Are you sure?"

"Yes, I'm afraid so. What can you tell me about Edgar Stevens?"

"Oh, not much," she said, surprised at the unexpected turn in the conversation. On the other hand, she was glad, because she'd wanted to talk about what Jake and Kyle had been doing at the bank, and she hadn't known how to broach the subject. Now that she had her opening, she took advantage of it. "He is rather tight, I've heard. Greedy, even."

"I can vouch for that," Jake responded, his dark eyes rarely straying from hers.

"I saw you coming from the bank," she said. "Is Mr. Stevens causing Kyle some problems?"

"Is he ever!" Jake exclaimed, his eyes suddenly flaring with fire. His anger was so intense it almost made her jerk back. "I think he's after this ranch, new house and all," he went on through clenched teeth.

"No!" Kara exclaimed in surprise.

"Yes!" he countered with rage in his voice. Then Jake Garrett told her all about the visit Kyle had made to the bank earlier that day. She listened in stunned silence.

Before Kara knew it, she was telling Jake all about her visit with Sammy Shirts. After she'd finished, he said, "I honestly doubt that Edgar kidnapped Cody. That seems more in character for this Buster guy. But Stevens is prepared to take advantage of the situation, and I expect him to try to foreclose on the ranch unless someone puts a stop to it."

"But who could possibly step in and do that?"

"I was hoping a visit from the sheriff might help," Jake stated. "If Stevens knew people were on to his game, maybe he'd back off and give Kyle an extension on the note—in writing, of course. And maybe he'd loan Kyle the money to pay the kidnapper to get Cody back. That's the only chance of saving the boy, I think. Don't you?"

"Probably," Kara admitted.

"Talk to the sheriff," he urged, the anger receding. His dark eyes were softer, pleading as he spoke. "We can't stand by and let that shark take everything Kyle has worked so hard for, can we? He's already suffered more than one man should have to suffer."

"I'll talk to Sheriff Hanks," she promised. "Maybe he can think of something."

"To start with, ask him if he'd try to convince old Stevens to write down the extension he promised Kyle on that note," Jake suggested.

"It's worth a try," she agreed. "I need to go now and meet with him." Reluctantly, she moved away from Jake.

"Kara," he said, calling her by her first name for the first time.

"Yes, Jake?" she said, turning back toward him and gazing into his dark, mysterious eyes.

"Do you have plans for dinner tonight?"

"No, but—" she began.

"No buts," he cut in with a chuckle. "I'd be honored if you'd have dinner with me."

For a moment, Kara felt breathless, but she recovered quickly and replied, "I'd like that very much."

"Good. Is eight too late?"

"Eight's perfect," she answered.

"Give me your address and I'll pick you up."

She jotted it down for him, and then he walked her to her car and opened the door for her. "I'll see you at eight then. And no uniform, please," Jake laughed. "You look great in a uniform, but I'm curious to see you in . . . well, in something less formal."

She blushed. "I'll try to find something," she giggled, and he gently closed her car door.

Ten minutes later, Kara was back in the sheriff's office. "Did you get the photos you wanted?" she asked.

"Sure did. I'm not sure yet why I wanted them, but who knows, they might be worthwhile someday. If nothing else, it seemed to make old Roscoe feel like I was doing my job. Maybe he'll leave us alone for a few days. Now, tell me what you've learned, Kara," Sheriff Hanks said, sitting back in his chair and watching her expectantly.

When she'd completed her report, he sat silent for a few seconds. "Edgar Stevens," he said thoughtfully. "You know, I never did like that man. He and I went to high school together. He's two years older than I am. I remember when he ran for one of the student body offices. He decided the name Edgar was too pedantic, maybe even intimidating, so all of his campaign posters proclaimed wonderful things about Ed Stevens—friendly Ed. But in the pictures he looked like a used-car salesman with a phony smile, and he sounded like one in his speeches. "Ed" just never caught on with anyone. And because he was so eager to change our impression of him, we all started calling him Eager Edgar. Looks like he's still the used-car-salesman type with the same phony smile. He hasn't changed at all in thirty-five years. I don't know if I can do anything or not, but I can sure try. And I will. But I can hardly see him as a kidnapper, even if Sammy can. It's too easy for Eager Edgar to steal with paper and pen."

"I agree," Kara responded. "But then, like you said, we can't rule anyone out until we have a good reason to."

Sheriff Hanks nodded. "And that includes Mariah Taylor, although I agree she's been bumped quite a ways down on the list of persons of interest. I also agree that Buster Ashton still looms large as the culprit in this thing, and he is one dangerous man."

"Do you think we can rule Gil Enders out?" Kara asked.

"Absolutely not. I'm disturbed at the way he reacted to your question about a typewriter. And if he's not ill, then why did he take time off work, and where was he last night? He could well have put that note in Kyle's mailbox." The sheriff leaned forward. "What do you think, Kara?"

"I tend to agree," she admitted. "But if Gil did something to Cody out of jealousy or hatred or whatever, why would he write a ransom note?"

"He may have written it to throw us off his trail. That's why I can't dismiss him. I'd sure like to know if he has a typewriter, and if so, get a sample from it to compare to the ransom note. That way, we'll at least know if he wrote it or not."

The sheriff sat back again. "Kara, have you noticed how every time we seem to get closer to a solution to this thing, we only get farther away? We have more suspects than ever now, if we count Edgar Stevens, and I suppose we have to for the time being. And I haven't dismissed Sammy, either. You never know what his game might be."

Kara nodded. "What now?" she asked.

"I'll take a turn with Gil Enders. You go home and get some rest this afternoon. You never know when you may be called out again at some unearthly hour."

"All right, but—uh—Sheriff?" she stammered.

"Yes, Kara?" he said, leaning forward again. "Do you have something else on your mind?"

"Yes, sir. I have a date tonight. Of course, if you need me to, I'll break it," she added quickly.

The sheriff smiled. "With whom, if I may ask?"

"With Jake. Jake Garrett," she said, blushing.

Sheriff Hanks settled back in his chair again with a grin. "I see. I thought this would be coming," he chuckled. "Well, go and have a good time. I won't disturb you unless it's absolutely necessary, and if it is, I'm sure Jake will understand."

CHAPTER 9

After school, Bridget walked Candi to her school bus. Earlier in the day, Candi had told Bridget about the ransom note. Both girls were more sick with worry than ever. Bridget had also seen Kara Smith's patrol car from the window before lunch, and she mentioned it to Candi as they walked.

Candi responded quickly. "She was here to talk to Miss Taylor, I'll bet." Her brown eyes hardened. "I just know she had something to do with Cody!"

Bridget agreed with her voice but not with her heart. Despite everything that had happened, she had a hard time picturing Miss Taylor as a kidnapper, especially one who would demand a ransom. When Candi had told her about the ransom note, it had two effects on her. First, she felt a surge of hope that Cody was still alive, but then the awful reality of Cody having been kidnapped was driven home. Even though she still felt ill, she doubted Miss Taylor's involvement.

Candi noted her friend's hesitation. "Don't you think it was her?" she asked harshly.

"I don't like her either, but I don't know," Bridget hedged. "I just can't get Gil Enders out of my mind. I shudder to think of him. He hates Cody! And he seems like a greedy guy to me."

"Maybe he and Miss Taylor are in it together," Candi suggested.

That made Bridget stop dead in her tracks. "Oh, no! Do you think that's possible?"

"Of course, it's possible," Candi replied. "We should have thought of it sooner."

"Candi, what can we do? I get sick thinking of Cody being tied or locked up somewhere, or worse, while . . . while . . ."

"While what, Bridget?" Candi asked.

"Well, you know, while the cops do their thing. They should have had him back by now. They should have found him. Maybe Sheriff Hanks doesn't know what to do. And I can't imagine that Kara Smith does," Bridget declared, shaking her head with doubt.

"Yeah, I agree. She's too . . . you know . . . too girly to be a tough cop!"

"And too nice!" Bridget added. "She doesn't even look like a cop. Of course, there are other deputies, but I haven't seen them around much."

"The sheriff and Kara are trying to do it all, I think," Candi agreed.

The two girls looked at each other thoughtfully for a moment. Then Bridget whispered, looking around to make sure she was not overheard. "Maybe we should do something to help find Cody."

"Like what?" Candi asked with wide, eager eyes.

"Well, let's see," Bridget began, brushing absently at her hair and wrinkling her forehead. "Well, I don't know."

The girls stood silently for a moment, thinking. "Hey, I have an idea!" Candi exclaimed suddenly. "I think my cousin—you know, Jake—I think he's got his eyes on that officer, Kara Smith. Maybe I can get him to pump her a little. I know he wants to help find Cody. He's worried to death. I'll go home and talk to him. Maybe with his help we can do something."

"Good idea," Bridget agreed quickly. "Call me later. You better run so you won't miss your bus. I'll be waiting by the phone."

"Okay, I'll call as soon as I talk to Jake," Candi called as she turned and ran for the bus.

As Bridget stood watching the bus pull away, she was deep in thought. She hadn't realized just how strong her feelings for Cody were, but she found that she was willing to take any risk if it would help him. She clenched a determined fist and turned to walk home, but she bumped right into Miss Taylor.

"Oh, I'm sorry," Bridget said hastily as she stepped to the side and tried to get by.

Mariah stopped her with one word, "Don't!"

"Don't what?" Bridget cried in sudden fear.

"Don't interfere. Let the sheriff handle things, Bridget. He'll catch the guilty party," Mariah ordered.

Bridget noted a catch in Miss Taylor's voice and looked up at her face to see tears in her eyes. Bridget felt guilty—Miss Taylor really didn't look like a criminal. But Bridget was determined to help Cody, so she burst out, "Somebody's got to do something!"

"The sheriff and his deputies are working hard. They're going to catch him . . ." Miss Taylor hesitated as her voice caught again.

"Who?" Bridget demanded. "Who are they going catch? You know something, don't you?" Her heart began to beat wildly and she stepped back. *Maybe,* she thought, *Miss Taylor really is involved, or maybe she knows something she isn't willing to tell.*

"Bridget, I know you girls think I'm terrible and that I hate Cody, but it's not true. You've got to believe me. And yes, I do know something. Do you have a minute?"

Bridget hesitated, looking around to see if there was anyone who could rescue her if she screamed. There wasn't, and her stomach knotted up. Then she thought of Cody. As she envisioned him tied tightly somewhere with his face in the dirt, her determination to help him came surging back. She squared her shoulders bravely. "Sure."

"Let's go back into the school, to my room," Mariah suggested.

"All right," Bridget complied. It seemed safe enough, since there were still plenty of people in the school, so she followed the English teacher up the walk.

Once they were back in the classroom with the door shut, Miss Taylor said, "Please don't be nervous. I love you kids. I wouldn't hurt you for the world."

"I . . . I know," Bridget stammered unconvincingly. She knew no such thing, much as she wanted to.

"Sit down and let me tell you a story, Bridget. It's a true story. Maybe after you hear it, you'll trust me. And maybe you won't. But I hope you do. I was married once to a guy by the name of Roger Griggs," she began.

Despite herself, Bridget relaxed as Miss Taylor emotionally told her about her disastrous marriage. She described how Roger beat her, and the fear she came to feel in his presence. Bridget's stomach knotted as she thought of the terrible things this woman had suffered. Then she sighed with relief as Miss Taylor said, "I got away from him at last."

"Does he still bother you?" Bridget asked breathlessly.

Miss Taylor nodded slowly. "In a way he does. Oh, he doesn't come around me or anything like that. He can't right now. He's in prison."

"Prison!" Bridget gasped.

"Yes. He writes to me when he wants something from me, which isn't very often. That's what I want to talk to you about. You see, Bridget, he's in prison for kidnapping."

The blood drained from Bridget's face. For a moment she thought she might faint. Miss Taylor sprang to her feet. "I'm sorry," she said. "Let me get you a glass of water."

"No, I'll be okay," Bridget responded as she rubbed her eyes and shook her head. Miss Taylor's hand rested on Bridget's shoulder, and it felt like a concerned touch, not an evil one. She stood there for a moment, and then Bridget said, "Okay, you can finish your story now."

Miss Taylor sat down again, gazed at Bridget, and finally continued, "He's in prison, and he can't hurt me while he's there. But . . ." she hesitated. "Bridget, please, don't let this frighten you."

"Okay," Bridget breathed, tensing again as she anticipated something even more terrifying from the lips of her English teacher.

"Roger has a younger brother, a half brother actually. His name is Buster Ashton. He was involved with Roger in the kidnapping. They did it several months after my divorce from Roger was final. The authorities caught them both before they collected any ransom, and the woman they'd kidnapped wasn't hurt, thank goodness."

Bridget interrupted with a burning question. "Is Buster in prison too?"

"That's the problem, Bridget. He got out on parole a few months ago."

"Oh! So is he the one—?" She couldn't finish.

"It's possible, although I have no way of being sure. But do you see, Bridget, why you and Candi must let the sheriff handle this? Buster is a hardened criminal, a very dangerous man. The police are looking for him, and they're questioning Roger in prison. I believe he could have something to do with it, even though he's still behind bars. I have agreed to help the police in any way I can," Miss Taylor concluded.

"Won't Buster hurt you?" Bridget asked fearfully, experiencing a strange new affection for Miss Taylor.

"I don't know, but for Cody's sake, I'm going to try to help law enfocement anyway. But that doesn't mean you and Candi should be involved in this at all. You need to leave this up to the police and me. You do see why, don't you?" Mariah asked, her eyes soft and pleading as she watched Bridget.

"Yes, I do," Bridget agreed. "I just hope . . ." Her voice broke.

"I know, Bridget. We all hope, and we all pray for Cody. I'm sure that Heavenly Father is watching over him. Now, would you like a lift home?"

"No thanks. I'll walk," Bridget answered as she rose on a pair of unsteady feet.

"Are you sure? I'd be glad to drop you off. It wouldn't be far out of my way at all."

"Thanks anyway, Miss Taylor, but it'll give me a chance to think. I'm . . . I'm really sorry I've been so awful. Thanks for telling me about Buster and your ex-husband."

Miss Taylor smiled. "I understand perfectly how you feel. And thank you for listening. Oh, and Bridget, it would be better if you didn't say anything about this to anyone for a while."

As Bridget walked in the door of her home several minutes later, the phone was ringing. Her mother answered it and then called out, "It's for you, Bridget. It's Candi."

"I'll take it in the family room," Bridget answered as she dropped her books and ran downstairs.

"Bridget," Candi said excitedly as soon as Bridget picked up the phone. "You won't believe the luck we're in. Jake has a date with Kara Smith tonight. He doesn't think we should get involved—he says it might be very dangerous for us, but he wants to himself. He's going to see what he can pump from her."

"I see," Bridget responded in a noncommittal tone. "Maybe he's right. Maybe we shouldn't—"

"Hey, what's the matter?" Candi interrupted. "You're the one that wanted to do something. Now maybe we'll be able to. Jake will let us. I'll make him."

"I'm sorry, Candi. Something has happened. I'm not so sure we should interfere," Bridget began, wondering how to convince Candi of Miss Taylor's innocence, while at the same time recognizing the strong feelings her friend had against her teacher.

"I don't get it!" Candi sounded upset. "What could possibly have happened?"

"I learned who's got Cody," Bridget declared, hoping to shock Candi into listening with an open mind.

"You did?!" Candi shouted so loudly that Bridget jerked the phone away from her ear.

"Yeah, but we've got to keep it quiet. I was told not to say anything."

"Who is it? It's Gil and Miss Taylor, isn't it? I just knew it."

"No, Candi, it's someone we never even heard of before. His name is Buster Ashton. And it's not the first time he's kidnapped somebody," Bridget explained. "The police are closing in on him, so we better stay out of it for now and let them catch him."

"Who told you? Has the sheriff been there?" Candi asked.

"No, it was someone else. It's got to be Buster Ashton though. If you knew the whole story, you'd understand."

"Then tell me!" Candi demanded.

"I can't."

"You can. Cody's my brother. Please, Bridget. If you're my friend, you'll tell me."

Bridget hesitated. She hadn't actually *promised* Miss Taylor she wouldn't say anything. "All right," she conceded, "but you can't tell anyone."

"I won't," Candi promised.

"Good. Miss Taylor overheard us talking about getting involved, and she—"

"Miss Taylor! You've been talking to Miss Taylor? Are you out of your mind? You can't believe her!"

"Listen to me," Bridget pleaded, and she told Candi the story Miss Taylor had told her.

When she had finished, Candi said, "You believed her?"

"Well, I think so. You should have seen her. She cried and everything. She feels awful because this guy was her brother-in-law. She's helping the sheriff."

"I'll just bet she is!" Candi hissed. "Bridget, she told you all this just to make you trust her. Think about it. Why would this Buster guy pick my dad to get money from? How would he know anything about our family? There's only one possible way. And that's because Miss Taylor told him about us. Why else would she be hanging around with Dad, kissing him and stuff?"

The tentative trust Bridget had recently developed in Miss Taylor went out of her like air from a deflating balloon. What Candi said made a lot of sense. Bridget began to tremble, and she couldn't think of a response.

"Bridget, are you still there?" Candi demanded.

"Y-yes," she stuttered.

"Are you okay?"

"I guess so."

"Am I right?"

"Probably. I never thought of that. But, Candi, what can we do?" Bridget asked in desperation.

"I don't know yet, but I'll talk to you in the morning. Jake will have some ideas," Candi said confidently. "Remember, he'll be with Deputy Smith tonight. And don't let Miss Taylor get near you. She could be dangerous."

* * *

Jake Garrett felt no danger in getting near Deputy Kara Smith that evening—very near. And she enjoyed it. After dinner they held hands and talked softly until it was late. She'd never been with someone who made her feel so good about herself. He not only complimented her with his words, but with his eyes and even his tone of voice.

It felt so natural to talk with Jake about the terrible crime that had brought him to Utah and into her life. And, yes, there was no longer any doubt in her mind that Cody Lind had not run away or gotten lost. He'd been kidnapped, and Buster Ashton had probably done it. Kara told Jake everything she and the sheriff had done, and he agreed with her that Buster was the most logical suspect.

For a long time Jake and Kara stood at the door to Kara's apartment. She had never kissed a man on the first date, but this night was different. Jake was different. She simply had no desire to resist him when he took her into his strong arms. "You make a guy want to settle down around here," he said after a lingering kiss.

"Thank you for a wonderful evening, Jake," she sighed.

"Can I take you out again?" he asked eagerly.

"Of course," Kara responded. "Anytime." Then reality hit her and she qualified her answer. "Actually, Jake, I won't have much time until this case with your cousin is wrapped up. After that, anytime would be great."

"We'll get it wrapped up soon," he promised. "You just let me know what I can do to help. I don't want to interfere, but I do want to be of assistance. After all, I love Kyle and his kids. They're my family—all that's left of it."

"They're lucky to have you, Jake. As for helping, for starters, you could keep Mr. Lind from doing something foolish, like paying the ransom without our knowing about it," she suggested.

"Oh, I won't let him do that," he said, his eyes flashing in the dim light. "That is a last resort. I can't let him lose his ranch. We've got to think of some other way . . ." He let that thought linger as he enveloped her once more in his arms.

*　*　*

"How was your date, Deputy?" Sheriff Hanks asked when she walked into his office the next morning.

She couldn't stop the smile his question evoked. Before she could answer, the sheriff laughed. "That good, huh? Well, don't be getting any crazy ideas. I don't want to lose one of my best deputies."

"Oh, Sheriff, you know me better than that," Kara scolded.

"Do I?" he asked, and she didn't respond.

"Well, sit down. We have work to do. No one has seen Buster Ashton lately. I've been on the phone this morning with a dozen agencies around the state and as many more in Wyoming. Nothing."

"He's the one, isn't he?" she asked confidently.

Sheriff Hanks looked at her sharply. "It seems likely, but Kara, we can't let one suspect pull us off the trail of the others—Sammy Shirts and Gil Enders, for starters. And who knows, maybe there's someone else out there who has a reason to hurt Cody or Kyle, someone we haven't yet discovered. We have to keep our minds open to every possibility. Now, I have some work for you to do, and it has to do with Sammy. I'm meeting Edgar Stevens as soon as he comes to the bank this morning. I want you to locate Sammy and stay on him, without letting him know you're there, of course. I want to know what he's up to."

"You want me to follow him all day?" Kara questioned.

"Unless I tell you differently. Follow him everywhere. I want to know every place that man goes. Shawn is already doing the same with Gil Enders. It'll be a long and boring day, I know, but we need to start eliminating suspects if we can. In the meantime, I've done everything I can to try to locate Buster Ashton, and I'll see that we keep that effort up."

"Okay," Kara agreed, but she was less than enthusiastic about her assignment.

"And Kara, drive your own car and take your portable radio and cell phone. I'll pay mileage. I don't want Sammy to even suspect that we're watching him."

She rose to her feet. "Okay. Good luck with Mr. Stevens. Jake is really worried that Stevens is going to get his uncle's ranch."

"So am I," the sheriff admitted. "I'm afraid that's a very real possibility."

After driving around town for several minutes, Kara finally spotted Sammy hiding in the shadows, watching the bank. Apparently, Mr. Stevens wasn't in yet. She settled in for a long, tiring day, feeling far from happy about it. *Buster Ashton is the one who's holding Cody. I'm sure of it. Or am I?* she asked herself as doubts began to enter her mind. There were definitely others who seemed to have motives for taking Cody, and there could still be others who might have a motive for hurting the Lind family. She told herself she had to keep an open mind, and she found herself getting more interested in seeing what Sammy Shirts was up to. He was certainly acting strange.

* * *

"Hi, Bridget," Candi called as Bridget was putting her books in her locker. "We'll be rid of our books today. Can you believe it? Last day of school tomorrow."

"None too soon," Bridget answered glumly. "I guess they still haven't found Cody. Candi, I'm scared."

"So am I. I can hardly stand it. They've just got to find him."

"What about Jake? Did you learn anything from him?"

"I'll say I did." Candi looked up and down the hallway to make sure no one else was listening before she stepped closer to Bridget. "Kara Smith told Jake everything that the police are doing," Candi went on, speaking very softly. "They're pretty sure it's Buster Ashton. Everything Miss Taylor said is true, except, of course, the part about her not being involved. Deputy Smith doesn't seem to think she is, but I don't agree. Miss Taylor pulled the same stunt on her that she did on you. Jake and I think she's in it up to her neck. We can't talk to Dad about it though. He's so gone on Miss Taylor that he won't listen."

"Okay, so what can we do? Did your cousin suggest anything?"

"He didn't want us to do anything, but I told him we were going to. He said for us to be awfully careful and not cause any problems." Candi looked around again before leaning closer to Bridget. "Listen. Here's what I think we might do . . ." And she quickly whispered her idea.

CHAPTER 10

As Sheriff Hanks rounded his desk to leave for the bank, his phone rang. "It's Chief Worthlin, Sheriff," his secretary said. "Do you have time to talk to him?"

"I'll take time," the sheriff said. "Hello, Chief. How's the town today?" he asked a moment later.

"Quiet, but on edge. I get the feeling everyone is watching everybody else, wondering who the kidnapper is. There's a lot of unrest and distrust growing in the community."

"I'm on edge too, and like everyone else, I'm not sure who we can trust. However, I'm leaning more and more toward the theory that this Buster Ashton has taken him. Has word of him leaked out?" the sheriff asked.

"Not that I've heard. My men and I hear a lot of whispering about Enders and Shirts, though. Of course, they're not popular fellows in this town, either one of them."

"But are they kidnappers?" the sheriff mused. "I'd sure like to know. That's why I have a couple of my deputies watching them closely. Did you let your men know what we're up to?"

"Sure did. Anyway, I know you're busy, Vince, but something curious happened this morning. I got a call from old Mrs. Barclay, you know, that retired schoolteacher. She's been out of town with her son's family for a week. Just got back last night. This morning she discovered that a rear window in her house was broken and someone has been in the house. That's not the curious part, though. What was taken is."

"And what was that?" the sheriff asked.

"Only one thing's missing as near as she can tell. A typewriter. She's had it for years, she says. Can hardly get ribbons for it anymore."

"My oh my," the sheriff mused as a chill went up his spine. "Now that is curious. Who would even know she had a typewriter?"

"I suppose a lot of people might know that," the police chief said. "She kept it right there in her living room, and it could be seen from her living room window. And, of course, a lot of people have been in her house. She's been sick quite a bit lately, but she used to host a lot of parties, and she always sent out invitations that she'd typed. And she's always been a good one for sending people notes when they have an illness or a death in the family, that kind of thing."

"But would Sammy Shirts or Gil Enders have known that? Or Buster Ashton? Seems like a stretch, that last one especially," the sheriff concluded.

"Well, I suppose that even people who haven't been to her place or received one of her notes may have seen something she typed. And she also said that she always types a list when she goes to the store. I specifically asked if that included the hardware store, and she said it did. She told me that if she didn't type up a note—even if she only needed a couple of things—by the time she got to the store, she would forget what she wanted. She said she always has to type them because she can hardly read her own handwriting anymore, her hands shake so badly now."

"So Gil Enders could have seen Mrs. Barclay's notes a number of times," the sheriff mused.

"Oh, yeah, and Sammy, too. He's all over town. He could have seen a note she gave someone, or he might have even seen the typewriter through her window."

"Yes, that's possible," the sheriff agreed. "But what about Buster Ashton? We don't even know if he's been in town."

"That's true. But you might want to talk to Mrs. Barclay yourself."

"That's a good idea. I'll do that," the sheriff decided.

"We've gone over her place carefully," the chief went on. "We can't find a single fingerprint that doesn't belong to the old lady. The burglar probably wore gloves. We did find a good boot print in the dirt near the house. We took some shots of it, and I took them over to be developed."

"I'd like to see that boot print myself," Sheriff Hanks remarked. Then he asked, "Is the print still there?"

"Sure is. We covered it with a box. The old lady said she wouldn't let anyone disturb it until I gave her the word. She's sure mad about the typewriter. She says it's is a good one, even if it is hard to get ribbons for it now. She really wants it back."

"Ron, I'd like to have a look at that boot print and talk to Mrs. Barclay. I'll slip over on my way to the bank," the sheriff said.

"The bank? It's not payday today, is it?" Chief Worthlin chuckled.

"No, but I have business there. I need to talk to Edgar Stevens. He's about to foreclose on Kyle's ranch."

"What? I thought Kyle was loaded."

"So did everyone else. Apparently his wife's illness cost more than anyone suspected. That, along with the mansion they built, made considerable inroads into their finances. At any rate, Edgar apparently can't wait to get his hands on Kyle's place. I'm going to try to stall him if I can. But I'll stop by Mrs. Barclay's place on the way."

Sheriff Hanks palmed a photo from his top desk drawer and hurried out the door. At the widow's house, after listening to her complain about her typewriter, he asked her if she happened to know Mariah Taylor.

"That sweet new English teacher," she responded. "Dr. Odell was here a few days ago. I haven't been feeling well lately, you know. But when he was here, he mentioned that Kyle Lind had a lady friend. When I asked him who it was, he told me it was Mariah. I told him I thought that was real nice. She was at my house in the fall. I always have a party here for the schoolteachers. She seemed like such a nice lady. That was before dear Ellen Lind got sick and passed away."

"The party was here at your house?" the sheriff asked.

"Oh, yes. I love to hold parties, but Dr. Odell tells me I shouldn't do that anymore, that my health is too frail. He was at my party too. It was just before Halloween—a costume party. He won the prize for the best costume. Of course, the prize wasn't much, just a bag of candy, but what does a man with an income like Dr. Odell's need anyway? The prizes I give are just a gesture. You know, Marshal

Odell's quite an actor, too. You must remember how good he was in the high school plays."

"Yes, he was good," the sheriff agreed, glancing at his watch. He'd forgotten how long Mrs. Barclay could spin out a story.

"You know, he didn't even wear a mask that night, and nobody knew who he was for quite a while. He'd disguised himself really well with a creative wig and a lot of work on his face. He's quite an artist, you know."

"Yes, I remember that too. He can paint anything. But now, back to Mariah Taylor," the sheriff urged. He didn't have time for dear old Mrs. Barclay to keep moving him away from the task at hand.

"Yes, Mariah. She's such a beautiful lady. I think Marshal's had his eye on her, at least he did before she started dating Kyle Lind. The two of them were really friendly that night at the party. She laughed more than anyone at the way he'd fixed himself up. He's such a dear. He was also one of my best students. I remember how much he used to like Ellen. That was before she fell for Kyle, of course. He and Ellen were both such good students. She was such a dear friend."

The sheriff suddenly realized that Marshal Odell had as much reason to wish harm on Kyle as anyone. But he dismissed the idea as quickly as it came. Marshal was his physician and a good friend. The sheriff directed his attention back to Mrs. Barclay. She was still reminiscing.

"I admit, Ellen was one of my favorite students. And so were you, Sheriff. You were in one of my very first classes when I taught first grade."

"Yes, I remember," Sheriff Hanks said. "And you were one of the best teachers I ever had."

"Oh, you're just saying that," she purred as she reached over and patted his hand fondly.

"No, I really mean it," he said. "So you got to know Mariah Taylor?" he asked, trying to steer her back on track once more while sneaking a peek at his watch.

"Oh, yes. And I just think it's so nice that Kyle might have found someone else." She had to swallow several times before she could speak again. "Oh, that poor man. I just heard that his boy is missing. That is so horrible and so unfair."

"Yes, it's a very serious matter," the sheriff agreed. "But we'll find him."

"Oh, you just must," Mrs. Barclay sighed. "Cody is such a nice boy. Reminds me a lot of his mother. Harry was smart, hiring him. That Enders boy that works with him is not a very nice person. I always try to get Cody to help me when I go to the hardware store. I know I shouldn't say bad things about anyone, but when Harry had Gil deliver my new vacuum cleaner last year, he was really quite rude. I asked him to help me take it out of the box, but he said he didn't have time, and he just left it sitting right there on the floor."

"Gil Enders has been in your house?" the sheriff asked in surprise.

"Oh, yes, but the next time I need something delivered, I'll ask Harry to send Cody," she said emphatically. "Oh, I hope he's okay. I'll bet Kyle is having a hard time. Maybe Mariah can be a help and comfort to him. And I wouldn't be surprised if that handsome nephew of Kyle's were to come and help him again."

"As a matter of fact, he's out at Kyle's place right now," the sheriff stated. "He's been keeping things up for Kyle."

"He would. He's such a nice young man. He was so thoughtful and sweet when he brought my casserole dish back after Ellen's funeral. I heard that he drew up the plans for that new house of Kyle's."

"Yes, that's right," the sheriff agreed. "He's apparently a very successful architect."

"And he's not even married," Mrs. Barclay sighed. "I'm surprised some pretty young woman hasn't latched onto him. He's a right handsome young man. You should introduce that nice Kara Smith to him. She needs to get married. Why, Vince, it's a shame that a pretty young thing like her is in such a dangerous business. You shouldn't be hiring young women like her. She should be teaching school like Mariah and me."

The laugh rumbled up from deep inside the sheriff's belly before he had a chance to quash it. "Times have changed," he said. "She wanted to go into law enforcement, and I feel lucky to have her. She's actually a very good officer."

"Well, she needs to find someone like Kyle's nephew and get out of police work before she gets hurt," Mrs. Barclay said firmly.

Sheriff Hanks rose to his feet. He had to cut this visit short. "Actually, Kara had dinner with Jake—that's Kyle's nephew—last night," he said, winking at his former first-grade teacher.

"Oh, really? Now that's nice," Mrs. Barclay cooed, as she too began to get up.

"No, you stay where you are. I can let myself out. However, with your permission, I would like to go around back and look at the boot print left by the person who stole your typewriter."

"Of course. Feel free to do that, Vince," she replied as she relaxed again on the sofa. "And I sure hope you police officers can find my typewriter. Why, I'll be lost without it."

"If we can't," the sheriff said. "I'll see that you get another one."

"You'd do that for me?" she asked.

"Of course I would," he responded. "I couldn't let my favorite teacher be without a typewriter." Then, as he reached the door, he said, "Oh, there's one more thing. Do you have something that you typed on your typewriter that I could borrow?"

"Of course," she answered. "If you'd open that drawer on the right-hand side of my desk, there will be several things."

He stepped over to the desk she pointed at. As she said, there were plenty of typewritten papers to choose from. He took the one on top, a list of people Mrs. Barclay intended to send letters to. He showed it to her and promised, "I'll see that you get it back."

"Of course you will," she said. "If I can't trust the sheriff, who can I trust? But what do you need it for?"

"I'd just like to study the way the type looks. Who knows," he said evasively, "maybe we'll find something typed by the thief, and if we have something to compare it to, then we'll be able to tell who stole your typewriter."

"Oh, I see," she replied. "But you might need my list for a long time."

"I'll copy it and bring back a copy for you to use until I can return the original," he offered. "Will that be okay?"

"That will be just fine," she responded, then briefly put her hand to her mouth. "But what good will that list do me? My handwriting is so poor now, and I don't have anything to type on. I can't write those letters anyhow."

"Like I said, I'll see that you have a typewriter," Sheriff Hanks promised, but Mrs. Barclay still seemed disheartened.

As he left her house, the sheriff couldn't believe how much he'd learned from her. Both Mariah Taylor and Gil Enders had been in her house. Heck, virtually everyone he knew had been in her house, even out-of-towners like Jake Garrett. And, of course, Sammy Shirts lived only a couple of blocks away. Instead of helping to narrow his list of suspects, this new information gave each of them more reason to be considered. The sheriff couldn't help feeling even more suspicious of Mariah.

If Buster has taken Cody, he thought, *and if Mrs. Barclay's missing typewriter turns out to be the one that was used to type the ransom note, then Mariah has to be considered as at least an accessory to the kidnapping. Of course, Mrs. Barclay's missing typewriter may have nothing to do with the note,* he admitted to himself. *And just because Mariah has been in Mrs. Barclay's home doesn't mean she's the one who stole the typewriter. That could've been just about anyone.*

A moment later he removed the box the police chief had used to cover the track behind Mrs. Barclay's house and stared at a perfectly preserved boot print. Then he held the photo of the print found at Roscoe's place beside it. "Hmm," he mused as he studied the two. "Now this is curious. Very curious indeed."

The missing typewriter, the interview with Mrs. Barclay, and the boot print in her yard were very much on the sheriff's mind as he entered the plush office of Edgar Stevens·a few minutes later. It appeared that the banker was not exactly delighted to see him. "What do you want, Sheriff?" he growled as Sheriff Hanks's boots sank into the rich, deep carpet.

"Just need to visit a minute, Edgar," the sheriff said with a smile.

"I'm a busy man, and I'm sure you have more important things to do than bother me," Edgar said, making no effort to offer Vince a seat.

The sheriff sat down anyway, drawing an even larger frown from Edgar. "Need more than a minute, do you?" the banker asked as he seated himself in what was easily the most expensive chair in Harrisville.

"I hope not," the sheriff stated calmly.

"Well, out with it," Edgar ordered.

"I came to discuss Kyle Lind," the sheriff began.

"With me?" Edgar asked incredulously. "This is a darn foolish place to be asking questions that relate to the disappearance of that son of his."

"Is it?" Sheriff Hanks asked. Then, before Mr. Stevens could answer, he questioned, "Can you give Kyle a little time on his ranch, Edgar? This is a poor time to be putting the squeeze on someone with as many problems as he has right now."

Edgar flushed, then settled his large frame deeper into the soft leather of his chair before speaking. "I run a business here, Sheriff. I can't be letting people's personal problems get in the way, or we'd lose our shirts."

"You mean *you* might lose your shirt," the sheriff replied crisply. "Anyway, I came to ask you to give Kyle a few weeks, or even better, a few months. He's a smart man, a hard worker, and a good rancher. He'll get his feet back under him and get his affairs with you squared away if you'll just give him some time."

"He's had time and I told him he could have a little more. His note's due in a few days. If he doesn't get his payment in shortly thereafter, I'll have to foreclose," Edgar fumed. "Now, if that's all, there's the door."

The sheriff leaned forward in his chair. "I know where the door is, Edgar, and I'll go through it when I'm right good and ready. Did you give Kyle his extension in writing?"

"He doesn't need that," Edgar declared.

"I think he does. Maybe you could just have one of your secretaries type something up for you to sign and I'll run it out to Kyle. I've got to get out there and see him in a few minutes anyway."

"He didn't tell me he needed it in writing. Until he does, things will stand as they are," Edgar announced sharply.

"Edgar, I'm trying to conduct a very difficult investigation. The life of Kyle's son could very well be in jeopardy. I need to have Kyle as alert as I can until we get the boy back, because I need his help. In the meantime, it would help immensely if you would remove the threat of losing his ranch. Should I call one of the girls in?"

"Sheriff, you can't badger me into signing something that would be detrimental to the interests of my bank. I appreciate your situation, but I have work to do, and I can't help you."

The sheriff stood. He knew he'd failed, and he was frustrated and furious. He wanted to grab Edgar Stevens by his fat neck and shake him until he passed out or agreed to help Kyle Lind. Stevens was one of the most cold-hearted men he'd ever encountered, and he'd known many in his career. The sheriff knew he'd have to find another way to save Kyle Lind's ranch. Perhaps another bank would buy the note or lend the payment to Kyle.

In the meantime, Edgar Stevens could not be discounted as a suspect. He needed to be watched more closely, even though he, of all people, would know that Kyle couldn't come up with a half million dollars in cash. The ransom note, the sheriff reasoned, if it came from Stevens, might simply be intended to put extra financial pressure on Lind. Or maybe it was a decoy meant to throw him and his deputies off in their investigation. He couldn't allow that to happen—Edgar remained very much a suspect.

Sheriff Hanks was surprised to see Marshal Odell waiting outside the banker's door when he left. "Good morning, Dr. Odell. I wouldn't think you'd need to be borrowing money from the bank," he said lightly.

The sharpness of the doctor's response surprised the sheriff. "He's killing Kyle Lind."

"He's what?" the sheriff wondered loudly.

"You know what I mean. He's about to foreclose on the Lind place. And Kyle tells me he won't even talk about lending him the money to pay the ransom. Kyle's in bad shape, and Edgar Stevens is making it worse. I was hoping I could get him to give Kyle an extension on the note and agree to lend him the money he needs for whoever the lowlife is that took Kyle's boy. If he doesn't, it's very likely that Kyle's going to have a stroke."

"Well, good luck, doctor. That's what I just spoke with Edgar about, and I got nowhere," the sheriff growled darkly. "Maybe you'll do better."

"I don't know if I will or not, but for the sake of my patient, I intend to try," Dr. Odell said. "That Edgar Stevens seems to think he owns this town."

"He practically does," the sheriff admitted and headed up the hallway.

* * *

Edgar Stevens had watched the two men through his one-way window. He knew exactly why Dr. Odell was here. And he was going to get the same kind of answer the sheriff did. He knew how to say no when it was in his own best interest. He invited the doctor in.

* * *

Edgar Stevens was being observed later that morning as he left his bank. Sammy Shirts was on duty, so to speak. So was Deputy Kara Smith. Sammy's old pickup followed Edgar's new Cadillac. Kara's light blue Geo Prizm followed Sammy's rusty pickup. They all ended up in Salt Lake City some time later, where Edgar parked and entered one of the sleaziest bars in the entire state of Utah.

Kara wondered how Sammy's truck had made it all the way without running out of gas. He must have stolen a tankful the night before, she decided. He got out of his truck, watched the bar for a few minutes, then reached into the back of his truck and pulled out a five-gallon gas can.

More than a tankful, she amended as she watched him gas up his truck from three such gas cans. He then climbed back into his cab, where he settled in to wait for his quarry. An hour later, all three vehicles, widely spaced on the freeway, were on their way back to Harrisville. The last of the three, Kara Smith's Prizm, carried a puzzled deputy sheriff. What possible business could a wealthy banker have in a Salt Lake bar, and what possible interest could the Harrisville town drunk have in following a wealthy banker there and back?

* * *

Early that afternoon, Sheriff Hanks received a visit from Chief Ron Worthlin. In his arms the chief carried a slightly dirty typewriter and a packet of photos. "What do you have there?" The sheriff smiled as Chief Worthlin placed both items on his desk.

"It's the boot print pictures and Mrs. Barclay's typewriter. And there's not a fingerprint on it," the chief announced.

"Where was the typewriter, Ron?"

"One of my men found it in one of the big garbage dumpsters behind Harry's Hardware. Thought you might be interested in typing a few words."

"Actually, I already have a sample that Mrs. Barclay gave me," the sheriff revealed. "Here, see what you think."

Ron studied the ransom note and Mrs. Barclay's list under a magnifying glass while the sheriff flipped briefly through the photos.

"What do you think, Chief?" the sheriff asked at last as he tossed the photos back onto the desk.

"I think this typewriter was used to type the ransom note."

"That's my conclusion too. We'll have to send both samples to the forensics lab to be sure, but I'd almost stake my job on it," the sheriff replied grimly.

"That means Gil Enders—" Chief Worthlin began.

"It could mean anything, but it doesn't help Gil's case any. He's looming large in my book," Sheriff Hanks interrupted.

"And in mine," the chief agreed.

"I guess I'll have him brought in. Would you like to stick around?"

"If you don't mind."

It took just ten minutes for Chief Deputy Fullman to deposit a very angry Gil Enders in the sheriff's office. Chief Worthlin shut the door, and Sheriff Hanks ordered, "Sit down, Gil," while he studied the young man's boots. Like half the men in Harrisville, Gil wore boots much of the time, and today was no exception.

The typewriter was out of sight behind the sheriff's desk. With his eyes on Gil's face, the sheriff picked it up and set it on the desk. Gil didn't flinch. "What's that for?" he asked after a moment of strained silence. "Figure you can make me type some kind of confession?"

"Ever see this before, Gil?"

Gil swore loudly as he denied any familiarity with the typewriter. Sheriff Hanks then stated, "It was found in the dumpster behind Harry's Hardware."

"So? Then go get Harry," Gil growled.

"Let me see your boots, Gil."

"My boots! You don't have no right . . ." Gil began angrily.

"I just need to look at the bottom of them," the sheriff told him patiently.

Gil stood and turned toward the door.

"Sit down, Gil. I just need to see the right one. Fullman, maybe he could use a little help," the sheriff said quietly.

Red faced and muttering, Gil glared at Deputy Fullman, then sat and pulled his right boot off. Sheriff Hanks took it from him, picked up a photograph from his desk, studied the boot and the photo momentarily, and then sighed. "All right. You can put it back on. Take him back to work, Shawn."

"I was at home," Gil corrected sullenly.

"Sorry, take him home then," the sheriff clarified with a frown.

After Gil and the deputy left, Chief Worthlin, who had watched the entire episode without saying a word, finally spoke. "Well?"

The sheriff explained what he had learned, and the chief left, saying, "You keep the typewriter for now. I'll try to appease Mrs. Barclay."

Shortly after Chief Worthlin left, Kara called on her cell phone. "Where are you?" the sheriff asked. "The last time you called you said you were following Sammy out of town."

"Yeah, and you won't believe this. He parked across the street from a bar in Salt Lake," Kara reported.

"A bar?" the sheriff queried. "Aren't there enough bars in this county to keep him occupied?"

Kara chuckled and explained, "He didn't go into the bar."

"If he didn't go in the bar, what did he do?" the sheriff wondered.

"Sat outside in his truck. Well, actually, he filled his gas tank from three cans he had in the back. Then he sat in his truck."

"Watching a bar?" the sheriff questioned in disbelief. "So, if he didn't go in, what was he doing? Or could you tell?"

"He was waiting for Edgar Stevens to come out of the bar. He—"

The sheriff interrupted. "Edgar Stevens?"

"Yes. Sammy followed him to Salt Lake, and I followed Sammy like you told me to. After about an hour, Edgar came out. We're all on our way back to Harrisville now."

"My, oh my, but this is getting interesting . . . and downright puzzling," the sheriff said as he laced and unlaced his fingers several times. "When you get back to town, call Shawn. He'll take over for you in keeping an eye on Sammy. I'd like you to come in so we can discuss this."

* * *

"Let's walk to my place together," Bridget suggested to Candi as the school day ended. "I'll get Mom to let me take the car and run you home in a little while to get your stuff—if your dad agrees, that is."

"Okay. We don't want to take any chances of being overheard by Miss Taylor," Candi answered.

"That's for sure," Bridget agreed.

"Do you think your dad will let you spend the night at my house?" Bridget asked as they strolled beneath the green branches of several towering elm trees that bordered the walk. "It's the only way we can do what we need to do."

"I'm sure he will. He's so worried and out of it right now that he won't even wonder why," Candi sighed.

"So what's Jake doing tonight?" Bridget asked.

"He didn't say. He's keeping busy all day. He's practically running the ranch by himself right now. I think he'd like to take Kara Smith out to dinner again. But he says she'll be pretty busy, so he won't get to see her much for a while. I think he really likes her."

"Maybe he'll take her back to Arizona with him," Bridget snickered.

"Maybe," Candi said. "And maybe he'll want to move here. Not that there's much work around here for a good architect. I think he's really good—he designed our house."

"Oh? I didn't know that."

"He hardly charged anything for it. But some people must pay him well. I know he makes good money."

* * *

"This is the place, isn't it?"

"Looks like it to me."

"Well, let's see if I can hook him again."

The fisherman cast and watched as he slowly fed out his line. He hooked something. He pulled hard. "A snag," he said, jerking harder. The line broke and he reeled it in, muttering angrily at losing his hook.

The two men both fished for another hour. They caught a couple of small trout, but the large, elusive one was apparently not biting. After losing several more baited hooks, the two fishermen moved a little farther around the shore.

CHAPTER 1 1

When she entered Sheriff Hanks's office an hour later, Kara found the sheriff frowning as he studied a notebook. An old typewriter sat on his desk. She stood quietly until he looked up and invited her to sit down. "Have a seat, Kara. You don't have to wait for me to invite you to sit, especially when I'm distracted."

She sat down and asked, "Are you making any progress on the case?"

The sheriff shrugged. "It just keeps getting more confusing. It's like a jigsaw puzzle with extra pieces mixed in. I'll tell you about it in a minute, but first, tell me about Sammy and Edgar. What did they do when you got back to town? Did Sammy follow Edgar to the bank?"

"Edgar didn't go to the bank," Kara revealed. "He went straight home. Then Sammy bought a six-pack of beer at the 7-Eleven and went to his home. That's where I left him when Shawn took over."

"That's it?"

"Strange, isn't it?" Kara said. "Both the fact that Edgar would drive all the way to Salt Lake just to spend an hour in a bar in the middle of the day, and that Sammy would follow him all that way."

"It's downright peculiar," the sheriff agreed. "And it may or may not have anything to do with Cody Lind. But at this point, we need to consider it a possible link to the case."

Kara's curiously glanced at the old typewriter. Finally, she asked, "Where did you get the typewriter, Sheriff? Isn't it a little out-of-date for our office?"

"That's for sure," the sheriff answered, smiling for the first time since she'd come in. "It belongs to Mrs. Barclay. It was stolen from her house, used to type the ransom note, and deposited in the garbage behind Harry's Hardware."

Kara stared. "You *have* had a day! So Gil—"

"You're not jumping to conclusions, are you?" the sheriff interrupted quietly.

"Well, I guess I—"

The sheriff smiled and waved his hand, interrupting her again. "It's hard not to, I know. And I did have a chat with Gil. As you can imagine, he denies knowing about the typewriter. In fact, he acted smart and told me to talk to Harry. But anyone could have put it in that dumpster of Harry's, including the elusive Buster Ashton."

"Did you dust it for fingerprints?"

"A city officer did. No prints. It had been wiped clean. Anyway, we have so many persons of interest doing suspicious things that I hardly know which way to turn. I talked to Stevens, as I'm sure you know."

"Yes, I saw you go in and come out of the bank. You didn't look very happy," Kara remarked.

"I wasn't, and I'm still not. Edgar Stevens is one callous man. And I'm convinced of one thing: he plans to get his hands on Kyle's ranch in any way he possibly can."

"He won't give him an extension?"

"Not in writing. He even ordered me out of his office. On my way out of the bank, I closed my account there," Sheriff Hanks declared with a grin. "That won't hurt him much, but it was all I could think of at the time."

"He'll definitely be heartbroken," Kara laughed, then immediately resumed a serious tone. "So now what?"

"I'm not sure. Maybe we can help Kyle find a bank somewhere that will either buy the loan or make the payment. That's probably a long shot, but this is turning into one too many things for Kyle to handle. I'm afraid he's going to crack on us. First thing in the morning, I plan to go to Salt Lake and see what I can do. I know a fellow there who works for Wells Fargo Bank. I helped him a year or so ago with a property dispute out beyond Roscoe's place, and he seemed like a really good fellow. I know it will be Saturday, but I'll call on him at home. Maybe he can help."

"If you don't tell him you know Roscoe," Kara muttered under her breath. Then she asked, "What do you want me to do now?"

"Go out to Roscoe's place and—" the sheriff began.

"You're not serious?" Kara interrupted.

"Yes, actually, I am."

"What do I do there? Has he complained about trespassers again?"

"No, I haven't heard from him today at all, but something has come up. It has to do with the typewriter," Sheriff Hanks began.

"The typewriter? You surely don't think Roscoe stole it!" Kara exclaimed in amazement.

"No, Kara, but take a look at this," he said as he leaned forward and handed her two photographs. "The one in your left hand is a picture I took out at Roscoe's, the one that was in the ditch. The one in your right hand, I took this morning at Mrs. Barclay's."

Kara studied the two photos. Each showed the clear print of a boot. She was no expert, but they certainly appeared to have been made by the same boot. Each had a peculiar checked pattern on the heel and a small but distinctive gouge in the sole near the toe. Puzzled, she looked up at her boss. "This seems crazy!" she stated. "It looks like the person who stole the typewriter is the same one that stepped in that ditch at Roscoe's."

"That's right, and it makes no sense at all," the sheriff agreed. "But there it is, and there must be a logical reason for it. Obviously, there's something that ties these two prints together. What we have to do is figure out what. We've got to find the connection between the two. Somehow, whatever is happening or has happened at the old Norman homestead is connected to the kidnapping of Cody Lind."

"Does that mean Buster Ashton's been in the area?" Kara questioned.

"If he's the one we're after, he obviously has been. Whoever took Cody was certainly around."

With a quick change of subject, the sheriff asked, "Have you had dinner?"

"No, I haven't had a bite since morning."

"Then go eat, freshen up if you like, and then get out there in time to look around again while there's still some daylight."

"What am I looking for?" Kara asked.

"Anything that might help" was the sheriff's vague answer.

Kara left and went straight home, exchanging her Prizm for a patrol car. At home, she microwaved a frozen entrée. Before it was ready, Jake called.

"What are you doing this evening?" he asked after a couple minutes of chatting.

"The sheriff asked me to go out to the west end of the county. You know, out there where that crazy farmer's been seeing lights. I told you about it, didn't I?"

Jake hesitated slightly. "Well, I think you did mention something, but that can't possibly have anything to do with the kidnapping, can it?"

"That's what we thought. Now we're not so sure. The sheriff found a boot print that matches. He wants me to go out and look until dark."

"For what?" Jake asked.

"Anything. Clues, I guess."

"Could you use some help?"

"Of course, but all the other deputies are busy, and the sheriff can't go either. It would be easier if there were two or three of us," she said.

"I mean me," Jake said.

"Do you have time?"

"For you, I'll make time. I think I've got things pretty well in hand here at the ranch. Where should I meet you?"

"I'll pick you up," Kara offered. "Your uncle's place is on the way. Give me half an hour to eat and drive out there."

"Thanks, Kara. I'll be ready."

Just the way Jake said her name made her shiver with delight. She wasn't sure what the sheriff would think about a civilian helping out with the case, but it surely couldn't hurt. And as Cody's cousin, Jake was as concerned as anyone about the boy. He'd be a tremendous help.

* * *

He *was* good help. At first Jake and Kara worked side by side, but then Kara glanced at the sinking sun and said reluctantly, "We're wasting time, Jake. At this rate we'll never get the whole area searched before dark. We need to split up the area and search separately. We'll cover more ground that way."

"You're right," Jake agreed with a sheepish grin. "I must admit, though, I've enjoyed working beside you. But we'll do it your way, and then, later, maybe we could go into town and I could buy you some ice cream."

The ice cream sounded good, but eating it with Jake Garrett sounded even better. She quickly agreed. "It's a date. Let's see . . ." she began as she straightened up.

"Would you like me to search below the ditch and from this side of the outhouse west?" he suggested.

"Sure, and I'll search above the ditch, around the old derrick, and over where the cabin used to be," she said. "But we need to be thorough."

For the next ninety minutes or so, they both worked diligently. Occasionally, she would look toward Jake. Almost every time, he was walking slowly, his head bent. Several times he stooped down, studied the ground, and then went on. He spent several minutes around and in the old outhouse, and then he worked back and forth through the weeds. She looked up once just as he was shutting the door to the ancient cellar.

Likewise, Kara covered every inch of her section of the old homestead. As much as she hated any place that might harbor spiders, she even pulled the lid off the cistern and peered inside. Finally, as the setting sun cast a bright pink hue on the few clouds that hovered near the hills to the west, she decided they'd done enough. She hadn't found a thing. "Jake," she called.

He was at the edge of the neglected pasture fence that bordered the area they were searching. Looking up, he waved. "Ready to quit?"

"I think so," she shouted back as she began to move in his direction.

They met beside the ditch. "Where was that track?" he asked.

"Right there," she said, pointing down. It was still clearly visible beneath the water.

"Somebody got a boot full of water," he chuckled. "Did you find anything?"

"No, did you?"

"Just this little flashlight," he replied, holding it by the strap that was secured to one end.

"Jake, where was that?" she asked as she reached for it.

"No, Officer," he said with a laugh. "It might have prints and you don't have your gloves on. I've only touched it myself by this strap."

Kara felt foolish. "Here, I have an evidence bag," she said as she retrieved one from her pocket.

She held the bag open, and he dropped the flashlight in. Then she studied it. It was small, dark blue, and rubberized. "It takes AA batteries," she commented.

"Yes. I've seen this kind of light before. They're really quite bright for something so small," Jake remarked.

"Hey, maybe it made the light that Mr. Norman saw," Kara suggested.

"Could be. I found it inside the outhouse."

"I guess you'd better show me where. I'll need to log it in as potential evidence, and the sheriff will want to know exactly what position it was in, and so forth."

Jake led the way as they returned to the outhouse. The door stood open exactly as it had when she'd been there the last time. Without taking the flashlight from the clear plastic evidence bag, Jake laid it on the floor against the doorway to the right. "It was right there," he explained.

Kara pulled a small notebook from her pocket and made a couple of notes beside a crude drawing she sketched. Then she bent down, picked up the bag, and put it in her pocket. "Let's get out of here. There are too many spiderwebs and far too many spiders for my comfort," she said, shivering and rubbing her arms.

"That's probably all you could see down that hole you were looking in," Jake said with a laugh.

"You mean the old cistern? It was creepy. Full of spiders," she agreed. "I hate spiders."

"Then you don't want to go in that old cellar. It's chock full of them, though I admit I didn't have the door open long enough to see any," he reported. "This place is not worth much except for raising spiders—and rats. One of them ran out when I opened the cellar door. It was enormous."

Kara let out a muted shriek. "I'd have passed out! I'm surpised you didn't yell or anything."

Jake looked startled for a moment and then grinned. "I sort of—grunted. It wasn't very loud. I guess you were so engrossed in your own search that you didn't hear me." He laughed and winked at her. "But you, a cop, and you'd faint? You probably face more dangerous things every day than spiders and rats," Jake teased.

"That's different," she laughed as they started back toward the ditch, side by side on the ancient stone walk.

"Why doesn't the farmer—what's his name?" Jake asked.

"Roscoe Norman," she answered.

"Why doesn't he level this place and make another field here? It seems to me like he's wasting good farming ground. And it would be easy to water with the ditch going right through here."

"If you were to meet him, you wouldn't ask. For that matter, look at the rest of his place," she invited, stopping and swinging her arm out over the acres of brush and dry grass and the few half-decent fields that Roscoe Norman called his farm.

"I see what you mean," Jake answered with a grin. "I guess I'm just used to the way Kyle does things. He'd install wheel lines for irrigation and soon have this spot producing good alfalfa hay." His dark eyes swept the farm before coming back and meeting Kara's. "Roscoe doesn't have much of a place to look at here, does he. I'd much rather look at you, Kara."

Kara's face flushed. "Oh, I'm sure you say that to all the girls," she joked.

"No, I mean it. I've met lots of girls in my time, Kara. But I've never met anyone that's as pretty and as smart as you." As he spoke he reached for her hand and pulled her close.

The kiss that followed felt so natural that she almost wished it would never end. At the same time she also felt a bit guilty kissing him, especially since she was on duty.

"Let's go have some ice cream," Jake suggested when she gently pulled away from him.

"Sounds good," she responded, and arm in arm they made their way back to the car.

"Hey," Jake said after they were in the car, "is that the old farmer—Roscoe Norman—turning in at the end of the lane?"

Kara turned her head. "Sure is. Rats!—and I don't mean the kind you saw. I was hoping we'd get away without having to meet him."

Jake threw back his head and laughed. "Someone who sees lights where there aren't any? You think he wouldn't see a couple of people rummaging around his property like some old prospectors?"

Kara laughed with him, threw her patrol car into reverse, and turned around. Then, since Roscoe's truck filled the lane ahead, she waited. As his old truck bumped and belched up the road, she said to Jake, "I'll try to hurry this up. That ice cream is sounding better all the time—"

Roscoe finally pulled up and stopped near her car. He got out just as Kara went over to meet him.

"Thought it was the sheriff," he started gruffly. "What are you doing here? Somebody else see trespassers on my place?"

"Not that we know of, Mr. Norman. The sheriff asked me to take another look around." Kara hoped her smile would disarm him.

"Who's the fella in the car?" Roscoe demanded.

"A friend of mine. He's been helping me search."

"Search? What you searching for?"

"Clues," she answered evasively. Kara didn't want to tell Roscoe Norman that this piece of property was now connected to the investigation of a kidnapping because of the boot print in the ditch. That would bring far too many questions from the old man, and at this point Kara had no desire to try to answer them.

"Clues? You mean you're gonna try to do something about those kids?"

"Somebody's been on your place, Mr. Norman, and we want to know who," she replied, knowing he would think she meant rabbit hunters while she really meant a kidnapper.

"Hmph. Only way to get them kids is to catch them in the act. I'll call when I see them again," he growled.

Kara remembered the flashlight. She retrieved it from the car, still safely encased in the plastic evidence bag, and held it up to Roscoe. "Does this look familiar?" she asked.

Roscoe squinted in the fading dusk. "A flashlight," he said. "Never seen it before in my life. Probably the one them kids was using—the one that made that light up in the sky."

"Could it be?" she prompted.

After Roscoe explained with a few choice swear words how certain he was, Kara reached into the car, dropped the light beside Jake, and declared, "Well then, I'll give it to the sheriff. Let us know if you see anyone around here. We need to be on our way now. We have an appointment."

"I got a few more questions, young lady," Mr. Norman began. "Seems like you cops are always in a hurry."

"Sorry, but there's a lot we have to do. Thanks for your time," she finished briskly as she climbed back in her patrol car and shut the door.

"An appointment?" Jake asked with a grin after they were on their way down the lane.

"Yes. With a bowl of ice cream, remember?"

Jake laughed. "I'll be awfully glad when we get Cody back, both for his sake and ours. I'd like to see a lot more of you."

She smiled in agreement. After driving in companionable silence for a moment, she asked, "Jake, what can we do to keep Kyle from having a breakdown, or even worse, a stroke or heart attack? The sheriff is really worried."

"So am I, Kara. And so is Dr. Odell. When he was there to see Kyle the other day, I told him about the ransom note and how Stevens is threatening the ranch and refusing to lend the money for the ransom. The doctor about came apart. He said that was all Kyle needed to cause him to have a stroke."

"If the doctor's that worried about Kyle, then I'm really afraid for him," Kara said with concern. "Surely there's something that can be done for him."

"There's not much more Dr. Odell can do short of putting him in the hospital, and Kyle won't hear of that. The doctor's right. It's that banker who's pushed him to the brink and driven his blood pressure so high. He was coping until he learned that he might lose his ranch. I'm going to find that banker myself tomorrow and talk to him." Jake suddenly sounded angry.

"What good will that do?" Kara asked.

"Maybe none, but I don't like to see my uncle pushed around like this. Maybe I can at least get an extension in writing."

"That would help. The sheriff tried today, but he got nowhere with Mr. Stevens. So the sheriff's going to Salt Lake tomorrow to ask someone he knows at Wells Fargo to either buy the loan or lend Kyle the money to make the payment that's almost due."

Jake straightened up. "Hey, that's great. I'd like to see that banker's face when they plop the money down. That would be worth a lot right there. The nerve of the guy. Why, Kyle's ranch has been in the family since the turn of the century! There's no way some greedy banker should get it now."

"That's just how the sheriff feels," Kara agreed.

CHAPTER 12

Sheriff Hanks had been trying to call Kara for over an hour, but she apparently had her cell phone turned off. And when he'd tried to call her at home, she didn't answer. It was nearly eleven o'clock that night before he finally made contact with her at home. "Kara," he said when she answered, "where have you been?"

"Out to Roscoe's," she replied.

"This late?"

"No, but I ran into Jake and he offered to buy me some ice cream."

The sheriff chuckled. "I see. I'm sorry to bother you, but I just wanted to ask if you found anything out there."

"Sure did. A small flashlight."

"You're kidding."

"I'm not. It works, too."

"Where was it?"

"In the outhouse."

"Kara, I'm still at the office. Would you mind running it over? I'd like to have a look at it," he said.

"I'll be right there," she agreed.

While the sheriff waited, his mind roamed. The few clues in this case seemed fragmented, and they led nowhere. He'd never had a case as puzzling as this one. He wasn't sure how much longer he could physically keep pushing the way he was, but he felt compelled. A young man had been missing for a full week, and his life now hung in the balance.

"I wonder why we didn't notice this there before," Vince stated a few minutes later as he turned the bag containing the flashlight over in his hands.

"It couldn't be seen unless you went inside the outhouse. It was on the floor and sort of against one wall," Kara explained.

"Does it make a *rigid light*?" the sheriff asked, and they both chuckled.

"I suppose it could," Kara said. "At least, it could be aimed straight into the air."

"Was there anything else out there?" he asked a moment later.

"Nothing that I could see."

"All right, thanks," he said, rubbing his eyes. "I guess we ought to check this light for prints."

While they carefully dusted the small flashlight, the sheriff said to Kara, "I called Kyle a little while ago. He's near a breakdown, I'm afraid. I explained what I wanted to do about saving his ranch, but all he said was, 'It doesn't even matter anymore, Sheriff. All I want is my boy back.'"

"You're still going to try to save the ranch, aren't you?" Kara asked as she remembered Jake's concern.

"Of course," he replied.

"What do you want me to do tomorrow?"

"Come in here and cover for me. Respond to whatever seems important. Shawn and Phil will be nosing around to see if they can learn anything new. They'll try to keep an eye on Sammy and Gil too, as their time permits. They've been told to let you know anything they see or hear that might be important to the case. As the acting detective, I want you to keep a log of what they report to you. I also want you to list everything that you've done and observed as well. Will you do that?" the sheriff asked.

"Of course. Doesn't look like we're going to find any prints, does it?" Kara said, eying the flashlight dejectedly.

"Nope, but it was worth a try. Kara," he said, suddenly standing upright, "there is something else I'd like you to do. Check with Harry in the morning. See if he might have sold this flashlight or one like it recently, and if so, to whom. Who knows, we might luck out yet. That's what it often takes to break a case like this—luck. And it often comes in the form of something seemingly insignificant."

Shortly after Deputy Smith left Sheriff Hanks's office, the phone rang. It was his chief deputy on a cell phone. "What is it, Shawn?" the sheriff asked.

"Sammy went out a little while ago." Shawn reported. "He drove over near Edgar Stevens's house, where he got out of his truck and approached the place on foot."

"At this time of night? Where is he now?"

"I don't know," Shawn confessed.

"You mean you lost him?"

"I couldn't help it. I followed him on foot. He went up to the door and knocked, and when the door opened, he went in."

"Edgar Stevens invited Sammy Shirts into his house at midnight? Absurd!" the sheriff scoffed.

"Well, they talked for a while at the door first, then Sammy went in. I wasn't close enough to hear what they said. I figured he'd be back out in a bit, but instead, the garage door opened and Stevens's Cadillac backed out. There were two people in it. They left in a hurry. One of them must have been Sammy. By the time I got back to my car and headed down the street in the direction they went, I couldn't find them anywhere. I'm sorry, Sheriff."

"It's all right, Shawn. Stay near that house, though, and wait to see if they come back, or if just Edgar comes back, or whatever."

After he'd hung up the phone, Sheriff Hanks stood and stretched, trying to relieve the muscle tension in his shoulders and neck. This case seemed to become more complicated with each tick of the clock. All of a sudden, everyone was acting suspiciously. Sammy Shirts and Edgar Stevens going somewhere together in the middle of the night? It was just plain crazy, and the sheriff was exhausted. He needed sleep in the worst way. Perhaps after he finally got some sleep he'd be able to think more clearly and make sense of the seemingly meaningless bits and pieces of this case.

The phone rang again.

"Sheriff, Kyle Lind here. I just got another ransom note. I've got to get the money or they are going to kill Cody," the rancher said in a broken voice.

"Sit tight. I'm on my way, Kyle."

He slammed down the phone, thought for moment, then dialed the phone. "Kara? I need your help. Come over to the office immediately and we'll drive there together."

"Where are we going?" she asked.

"We're going out to Kyle's. Please hurry."

* * *

Kara Smith could scarcely breathe. The sheriff had given no explanation, just said he needed her to go with him to Kyle Lind's. *Something must have happened, and it must be serious,* she thought. When she pulled into the office parking lot, Sheriff Hanks was already outside, waiting beside his patrol car.

"What's happened?" she asked as soon as she'd gotten into his car and closed the door.

They were already rolling by the time he answered. "Another ransom note."

"This time of night?" Kara exclaimed.

"That's what Kyle told me. And they've threatened to kill the boy."

Kara sank back into her seat, speechless. Suddenly things were moving too rapidly. She closed her eyes and prayed silently.

* * *

"Is she home?" Candi asked breathlessly.

"I don't think so, do you?" Bridget whispered.

"No—so now what do we do?"

"I don't know."

Candi looked serious, then said, "I was thinking that we should just watch her place and see what she does tonight and who comes to see her. Who knows, Buster might come. If he does, or if somebody else does, we'd better call the sheriff and not do anything else."

"But since it looks like she isn't here, we can't stay and watch nothing. So, I wonder if maybe we'd just better go home," Bridget suggested.

"Maybe . . . no . . . I don't know. I really thought she would be here." The two girls were caught up in their own thoughts for a moment. Then Candi whispered, "Bridget, maybe we should go in and see if we can find any papers or anything."

"That's illegal!" Bridget gasped.

"I know, but so is kidnapping. It's my brother they took. Nobody will ever know if we're really careful and don't disturb anything that Miss Taylor might notice," Candi reasoned.

"I don't know, Candi. Maybe one of us should wait out here and keep watch while the other one goes in, just in case she comes home."

"Good idea. You wait. Whistle loud if you see a car coming, and I'll come out," Candi suggested. "No, wait. That won't work. She might hear you. I know, we'll both go in, and you can watch from in there while I look."

"Well, okay. But how will we get in?" Bridget asked, her heart racing with an exhilarating mixture of fear and excitement.

"I don't know. Break the glass or something."

"Then she'll know someone's been in there," Bridget fussed.

"You're right. But she'll only know that *someone* has." Candi wrinkled her nose. Then she said, "Let Miss Taylor worry. It serves her right. No one would ever suspect us. Anyway, we're at your place asleep for all anyone knows."

"Right." Bridget chuckled nervously. "My folks would certainly never believe we would be out here doing this, and they think we went to bed early. Okay, Candi, if we're going to go in, let's do it before I chicken out."

"You can't chicken out. This is for Cody," Candi reminded her. "We've got to be willing to take a risk for his sake."

"Yeah, it's for Cody," Bridget agreed.

* * *

"Jake, tell them what you saw," Kyle prodded.

Kara, seated beside Jake, turned her eyes up expectantly. He explained grimly, "I saw a car stop . . . that is, I saw car lights. It stopped right there by the mailbox for just a few seconds. Next I heard a car door close, and then the engine accelerated quickly as the car turned and sped off."

"What direction did it go?" Sheriff Hanks asked.

"Back where it came from. It went toward town."

"Where were you when you saw it?" the sheriff pressed.

"I was out by the barn. I couldn't sleep, so I walked outside and was wandering around when I saw the lights on the road. Anyway, I thought it was rather curious, so I walked up there. The note was in the box, not even folded. It was just like you see it there," Jake reported as he pointed to the paper the sheriff was holding carefully by one corner.

The sheriff nodded, and Kara tore her eyes from Jake's worried face. "What does it say?" she asked.

The sheriff adjusted his glasses. "Typed, as you can see. It says, 'Time is running out. Produce the money or the kid dies. Instructions as to where you'll leave the money will follow.' That's all," he said as he looked up.

Kara jumped as Jake suddenly slammed a fist into the arm of the sofa. "Sheriff, we've got to find Cody! Either that, or get the money so he'll be returned. This guy is getting desperate. We can't risk Cody's life!"

"And you think if we produce the money the kidnapper will produce the boy like he says?" the sheriff asked.

"Well, I suppose—I don't know—Will he?" Jake stammered. "You're the expert here."

"Maybe he will. Maybe he won't. It would be a terribly dangerous gamble. Kara, let's get back to town. We've got a long night ahead of us. Kyle, we'll find Cody. So help me, I won't rest until we do," the sheriff declared with fierce resolution.

Kara looked at him in surprise. She wondered how he could actually make and follow through on that commitment. They didn't seem any closer to a solution now than they had been the morning Kyle reported Cody's disappearance. A week had passed, and all they had was a longer list of suspects. There was no way it could be all of them. *But it could be any of them,* Kara thought, *or perhaps none of them.*

Sheriff Hanks and Deputy Smith stopped at the mailbox on their way back to town. "No chance of a tire print or boot print," the sheriff complained. "It's paved right up to the box. Well, let's get back and check this note against the other one and the sample I got from Mrs. Barclay."

"But it couldn't have been typed on that one," she protested. "We have it."

"So we do," he stated, glancing at her in the near darkness of the patrol car. "That doesn't mean it wasn't used to type this note. In fact, the kidnapper may have typed a whole series of notes before he or she discarded the typewriter."

* * *

"Hurry, Candi! I'm getting scared," Bridget whispered loudly. "What's taking you so long?"

"I'm trying, but she has lots of stuff and it's hard looking with nothing but this little flashlight to see by," Candi whispered back.

Bridget strained as she looked into the darkness beyond Miss Taylor's bedroom window. For the past hour, while Candi searched, Bridget had moved from window to window, peering outside, fearful that at any moment she'd see the lights of the teacher's car.

She left the bedroom and hurried back into the kitchen where she could look directly into the driveway. Then a minute later, she went into the living room, where Candi was busy at a small desk. She'd scattered everything it contained across the carpet. Candi looked up. "I can't find anything," she moaned. "There has to be something."

"We've got to go. We've tried our best, and that's all we can do," Bridget insisted.

"No, we've got to hunt a little longer. Miss Taylor isn't back yet, and it's really late. She's probably staying somewhere out of town for the night. Relax and just keep watch. Or else you could help me. We'll hear a car if it drives up, and then we can run out the back way like we decided," Candi declared.

Bridget hesitated momentarily, then acquiesced. "All right, but if we don't get out of here soon I'll die of fright. Where should I start looking?"

"See that bookcase over there?" Candi said, shining her light for a brief moment across the small living room.

"Yeah."

"See what you can find there."

"What should I look for?"

"Anything. A paper with a message from Buster or something like that, I guess."

Bridget turned on her own small flashlight, moved to the book-case, and pulled a book from the lowest shelf. She leafed through it.

When nothing fell out, she put it back and tried the next one, not at all sure what she was accomplishing. But as she busied herself, the tension slowly left her body. For several minutes the two girls worked in silence. Then Candi joined her at the bookshelf. "Nothing over there. Have you found anything?"

"No. Let's go now," Bridget whispered fiercely.

"Okay," Candi agreed at last, and together, they turned quietly toward the rear of the house where they had entered.

Just then, a hinge squeaked. The back door!

Bridget and Candi stopped in unison. Bridget thought she would faint. The door shut almost soundlessly, but the floor creaked in the back hallway. Candi grasped Bridget's arm tightly. They were no longer alone in the house, and now their exit was blocked. Whoever had just come in hadn't parked in the driveway, and he or she didn't turn on any lights in the house. Surely if it were Miss Taylor, she wouldn't try to move around her own house in the dark, Candi thought. *Unless she knows we're here.* Maybe she'd seen the light from their small flashlights. It took all the willpower Bridget could muster to suppress a scream of terror.

The girls huddled together as the floor continued to creak. Then Bridget heard the unmistakable sound of shuffling feet approaching them. Hoarse breathing accompanied the shuffling as the intruder drew closer.

The back door was out of the question, so Bridget tugged at Candi, and then the two girls bolted for the front door. Bridget grabbed the doorknob and turned it easily, but when she yanked on the door it didn't move. Just before a hand grabbed her by the hair, she realized that the dead bolt was locked. She and Candi screamed in unison.

* * *

Sheriff Hanks looked up from the ransom notes he'd been scrutinizing through a magnifying glass. "You look, Kara. I think they were both typed with this typewriter."

She examined them also. "You're right. But how can that be? We have the typewriter."

"Like I told you before, Kara, the kidnapper typed both notes, and probably more, before he got rid of the typewriter. Whoever it is, he . . . or she . . . has a plan, and no matter what we do, it will be carried out."

As he spoke, the phone rang.

"Sheriff Hanks," he said wearily as he pressed the handset to his ear.

"Sheriff. This is Houston Harrison. My daughter's gone! She and Candi Lind are both gone." He spoke rapidly, obviously panicked.

"Slow down, Houston," the sheriff admonished. "Where were they and how long ago were they last seen?"

"Candi was spending the night with Bridget. They went to bed fairly early. For some reason, I woke up and found that my wife had left our bed. I called her name and she came running. She'd just checked the girls' room and they weren't in it! We called Kyle Lind, and he hasn't seen or heard from Candi since this afternoon when she asked him if she could stay at Bridget's. Please hurry. As you can imagine, we're terribly frightened."

"I'll be right there," Sheriff Hanks assured him as he put the phone down. "Come on, Kara. You take your car and I'll take mine. Bridget Harrison and Candi Lind are missing. We'd better call Kyle Lind and let him know we're looking for them. I sure hope this doesn't push him over the edge." Then the sheriff added with frustration, "And I sure wish I knew where Buster Ashton is right now."

CHAPTER 13

Buster Ashton's location was not unknown to everyone. Bridget and Candi knew exactly where he was, or at least they knew the location of someone they both thought must be Buster. He was glaring at the two of them in the beam of the flashlight he'd pulled from his pocket. "I don't know what you two are doing in here," he said gruffly, "but I'm quite certain Mariah didn't give her approval."

"Who are you?" Bridget managed to squeak out.

"That's none of your business. I'm just a friend of Mariah's. She has something I need. She told me to come get it tonight."

"You're Buster Ashton!" Candi suddenly cried out in fear.

"Well, well. Aren't you the smart one? But it doesn't matter. I'll just get what I came for and then we'll leave—together, the three of us."

"We won't tell," Bridget stammered as she realized he intended to kidnap them. "Please don't make us go with you." Her voice trembled uncontrollably.

"That's probably true," Buster chuckled. "You won't tell. After all, you girls are burglars. You could go to prison for what you've done tonight."

"Please," Candi begged. "Let us go."

"No, that would not be smart, now would it, to leave two witnesses," he said. "You two will have to come with me."

"But . . . but you said Miss Taylor—" Bridget started.

"I know what I said!" Buster hissed angrily. "Now you two shut up while I think."

Bridget had never regretted anything in her life as much as she regretted coming here this night. *This is the man who helped Miss*

Taylor kidnap Cody, and now he has us, too, she thought. She was absolutely certain he had kidnapped Cody. Tears flowed in small streams down her face.

A bright light suddenly pierced the living room window and cut across the room as a car pulled up outside. Buster Ashton acted quickly. "You two in there," he ordered, shoving them toward Miss Taylor's bedroom. "And keep still!"

They kept still, except for the dreadful pounding of their hearts, which seemed loud enough to be heard next door. Bridget felt Candi's hand suddenly grab her arm and squeeze when someone opened the front door. Then they heard a loud gasp in the living room. Buster laughed, and the familiar voice of Miss Taylor asked, "What are you doing here, Buster?"

"You know why I'm here," he answered.

The conversation soon escalated into a bitter argument. Bridget could hear very little that actually made sense, since the two kept talking at the same time. What she could make out convinced her that although Miss Taylor had not expected to find Buster in her house, there was no doubt that the two of them were well acquainted.

Suddenly, the argument ceased and footsteps came in their direction. Bridget heard Miss Taylor ask, "What girls, Buster?"

"I don't know their names. What do you think I am? A schoolteacher?" Buster sneered. "They were just here when I came in. Looked like they broke the window out of your back door."

"I see," Miss Taylor said as the footsteps came to a halt not far from the bedroom door. "I believe I know who they are. Where are they now?"

"In your bedroom."

"What did you intend to do with them, Buster?"

"Take them with me, of course, but now I'll let you take them."

Bridget had heard enough. "Candi," she whispered frantically, "let's try to get away."

Candi nodded. They moved instinctively toward the bedroom window. It opened easily.

So did the bedroom door.

"Are you two o—hey, what are you doing?" Miss Taylor demanded.

Frantically, Bridget pushed out the screen and the two girls scrambled through. Once outside, they ran for the nearest fence. "I'll get them," they heard Buster shout as they attempted to scale the tall wooden fence.

Bridget glanced behind her as she gained the top and prepared to leap to the other side. Buster was out the window and running hard toward them, with Miss Taylor close behind. "Run!" Bridget screamed to Candi as she dropped to the ground.

"Stop, girls!" Mariah shouted.

Her voice gave them added impetus, and they shot up the street at a dead run. But they were not gazelles, or even Olympic runners. Not accustomed to running at that pace, Candi stumbled and fell. Bridget ran back and helped her to her feet. Buster was losing ground, but Mariah was closing in on them. Bridget grasped Candi's hand and propelled her forward again.

"Stop!" Mariah shouted from right behind them. Her voice was ragged and gasping for air, and it gave Bridget new hope.

"Hurry!" Bridget shouted desperately.

"I can't. I hurt my ankle. I'm going to fall," Candi gasped as she lost her balance and dropped to the ground. Bridget spun like a cornered animal, crouching and ready to defend both of them as Miss Taylor stumbled up to them. She was still gasping for air and couldn't speak.

"Don't touch us!" Bridget shouted angrily as she again helped Candi to her feet. The two girls began to slowly back away.

Buster was still running slowly toward them, and in the street-lights his face looked twisted and churlish. Miss Taylor managed to say in short bursts, "Please . . . don't run . . . I won't . . . hurt you."

Then Buster reached Mariah and tried to dash past, but the schoolteacher extended her leg and tripped him. He fell with a loud thud. The girls continued to back away. Cursing, Buster lay still for a moment before he struggled to his feet. Much to the girls' surprise, instead of pursuing them, he faced Miss Taylor, shaking his fist in her face.

"You shouldn't've done that," he threatened.

"Buster, you're in enough trouble already. The police know all about Cody. They even—"

Buster cut her off with a backhand slap that sent her reeling to the ground. "Shut up, woman. I don't know what you're talking about!" he shouted.

The girls continued to back away. Then Bridget said, "We've gotta run again," as she yanked at Candi's hand.

Limping badly, Candi tried her best to run. As they rounded a corner and lost sight of Buster and Mariah, they heard the welcome sound of sirens piercing the night. "Cops!" Candi yelled. "They're probably after us. We'll be in trouble."

"Maybe, but not as much trouble as we'll be in if Buster and Miss Taylor catch us again."

A moment later, a patrol car screamed by. Then its brake lights flashed and the car screeched to a halt. Prison sounded better than being caught again by Buster Ashton and Mariah Taylor, and Bridget hurried toward the car, Candi limping along behind her.

"Officer!" she screamed in relief as Kara Smith leaped from the car. "Help us!"

"That's what I'm here to do," Kara said calmly. "Where have you girls been?"

"Buster . . . Buster Ashton kidnapped us!" Candi blurted.

The young deputy's face darkened. "How did you get away?"

"We jumped out of Miss Taylor's window," Bridget answered tearfully, "but he and Miss Taylor chased us. They're right around the corner!"

"All right now, calm down," Kara instructed as she stepped back to her car and grabbed the mike to her radio.

"Sheriff," she fired into the mike, "I've got the girls. Mariah Taylor and Buster Ashton had them, and they're still close by."

"What's your location?" Sheriff Hanks called back.

"Near the corner of Fifth South and Oak." Then the deputy whirled. "Get in!" she ordered the girls.

Bridget had scarcely fastened her seat belt before the big patrol car came to life with a surge of power unlike any she had ever experienced before. They rounded the corner, tires squealing. There was no sign of Buster or Miss Taylor. Kara keyed the mike again. "I can't see them, Sheriff," she reported.

"I'm almost there," he replied. A moment later his patrol car sped up the street and slid to a stop.

He leaped out and ran to Kara's car. "Where were they, girls?" he asked.

"Right here in the street," Bridget sobbed.

"Kara, I'll search. The city will have an officer here in a moment to help me, and any other officers the dispatcher can contact will be coming soon. You take the girls to the Harrisons' and then head for Mariah's house. It's only about three blocks east," the sheriff said as he turned and ran back to his car.

As they drove, Kara asked, "Do they have a car?"

"I don't know," Bridget answered. "We only saw Miss Taylor's. She left it in the driveway."

"All right. We'll find them," she assured the girls as she rolled to a stop in front of the Harrisons' house, where Bridget's folks stood anxiously waiting.

"You girls stay here. I'll be back," Kara ordered tersely. Then to Bridget's parents she shouted, "Take them inside, lock the doors, and wait." With that, the deputy roared back up the street.

* * *

Within a couple of minutes Deputy Smith was pulling up at Mariah Taylor's house. The living room window glowed yellow, but the rest of the house appeared to be dark. Mariah's blue Pontiac Tempest was parked in the driveway. Kara waited impatiently for a couple of minutes until a city police officer and Sheriff Hanks joined her. They approached the house together. There was no response to the sheriff's knock. Kara circled the small yard and discovered the screen belonging to the window the girls had escaped through.

Finally, after checking inside and assuring themselves that Mariah and Buster hadn't returned, the sheriff asked the city officer to stay and keep an eye on the place. Then he told Kara to begin searching for the missing suspects. "I'll go talk to the girls," he said. "I'll see if they can give us anything else to go on."

Kara felt helpless as she drove through the neighborhood. It was quite likely that Buster would have had a car parked nearby, and if so, he and Mariah were long gone. There wasn't even a description of a car to broadcast, unless the girls could give them one—and she doubted that.

* * *

After listening to the amazing story of the two tearful girls' self-appointed mission to find evidence against Mariah Taylor, the sheriff turned to Houston Harrison. "I hope that when we find Miss Taylor, she won't want to press charges against Bridget and Candi. They could be in serious trouble, despite their good intentions."

"I understand, Sheriff," Houston said with a long face. "It does look like she's involved in the kidnapping though, doesn't it?"

"Possibly. I wish we knew for sure that we're on the right track, because from what the girls say, Miss Taylor probably didn't know Buster would be in her house, and she doesn't seem to like him much. At any rate, we're doing all we can to find them. Keep the girls home the rest of the night. I'll be in touch tomorrow."

After several more hours of searching in vain for Mariah and Buster, Sheriff Hanks finally grabbed a few hours of sleep. When his alarm awakened him at noon, he rolled out of bed with a groan. After a quick shower and a bowl of cold cereal, he kissed his wife and returned to the office. A few phone calls assured him that there were no new developments in the case.

He was almost convinced that Buster Ashton and Mariah Taylor were the only serious suspects in the case. *Almost.* As he reviewed the notes he'd written to help him keep abreast of every suspect he had identified, the mystery of drunkard Sammy Shirts following the shyster Edgar Stevens to a bar in Salt Lake jumped out at him.

With it, the concern over Edgar's foreclosure on Kyle's ranch moved the sheriff to pick up the phone. A minute later he was speaking with a police lieutenant in Salt Lake City whom he had worked with before. After exchanging greetings, the sheriff got to the point, explaining what was happening with Edgar Stevens and about his mysterious trip to the bar in Salt Lake City.

"Sheriff, can you give me the name of the bar?" the lieutenant asked.

The sheriff did so. The line was quiet for a moment before the lieutenant revealed, "That bar is owned by a questionable character by the name of Ken Treman. We suspect him of extortion but have never been able to make a case against him."

"I was planning to go to Salt Lake today, but I was pretty much up all night. Is there anyone in your department who could do a little discreet checking up on this Ken Treman?"

"We're always looking for a reason to go after him. I'll have a couple of my men do a little nosing around this evening. If we learn anything of interest, how do I get hold of you?"

Sheriff Hanks gave him his cell phone number and the number of his dispatcher. "They can always find me if you can't reach me on my cell phone, and I'll return your call," he promised.

His next phone call was to an officer of a Wells Fargo Bank branch office in Salt Lake City, where he hoped to get help in saving Kyle's ranch. Fifteen minutes later he hung up, sorely disappointed. As much as the bank officer wanted to help, it just couldn't be done. It appeared that Kyle Lind was about to lose his home, his ranch, and everything else he owned.

When Kara came in looking fresh and bright a few minutes later, he told her of his failure to find a way to save Kyle's ranch. "It might have helped if I could have made my request in person, as I'd planned. But there's nothing I could do about that, I'm afraid."

"There has to be some way," Kara moaned as her brightness faded with the disappointing news.

"I can't think of another soul to call. Anyway, he said that what I wanted just couldn't be done without undergoing a lengthy process. And we don't have much time, I'm afraid, before the kidnapper will be expecting the ransom."

"Surely there's someone who can help Kyle," Kara insisted. "Maybe Jake knows someone in Arizona."

"I would think he'd have tried already," the sheriff stated with a sigh. Then he said, "Ken Treman."

"What?" Kara asked, puzzled.

"A strong-arm man by the name of Ken Treman owns the bar Stevens led you to. He intimidates folks for those who have the need and the ability to pay. At least that's what the police in Salt Lake think. They're checking on him for me right now. In the meantime, since Buster and Mariah seem to have vanished, I guess we should see what Sammy and Edgar are up to."

"Does that mean I get to follow Sammy again?" Kara asked, sighing.

"Afraid so, Kara," the sheriff responded.

"All right," she answered, trying to appear enthused.

As she started to rise from her chair, her cell phone rang.

Vince scanned his notes again as she said into the phone, "I had a long night. I'm sorry."

She was silent for a moment before continuing. "No, I'm afraid not. I'll be watching one of the suspects again."

More silence. The sheriff glanced up at her. Her lips were tight and her eyes screwed shut. "I know that," she said at last. "We have people looking for them everywhere. In the meantime, there are still other suspects."

Another pause. Then Kara said, "Sammy Shirts."

As the other party again spoke, Kara opened her eyes and looked at Sheriff Hanks. Her voice was soft when she answered again. "No. The sheriff has done everything he can, Jake. It looks like Stevens is going to get his way, unless you can think of something. I have to go now. I'll call when I get a minute . . . maybe this evening sometime."

After she'd closed her phone, Kara sighed, "That was Jake Garrett. He's really upset. He thinks we should be concentrating more on Buster after what Candi told them this morning about the little stunt she and Bridget pulled last night. And he is really upset with Edgar Stevens."

"Aren't we all," the sheriff mumbled. "You better go find Sammy. Keep me informed. And Kara, call me if you head for Salt Lake again."

After Kara left, the sheriff went over his notes again, then added a few more. Several things disturbed him, not the least of which was the episode with Mariah Taylor and Buster Ashton the previous night. Somehow, he just couldn't see Mariah Taylor as a kidnapper, despite what had occurred with Bridget and Candi. Buster, yes, but Mariah, no.

His secretary paged him. "There's someone here to see you, Sheriff," she said in a strained tone.

"Who is it?" he asked gruffly.

"Mariah Taylor."

CHAPTER 14

"Good afternoon, Mariah," the sheriff said as the English teacher entered his office.

"Hello, Sheriff," she said in a voice choked with emotion. Her long hair was windblown, her face drawn and pale. One eye was black and swollen. There was ground-in dirt on her khaki slacks, and a rip in one sleeve of her light blue blouse.

"How can I help you?" Sheriff Hanks asked as he waved her to a chair across the desk from him.

"You're looking for me, aren't you?" she said with downcast eyes.

"Not anymore," he responded. "Perhaps before you say anything else, I need to advise you of your rights."

"Am I under arrest, then?"

"Not at the moment, but you could be at any time. You have the right to remain silent. Anything you say can and will be used against you in a court of law," he began. As he droned the rest of the standard Miranda warning, Miss Taylor sat with her head lowered and her hands folded in her lap. She finally looked up when he asked, "Do you want an attorney now, or would you like to answer a few questions without one?"

"I've nothing to hide, Sheriff. I came to talk, and that's what I intend to do," she declared, squaring her shoulders and sitting up straighter.

"Fine, let's begin then," he replied as he picked up a pen and leaned forward.

"Don't you want to record this?" she asked.

"I'll take notes. Now, why don't we begin with last night. Where had you been before you came home and found Buster Ashton, Bridget Harrison, and Candi Lind in your house?"

"Driving around," she answered.

"Alone?"

"Yes. I was just so worried, Sheriff. I know everybody thinks I helped kidnap Cody, but I swear to you, I didn't. Please, you've got to believe that, Sheriff. I wouldn't hurt Kyle or any of his family for anything. I'm so worried about Kyle. He's about to lose everything."

"Yes, he is. So you are aware of what Edgar Stevens is doing?" the sheriff asked.

"I talked to Kyle on the phone last evening. I've avoided returning his calls, but I finally felt that I just had to," she blurted.

The sheriff noted the tears forming in her eyes and the slight reddening of her face. Then he lowered his head and made a few notes, and as he wrote he thought how sincere this lady sounded. She either was telling the truth or she was a very good actress. He looked up and asked, "Were you expecting to meet Buster?"

"No!" she exclaimed with a firm set of her jaw. "He still wants money from me. I guess he came to steal some."

"I see. What about the girls? Did you have any idea they were at your house? Did you have any idea they'd be in there?"

Slowly, she nodded. "I did. I was down the street when they first arrived at my house a little after midnight."

"You watched them go in?" he asked in amazement.

"Yes."

"Why didn't you stop them?"

"I knew what they were after, and I knew they wouldn't find it," she stated simply.

"What were they after?"

"Something that would prove I kidnapped Cody, or that at least would show that I helped. I guess I hoped that by finding there was nothing like that in my house they would begin to believe me."

"Why did you finally go in?"

"I left town after they'd been in there for about half an hour. I drove out of town to the west, past Kyle's place, then back again." She smiled briefly. "I passed you and Deputy Smith at the edge of town."

The sheriff nodded. "Do you know where we were going?"

"Kyle's?"

"That's right. Why do you suppose we did that?"

"I have no idea. Tell me," she said pleadingly.

"To pick up another ransom note," the sheriff informed her, watching her face intently.

Her surprise seemed genuine. "Oh, no! And what did he say this time?"

"What did *who* say?" the sheriff asked.

"Buster. Who else could have written the note? It has to be him, Sheriff. He says he doesn't know anything about Cody, but he's lying. I swear, he's lying," she said emphatically.

"Okay, let's back up again, Mariah," Sheriff Hanks said as he scribbled a few more notes. "After you returned home, you went inside your house, correct?"

"Yes."

"Which door?"

"Don't you already know?" she queried.

"I want to hear it from you."

"All right. I went in the front door."

"Did you think the girls were still there?"

"No. It had been so long by then that I thought they surely would have left. So I just unlocked the door and stepped in. Buster grabbed me as soon as I reached for the light switch."

"And did it surprise you that he was there?" the sheriff wondered.

"Surprise me? It shocked and scared me."

"What did he say? Did he explain what he was doing in your house?"

"He said he came to borrow some money. He was desperate, he told me. We got in a terrible argument. I was very angry, but I was afraid, too. Even in the best of circumstances, Buster is pushy, rude, and arrogant. He would never be called a nice person, Sheriff."

"I gathered that," Sheriff Hanks responded. "What happened next?"

"He said he caught two girls in my house. Then I was really worried. I figured they'd already left. I asked him what he did with them. He said he'd put them in my bedroom. I assumed he'd tied them up or something, and I knew they must be terrified. I was praying that he hadn't hurt them. When I opened the bedroom door, they were scrambling out the window. I shouted for them to stop so I could explain that it was all right that they were in my house and that I wouldn't let Buster hurt them, but they ran."

"How did you plan to defend them from Buster? You weren't armed, were you?" the sheriff asked.

"Of course not. I don't even own a gun. I don't know what I'd have done, but he'd have had to kill me to hurt them."

"Okay, so you chased them?"

"Followed them," Mariah corrected. "Buster went out the window after them, so I followed. The poor kids were so scared that they wouldn't stop for me. I swear, I would never have let Buster hurt them." Her voice caught as she replayed last night's events in her mind.

"The girls said you caught up with them before Buster did," the sheriff prompted.

"Buster smokes too much, and he'd been drinking last night." She smiled wanly. "So I was able to outrun him. Maybe I was just more desperate. I don't know, but yes, after Candi fell and Bridget helped her up, I knew I could get to them before Buster did."

"And you did. What happened then?"

"My lungs were on fire. I don't usually run like that," she admitted with another weak grin. The sheriff found himself starting to warm up to this woman, but he forced himself to remain objective. She continued. "I couldn't speak for a moment, and they kept moving away from me. I finally said something, I don't know just what, and then I heard Buster running up behind me. I stuck out my foot and tripped him as he tried to pass me."

"And the girls took off again," the sheriff finished.

"Yes. Not very fast though. Is Candi going to be all right? I'm worried about her."

"It's just a minor ankle sprain. She'll be fine. What did you do then?" the sheriff pressed.

"I tried to go after them, but Buster hit me . . . knocked me down. When I got up he grabbed me and dragged me off the street. That was when we heard the sirens. We fought. That's when he gave me this attractive black eye. I tried to get away from him, but he pulled a gun on me. His car was about a block from my house, in an alley. He made me get in with him."

"Where did you go after that?" the sheriff asked as he took notes.

"To Wyoming. Evanston. I asked him where he had Cody, but he said he didn't know anything about any Cody. I told him you were after him, and he became really nervous. He said that just because he got arrested for kidnapping once didn't mean that he'd ever do it again. I asked if that wasn't what he had done to the girls at my house."

"What did he say to that?" the sheriff inquired with more than a little interest.

"He said that was different. They were breaking the law. I guess they were, at that, but I'd never want them arrested for it."

"You wouldn't?" Sheriff Hanks raised his eyebrows.

"Of course not. I told you before, I don't blame them. I realize how bad it looks for me. If I were in their shoes, I'd suspect me too. Anyway, then I asked Buster what he thought he was doing to me if it wasn't kidnapping. 'You're my sister-in-law,' he said, as if that excused him from forcing me to go with him."

"Were you afraid he might hurt you, Mariah?" the sheriff asked with concern.

"He would have if I hadn't gotten away from him. He still will if he catches me again. If you want to put me in jail, I won't object," she exclaimed, to the sheriff's amazement.

"I haven't said anything about putting you in jail," he responded quickly.

"I know that, but I'd be safer there. Not that it matters. If I thought he'd take me and let Cody go, I'd let him."

"But you said he'd kill you," the sheriff reminded her.

"Better me than Cody," was her answer, and again the sheriff felt a ring of sincerity in her voice.

"Tell me what happened after you got to Wyoming."

Just then his intercom buzzed. "I'm sorry to interrupt, Sheriff, but Kara is calling on her cellular. She says it's urgent."

"Transfer the call in here," he instructed. "I'm sorry," he said to Mariah. "It's Deputy Smith."

As Mariah nodded, Kara came on the line. "You won't believe this, Sheriff, but I think we're going to Salt Lake again."

"I see," he responded.

"Sheriff, are you not alone?"

"That's right, Kara. I'm visiting with Mariah Taylor," he explained. The silence on the other end made him grin despite himself.

Finally, his young deputy said, "You're kidding me, aren't you?"

"Not at all. So tell me, what exactly is happening?" he prodded.

"What's she doing there? Do you want me to come in, or—" Kara began.

The sheriff cut her off. "No. Fill me in."

"All right," Kara agreed, and the sheriff could hear the reluctance in her voice. "Sammy watched the bank again. Stevens came out, got in his Cadillac, and drove off. Sammy followed him. And I followed Sammy. We're ten miles out of town already. That's all I know."

"Keep me posted," Vince ordered and hung up. "I'm sorry," he said to Mariah. "Where were we?"

"You were asking about what happened after I got to Evanston. It's simple, really. I could see he wasn't going to tell me anything about what he'd done with Cody, so I decided I needed to try to get away from him. He got careless, and I got away," she stated flatly.

That was too easy, the sheriff thought, so he pressed her for details, wondering doubtfully if she could provide them.

"He was tired, and he was drunk," she started. "He parked the car behind a warehouse of some kind and said he had to . . . well, you know . . . go to the restroom. Only there wasn't a restroom nearby. He stepped out of the car, but in his hurry he forgot to take his gun. It was on the dashboard above the steering wheel. So I reached over and shut the door and locked it. He pounded and screamed, but I was able to drive off." She opened her purse. "Here, you can have this," she offered, pulling a 9mm pistol by the barrel from her purse and carefully offering it to him.

Vince accepted the gun, unloaded it, and slipped it into a drawer beside him, making a mental note to check it in as evidence later. "Thank you," he mumbled as he shook off the shock the incident had cast over him.

"Would you like this, too?" she asked, reaching into her purse again and producing a single car key.

"Thanks. Is it to Buster's car?" he asked, eyeing the purse nervously, wondering what else it might contain.

"Yes," she answered. "It's parked in your parking lot. Here, you can check this if you like," she offered, sliding the purse across the desk toward him.

"I'm sure it's fine," he indicated, but he had a quick look inside anyway, before pushing it back toward her.

Vince took a minute with his notebook while he collected his thoughts. Then he said, "What time did you get the car away from Buster?"

"I don't know. I lost my watch when he and I were scuffling, and his car doesn't have a clock." She grinned. "It was made before clocks were invented, I think. It was after sunrise, though. I started right back, but I forgot to look at the gas gauge. Not that it would have helped. It doesn't work. Anyway, I ran out of gas on the freeway."

"That's what took you so long getting here?" the sheriff asked curiously.

"Yes, that and a flat tire. It took over an hour before I was able to get someone to bring me some gas in a can. Then I had to drive back to the nearest service station and fill up. I had the flat after I got back in Utah. Buster had a spare tire but no jack. A truck driver helped me change it."

"How long did that take?" the sheriff inquired.

"Quite a while. One of the lugs was rusted on. I got really tired a little later and stopped in a rest area. I'm sorry it took so long, but here I am," she sighed, spreading her hands, palms up. "Now, what else do you want to know?"

Sheriff Hanks wrote a few more notes in his notebook. "I guess that's all for now. Let me give you a lift home."

Miss Taylor tensed. "Sheriff," she began, but said nothing more.

"What is it, Miss Taylor? Are you worried about Buster?"

"Well . . . yes, in a way, but—"

The sheriff interrupted. "How about if I take you home and then have someone watch your house around the clock? If Buster comes, then we can nab him. If he is the one who's holding Cody Lind, maybe we can persuade him to lead us to Cody."

"I can't imagine it being anyone else," Mariah said as she ran one hand through her long, blonde hair. "I hadn't thought about your catching him if he does come for me again. If you want me to, I'll go home and wait. Anything I can do that might help, I'm willing to do."

"We'll protect you, Mariah," the sheriff assured her.

"Thank you," she mumbled. "I may need it. If we can just get Cody back for his dad, it won't matter what happens to me," she added as her eyes misted again.

"One more thing, Mariah. If you can tell me how Buster was dressed when you last saw him, I'll put that information out over the air. I suppose he'll come up with another car."

"He'll steal one. I don't think the one outside is actually his," she revealed.

It wasn't. The sheriff soon learned it had been stolen two days ago in a neighboring county. The case against Buster Ashton was looking stronger all the time. If he could just be sure about Mariah Taylor. At least he had a way to keep her, with her own permission, under around-the-clock surveillance. The biggest problem the sheriff had now was lack of manpower. His handful of deputies were, like him, wearing down.

He needed help, so he called Chief Ron Worthlin, who met him in his office half an hour later. After bringing the chief up-to-date on his interview with Mariah, the sheriff asked, "Could you lend me some manpower to keep an eye on her?"

"I thought you'd never ask," Ron chuckled. "Of course we'll help. I'll take that as an assignment if you like and keep her under surveillance until you say otherwise."

"Thanks, Ron," the sheriff said gratefully. "That would be great."

"Anything we can do, we'd be glad to," the police chief offered.

"There is one other thing," added Sheriff Hanks.

"And what's that?" Chief Worthlin inquired.

"Help me reason through a couple of things, will you? I could use your brainpower for a few minutes," the sheriff said as he fingered his steadily filling notebook.

"I don't know how much I can help you there, but I'll give it a try."

"Thanks. Let's get Mariah home and one of your people watching her place. Then maybe you and I could spend some time going over my notes."

Thirty minutes later Ron and Vince were in the sheriff's office again, discussing the suspects in the case one by one. When they got to Mariah, Ron said, "One thing bothers me about her. I know she seems to be coming off as very much a victim herself, but who better to have put the note in the mailbox out at Kyle's place than her? The time frame's about right."

Sheriff Hanks took a deep breath and exhaled slowly before saying, "The same thought occurred to me. I already know she was driving out that way. I've tried to brush the thought away, but it nags at me. That's one reason I'm glad to have her under surveillance. If it was Mariah who left the other notes, she can't leave any more, now that we're watching her."

"Then again, Buster was in the area. He could have left it just as easily, I suppose," the chief pointed out.

"Or both of them together," the sheriff mumbled, but he didn't really believe that.

After talking more about Mariah Taylor and Buster Ashton, they moved on to Sammy Shirts. "Kara Smith is following him at this moment," the sheriff revealed.

"Following?" Ron asked with an arched eyebrow.

"Yes. She called earlier on her cell phone. It seems that Sammy is tailing Edgar Stevens again, who was headed toward Salt Lake, just like before. As much as I suspect Buster is our man, I can't rule out Sammy or Edgar. I wonder where they are right now," the sheriff mused aloud.

He didn't wonder for long, because Kara called again. "I'm puzzled, Sheriff," she admitted.

"Where are you calling from?" he asked.

"We're about fifteen miles from Salt Lake. Edgar turned onto a side road here. I had to stay back because Sammy did, too, so I couldn't see who Edgar met, but he met someone. They talked for only two or three minutes, and then Edgar headed back toward Harrisville. We're still on our way in your direction."

"I wonder if he met our mysterious bar owner, Ken Treman," the sheriff remarked.

"I couldn't say. Whoever it was came from the other direction on this little county road we were on, and he left the same way."

"What was he driving?"

"I watched through my binoculars, but I couldn't tell for sure. It was a sedan, light-colored—that's all I know."

"Thanks for calling in," the sheriff said. "And keep in touch."

After hanging up, the sheriff turned again to the chief. "I just thought of something. I don't know why I didn't think of it before. I'm too tired, I guess."

"What's that, Vince?"

"I haven't looked for any boot prints Buster may have made last night. That could be a prime bit of evidence."

"You're right. I'll help you do that right now if you'd like me to."

"Let's go," the sheriff said, rising and reaching for his felt hat.

They found some footprints, photographed them, and returned to the office. "Definitely not a match," the chief observed a few minutes later as he straightened up from his study of the various photos of boot prints. "But then, Buster may have more than one pair of boots."

"That's true, but I sure did have my hopes built up. A match would have helped our case against him, and it would have helped eliminate other suspects," the sheriff moaned. "Seems like nothing is making this case any easier."

By the time Chief Worthlin left, the afternoon was wearing away. Kara had called in a little earlier to report that Edgar was back at the bank and that Sammy was drinking a beer not far away. Sheriff Hanks could sense the boredom in her voice, but he needed her to continue to keep watch.

Sheriff Hanks drove over to Harry's Hardware. He wanted to check on the purchase of a flashlight like the one Jake and Kara had found out at Roscoe's old outhouse. He had it in a bag in his pocket when he entered the store. Gil Enders was at the register with a customer when he walked in.

"Afternoon, Gil," he greeted. "Your boss around?"

Gil just grunted and kept on with his work, and Sheriff Hanks looked at him more closely. Gil appeared worn out and tired. The sheriff wondered if he might have been up late the night before, possibly delivering a ransom note?

The customer gathered her bags and left. The sheriff commented, "You look tired, Gil. Up late, were you?"

Gil swung his head slowly toward Sheriff Hanks. "None of your business." He swore and stormed toward the nearest aisle.

"Looking for me, Sheriff?" Harry said from behind him. The sheriff turned and extended a hand as Harry added, "Or are you just interested in my help?"

"Both," the sheriff responded.

"Gil's getting to be a real bear," Harry revealed. "I'm about ready to let him go. Something's sure eating at him. And I don't know what it is, unless he's involved some way in this terrible thing with young Cody. Every time I mention Cody, Gil blows up."

Vince shrugged. "Seems like everyone's blowing up lately. I know I'm sure on edge." He pulled the flashlight from his pocket, "Do you sell flashlights like this one?"

Harry took the evidence bag from Vince, peered closely at the small flashlight it contained, and then handed it back. "Sure do."

"I don't suppose you could tell me anyone who might have bought one around the time of Cody's abduction?"

Harry laughed. "Sheriff, that's a hard question. The simplest answer would be to say everybody."

"You've sold a lot of them?"

"Dozens," Harry said as the sheriff grunted in disappointment. "But to say exactly who bought them would be next to impossible." He paused for a moment, then his eyes narrowed suspiciously. "Gil has one. Where did you get that one?"

"I can't really say right now, but it could be important. Is there any way you could find out if Gil still has his?" the sheriff asked as his pulse quickened.

"Short of asking him, you mean? I don't think so. Cody bought one too. Of course, he doesn't count."

The sheriff stared at Harry for a moment. "Are you sure?" he asked.

"About what?" Harry queried with a puzzled frown.

"Are you sure Cody had one?"

"Oh, yeah. He and Gil bought them the same day. I remember, because they rang them up for each other."

"I lost mine," Gil stated with a sneer as he appeared from a nearby aisle. "If you're talking about the flashlight you have in that bag, anyway."

Sheriff Hanks turned to Gil. "When did you have it last?"

"Last I remember it was under the seat in my truck. I figure it must've rolled out. Why, you figure on arrestin' everybody who has one of 'em?"

"No, but who else bought them that you can remember?" the sheriff questioned.

"Half the town."

"Name a few people," the sheriff urged.

"Oh, Mrs. Short, for one. Mrs. Stevens, too." The sheriff stared, but Gil went on. "And I think I sold one to one of the city cops. Oh, that Miss Taylor, the English teacher, she bought one."

The sheriff stared again. "When did she buy one, Gil?" he asked.

Gil's face broke into a complacent grin. "The day before Cody took off. There, I've helped you. Now will you stay off my back?" he demanded. "I don't know anything about what happened to Cody." He turned his back and strode away again before the sheriff could respond.

CHAPTER 15

When Shawn relieved Kara from her shift at seven that evening, she didn't care if she ever saw Edgar Stevens or Sammy Shirts again. This was the kind of police work that would make even the most devoted officers in the business rethink their employment choice.

She had more than a few serious doubts herself a few minutes later when the sheriff ordered, "Go home, get some sleep, and then take over again on the Sammy Shirts detail at three in the morning. And by the way, I just got a call from the Salt Lake police. They say they can't find Ken Treman."

"All right," Kara agreed reluctantly, and a pleasant evening with Jake Garrett was shot to pieces.

She did call the Lind place, and Candi answered the phone. "Hey, how's your ankle?" Kara asked.

"It's fine. That was so stupid of Bridget and me. Dad and Jake threatened to lock me up if I even thought about doing anything like that again. Actually, we're lucky Miss Taylor doesn't have us locked up . . . in jail, I mean. But can you believe the sheriff let that woman go home?" Candi queried in the very next breath.

"She's being watched," Kara assured her. "Is Jake there?"

"Yes. I'll get him. He keeps asking if you've called," Candi replied in a lighter tone. "He's awesome, isn't he?"

Kara agreed, and a moment later Jake's soothing voice came on the line. "Hi, Kara," he said. "You sure know how to make a guy lonely."

"I'm sorry. The sheriff's keeping me busy. I have to go back on duty at three in the morning. I was planning to come out and see you—until the sheriff told me that."

"Oh, no," Jake moaned. "I'm disappointed. I was going to offer to take you to dinner again tonight."

"Sorry, but I've got to get some sleep. After chasing Sammy and that creep Edgar Stevens all day, I'm beat," she explained.

"What were you doing following them around?" Jake wondered. "It's seems rather obvious that Buster Ashton has Cody. Why is the sheriff wasting everybody's time on those two? I'm beginning to wonder about that boss of yours, Kara."

"He's okay, Jake," she said defensively. "I admit that I'm having a hard time with it myself, but Sheriff Hanks has been a cop for a long time. I have to believe he knows what he's doing."

"Okay, okay. I don't want to start an argument. The last thing I want is to argue with you. I was just hoping to spend the evening with you, Kara." Then he added tenderly, "I'm getting kind of hooked on being with you, you know."

"I enjoy being with you, too."

"So what's he got you doing at three in the morning?"

"Following Sammy again, which is almost sure to mean following Edgar, unless of course Sammy gets too drunk and falls asleep in his apartment. If they both act like normal people and sleep at that time of night, I'm afraid I'm in for a boring time of it. I wish you could be with me. It would sure make the time go by faster," she said wistfully.

"I wish that too, but I've got to be here to do the chores in the morning for Kyle. I went in to see Dr. Odell today about him. He'd left his office, so I had to find his house. But anyway, Odell says that if Kyle will take the medicine he prescribed, he'll be all right. I'm not so sure, though. Kyle's almost a basket case now. This thing with Stevens is the final straw. It makes me so angry—I wish I could think of something I could do. It's tearing me up, seeing Kyle losing his ranch and everything. The poor man doesn't deserve all this."

"No, he doesn't. Well, I better get some sleep, Jake. Maybe I'll see you tomorrow," Kara offered hopefully.

"You'd better," Jake agreed with a chuckle. "I'll be as bad off as Kyle if I don't see more of you pretty soon."

"Oh, sure," Kara responded, but it pleased her to hear his words. *Jake Garrett is one great guy,* she thought as she hung the phone up a minute later. The word *love* kept rolling about in her head, making her dizzy with pleasure. Could this be love? It seemed too good to be true. After all, she'd known Jake for only a very short time.

When Kara took over the surveillance again from Shawn at three on Sunday morning, he reported that Sammy had been in his house with the lights off for several hours. "He's sleeping, I suppose," he explained with a tired smile. "Which is exactly what I intend to do now."

Sammy Shirts apparently slept until nearly four in the morning—at least the lights were off until then. When they came on it was only for a few minutes, and then the house went dark again. Kara's heart started beating faster and her palms began to perspire when, at just one or two minutes before four, Sammy came out of the house, climbed into his old truck, and drove off. Kara followed him with her lights off, keeping a discreet distance behind him. Sammy didn't go far. He parked a block away from Edgar Stevens's house and walked furtively to the banker's back door, with Kara following at a distance in her unmarked car. The door opened with a quick wash of yellow light, swallowing Sammy in the blackness of its closing.

A few minutes later, Sammy came out again, holding what looked to Kara like a small package. He stuffed it beneath his ragged jacket before he reached the street. *That's strange. Could Sammy Shirts be involved in some kind of shady deal with Edgar Stevens?* Kara wondered. It seemed unlikely, but one thing was certain: something shady was going on.

Kara watched as Sammy hurried to his truck and pulled away from the curb. She was almost ready to follow when a car with its lights off slid from the darkness beyond Edgar Stevens's house and fell in behind Sammy as he passed in his truck. It looked like a Cadillac, although she couldn't be sure because of the darkness. *Edgar drives a Cadillac.* Kara felt a sudden shiver of apprehension. Sammy might be a creep and a small-time crook, but if he was in danger—and she couldn't help thinking that he was—then she had a duty to protect him.

With this frightening thought in mind, Kara pulled into the street with her lights off and followed the two cars. The temptation to call the sheriff was intense, but she forced herself to refrain, knowing how tired and worn out he was. She'd let him get his rest.

The Cadillac kept its lights off as Sammy headed out of town. Kara did the same, although it was difficult driving with nothing but a quarter moon to light the way. Kara could not imagine where Sammy might be going. Why didn't he just go back to his apartment? And why was the Cadillac following him? Sammy's old truck rumbled east on the highway for several miles before turning south on a dirt road in a remote, hilly area of the county.

Several rough, twisting, uphill miles later, the car following Sammy stopped behind a small stand of juniper trees just as the first light of dawn appeared as a dim gray line on the horizon. Kara couldn't see Sammy's truck, but she assumed he too had stopped. There was nothing out here, as far as she knew, but juniper and piñon pine, sagebrush, hills and deep ravines, and a smattering of wildlife.

Several minutes passed before a shadowy figure emerged from the Cadillac and slipped into the shadows of the trees. With the daylight now increasing, Kara followed quickly and easily on foot. Too quickly, for she stepped on a brittle piñon branch that snapped with a sound not unlike a small rifle firing. Ahead of her, Edgar, or whoever had been stalking Sammy, spun on his heels. She dropped to the ground, but not before he'd caught a glimpse of her. Immediately, he abandoned his mission and sprinted for his car. The way the man ran, Kara realized it could not possibly be Edgar Stevens—the banker was far too heavy to run like that. *So who is it?* she wondered.

Kara was torn between following the stalker and following Sammy Shirts. Recalling the sheriff's admonition to stay with Sammy, she listened for a moment as the stranger quickly started his car and roared back the way they'd come. After listening long enough to assure herself that he didn't stop at her patrol car, she proceeded forward more cautiously. Walking slowly and guardedly for several minutes, she hadn't gone far when she heard footsteps approaching in the trees.

She ducked behind a large piñon tree and waited. In a moment Sammy Shirts appeared, walking quite briskly and humming to himself. Apparently he hadn't heard the engine of the car of the man who'd left so hastily several minutes before. Suddenly, Kara realized that if Sammy left here before she did, he was likely to turn back toward town. If he did that, he would see her car, which was parked in plain view a few hundred yards back down the road. Since there was no way now for her to get back there in time to leave before he did, she did the only other thing she could think of. She stepped from behind the tree and called out, "Hi, Sammy, it's Deputy Kara Smith. I'd like to talk to you for a minute."

Sammy spun, almost falling as he did. "I'm sorry," she called out again. "I didn't mean to frighten you, Sammy."

"You didn't," he said in a voice that was both slurred and quaking. "What are you doing out here?"

"Well, Sammy, I thought I'd ask you the same question. And I also planned to ask you what you did with that package you were carrying earlier."

Sammy's face registered alarm in the dim light of the early dawn. He looked around as if searching for a way to escape, but Kara had already closed to within a few feet of him. He stammered when he finally spoke. "Wh-what p-p-package?"

"You know which one, Mr. Shirts. The one you picked up at Mr. Stevens's house," Kara stated.

For a moment, she thought Sammy Shirts would faint. He stumbled backward several feet before sitting heavily on the ground. Kara advanced, one hand resting ominously on the butt of her pistol. Sammy sat there trembling.

"All right, Sammy. Get on your feet. We're going to go back to where you just came from."

Sammy shook his head as tears started to roll down his whiskered face. "No, please don't do that, lady cop," he begged. "It ain't nothing bad."

"If it's not bad, then you have nothing to fear," she insisted authoritatively, and reaching for his arm she half dragged him to his feet, spun him around, and started pushing him in the direction from which he'd come.

Sammy balked, but as Kara pushed him firmly, she said, "You and I can go now, or I'll call for help and we'll carry you."

"Okay, I'll go, but it ain't nothing. I swear it ain't," Sammy insisted.

After walking several hundred yards up a ridge and down the far side, they approached a heavy shale ledge overhanging a dark, shallow, recessed area, not really deep enough to call a cave but nevertheless a low-ceilinged shelter. A glance told the deputy that Sammy had been on his hands and knees as far back as he could go beneath the ledge. She ordered, "Crawl back in there, Sammy, and get whatever it was you left. And don't get smart with me, because—"

"Please, Deputy Smith," he begged, once again close to tears. "Don't make me do this."

"Fine," she said with disgust. "I'll do it myself. Don't you move an inch until I tell you to," she added gruffly.

Sammy whimpered but stood still as she crawled quickly beneath the shale outcropping. Keeping a cautious eye on Sammy, she felt around the rock at the back of the sheltered area. She retrieved a large leather bag and crawled out from under the rock.

It was a money bag. As Kara swung Sammy's bag into his view, she asked, "Is this what that fellow who followed you from Edgar's house was after?"

For a moment, Sammy Shirts's face was stricken with a look that could be nothing less than sheer fear. Then he bolted. Kara hit her head hard on the rock above her as she attempted to leap after him. The blow brought her to her knees. For a moment, the world spun around her and she felt darkness closing in. After a minute, however, the pain subsided and her head cleared. On weak arms and legs, she crawled out and carefully stood up, shaking violently.

When she touched the painful area on the crown of her head, her fingers came away bloody. The sight of her own blood on her hands sent a surge of anger and adrenaline through her. She jogged down the trail after Sammy, but long before she returned to her car, he'd reached his old truck, turned around, and rumbled down the rough, winding road.

After pausing to wipe the blood from her head with some tissues from her glove box, Kara jammed her accelerator to the floor and began to pursue Sammy. He wasn't hard to follow, although he turned off the road they'd driven over coming up. His wide dust trail gave sufficient indication of his whereabouts. Once Kara had his truck within sight, she slowed down, content to simply follow him.

Picking up her cell phone, she called Sheriff Hanks, who sounded groggy. "I need some assistance," she told him. "I'm chasing Sammy Shirts right now, and I could use help stopping him."

The sheriff didn't ask why, but simply requested her location. Ten minutes later, just before reaching the highway and shortly after the sun had appeared on the eastern horizon, Sammy drove into a hastily constructed roadblock. Sheriff Hanks sauntered from behind his car as Sammy slid to a stop and pounded his steering wheel fiercely with both hands.

Kara pulled in behind his ancient truck and got out of her car, her hands cradling the money bag. "What's Sammy been up to?" the sheriff questioned good-naturedly as Kara joined him beside the pickup. Sammy reached through the open window, grabbed the outside handle, and opened the door. Apparently, the inside handle mechanism had fallen prey to years of abuse and neglect.

"He didn't want me to know what was in this," Kara answered, waving the large bank bag in front of her.

Sammy moaned. "That's mine. I earned it," he said, his eyes bloodshot.

The sheriff took the bag and opened it. He peeked inside before turning solemnly to Sammy. "This looks like a lot of money, Sammy. Where did you get it?"

Sammy clenched his teeth defiantly and barked, "I told you, it's mine."

Kara clarified, "He got it from Edgar Stevens's house a little after four this morning."

Sheriff Hanks handed her the bag and she peered in. The outside bill of a large stack had the portrait of Benjamin Franklin engraved on it—one hundred dollars. "We'll count them when we get back to the office. Sammy, I'm going to have to take you in for questioning."

At that moment the radio came to life, calling both the sheriff and his deputy. Kara hurried back to her car. "Chief Worthlin would like you or the sheriff to meet him at Edgar Stevens's house," the dispatcher told her.

"We're tied up at the moment," she responded. "Is it urgent?"

"Just a moment," the dispatcher said.

When she came back on the air, she declared, "It is. If at least one of you could wrap up what you're doing and come in, he'd appreciate it."

"You stay here with Sammy while a tow truck comes," the sheriff said after Kara explained the situation. "I've cuffed him and read him his rights. Take him to the office as soon as the tow truck arrives, and I'll meet you there later. I'll go see what the chief needs."

It was thirty minutes before a tow truck arrived at her location and twenty more before Kara finally pulled up outside the sheriff's office. Sammy had lapsed into a stubborn, unbroken silence from the time Sheriff Hanks left, and Kara had said very little to him. Now she commanded, "Get out of the car, Sammy. We're going to find out what gives with your sudden accumulation of wealth that you don't seem to want held in Edgar Stevens's bank."

Glaring at her malevolently, Sammy nevertheless did as he was told, and Kara followed him into the sheriff's office. The sheriff was there already, sitting behind his desk with his head in his hands. He raised his head as the two of them entered and said, "Sit down, Mr. Shirts. We have a few things to talk about—like why you're hiding large amounts of cash way up in the hills."

"It's none of your business," Sammy sneered.

Sheriff Hanks ignored him and turned to Kara. "It seems that Edgar Stevens is missing. His wife reported that he had visitors around four this morning. After they left, she went to sleep again. When she awoke just before daybreak, Edgar was not in bed, so she got up and went to the living room. She found blood on the carpet, and Edgar was gone."

Kara caught her breath as the sheriff turned back to Sammy, who had grown very pale and, if possible, even more withdrawn. "We know you were one of the visitors, Sammy, because Deputy Smith saw you go in the house and then come back out a few minutes later carrying this." He pointed to the bag full of money sitting on his desk.

Sammy finally broke his silence with a flood of words. "I didn't do nothing to Mr. Stevens, I swear, Sheriff. He gave me that money because I earned it, but when I left the house, he was fine. It was probably that other guy that—"

"What other guy?" Sheriff Hanks broke in.

"Treman, I think his name was. I wasn't never introduced proper-like. But I heard Mr. Stevens call him Treman—or Truman. I don't know if it was his first name or his last name. "But he was big and mean looking. It must have been him that hurt Mr. Stevens."

Kara and the sheriff exchanged glances. Then the sheriff said, "Tell me something, Sammy. What was it you did to earn all this money? I counted it while I waited for you to arrive. There is exactly ten thousand dollars in this bag."

As Kara stared in astonishment, the sheriff continued, "That's a lot of money, Sammy. You've never seen that much money at one time in your entire life, have you?"

Sammy shook his head.

"What did you do to earn it from Mr. Stevens?" the sheriff pressed.

Sammy remained silent but ground his teeth and stroked his whiskers nervously.

Kara broke the silence. "Sheriff, Sammy was followed from Edgar's house by someone besides me. I thought at first that it was Edgar, because it looked like a Cadillac. But I was wrong about that. The guy, whoever he was, saw me up near where Sammy tried to hide the money. He was a big man and ran a lot faster than Edgar would have been able to."

"Ken Treman," the sheriff said as he picked up the phone and punched in a series of numbers. While he waited for someone to answer at the other end, he declared, "You're lucky he didn't get to you before Deputy Smith did, Sammy. He's not known for his gentle ways." Then, looking at Kara, he asked, "I take it he saw you and left?"

"Yes, and he was in a hurry," she confirmed. "But I didn't get a good look at him, I'm afraid. I'd never be able to identify him."

Kara wouldn't have believed Sammy could go any whiter, but as they talked about Ken Treman, he did. In fact, his face looked as lifeless as wax. The sheriff spoke into the phone. "Chief? Vince here. You may be looking for a fellow by the name of Ken Treman. When you find Edgar—if you find him—he may very well be with this Mr. Treman from Salt Lake." The sheriff explained the situation further, then finally hung up the phone and turned to Sammy Shirts.

Thirty minutes later, Sammy Shirts finally agreed to level with the sheriff, or, Kara guessed, at least he pretended to level with him. After being advised of his rights, he made a serious confession.

CHAPTER 16

When Kara finally went home later that morning to get a little more sleep, she tried to call Jake, but the Linds' phone was busy. If Jake had a cell phone, Kara didn't know the number. She found herself missing him more than she would have expected, so she dialed the number repeatedly until she finally got through. Candi answered. "Hi, Kara," she said. "Have you been trying to call?"

"For about ten minutes."

"Sorry," Candi replied with a coolness to her voice. "Dad's been on the phone with Miss Taylor."

"Really?" Kara asked in surprise.

"He called her," Candi disclosed with obvious disgust.

"I see. Well, I guess that's his right. Is Jake there?"

"Yes. He's right here," she responded.

"Hi, Kara," Jake said. He sounded as tired as she was. "Have a long night?"

"Terribly long. What did Kyle talk to Mariah about, or can't you say?" she asked curiously.

"He just went outside, so I can't ask him right now, and probably shouldn't anyway. So I don't know what they talked about. Whatever it was, it worries me. Despite all the evidence against Mariah, Kyle still thinks there must be some explanation. By the way, you sound really tired, Kara. Are you okay?"

"Yes, I'm okay, but I am tired" Kara admitted. "But I wanted to talk to you before I caught a few hours' sleep. I've missed you."

"I've missed you, too," he replied sweetly. "I don't think I got much more sleep than you did."

Surprised, Kara asked, "Why not? What were you doing all night?"

"Tossing and turning in my bed. I was worrying about you, Kara."

"About me? You don't need to do that. I can take care of myself. I'm a big girl."

Jake chuckled, then became serious. "And a very attractive one, too—one that I like very much. That's why I worry."

Kara caught her breath and her spine tingled. Did he mean that? Did he really care about her?

"You still there, Kara?" Jake's voice was filled with mirth. "I didn't mean to startle you."

"I'm still here."

"So how was your night? You said you had to work."

"Long," she sighed. "Have you heard about Edgar Stevens?"

"No, did Sammy follow him somewhere again?"

"No, but I followed Sammy to Edgar's house. It seems that Edgar Stevens was being blackmailed by Sammy Shirts. Edgar paid him ten thousand dollars to buy his silence about something. After that, Sammy left. I followed him out of town, but so did a fellow we believe is Ken Treman, a guy from Salt Lake City who frequently seems to find himself on the wrong side of the law."

"What in the world would a loser like Sammy have on someone like Edgar?" Jake wondered.

"It has to do with Kyle," Kara revealed.

"Really? What?"

"This may surprise you, but Sammy said he knew that Edgar had kidnapped Cody, and that he—Sammy, I mean—needed money. Since Edgar had a lot, he thought it might be worth ten thousand to the banker to have Sammy keep his mouth shut."

"You're right. It does surprise me," Jake said. "Buster Ashton and—"

Kara interrupted. "I'm not so sure now, Jake. Sammy says he saw Edgar out and about late the night that Cody disappeared, and we all know that Edgar covets that farm more than seems reasonable. I know the ransom notes don't make sense unless he's just been trying to keep us off his track and interested in someone else—namely

Buster Ashton—while Kyle becomes so deranged with worry that the time gets away and the ranch just naturally reverts to the bank."

"And thus to Edgar Stevens," Jake finished fiercely.

"That's right, but Jake, there's something else."

"There is?"

"Yes. Edgar has disappeared. So has Ken Treman. We think they were working together somehow, but that things went sour between them early this morning. Anyway, Edgar is missing from his house, and there's blood in his living room."

There was silence on the line for a long moment. Finally, Jake remarked, "That's interesting. I wonder what's happened. And Kara, what happens to Cody if Stevens did kidnap him and now this Treman guy has done Stevens in? Oh, Kara, I don't know what Kyle will do when he hears this, but it really alarms me."

"Jake, please don't say anything to Kyle. The sheriff wants to tell him himself. He'll be out in a little while. And don't tell him I told you about it, either. I don't know that he wants me talking about it yet."

"Okay, Kara. I'm mum," Jake said. "You get some sleep. I'll see you in a few hours."

It was with conflicting emotions that Kara climbed into bed a few minutes later. On the one hand she felt elated, because Jake had declared that he liked her a great deal. But on the other hand, she also felt sick over the situation with Kyle Lind and his missing son. Jake was right—this might be the thing that pushed Kyle over the edge, even though it appeared that they'd finally found out the identity of the kidnapper. The worst thing was that they might have found out too late, since Edgar's disappearance could also spell death for Cody.

Kara was extremely angry with Sammy for not coming forward sooner. If he had, he probably could have saved both Cody and the ranch. If only he hadn't been so greedy! Kara had one fleeting but encouraging thought just before she fell into a worrisome sleep. What if Sammy Shirts had lied? What if Edgar Stevens had actually paid Sammy the ten thousand dollars to kidnap Cody Lind for him, to put pressure on Kyle while he went about the business of getting the ranch for himself?

* * *

It was a troubled Sheriff Hanks who turned his car off the highway onto Kyle Lind's lane. In some respects, everything seemed so clear now, like the water-protected boot print, and yet the case still seemed very muddy. Buster Ashton had been a person of interest until this latest episode with Sammy Shirts and Edgar Stevens. Now it appeared that Stevens, with the possible help of Shirts or Ken Treman, was the man he was after. And Stevens was gone! But still, the sheriff didn't want to rule out Buster Ashton as a player in what may have been a complicated crime.

The sheriff parked his car beside Jake's and climbed out. Seeing no one in the yard and corrals, he headed up the long walk to the house. The door opened before he reached the porch, and Candi came out to meet him.

"Good morning, Candi," the sheriff greeted with a tired smile.

"Good morning, Sheriff," she returned with a frown. "Jake says it might have been Edgar Stevens who kidnapped my brother. What are you going to do about it?"

The sheriff shook his head. "How did Jake know that?" he asked, but even before Candi spoke, he already knew.

"Kara Smith called," Candi responded.

"I see, and how is your dad taking the news?"

"He doesn't know yet. Jake said Kara told him that you wanted to tell Dad. He's not doing very good, Sheriff, and we're all really scared for him," Candi explained as she bit her trembling lower lip.

Sheriff Hanks put an arm around the girl's shoulders. "We're going to get things taken care of somehow, Candi. And your father will be all right. Maybe I should talk to Jake before I talk to your dad. Think that'd be okay?"

"Sure, but I'll have to wake him."

The sheriff looked at his watch. "Wake him? At this time of the morning?"

"I think he's in love," Candi crooned dramatically. "He couldn't sleep last night because he was worried about Kara—you know, with her out working all night and all. Until after he talked to her this morning and made sure she was okay, he says he didn't sleep a bit. He did the chores a little while ago and went back to bed."

"Don't disturb him," the sheriff stated as Candi swung open the front door. "Just let me talk to your dad."

"He's in the kitchen with Agnes. She's been great through all this," Candi revealed. "I don't know what we would ever have done without her and Jake."

The sheriff nodded. A moment later, he entered the kitchen and a worried Agnes rose from her place beside Kyle. Kyle didn't even look up until the sheriff spoke.

"Good morning, Kyle."

The rancher lifted his head and stared at the sheriff through unseeing eyes. He grunted and lowered his head again, as if the energy it took to hold it up was more than he could manage. Sheriff Hanks's eyes met those of the good lady who had made it her mission to care for Kyle's troubled family. Agnes shook her head sadly. "He's not too well this morning, Sheriff," she indicated quietly. "I hope you're not bringing him more bad news."

"I hope not either," the sheriff responded.

"What does that mean?" Agnes shot back, her kindly eyes narrowing suspiciously.

"Don't you know?"

"Know what?" the housekeeper asked.

"She doesn't," Candi replied from the position she now occupied beside her father, where she was kneading the muscles of his neck with her fingers.

"I see. Well, there have been some rather significant developments," the sheriff began. He sat at the table opposite the distraught rancher. "You might as well sit down too, Agnes. This might come as a bit of a shock to both of you."

"I got work to do," she interjected as she reached for the half-full plate in front of Kyle Lind.

"It can wait. You really do need to hear this. You're a part of this household, Agnes, and as concerned as anyone about what's going on."

"Maybe I should wake poor Jake," she suggested. "He'll want to hear whatever it is you have to say."

Before he could speak, Candi declared, "Kara Smith already told him. She called a little while ago."

Agnes nodded and took a seat next to Kyle. "Jake sure is smitten by that young woman. Not that I blame him. She's a right good catch for anyone. And for that matter, so is he. We're grateful to Jake for all he's doing to help out. He's more like a brother to Kyle than a nephew. I don't know what we'd ever do without him."

The sheriff made no response to her remark, instead addressing the matter pressing on his mind. "Kyle, look at me and listen to what I have to say. It's very important."

Kyle slowly lifted his head. His eyes still looked glazed, but when he finally spoke, he seemed more mentally stable than the sheriff had first supposed. "I'm mighty tired, Sheriff." He smiled weakly, then said to his daughter, "That feels better, Candi. Honey, why don't you sit down too."

"That's okay, Dad. I'd rather stand," she replied.

Kyle nodded and turned to Sheriff Hanks. "Anyway, Sheriff, I can't sleep, I can't eat, and I'm so worried about my boy that it's killing me. Please, tell me, what has happened now?" The despair in his voice was clear; it was as if the rancher had concluded that nothing but bad news could possibly enter his house.

"Well, Kyle, this is about Edgar Stevens."

"That devil!" Agnes erupted uncharacteristically.

"He is that," the sheriff affirmed.

"So what you have to say is about the ranch, not my son?" Kyle asked bitterly. "I don't care about the ranch. All I want is my son back."

"This may have something to do with both," the sheriff clarified. "Let me explain." For the next ten minutes, he told them about Ken Treman and Sammy Shirts, and he explained about Edgar Stevens's suspicious contacts with both of the men. As the story unfolded, Kyle's eyes lost their glaze and the sheriff thought he could see hope returning, until he mentioned the fact that Edgar had disappeared.

"Oh, no! Then how can he ever tell us where Cody is?" Kyle asked in dismay.

"We'll find him," a deep voice said from the doorway.

Sheriff Hanks glanced over, surprised to see Jake Garrett standing there. He was fully dressed, from his dark western-cut shirt to his shiny black boots. The sheriff's eyes lingered on the boots—that was the third pair he'd seen Jake wearing. He also had a pair of very expensive alligator-skin boots and some dusty riding boots, the ones he used for ranch work. The shirt he was wearing was new too, the sheriff noticed. He could see the creases from where the shirt had been folded in the store. Jake had money, but that was to be expected, since everyone said he was a very successful architect. The sheriff glanced back at Jake's face, thinking that the man must have enjoyed a good nap. Although his eyes betrayed his fatigue, he still looked energized and ready to go.

"Good morning, Jake," the sheriff said. "Won't you join us? I was just bringing the rest of the family up-to-date on what Kara filled you in on earlier."

Jake frowned. "I'm not sure what all this means . . . this talk about Edgar's disappearance. I suspect he has a lot of enemies in this town. Only one thing has been solved by his disappearance, and that one thing is that we can probably save Kyle's ranch now. I intend to personally speak with someone at the bank as soon as possible and get everything put on hold until Cody is safely returned. And I'll see about an additional loan to cover the ransom, if it's needed." He glanced at his uncle and added, "The ranch is safe now, Kyle. And you'll get Cody back. I'm sure of it."

The sheriff wished he were as sure. Even though it looked bad for Edgar Stevens, there was still the possibility that he could show up again and continue his campaign to confiscate the ranch. But Sheriff Hanks suspected that Jake was right about the ranch, so he voiced that opinion, adding, "I can put all my resources into finding your son now, Kyle. And believe me, I intend to do just that."

As the sheriff rose to his feet, his cell phone rang. He stretched a hand over the table to Kyle. "I'll be in touch," he said before answering his phone and stepping around the table.

"Sheriff, this is dispatch," the woman on the line said. "A young fellow called looking for you a few minutes ago. He says he's Cody Lind's best friend. I told him you were out there right now, at the Lind place, and that I would have you call him as soon as you were back in town. But he said he'd meet you there and hung up before I could say anything else."

"I see. I was just leaving here. Did he say what it was about?"

"Yes. He says he thinks he knows something about Cody. He was very excited. Wouldn't talk to anyone but you."

"What's his name?" the sheriff queried.

"Josh Schwarz."

"All right, thanks. I'll wait here for him," the sheriff responded and hung up the phone.

Sheriff Hanks knew Josh. He was a priest in his ward and a faithful young man who came from a strong home. "Candi, what can you tell me about Josh Schwarz?" he asked.

Her face lit up with just enough red in her cheeks to hint at more than a passing interest in the young man. "He's Cody's best friend," she replied.

Jake noted her blushing reaction, and he remarked with one of his handsome grins, "But you don't like him, do you?"

"Oh, Jake," she retorted, punching her cousin lightly on the shoulder as she turned an even deeper shade of red.

"He's on his way here to see me. I'll wait for him outside," the sheriff announced.

"And I'll head for town. I want to see if I can track down the vice president at the bank, even if it is Sunday," Jake explained.

"It's time your little sisters were up. They can't sleep 'til noon, Candi," Agnes declared. "You go wake them up while your father and I fix some breakfast for them."

Reluctantly, Candi did as she was told. Kyle Lind, however, arose and said to Sheriff Hanks, "Mind if I come with you to talk with Josh? Agnes doesn't need my help, and I suspect he wants to talk about Cody."

"Of course, Kyle," the sheriff said, pleased to see the rancher acting more alert. Even though the developments in the case were not conclusive, the fact that something was happening was apparently good for Kyle. Either that or the possible salvation of his ranch and home was far more important to him than he'd been letting on. At any rate, he seemed better, and the sheriff was glad for that.

When Josh Schwarz arrived, he leaped from his rusty Ford Ranger with the boundless energy of a teenager. Although he was quite short, Josh made up for his lack of height in muscle, energy, and sheer exuberance. He was also a good-looking young man, Vince realized as he recalled Candi's reaction.

"Good morning, Sheriff," Josh began with a serious face. "You too, Mr. Lind." He offered his hand to both men. Then he said,

"Sheriff, my dad told me to stay out of this and not to pester you unless I had something to say that was worth your time. That's why I haven't bothered you until now."

"I take it you know something, Josh," the sheriff stated, trying to match the young fellow's seriousness.

"I sure do! I've been pretty sure all along," Josh replied with a clenched fist. "Now I'm positive."

"About what?" Sheriff Hanks pressed hopefully. He didn't care where his leads came from, as long as they led to the recovery of Cody Lind.

"About Gil Enders," Josh responded ominously.

The sheriff's hopes sank. At this point, his interest in Gil was minimal. "What about Gil?" he asked, trying to act more interested than he was.

"I probably shouldn't have done this," Josh admitted sheepishly, "but after all, Cody is my best friend, Sheriff. Isn't he, Mr. Lind?"

Kyle mumbled his assent, and the sheriff questioned, "What shouldn't you have done, Josh?"

"I shouldn't have followed Gil last night," he admitted.

The sheriff's interest picked up. "What time of night?"

"Well, actually, early this morning. He's been going somewhere almost every night, and me and some of the other guys have been wondering why. So we decided to find out."

The sheriff moaned to himself. First the girls—Candi and Bridget—and now the boys. Couldn't anyone just let him do his job? "And what did you learn?"

"Where Gil's been going."

"And where is that, Josh?"

"Well, actually, Sheriff, he went several places. He walked, you know."

The sheriff hadn't known. "Where did he walk to?" he pressed impatiently.

"First, he went to Harry's Hardware. He has a key, you know."

I'm learning all sorts of valuable things, Sheriff Hanks thought wryly. "Did he go into the store?" Prying information from Josh was becoming as difficult as appeasing Roscoe Norman.

"Yes."

"How long was he in there?"

"Not long. When he came out, he headed straight for Mariah Taylor's house."

The sheriff groaned, and Kyle Lind perked up. "Why would he go to her place?" the rancher queried suspiciously.

"I don't know," Josh admitted. "But he didn't go in or anything like that. He just stood and watched the house for a while, you know, like that one city cop was doing. Maybe that's why he didn't go in, because he saw that cop."

It wasn't a secret, the sheriff supposed, that he had Mariah under surveillance, although it did appear that Gil might not have known. "Did the officer see him?"

"I don't think so," Josh answered. "And I'm sure neither of them saw me."

The sheriff asked Josh what occurred next.

"Gil walked to Sammy Shirts's dump—I mean, his place."

Does Gil Enders think he's a cop too? The sheriff wondered. This was more than coincidence. "What time was that?" he questioned.

"About four or so in the morning."

Sheriff Hanks already knew that Sammy had left, with Kara on his trail, a little before that. "Did Gil watch Sammy's place, too?" he asked.

"No, he went in."

"He went in?" the sheriff wondered in amazement.

"Yup. He had a key, I guess."

"To Sammy's place?"

"Yup. It took him a minute, like maybe the key didn't fit right or something, but he finally unlocked the door and went in. Course, Sammy wasn't home."

"How do you know that? You didn't ask Gil, did you?"

"Oh, no. I didn't dare let him know I was following him. Sammy's truck wasn't there—you know, that old beater he drives. Sammy never walks anywhere. He was probably out stealing gas or something," Josh guessed.

Not true this morning, but likely true on many previous occasions, the sheriff thought. "Did you actually see the key he used?"

"No, but he must have had one."

"I see, and what did he do in Sammy's place?"

"I don't know. Like before, I couldn't follow him in. And Gil never did turn on any lights. He had a flashlight, you know. Of course, I still couldn't see anything, even though I tried, because all the windows had blinds pulled down over them."

"What kind of flashlight did Gil have?" Sheriff Hanks queried.

"I didn't see it close up, but it looked just like mine. Here, I'll show you." Josh stepped back to his truck, opened the door, and took a flashlight from the jockey box. "Like this, I think. I bought mine at Harry's Hardware."

The sheriff was not surprised to see that the flashlight Josh handed him was identical to the one Kara had found in the old outhouse at Roscoe Norman's abandoned homestead. He studied it for a moment and then returned it to Josh. "What happened next, Josh?" the sheriff asked.

"Gil went home, got in his car, and drove out to Edgar Stevens's house on the other side of town. That was too far for him to walk before it got light, I guess."

If Josh had only a portion of the sheriff's attention before, he certainly had all of it now. "What time did he get there?" he questioned eagerly.

"I don't know, because I had to go home and get my pickup. I ran as fast as I could, but it still took me ten minutes or so. Anyway, Gil's car was just pulling out of the alley behind Mr. Stevens's house when I got there."

"Wait a minute, Josh. You mean you didn't actually see him go to Edgar's, but you saw him leave there?"

"That's right."

"How did you know that you would find him there?" the sheriff asked, puzzled.

"Where else would he go? Candi told me what Mr. Stevens was doing to her dad. So I figured that since he'd already been to Miss Taylor's house and to Sammy Shirts's, he would probably go to Mr. Stevens's. And I was right," Josh declared proudly.

"You were, at that," Sheriff Hanks agreed, wondering if the entire county knew who his suspects were, or just those people who were close to the family.

"Sheriff," Kyle Lind started.

He had almost forgotten the rancher was standing there with them—he'd been so quiet. "Yes, Kyle?" the sheriff asked.

"There is some kind of conspiracy," the rancher said bitterly. "They're all in it together, even Mariah."

The sheriff had to admit that he was shaken by Josh's story. While the idea of a conspiracy seemed ridiculous, how could he not consider it? "Maybe so," he agreed reluctantly after a long hesitation.

"It's got to be, Sheriff," Kyle insisted.

"That's what I think!" Josh exclaimed. "One thing's for sure—Gil Enders is in it up to his stinkin' eyeballs!"

"Josh, where did Gil go after he left the alley behind Mr. Stevens's house?"

"I don't know. He drove really fast and I lost him."

"Where was he headed before you lost him?"

"West through town. I checked his house after he got away from me, but he hadn't gone back there. Not until later, anyway. When I drove by his house a little while ago, his car was there. I went to the store, and he was working. So that's when I called the dispatcher."

"Josh, think very carefully. Did you see any other cars around Mr. Stevens's house when you were there?" the sheriff asked, thinking of Ken Treman.

Josh wrinkled his face thoughtfully. Finally, he said, "There was the one that passed me going the other way a couple of blocks before I got there."

"What did it look like?" the sheriff asked.

A sheepish look came over Josh's face as he looked up at the sheriff. "Gee, I don't know. I was so busy thinking about whether I'd find Gil at Mr. Stevens's that I didn't pay much attention. It seems like it was quite big, but that's all I noticed."

"Do you remember anything else you think I should know, Josh? Anything at all?"

"I don't think so," Josh replied, "but if I think of something, should I call you?"

"By all means, Josh. I appreciate what you've done, but a word of caution now. Leave the rest of this up to me and Chief Worthlin and our officers. It could get very dangerous. Please, don't follow anyone again," the sheriff stressed.

"Okay," Josh answered soberly. Then, turning to Kyle, he asked, "Is Candi in the house?"

"She is. Run on in. She'll be glad to see you," he said kindly.

After the boy had jogged up the walk, Kyle Lind turned to the sheriff and queried, "What are you going to do now?"

"Talk to Gil Enders. He's got a lot of explaining to do. Maybe he's just interested in the same people I've been interested in. But again, he may have his own agenda, and like you said, there could conceivably be several of them working together."

CHAPTER 17

When Sheriff Hanks entered Harry's Hardware late that morning, Gil Enders scowled at him with obvious dislike. Ignoring his stare, the sheriff asked, "Is Harry in?" He had just decided to talk to Gil's boss first.

"He's in the back," Gil said, turning away sullenly.

"Thanks," the sheriff said and went in search of the store owner.

When the sheriff found him in the office hunched over a computer terminal, Harry looked up, saved what he was working on, and stood. "What can I do for you today, Sheriff?" he asked pleasantly.

Sheriff Hanks closed the door and turned to Harry, who waved him to a chair. "I hear Edgar Stevens is missing," Harry declared.

"I suppose that's all over town by now." The sheriff sighed as he sat down.

"Mrs. Thompson just told me. Her daughter works at the bank, you know. Stevens didn't come in at all today. I guess he had an important meeting with some folks from out of town, but he didn't show up for it, so they called his house, and Chief Worthlin answered the phone!" Harry sat down across from the sheriff.

"That's right, Harry. And one of the last persons seen there early this morning was none other than your employee."

"Gil?"

"That's right. What would he have been doing there?" the sheriff questioned.

"I have no idea!" Harry replied, obviously perplexed.

"Harry, what would Gil have been doing here in the store around three or three thirty this morning?" the sheriff asked.

Harry's mouth dropped open. "Nothing that I asked him to do," he said emphatically. "If he was here at that time of night, it was on his own. What makes you think he was?"

"He was seen here. He does have a key, doesn't he?"

"Yes, but I can't imagine why he would be here at that time of night. Why, he'd have to disarm the alarm and everything."

"Can he do that?"

"Oh, yes. He helped install it," Harry reported. "But he has no business in here at that time of night, and he knows it. I'm going to have to have a talk—"

"Not yet, Harry. I need to speak with him first. And I'll need to take him down to my office to do so. One more thing, Harry. Would he have access to keys that could be used to open doors in town? You know, some sort of master key or something?"

"No. We don't . . ." Harry stopped short. "Why do you ask that?"

"Because he was seen entering a locked house last night after he left here," Sheriff Hanks explained.

"Let me see," Harry sighed, rising to his feet and hurrying to a file cabinet across the room. When he opened the top drawer and looked in, his face grew red. He shut the drawer and turned to face the sheriff, who had followed him across the room, then declared, "Vince, I keep a lock-picking set in there. People often lock themselves out and call on us to help them."

"Is it there?" The sheriff questioned.

"No, it isn't, but it should be," Harry stated despairingly. He explained that Gil was familiar with the lock-picks and used them all the time. The sheriff and Harry then went in search of Gil so the sheriff could take him in for questioning.

But Gil was gone—he'd left the store, apparently in a frenzy. The boxes he'd been neatly stacking on shelves lay scattered on the floor, almost as if someone had run through the aisle and kicked them. The sheriff drove to Gil's home, but he didn't answer the door and his car was gone. Gil Enders was looking very guilty in the eyes of Sheriff Hanks—and the sheriff was looking very foolish in his own eyes. He couldn't believe he'd let Gil slip right through his fingers. If he thought he'd been troubled earlier in the day, it was nothing compared to now. And the muddiness of the case was looking more like tar. How would they ever find Cody Lind now?

The sheriff returned to his office and, between fielding phone calls, he reviewed all his notes on the Cody Lind case. Most of the calls were inconsequential, but when his secretary told him that Mariah Taylor was on the line, he had a feeling it would be important.

"Ring her through," the sheriff instructed his secretary. A moment later he began, "Hello, Mariah. How are you this afternoon?"

"I'm fine, under the circumstances." She sounded cold and bitter. "Buster called."

Immediately alert, the sheriff asked, "Where did he call from?"

"He wouldn't say."

"What did he want?" The sheriff poised a pen over paper and prepared to write.

"Money. Same as before. Except now he says he needs a thousand dollars instead of five hundred."

"Is that all he talked about?" the sheriff questioned.

"No, we talked about other things," Mariah answered. Sheriff Hanks sensed that she was being cautious about what she said, and he noted that in his notebook as she went on. "He wondered if I had turned him in for kidnapping me. That was after he'd berated me for taking his car and leaving him stranded."

Mariah went on to explain that she told Buster she was frightened, uncertain as to what she should do, and that she wondered where he'd been since she left him stranded. She also explained to the sheriff how Buster had flatly refused to tell her where he'd been. However, she said, Buster did admit that he had been staying out of sight, even though he knew nothing about the kidnapping she'd accused him of. Finally, Mariah stated, "He asked me what exactly was going on."

"Did you tell him?"

"Of course not." Mariah sounded offended. "I promised to help you catch him, didn't I?"

"You did," Vince affirmed. "So what did you say to him? Did you try to get him to come see you?"

"After he told me that all he needed was some money, and insisted that I was in a position to help him out, I told him to come and I'd see what I could do for him. He said that as family, giving him a little money was the least I could do. I almost lost it with him then," Mariah confessed. "He is *not* family!"

The sheriff said nothing. He listened as Mariah breathed sharply, apparently trying to control her emotions. *Is this for real, or is she putting on an act?* he wondered.

"I controlled my temper," she explained after several seconds. "I said nothing more about the kidnapping, and he didn't mention it again either. All I said was, 'Buster, if you'll promise to leave me alone from now on, I'll give you the money.'"

"What arrangements did you make?" the sheriff asked quickly. The sooner he could take Buster into custody, the quicker he could begin to put together the fragmented pieces of this most unusual puzzle.

If Buster wasn't Cody's kidnapper, there was certainly plenty to hold him in jail on, including grand theft auto, felony kidnapping of Mariah, and breaking and entering. Buster had also held Candi Lind and Bridget Harrison against their will.

"I told him to come tonight and I'd have the money. He said he wasn't setting foot in Harrisville again. He said it wasn't safe for him. Sheriff, I'm sure he has Cody."

The sheriff remained silent again. Everyone else seemed to be certain about something, but he wasn't sure of anything. When Mariah spoke again, her voice was filled with doubt. "Actually, Sheriff, I'm not so sure, really. I know this sounds crazy, but if Buster was about to get a half million from K-Kyle . . ." She stopped short. Sheriff Hanks heard the quavering in her voice and her sniffling as she tried to cover her sobs, and he waited patiently. "I'm sorry," she finally continued. "If he was about to get a large ransom, why would he worry about a measly thousand dollars?"

The sheriff's eyes fell to the sheet of paper where he had just penned that same question. If Miss Taylor was telling the truth, Buster's demands made no sense. If, however, she was lying, they made perfect sense. This could be her way of putting blame for the kidnapping on Buster while shifting the focus from herself. Or it could be Buster and Mariah's way of shifting blame to anybody but themselves. Mariah went on. "Maybe he's not the one after all." Suddenly, the sheriff was concerned. He certainly had enough to hold Buster on, but he feared that Mariah might be backing down. If so, he would need to bring her in to the office right away.

As if Mariah were reading his mind, she said, "I know this probably sounds to you like I'm getting cold feet about helping. I'm not. Buster frightens me, I'll admit that, and I want him arrested, even if you have to arrest him for kidnapping me. Can you do that?"

The sheriff reassured her that he could, then directed her back to the main point at hand. "Mariah, if he's afraid to come to your house, what arrangements did you make?"

"I told him I'd get the money and meet him somewhere tonight. Sheriff, you will protect me, won't you?" she asked, sounding genuinely afraid.

He shook his head in frustration as he replied, "Absolutely. So where will you be meeting him and what time?"

"I don't know yet. He told me to call him from a pay phone at two o'clock in the morning, and then he would give me instructions. I'm to have the money, he said, and I'm not to be followed by anyone. He said I'd regret it if I involve the police. That's why I'm so frightened, Sheriff," she confessed sincerely. If she was not telling him the truth, she was one top-notch actress.

Sheriff Hanks then instructed Mariah to do as Buster had requested, except for one thing. She was to take no money, just an empty envelope. She wouldn't need the money because there would be a police officer, armed and with a warrant, hiding in her car when she met up with Buster. The sheriff assured her that the arrest would occur quickly so that she would not be forced to take any unnecessary risks.

"It sounds like I'll be safe enough," she said, still sounding a little skeptical.

"As safe as I can make you," the sheriff stated as an uncomfortable doubt reminded him that there was always the chance that something could go wrong. There were too many variables that could never be completely controlled.

* * *

Kara awoke to the annoying ringing of her telephone. "Are you up and ready for another assignment?" the sheriff queried when she finally answered it.

"No, and no," she responded. "I was sound asleep, and your assignments make me nervous." She chuckled to let him know she wasn't serious and then asked, "What am I doing tonight?"

"Going for a ride with Mariah Taylor. I was going to send Shawn, but he's suddenly really sick. His wife said he's so ill he can hardly get out of bed. I'm afraid it's going to have to be you. I would go myself, but with all the other things happening in this case, I think I'd better stick close to home," he explained. "I just don't dare get far away."

"Where are Mariah and I going?" she asked.

"I wish I knew," he said. Then he quickly filled her in on the details he did have. "You will, of course, take your cell phone so you can keep me posted. And we'll have another officer nearby, out of sight but close in case you need help. That will be Phil."

"I can handle Buster Ashton," Kara answered confidently. "When and where do I meet Mariah?"

"At one thirty tonight. Be on foot at the corner of Elm and Third Street. She'll pick you up there. And Kara, I want you to be rested, so get some more sleep. I'll be doing the same. It could turn into a long night," the sheriff stressed.

"Okay," she agreed, even as she planned a romantic evening with Jake Garrett. Thinking back on the events of the morning, she asked if Edgar Stevens had turned up yet.

When the sheriff explained that Edgar was still missing, Kara asked about Ken Treman, and the sheriff told her that Ken had not been seen or heard from, even though his home and bar were under surveillance. Then she asked if anything else had happened that day.

The sheriff sighed before saying, "Yes, as a matter of fact, it has. Kara, did you notice anyone out roaming around early this morning when you were watching Sammy?"

"No. Was there someone?"

"Two someones," he answered.

"Who? And what were they up to?"

"Josh Schwarz, for one. He is, he claims, Cody's best friend. He was playing cop and following Gil Enders."

"Gil Enders? What was Gil doing?" Kara asked with great interest.

"Gil apparently checked up on Mariah for a few minutes. At least, he stood outside her house and watched it. Then he visited Sammy's house and—"

"Sammy's? What time?" Kara broke in. "I was there. I should have seen him. Or else Shawn would have if it was earlier."

"Gil went around four. You must have already been gone. He went inside Sammy's house and had a look around."

"How did he get in?" she questioned, shaking her head in amazement at what the sheriff was telling her.

"I have reason to believe he used a lock-picking set of Harry's. After that, Gil followed your lead and went to Edgar Stevens's home," Sheriff Hanks revealed.

"You've got to be kidding!" Kara exclaimed, reeling.

"I'm afraid not. What he did there, no one knows, because Josh got there himself only as Gil was leaving. I'll fill you in more later."

"I assume you've talked to Gil. He must have some kind of explanation."

"I planned to, but he hightailed it to parts unknown," the sheriff sighed.

Kara was speechless.

"Now you can see why I have to stick around, Kara. The chief of police will be out tonight with at least one of his officers. Anything could happen. You be careful, and let me know as soon as you leave. Keep an eye on Mariah. I think she's on our side, but we can't be sure, so don't take any chances. I'll drop off a warrant for Buster's arrest before you go. If you're asleep, I'll lock it in your patrol car."

"What's the warrant for? Kidnapping Cody?"

"No, we don't have nearly enough for that. There are still too many other suspects, and we have no evidence against him. It's for kidnapping Mariah Taylor and for breaking into her house. The chief is getting it right now. You get some sleep, Deputy," he ordered, effectively cutting off the conversation.

As soon as they hung up, Kara dialed the Lind residence. Candi answered. "Have you heard all that's going on?" she said breathlessly.

"I just talked to the sheriff," Kara responded. "I guess he told me most of it."

"Well, Jake just got back. He's been with the bank officer for hours. He says our place is safe. The guy just under Mr. Stevens, whoever that is, signed a paper giving Dad another two months on his note. Now if we can just find Cody," the girl said in more subdued tones.

"We?" Kara interjected.

"Well, you know, you guys. I'll stay out of it. So will Josh and Bridget. The sheriff made us promise. So did Dad and Jake."

"Good," Kara replied firmly. "And we, the real cops—the trained officers—are doing our best, Candi, believe me. May I speak with Jake?"

When Jake came on the line, he was chuckling. "Hi, Kara. Have a good nap?" he asked.

"I guess, but I'm still tired. What are you so happy about?"

"The small part of the battle's won," he stated. "The ranch is safe—for at least two more months, anyway. Now, if we can just find Cody. I sure hope he's okay."

"So do I," Kara agreed. "It's been way too long since he disappeared."

"It really has," Jake affirmed with a note of sadness in his voice. "Are you busy?"

"Just lonesome," she replied wistfully.

"I'm on my way," he said. "Don't move till I get there."

"I'll be waiting," she replied and softly replaced the receiver.

When Jake arrived at Kara's house a few minutes later, he looked more handsome than ever, wearing a black western shirt, black bootcut pants, and his alligator-skin cowboy boots. He took Kara in his arms and held her tightly for a moment. She shut her eyes in anticipation, and when his lips met hers, it was like nothing she had ever experienced. She kissed him back, and several minutes passed before either of them spoke.

"Oh, Jake," was all Kara could say when she finally found her voice.

"Kara, I've missed you terribly."

"It hasn't been that long," she teased.

"It's been too long," he countered as his dark eyes drilled into her face with such intensity that she actually felt weak.

"Yes it has," she murmured. "Can I get you a Sprite or something?"

"Sure," Jake replied easily as he moved back, his eyes still taking in every inch of her. "Why didn't I find you years ago?"

"I guess you didn't look in the right place," she laughed, and he laughed with her.

The next few hours flew by as they talked and prepared dinner together. Neither of them broached the tragic subject of Cody Lind.

But the time passed too quickly, and at length, after they had eaten dinner, the doorbell rang. Kara opened the door to see Sheriff Hanks standing there. "I thought you were getting some rest," he said gruffly, glancing at Jake and nodding his head in greeting.

"I will, in a little bit."

"How are you this evening, Jake?" the sheriff asked.

"I'm doing okay, Sheriff," he answered in a friendly voice.

The sheriff held a large white envelope in his hand, which he offered to Kara. "Here's the warrant. Be careful, and get yourself some rest. That's an order. I'll be leaving now. I'm going to run home and try to catch two or three hours of sleep myself."

"I'll keep in touch tonight, Sheriff," Kara called awkwardly as the sheriff turned and started toward his car. She knew Sheriff Hanks was not happy that she wasn't resting as he'd requested earlier, and her reason for not resting suddenly seemed questionable.

"So what's the sheriff got you doing tonight, Kara?" Jake asked as soon as the sheriff was out of earshot.

"I have to meet Mariah Taylor at one thirty. We're going to meet Buster Ashton."

Jake's face darkened and his easy smile hardened into a scowl, the muscles of his jaw firm. "Kara, he's dangerous. They both might be. I don't think you should go."

"Jake," she said, slightly annoyed. "Of course I should go. It's my job. I can handle myself. I'm trained and experienced." Suddenly she felt defensive, and she waved the envelope in her hand. "And I will have this warrant for his arrest in my purse. I'll be bringing him in, Jake."

"Really?" The set of his jaw slackened a little. "That's good news," he said, but he didn't sound very enthusiastic. Then he added, "I want you to get out of police work, Kara."

Kara stepped back and dropped the envelope on an end table, surprised at how strongly she resented Jake giving her orders. "Why should I do that? It just happens that I really enjoy my job," she said icily.

His face continued to soften. "Hey, don't get mad, Kara. I'm not saying you have to quit it right now, but I was hoping that later, when . . ." His voice trailed off, and his eyes looked deep into hers.

"Wh-when what?" she stammered.

"Oh, you know. Someday," he said softly as he leaned toward her.

Kara's lips trembled as Jake covered them with his own, and she was carried away in her imagination, dreaming of a wonderful future with Jake Garrett. Of course, she still needed to get to know him better, and she was anxious to do so. But so far, they seemed to be well suited for each other.

Another hour passed as the two of them simply sat and talked. In Jake's charming presence, Kara easily forgot her earlier dismay at his attempt to control her life. When she finally remembered her one-thirty appointment with Mariah Taylor, it was already late.

"Jake, I'm sorry, but I have to get some rest before I go to work. I'll call you when I get back."

"Oh, please, Kara. I'm afraid for you," he protested. "Call the sheriff. He can send someone else to arrest Buster."

"No, Jake. It's my duty, but I'll be careful," she reassured him as she jumped up from the sofa. She grasped Jake's hand and pulled gently.

"Okay, I'll go now, but you be really, really careful," he stressed.

He kissed her again at the door. "This business with Cody will soon be over," he declared with confidence. "Then you and I can get to know each other better. I'll be waiting anxiously for your call." With that he turned and walked to his green Mustang.

Kara stretched out on her bed under a down quilt and closed her eyes. She had only two hours before she had to meet Mariah and be ready for what could be a very difficult and dangerous encounter with Buster Ashton. But sleep would not come, as pictures of Jake Garrett flashed through her mind like a slide show. She wondered if he could be the one—the man she'd been waiting to meet, the man of her dreams.

Later, when Kara climbed into Mariah Taylor's car a couple of blocks from her apartment, she was still thinking about Jake. As they pulled away from the curb, she experienced an uncomfortable tightness in her stomach. *Something feels wrong,* she thought. Was Jake right? Was she walking into a situation tonight that she couldn't handle? Maybe she should have asked the sheriff to send someone else. But it was too late now.

CHAPTER 18

Sheriff Vince Hanks, after a few hours of sleep, entered his office shortly after midnight. Immediately, he called Phil Simmons, the deputy whose assignment it was to keep within a reasonable distance of Kara in case she called for help. Phil's voice was slightly broken, an effect of the imperfect transmission from the deputy's antiquated cell phone, but he sounded calm. He assured the sheriff that all was well—that he shouldn't worry—and gave him their location and the direction in which they were traveling.

Phil was a good man, the sheriff thought. A little slow at resolving some of their more complex cases, but experienced and dependable nonetheless. The sheriff had considered having Phil ride in the car with Mariah when he'd learned that Shawn was ill. But then he remembered Phil's propensity for car sickness, and he knew the idea would never work. Still, he felt that Phil was the right man to be Kara's backup. Even with his confidence in Phil, however, the sheriff had a nagging worry that ate at him until he thought he'd be sick to his stomach. As important as he felt it was to remain close to town in case anything broke on the case, he now wished that he would have gone with Mariah himself. If Buster Ashton really was the kidnapper, he could prove to be one dangerous individual. Even if he wasn't the kidnapper, Kara could still be in a perilous situation, and so could Mariah.

As a diversion, Sheriff Hanks picked up his notes and, as the clock ticked off the minutes, immersed himself in another review of everything he'd jotted down about the Cody Lind case. Logic told him that either Buster Ashton or Edgar Stevens was behind the whole monstrous affair. They both had motive and the propensity for doing whatever it took to get ahead financially. If it was Edgar, he had probably enlisted help from Sammy Shirts, Gil Enders, or Ken Treman, or perhaps all three. Buster, as much as the sheriff didn't like the thought, might have been assisted by Mariah Taylor.

As the sheriff weighed the pros and cons of each suspect, something nagged at him. He was missing something, and though the thought would not go away, he could not put a finger on what he was overlooking.

Over and over, he reviewed the mystery of the lights at old Roscoe Norman's place and the boot print in his ditch. As he thought about that boot print—one matched perfectly by another found behind Mrs. Barclay's house, where the typewriter used to write the ransom notes had been stolen—his worry increased. That boot print had tied Roscoe's farm to the disappearance of Cody Lind. *What is it about that print that I can't quite figure out?* he wondered. All of his suspects wore boots—he already knew that. So it was something else. But what that something was he just couldn't quite figure out.

The phone rang, and the sheriff grabbed it with a start. The line was full of static, but he was able to hear his young deputy. "Sheriff? Kara. We're about to meet Buster. We are just beyond—" Her voice faded as the static became more persistent, filling his ears with meaningless noise. Then the phone went dead. He closed it and wished he had better communications with Kara. Cell phones could be so unreliable, despite the cell phone companies' claims to the contrary on TV commercials. A clap of thunder shook his office. He didn't remember a storm brewing as he'd entered the building an hour—he looked at his watch—two hours ago. Frantically, he dialed the number of the phone Kara carried. Nothing. Where was she?

He tried the number of Phil's phone, but that call would not go through either. Wherever they were, it appeared that there was no cell phone service. Phil did have a two-way radio, so the sheriff walked up front and tried him on that, but again, he couldn't make a connection. *He must be out of range,* the sheriff concluded as he returned to his office where he began to pace, almost overcome with anxiety. *Kara might be on her own too. And what if Mariah is actually in league with Buster? Could I have sent Kara directly into harm's way?* Suddenly, the sheriff was terrified for Kara. She was bright and capable, but lately she was also very distracted by Kyle Lind's nephew. Not that the sheriff resented Kara's friendship with Jake, but the timing was certainly unfortunate. Tonight she might well need every bit of her law enforcement training and every trace of her five senses, as well as common sense, if things went awry with Buster Ashton and Mariah Taylor. Especially if she was alone against the two of them!

* * *

Lightning danced about the remote canyons and tree-lined ridges where Buster Ashton had directed Mariah Taylor. Thunder crashed so loudly that it shook Mariah's old Pontiac Tempest, and the rain, when it finally came, could have floated a small ark. It seemed to fall by the barrelful across the windshield.

Kara, hidden on the backseat, dialed her cell phone frantically, but she was unable to get service. "I see the old cabin Buster said to watch for," Mariah announced. Her voice sounded full of panic, equal, Kara thought, to what she herself felt. What was it about a storm in the dark of night that drove fear into even the bravest hearts?

"The car doesn't want to stop, and I can hardly steer it. This mud is straight clay!" Mariah complained a moment later. The car slid, bumped, slid some more, then abruptly stopped, throwing Kara from her prone position on the backseat.

Shoving the useless phone into her pocket, she pulled out her pistol. Mariah's car shuddered and settled dangerously to the driver's side. "I think I hit a tree. I must have run off the road," Mariah said as the rain pounded mercilessly on the car.

"See anything of Buster?" Kara asked as she pulled herself awkwardly back onto the seat with her gun in one hand. She was shaking, and she scolded herself silently. *I've got to stay in control.*

"No, I don't see him . . . yes!" Mariah whispered frantically.

At that instant, the dome light came on as the passenger door was jerked open, and Buster Ashton shouted, "Get out, you fool! You're about to drop into a canyon. Can't you even stay on the road?" The car teetered precariously as Mariah struggled to climb across the seat.

Kara fought off the panic that threatened to overcome her. She knew she had to get out of the vehicle, but it was a two-door car and the driver's side door was obviously not a safe exit. That meant she couldn't get out until Mariah did. Anyway, she had to take Buster by surprise, and that wasn't possible at the moment. She caught a glimpse of Buster Ashton's head, dripping with rain, as he leaned into the car. "Grab my hand," he shouted to Mariah.

A moment later, the car slid again. Kara caught a glimpse of Mariah's blonde hair as she left the car, half dragged by Buster. Kara twisted, reaching for the seat in front of her to push it forward so she could reach the door, still holding her pistol in one hand.

The car slipped again . . . and kept sliding, tipping farther and farther. "Kara!" she heard Mariah scream.

"You witch!" Buster cursed. "You brought a cop, didn't you? I said no cops! I'll shove your car down the mountain, and that will be the end of your cop friend."

"Don't, Buster! You lunatic! Are you insane?" Mariah cried. "Let me help her. She could be killed." But Buster was already pushing against the precariously balanced car.

The Tempest slid until it stood almost on its side, leaving Kara helpless, trapped, terrified. Her gun slipped from her hand. For the briefest moment she remembered Jake's concern and how cocky she had been about her ability to handle the situation. Then slowly, the Tempest went over, crashing onto its top and picking up speed as it first slid and then began to roll, accelerating down the muddy mountainside.

Kara screamed. Her head struck something hard, and blackness wiped out the terrifying sounds of rending steel, shattering glass, and her own panic-stricken shrieks.

* * *

"You murderer!" Mariah screamed as the sound of her rolling Pontiac was smothered by the ferocity of the storm. Slowly, she crumpled to the muddy ground on the mountain road, silently pleading with God for the life of Deputy Smith.

"The money, Mariah. Hand me the money!" Buster shouted.

She shook her head in despair. What little doubt she'd had about Buster's involvement in the Cody Lind affair had now vanished. Buster was an evil man—a kidnapper, and now a killer. Mariah doubted that Cody was even alive. More than anything, she wished she'd been in the car with Kara, because she didn't want to live and have to face Kyle Lind and his family again. She'd come to care a great deal for him in the short time they'd known each other, and she would never intentionally do anything to hurt him. But Kyle would never believe that she'd had nothing to do with Cody's kidnapping. Not after this. And she couldn't blame him.

"Give me the money, you stupid woman!" Buster shouted again.

He doesn't need the money, Mariah thought, figuring he'd soon have every penny Kyle could scrape up. And when they found the deputy in that canyon below, the police would come looking for her. No one would ever believe she was not as guilty as Buster in the terrible thing he had just done. She'd tried to stop him, but he'd pushed the car until it began to slide down the mountainside. Hopelessly, she sank farther, sitting finally in the cold mud, her head bowed in despair.

Buster grabbed her by the hair. "Stand up, woman!" he ordered. "Give me the money, and then you can sit in the mud all you like." He jerked his hand, and she thought her hair would tear from her scalp. Yelping in pain, she struggled to her feet.

"I'll only ask one more time," Buster said fiercely, letting go of her hair only to grab her arm. She could see his face faintly, and she quickly glanced around, wondering where the light was coming from. A light glowed dimly in the little cabin on the upper side of the road, and she realized that was where he'd waited for her.

"Now!" he demanded.

Mariah turned to face him, shaking her arm loose from his painful grip. "I don't have it," she announced with a small smirk of satisfaction. "It was in the car."

His face, now only inches from hers, filled with rage, and he doubled his fists. For a moment she thought he would strike her. But as reason overcame rage, he finally said, "Then we will just have to go down and get it out of the car. You go first."

Mariah had ignored the sheriff's instructions to bring no money. Instead, she had brought one thousand dollars. The money was in an envelope in her purse, which had been on the seat of the car but could be anywhere on that muddy mountainside by now.

So could Kara Smith! That thought galvanized her. What if Kara was still alive down there? It seemed unlikely, but if she was, Mariah knew she was Kara's only hope. "I'll get the money," she shouted to Buster. "I'll go alone. You don't need to come." She had remembered Kara's gun, and she no longer wanted to die. She wanted to fight back, to stop Buster before he hurt anyone else. No one would ever believe her, but if she somehow defeated Buster and lived, she would tell her story, anyway. *And if I die, at least I won't have died a coward,* she told herself.

"We're both going," Buster announced.

"Fine," she responded, realizing that somehow she would have to beat him down to the car. "Do you have another flashlight?" she asked, even as she thought of how badly he wanted that thousand dollars. If she could find it, he could have it. But if she could find the gun, he'd also get something he wasn't expecting.

"There's one in my truck," he said. "I'll get it. You take this one."

Mariah took the flashlight he shoved at her and looked up to see a truck parked beside the cabin not more than thirty feet from where she stood. She hadn't noticed it until that moment. As she shined her light toward it, she could see that it was a late-model four-wheel drive—stolen, no doubt.

As Buster hurried to the truck, Mariah turned and scrambled over the edge of the ravine. She slid on the slick mud, falling a few of times, but she kept going at breakneck speed. Mariah knew Buster was coming, so she didn't waste time looking back.

As she descended the precarious slope, her mind raced. *If Kara's alive, I'll fight Buster with my bare hands if I have to, to protect her. If Kara's dead, I'll run down the mountain alone. Buster can have the money if he can find it.*

Suddenly she saw her car, a crumpled mass of steel, in the wavering beam of her flashlight. It rested on its wheels against a large pine tree. The tree had stopped the car from toppling even further down the mountain. Kara must be inside, Mariah decided, as she hadn't seen her on the way down, so she aimed the flashlight's beam inside the car.

Kara Smith lay like a lifeless rag doll in the front seat, obviously thrown there as the car rolled. Mariah reached through what was left of the space that had once held the car's windshield. Stretching hard, she placed a hand on the deputy's neck. A wave of relief passed through her as she felt the faint throbbing of a pulse beneath her cold, muddy fingers.

A cruel hand struck her shoulder. "Find the money?"

Mariah spun, pulling her own hand out of the car. "Buster, she's still alive! You've got to help me get her out. And you've got to go for help."

Buster laughed. It was a frighteningly corrupt sound, easily audible above the rain, which had eased in intensity. "And you thought you could get away from me."

"Please, Buster. We can't just let her die," Mariah begged. "You've got to help her. You will be a killer if you don't."

"Don't blame me. It's your fault if she dies, not mine. You should never have brought her. I told you not to. I warned you, Mariah. I should kill you and leave you here with her," he growled. "But Roger would never understand. The fool still loves you, you know."

Mariah was shocked—she hadn't thought her former husband, Buster's brother Roger, had ever loved her. But Buster thought so, and right now her life—and Kara Smith's—might very well depend on that belief. Turning back to the crumpled car, Mariah said, "Roger would want you to help me, Buster. Look, this door is in fairly good shape. It's the only part of the car that is." She gripped the door handle. "Let's see if we can pull it open," she suggested, hoping Buster might have an ounce of goodness left inside him.

"Maybe we can find your purse," Buster said as he laid his flashlight on the muddy ground. "Let me have that handle." She let go and he grabbed it, pulling fiercely. It gave just a little. Mariah grasped the door at the open window, where glass shards cut her hands. She pulled so hard that the muscles in her back burned and her fingers stretched painfully. The door gave a little more, then opened so suddenly that they both fell backward onto the ground.

On his feet in an instant, Buster yelled, "Is the money in your purse?" and picked up his flashlight.

"Yes, but help me get Kara out first."

Paying no attention to her, Buster climbed into the car, practically lying on top of Kara. Just as quickly, he burst back out. "I found it," he declared gleefully.

To Mariah's dismay, he opened her purse and poured the contents, including the envelope of hundred-dollar bills, on the muddy ground. He snatched up the envelope, inspected its contents, and barked, "Thanks, woman."

"Now, will you help me?" Mariah pleaded.

"Nope," he laughed as he started back up the slope.

At least, she thought thankfully, *he didn't kill me.* She turned to Kara and again found the deputy's pulse, which seemed a little stronger. With aching fingers, she methodically checked the deputy for broken bones and other serious injuries. Both arms and both legs felt like they had no breaks, but Mariah worried about Kara's back and neck. Before she could decide how to move her without risking further damage, Kara groaned and stirred.

"Kara, can you hear me?" she asked.

"Mariah . . . is . . . it . . ."

"Yes, it's me. Lie very still. I'm going to help you." As she spoke, Mariah heard the roaring of an engine. She looked up the steep incline and saw headlights momentarily fill the air overhead as Buster turned his stolen truck onto the road. Then he drove off and Mariah choked back tears of gratitude, knowing they were safer with Buster gone. Though they were stranded, she knew that they'd make it with the Lord's help.

Mariah turned back to Kara and continued her examination. Miraculously, it appeared that she had suffered no broken bones, and she had sensation in her hands and feet. In fact, despite Mariah's warnings not to, Kara moved on her own, then climbed out of the car. Soon they had struggled together up the steep slope, with Mariah bearing the young deputy's weight most of the way.

Fortunately, Buster had started a fire in the cabin stove before the women had arrived a long hour earlier. As Mariah and Kara finally staggered through the door, the fire's warmth enveloped them, and they both collapsed, side by side, on the only bed in the cabin. They were muddy, bruised, and exhausted. Kara's head was covered with blood from a shallow cut on her scalp, and she had smaller cuts on her arms and legs, but other than that she seemed uninjured. Still, there was always the possibility of internal injuries, so Mariah knew it was critical to get Kara to a hospital right away.

Of course, there was no phone in the remote cabin, and the cell phone Kara had carried had disappeared from her pocket, along with her pistol, in the mud of the mountainside. With no other choice, Mariah determined that she'd walk out to look for help at daylight.

* * *

Sheriff Hanks nervously paced his office from one end to the other. Every few minutes he stopped at his desk, reached for the phone, and dialed Kara's cell phone number. Then he'd wait a minute and dial Phil's. It was Phil that he eventually reached. "Where's Kara?" he demanded as soon as his deputy answered.

"I don't know. The phones were useless. I lost her two hours ago," Phil admitted. He sounded as worried about Kara as the sheriff was.

"Where was she the last you knew?" the sheriff asked.

Phil named a town just over an hour's drive from Harrisville. "What do you want me to do, Sheriff?"

"Come on home," Vince said after considering for a moment. "I'll put a bulletin out for Kara, Buster, Mariah, and the car. I'm afraid there is nothing more we can do right now."

After hanging up, Sheriff Hanks felt ill, fearing that he had sent his bright young deputy to her death. He had been so sure about Mariah—that she wasn't a criminal—and even now he didn't understand how he could have been wrong. Kara had known the risks and had accepted them, he reasoned, but that thought did little to console him. With bitter recriminations he worried away the next few hours.

Shortly after daybreak, his phone rang. "Sheriff. This is Gil Enders," a very tired and strained voice said. "I've got to talk to you."

"Where are you, Gil?" the sheriff demanded.

"I can't say. I'll meet you somewhere."

"What do you need to talk to me about?"

"It's about . . ." Gil hesitated. "It's about Cody Lind. I know who took him."

"Tell me, Gil. Right now."

"I can't. It's too dangerous. I'll meet you in a couple of hours and explain."

"Where at? Name the place and I'll be there," the sheriff urged.

"At . . . at . . . I don't know if this is such a good idea, Sheriff. Maybe I need to think about it a little longer. I've got me to think about, too," Gil stammered. "I could get hurt, you know, or even killed."

Gil sounded both tired and frightened, and the sheriff's heart beat faster as adrenaline rushed through his body. "Please, name the place, Gil. I'll come alone to meet you. You have my word on it."

"I don't know. I think I better not."

"Please, Gil. If you know anything that will help, let me know."

"I know you think I did it," Gil started.

"I don't know who did it!" the sheriff cried out in frustration. "If you can help me, please do."

"Well, I saw . . . a guy. He was at the banker's house."

"Edgar Stevens's house?"

"Yeah. It was in the night and dark, but I'm pretty sure who it was," Gil explained and then he hesitated.

"Who?" the sheriff pressed gently, not wanting to intimidate Gil.

"The same guy I saw the night . . . Gee, I don't know. I better not say yet. I could get killed, I tell you. I gotta have time. I gotta think some more." Before the sheriff could say anything else, the line went dead.

Sheriff Hanks slammed the phone against his palm in frustration before hanging it up. His mind was reeling with possibilities. *Could it be Gil who took Cody after all? Is he just now realizing what a terrible thing he's done, and now he wants to confess? Or is it someone else, and does Gil honestly possess the information I need to break this case open and find the real culprit? Did he see Buster at Edgar's? Or did he see Ken Treman? And why did Gil go there in the first place? Why did Sammy follow Edgar and make the claims he did? If Gil has been seen spying, he could very well be in danger, if he is innocent himself. Sammy Shirts could also be in danger.*

The sheriff had no idea how everything fit together. If only Gil would call again and tell him who he'd seen and what, if anything, he'd seen him do.

Once more the sheriff sat at his desk, this time writing down impressions and thoughts rather than things he logically knew. When the phone disturbed him again, he was astonished to find that his secretary was already there taking the calls. She was paging him. It was already past eight, he noted, as she said, "Sheriff, Mariah Taylor is on line one."

"Transfer it," he exclaimed. Then he said as calmly as he could, "Good morning, Mariah."

"Sheriff, Kara and I are both all right, but we lost Buster. He took my money and fled. He must have Cody somewhere, but if he does, I don't know where," she explained rapidly.

The sheriff cut in. "Okay, okay, Mariah. Slow down, and let's take this one step at a time. First, where is Kara? Why isn't she calling instead of you?"

"She was hurt. I didn't think she could walk out of the mountains where Buster left us."

"What mountains?" The sheriff asked calmly, although he was anything but calm. It was all he could do to refrain from shouting into the phone.

"I don't know what they call the mountains, but this guy whose house I'm at says it's about eighty miles from here to Harrisville. I thought it was farther, but then I don't know this area very well."

"Who's with Kara?" Sheriff Hanks demanded a little more sharply than he intended.

"She's alone in a cabin on the mountain. She's all right . . . at least she was when I left her. She's just badly bruised and has some cuts and scrapes."

"Okay, Mariah, let me speak with the fellow whose place you're calling from. I've got to get help to her, and to you. Then you and I will talk."

It took only a few minutes to learn where Kara was. The sheriff asked the man to hold the line while he made some calls on another line, getting a deputy from the neighboring county headed in the direction of the cabin where Kara waited and another deputy headed for the farmhouse from which Mariah was calling. The sheriff then spoke to Mariah again. "Okay, tell me what happened. Start from the beginning."

While Mariah talked, Sheriff Hanks listened, taking notes and interrupting only occasionally. When she'd finished describing the events of the last several hours, she begged, "You've got to believe me, Sheriff. I didn't have anything to do with Cody's disappearance."

"I don't have any reason to doubt you," the sheriff responded.

"You don't?"

"No, and I'll be anxiously awaiting Kara's story to confirm what you've told me. A deputy will be there to pick you up in a few minutes, Mariah. He'll take you to the sheriff's office there, and another officer will go pick up Deputy Smith."

Sheriff Hanks kept Mariah on the line until the officer arrived to pick her up . . . just in case, he kept telling himself. After he'd allowed Mariah to hang up, he sent Phil west to meet Kara and Mariah and bring them back to Harrisville.

After the sheriff's last call, his secretary paged him again. "Jake Garrett wants to talk to you," she announced. "He's been holding on line two."

"Sheriff, where is Kara?" Jake demanded. "She isn't home yet, and your dispatcher tells me her whereabouts are unknown."

"Calm down, Jake. She's fine and will be back in a few hours. She did run into a little trouble, but everything is okay now," the sheriff stated.

"Is she bringing Buster in?" Jake asked, his voice full of tension.

"I'm afraid not, Jake. He managed to get away."

"Get away? You mean we still don't have the guy who took Cody?"

"I'm afraid not, Jake. But we're working on it. We're doing every-thing in our power," the sheriff indicated with frustration.

"Working on it!" Jake thundered. "What about Kyle's money . . . and the kid's life? Kyle is going to have to pay out if you don't get this thing solved right away. And even if he does, that's no guarantee that we'll get Cody back."

"Why do you say that? Has there been another note?" the sheriff questioned.

"No, but when there is, I'm sure we'll find ourselves out of time. This thing is going to come to a head real soon. I can feel it in my gut. So can Kyle and the girls. You've got to do more."

"Jake, we're doing everything we can. Believe me, nobody wants this guy, whoever he is, caught more than I do."

"I'm sorry, Sheriff," Jake responded, sounding a little less tense. "I'm just so worried about Kara and Kyle and Cody that I feel like I'm going to explode."

"Of course you're worried, Jake. And speaking of Kyle, how is he this morning?"

"He's holding up okay, better than can be expected. He wants to pay the ransom if he can somehow get the money. He's tired of waiting, Sheriff."

"Tell him he's got to be patient a little longer," the sheriff urged. "I'll be in touch."

After hanging up, the sheriff rubbed his head thoughtfully and jotted down a few more lines in his rapidly filling notebook. Soon, several more unanswered questions were written there. *Yes,* he thought after he'd finished, *this case is going to drive me crazy.*

CHAPTER 19

From the moment Mariah Taylor had descended alone on foot down the muddy mountain road, Kara had been frightened. Because her gun had disappeared on her terrifying trip down the mountainside, she was not only alone but also unarmed. And she was afraid for Mariah. *What if Buster comes back and catches her walking out for help?* Kara kept thinking. Undoubtedly, Buster would hurt her or even kill her. Kara could only pray that Buster didn't come back.

She'd wanted to go with Mariah to find help. But with the pain she was in, she knew she would have only slowed the schoolteacher down. Kara finally agreed to stay and lock the cabin door behind Mariah when she left at daybreak.

As she relived the terrifying ride down the mountain, Kara remembered praying out loud, practically shouting so God could hear her over the sound of the rolling car. She realized now how unnecessary that was, for she knew that the Lord could hear her very thoughts. She also thought about the prayers Mariah had said she'd offered in Kara's behalf. Kara had plenty of time to express gratitude to her Heavenly Father while she waited for help to arrive. She knew she had been spared what could have been a much worse fate.

Kara also realized that the Tempest had begun its dangerous descent down the mountainside from a standstill rather than from a headlong moving start, so the ride, as terrible as it was, hadn't been nearly as bad as it could have been. She was grateful for that, too. And she was grateful for the sturdy evergreen that had stopped the car when it did. She'd truly been blessed.

Her ears perked up at the sound of a slow-moving vehicle working its way up the mountain road, and she knew she'd better have a look before it got too close. If it was Buster, she still had time to escape and hide in the forest behind the cabin. If it was help coming, she could finally relax.

Relief filled her sore, exhausted body when she saw a Dodge Ram from a neighboring county sheriff's department. That could only mean that Mariah had made it out safely, so Kara offered still another silent prayer of gratitude. A few minutes later, the deputy confirmed that Mariah, though fatigued and very chilled, was fine. He called on his police radio for a wrecker and another officer to assist in retrieving the badly mangled car from its resting place on the mountainside.

With the other assignments covered, the deputy drove Kara to town, where his first stop was the local emergency care center, per his boss's orders. Dr. James Elliott, an older gentleman, examined her gently, twisting her limbs carefully. "How does that feel, child?" he asked as he applied pressure along her spine. Kara laughed. No one, not even her grandmother, called her "child" anymore. Miraculously, everything checked out fine—Kara had no broken bones, and the doctor ruled out any internal injuries. Her scalp wound required nothing more than a good cleaning and a dozen stitches, while her other cuts needed only simple bandages. When Dr. Elliott had finished examining her, the deputy drove her to the county sheriff's office. Kara and Mariah hugged each other in relief.

Ninety minutes later they walked into the office of Sheriff Vince Hanks. Kara was touched at the relief in the sheriff's voice and on his face at her safe return. "I don't know how much more of this I can take," he joked. "I should have left you here and gone myself."

"You would have been busted up, being as old as you are," Kara kidded. "Miss Taylor's car doesn't take hills very well—going down where there's no road, that is."

"Who says I'm old?" he grinned. The sheriff turned to Mariah before Kara could say more. "I'm sorry about your car, Mariah."

"I wanted an excuse to get a new one anyway," she responded.

"Kara," he said, turning back to his deputy. "I'll have Phil stay with Mariah in the squad room while you and I talk. Then it's home and some much-deserved and needed rest for you."

For the next sevral minutes, Kara briefed the sheriff on her encounter with Buster, and the ordeal that followed. "Mariah's a good person," she declared at one point. "She risked her life for me. I'm certain now that she's not involved with Buster, if he's even involved with the kidnapping himself."

"I suspect you're right," the sheriff agreed. After she'd finished her account of the night's events, he told her about the call he'd received from Gil Enders. "So I'm really puzzled now," he concluded. "What about you?"

Kara admitted being more confused than ever about the case, then asked, "How are Kyle and his family?" She really wanted to ask about Jake, but that seemed too direct.

The sheriff seemed to discern her true motive anyway. "They're about the same, but Jake called. He's not happy with me for sending you on this assignment. When you talk to him, Kara, don't say too much about what's happened. Not yet, anyway."

"But he's family," Kara stated defensively.

"I know, but still, I want to keep things between us for now," he replied gruffly.

Thinking that such a comment was out of character for the sheriff, Kara realized that perhaps he didn't approve of her relationship with Jake.

"I think the less you tell him, the less he'll have to worry about. And at this point, as muddled as things are, we've got to be careful what we say to any of the family, Kyle included. Now, you need some rest."

"And so do you, Sheriff," she commented with concern as she observed the dark circles under his eyes.

He smiled. "You're right. And I intend to get a little. Haven't time for much, though. Let me know how you feel tomorrow."

"Tomorrow!" she exclaimed, glancing at her watch and realizing that it was still early afternoon. "That's a long time from now."

"That's right, Kara, and it may not be long enough. You have been through a lot in the past few hours. Go home and take it easy, and that's an order."

She went home, but the first thing she did was place a call to the Lind ranch. One of the little girls answered and told Kara that they all had orders to call Jake to the phone when she called, no matter where he was working. It took several minutes for Jake to come to the phone, and Kara waited as patiently as she could.

When he finally said hello, Kara said, "I'm sorry. Were you outside?"

"Yes. One of Kyle's bulls busted a hole in the bull corral, and I was fixing it," he said. He was breathing hard, and she guessed he'd run all the way to the house.

"I'll bet Kyle's glad to have you around. What would he ever do without you?" she asked fondly.

"I'm just glad to be here," Jake replied. "And I'm especially glad you called. I've been worried sick about you. I'll be so relieved to have this thing over."

"So will I," Kara sighed, "but I sure don't know when that will be. I'm sorry you worried about me, but I'm fine. The sheriff says I have to take some time off and to not even call in to the office until tomorrow."

"Then you do as he says," Jake ordered forcefully. "Could you use a little company?"

"Well, to be honest, I'm awfully sore and tired. I think I need to sleep—"

"Sore?" he broke in. "Kara, I'm on my way to town right now. I want to know what happened."

"Oh, it's nothing really," she responded, remembering the sheriff's admonition. "You better finish fixing that corral."

"It can wait," Jake answered almost angrily. "I want to see you."

"But—" Kara began again, wavering.

"No buts. I'm on my way," Jake insisted.

"All right, but I can't see you for long," she acquiesced. Before she could say anything more, he hung up. Kara realized it would be good to see him for a few minutes, even though she really needed to rest.

* * *

Sheriff Hanks also went home, eager to get the sleep his body craved. "Do you want me to take messages if anyone calls, Vince?" his wife asked. "I hate to have you disturbed."

"Yes, please. If it's important, you'd better wake me," he decided.

"What's important?" she questioned. "I can't tell. When people call you, to them it's always important, or they wouldn't be calling."

The sheriff nodded. "Find out who they are and what they want. Then decide. But if it's about the Lind case, it is important."

"All right," she replied. "I hope I don't have to wake you, because you need your rest. I'm really worried about your health. You can't go on like this."

"You're right," he agreed as his head hit the pillow. He was asleep before his wife had left the room.

It seemed as though he had barely fallen asleep when he was gently roused from his slumber. His wife was shaking his shoulder and saying, "I'm sorry, Vince, but there's a phone call that I think you'll want to take."

For a moment he tried to convince himself he was dreaming and that he should close his eyes and ignore her. But she persisted. "Dear, the caller is Gil Enders. He says it's very important. He sounds desperate. He wants to talk to you at once."

That brought the sheriff fully awake, and he took the phone from his wife's hand.

"Sheriff, I'm sorry I got scared before. Don't take me wrong, I still don't like Cody Lind, but wrong is wrong. Can I meet you somewhere?" Gil sounded desperate.

"Of course," the sheriff answered, glancing at his watch and noting that he'd been asleep for less than two hours.

"I'll be at the view area overlooking . . . No, that's too public and too close to Harrisville. "Let's see— "

"Why don't you just come to my office, Gil?"

"Oh no, that's the last place I'll meet you! I don't dare come there," Gil exclaimed. "I can't come anywhere near town."

"That's silly, Gil. You'll be safe there. I guarantee it," the sheriff assured, wondering at the genuine fear he sensed in Gil's voice.

"You don't get it, Sheriff. I can't come anywhere near Harrisville. I'll meet you in Salt Lake City. That's where I'm calling from right now."

Sheriff Hanks groaned, unsure whether he was alert enough to drive to Salt Lake. He had to arrange something better. "Are you sure we can't just talk over the phone?"

"No. Absolutely not! I've already said too much. If you don't want to come, then just forget it!" Gil shouted.

"I'll come, Gil," the sheriff said quickly. "Name the place."

"There's a ShopKo just off I-80 at 13th East," Gil stated.

"Yes, I'm familiar with it."

"Meet me there. I'll watch for you from the parking lot. Then I'll meet you just inside the south doors. Be there at seven o'clock sharp. If you're late, I'll be gone. I'm not taking any chances. Understand, Sheriff? I'll be gone if you're late."

"That doesn't give me much time, but I'll try to be there," the sheriff responded.

"And come alone," Gil added.

"Alone? I'm awfully tired, Gil. I'll need someone to drive me."

"No way. If you're not alone, you'll never see me again. Alone. Seven o'clock," he repeated. "Drive a private car, not a police car, and don't wear your uniform." Then Gil hung up.

While Gil's last requests greatly concerned the sheriff, at this point he had no choice but to comply. He was desperate to learn what Gil knew.

"Was that an important call, dear?" his wife asked as she reentered the room. She always left when he took a work-related call.

"Very. I've got to run to Salt Lake."

"Oh, Vince, you can't possibly," she moaned, her eyes wide with alarm.

"I have to. Fix me a sandwich if you will, and some cold water. I'll be leaving as soon as I make a phone call and get dressed."

He hated to make the call, but Kara was currently the most informed of any of the deputies on the case, and his chief deputy was ill. Someone had to know he was gone in case something important came up before he returned. Kara sounded groggy, and the sheriff asked, "Did I wake you?"

"Yes. I thought you wanted me to rest until tomorrow," she mumbled with a touch of irritation in her tired voice.

"I'm sorry, Deputy. Something has come up and I have to run to Salt Lake. I hated to go without letting you know in case something happens while I'm gone. I know you've been through a great deal the past few hours."

"Sheriff, you can't drive to Salt Lake," Kara declared, concern overriding her irritation. "You're too tired. Or is someone going to drive you?"

"I have to go, and I have to drive myself. I'll be in my personal truck but I'll have my cell and a handheld radio with me. I'll instruct dispatch and the office not to disturb you unless it's urgent."

"You'll fall asleep at the wheel," she protested again. "You can't do this."

"I've got to. It's critical. But I'll be okay," he said, hoping it was true. "I've got to meet Gil Enders."

"Gil!" Kara exclaimed. "What does he want, and why can't he talk to you here?"

The sheriff explained briefly, and Kara responded, "I see. Well, be careful. Don't take any chances."

The sheriff remembered his deputy's counsel an hour later when he was so sleepy that he could barely see straight. He finally looked at his watch, figured he could safely spare ten minutes, and pulled over to take a quick nap. Perhaps that would be enough to help him stay alert the rest of the way.

Ten minutes turned into twenty, and when he awoke, the sheriff couldn't believe what he'd done. Angry with himself and praying that Gil would wait, he pulled onto the highway again. He drove much faster than he should have, but even then, it was five minutes after seven when he pulled into the ShopKo parking lot.

He looked around for Gil but didn't see him. Jumping out of his truck, he rushed to the store's south entrance and went inside. Gil wasn't there. He waited for ten minutes, nervously pacing, looking over the parking lot, and checking his watch. Finally, when it became apparent that Gil had meant what he said about being on time, Sheriff Hanks walked through the entire store. Gil simply wasn't there.

Thoroughly discouraged, the sheriff headed back to Harrisville. But exhaustion again overtook him, and he eventually realized that he simply couldn't drive without substantial sleep. He stopped at a motel, rented a room, called both Kara and his wife to explain what had happened, and then dropped onto the bed in an exhausted sleep.

* * *

"Cast over there, Bob, and I'll move a bit this way. That big one's got to take our bait sometime. He can't be that smart."

The two men had been fishing for over two hours, and there was still plenty of time before dark. They were determined to catch the fish they believed to be the biggest one in the lake.

Bob moved over to where his pal had pointed and cast. He let his line sink until he was certain that it was on the bottom of the lake, then began to slowly reel it in. It stopped short, and he tugged. The pole bent, but it didn't give. "I've either got a big fish or a snag," he shouted to his pal.

He heaved and turned his pole one way and then another for a minute or two before his friend shouted, "Looks like a snag, Bob. You'll have to cut your line."

Just then, Bob heaved harder and the line came free. "I must have broken my line and lost my hook," he lamented as he reeled in the remaining line. "Hey, it still feels like there's something there," he called out a moment later.

"You've got something on the line!" his pal agreed with a shout.

A few moments later the two fishermen were studying a piece of yellow cloth. "It's part of a shirt," Bob's pal said.

The two men looked at each other. "We'd better call the sheriff."

* * *

When dispatch couldn't reach the sheriff, the call was routed to Kara. Because she'd been sleeping for several hours, she had to rub the sleep from her eyes before she answered the phone. "Deputy, the sheriff said we were to call you if anything important came up before he got back, and his wife says he won't be back for several hours," the dispatcher explained.

"What do you have?" Kara asked as she massaged a sore leg with her free hand. She had stopped trying to count the places that hurt.

"A couple of fisherman over by the lake on the west end of the county just pulled up what looks to them like a piece of yellow shirt. They're pretty agitated, and they want the sheriff to come right out."

A chill descended on Kara. Cody Lind had been wearing a pale yellow shirt when he disappeared. The lake was near Roscoe Norman's farm, so it would take her several minutes to get there. "Tell them to stay put. I'll be on my way as quickly as I can get dressed," she replied with a trembling voice. "And don't mention any of this on the radio."After hanging up and realizing how difficult it was to move her battered body, she had another thought and reached for the phone.

"Dispatch, call the search-and-rescue divers, would you please? Have them meet me at the lake," she instructed. "And again, nothing on the radio. I know Sheriff Hanks. That's what he'd say."

"It certainly is," the dispatcher affirmed.

After hanging up again, Kara kept her hand on the phone for a moment. The sheriff had said he was shutting his phone off, but he'd given her the number of the motel where he was sleeping. She was tempted to call him, but decided against it, knowing that he would try to drive home. From the way he'd sounded earlier, he was in no shape to do that.

Kara dressed as quickly as she could, but it still took more time than she had. In the car a few minutes later, she began to tremble. The combination of her bruised, sore body, fatigue, and the anticipation of finding Cody's body was enough to make her shake like a leaf.

Maybe it wasn't Cody in the lake, she tried to convince herself as she drove, but logic told her it had to be. Passing the Lind ranch, she wished Jake was with her. But remembering the sheriff's counsel to not share case details with Jake—and her own orders to the dispatcher to keep any word of what she was doing off the police radio—she knew she shouldn't inform Cody's family of the impending tragic news until it was confirmed. Even then, she wouldn't let them know until the sheriff gave his permission.

By the time Kara finally pulled up to the remote area of the lake's shore where the fisherman stood waiting, she'd managed to calm down. Steeling herself and ignoring her pain, she hurried over to the two men. "Here's what's left of the shirt we found, Deputy," one fellow said, handing it to her.

Pale yellow! The report had been right.

She nearly retched, but she prayed for control and instructed the men, "Show me exactly where you pulled it in."

"Right over there. I was standing on them rocks. The water's pretty deep here," one fisherman told her.

"Were you the one that found it?" she asked.

"Yup. Name's Bob," he said, offering her a grimy palm.

Kara shivered. "All right, fellows," she said in as businesslike a tone as she could muster, "there'll be divers here momentarily, and we'll see what you've found."

"Probably the Lind kid," Bob commented, shaking his head. "Makes me sick. If it is, I don't think I'll ever fish again."

"I hope it isn't Cody," Kara replied softly, figuring it was.

It wasn't.

An hour later, two divers pulled to the surface the wrinkled body of one Edgar Stevens, clad in what was left of a pale yellow shirt and gray pants. Not until she saw the grotesque body did Kara remember Edgar's wife mentioning that a yellow shirt she'd given him on his birthday just a week before was missing from his closet.

Tied to one of Edgar's feet was a heavy tire rim. "That was obviously meant to keep him down there," one of the divers surmised. "Whoever did the banker in didn't want him to surface."

Kara could see that for herself, but she was torn between feeling relieved that it was not Cody lying on the ground, and feeling guilty that she was not more horrified over the death of Edgar Stevens. When she said nothing but just stared at the dead body, the diver said, "Deputy, with your permission, we'd like to go down again. We thought we saw what could be a car not too far from where Mr. Stevens's body was."

"A-a car?" Kara stammered.

"Yes. Of course, we could have been wrong—the water is quite murky down there."

"Oh, I see. Well, by all means, go back down."

The divers returned immediately to the lake, leaving Kara with the body of the late banker at her feet. The fishermen both stood nearby with gaping mouths. Finally, Kara forced herself into action. "Gentlemen," she began, "I'll need statements from both of you. I'll get you some paper to write on, then I'll see about the body. And you are not to say anything to anyone about what we have here until the sheriff gives his okay—not even your wives. We'll need to notify his relatives, you know, before anything is said to the public. You do understand, don't you?"

They hurriedly nodded in agreement and promised not to say a word until either the sheriff or Kara called them.

As soon as the fishermen were busy chewing on a couple of her pens and staring at the note pads she'd given them, Kara directed the dispatcher to send someone out from the medical examiner's office. She also requested the help of another deputy, either Shawn or Phil. She did everything by phone, not wanting to make public any of the gruesome details about the most recent discovery until the sheriff gave his okay. Then she began to take photos while she waited for the divers to come up again.

She didn't have to wait long, and what the divers reported caused her to reel. "It's a car, a light green Buick. At least, we think that's the color," one of the divers said. "And we got the license plate number."

When he recited it to Kara, it was all the confirmation she needed. The car was the one Cody Lind had been driving the night he disappeared. "Is there a body in it?" she asked with grim apprehension.

"Nope. The driver's window was down, and we disturbed a school of fish. One was a monster. But other than that, the car was empty."

The other diver added, "If the Lind boy had been in it when it went into the lake, it is doubtful, the way the car was sitting, that his body would have floated out. But if it had, it should have surfaced, because the water is not very cold."

"Unless he had a . . ." Kara began, but her voice trailed off as her eyes drifted to the tire rim still tied to the leg of Edgar Stevens's corpse.

"That's right," one diver agreed, "but then he would have still been down there. We searched the lake bottom immediately surrounding the car, too. There was no body. Frankly, I don't think the boy went in with the car. There weren't any signs of a struggle that we could see."

When Shawn finally arrived to assist Kara, he was still not completely over his illness and the sight that confronted him didn't help his condition. Kara told Shawn that she'd do whatever he asked, since he outranked her. He chose to leave the car where it was until the sheriff came back. "I don't think we want anyone else seeing the car until the sheriff has a chance to decide how to proceed. But I think it is time to call him. And I'll let you do that, Kara."

She dialed the number of the motel where Sheriff Hanks had stopped.

After she'd recited the events of the past hour and expressed her concern for his safety on the road, the sheriff declared, "After what you just told me, I couldn't go back to sleep if I had to. I'll be there in ninety minutes or so. And Kara, call Chief Worthlin. After all, Edgar was last seen by his wife in Worthlin's jurisdiction. Anyway, we'll need all the help we can get, so ask him to call out his men. And make sure the body is sent for an autopsy. And first thing, get the forensics people there to check out the crime scene. We'll need more than just photos. Oh, and have the chief send someone to notify Mrs. Stevens. Also, please get Phil moving. Either he or one of the chief's officers will need to pick up Sammy Shirts, if they can find him. Have dispatch broadcast another bulletin on Buster Ashton and one on Ken Treman. It needs to go statewide and beyond. If they are found, they need to be picked up and held for questioning. And keep what you've found there at the lake as quiet as you can for now. Put nothing on the radio that you haven't already."

"Nothing has been over the radio yet," Kara replied. "I knew that's what you'd want, since so many people have police scanners."

"Good work, Kara. Sounds like you're doing what you can. I appreciate it."

"Should I call Kyle Lind and tell him about the car?" she asked hesitantly, hoping for a negative answer.

"Absolutely not!" the sheriff exclaimed. "And if the divers are absolutely sure Cody isn't in the car, leave it where it is for now. I wish I was there right now. I feel so helpless so far away. Oh, include a bulletin on Gil Enders, Kara. I'm still kicking myself for missing him. There's no doubt that he knows something of importance."

"I'll do that," Kara agreed.

"You're sure there's no body in the car?" the sheriff queried.

"That's what the divers said."

"Not even in the trunk?" he asked.

"Oh, I don't know," she answered. "I didn't think about that."

"Send the divers back down to see if they can open the trunk. If they can, and the boy's body's not in there, leave the car for now. But if he's in there, or if they can't open the trunk underwater, then I guess you'll need to have the car pulled out immediately."

As the divers went back down to check the trunk, Kara, Shawn, and the two fishermen waited tensely.

"The kid's not in there," one of the divers announced as he surfaced a few minutes later.

CHAPTER 20

Late that evening, Kara sat in the sheriff's office with Sheriff Hanks and Chief Worthlin. So far, they'd successfully kept the public from learning about the discoveries at the lake, and the sheriff hoped to be able to maintain the silence until the next day. Edgar Stevens's wife had been notified of his death, and she'd gone with the couple's only daughter to Salt Lake City. They didn't object to keeping the matter quiet—whatever it took to find Edgar's killer and bring him or her to justice.

Although Sheriff Hanks, Deputy Smith, and Chief Worthlin were exhausted, none even considered going home. A city police officer had just called to report that he had Sammy Shirts in custody, and all three officers wanted to hear what Sammy had to say.

The sheriff took the lead as soon as Sammy was ushered into his office. After advising him of his rights, the sheriff asked, "Do you want to call an attorney before we begin?"

"Am I being accused of something else?" Sammy queried shrewdly. "You already said you was going to charge me with blackmail."

That was true, but Sammy Shirts had been freed after agreeing to assist the sheriff in proving the case against Edgar Stevens. Now things had taken a vastly different turn.

"No, I'm not accusing you of anything else yet, but you certainly have a lot of explaining to do," Sheriff Hanks stated. "We found the body of Edgar Stevens a few hours ago. He'd been shot before he was dumped in the lake."

"I didn't kill him," Sammy replied sullenly. "I wasn't even there when Edgar was taken from his house. You are my witness, young lady," he said, looking at Kara. "When he gave me the money he was just fine. It's that Treman guy—Ken Treman—that killed Mr. Stevens."

"You don't know that, Sammy, because you were with Deputy Smith when Stevens came up missing," the sheriff reminded him sharply. "Now, are you willing to answer a few questions?"

"Sure. I ain't got nothin' to hide," Sammy answered. "I already admitted that Mr. Stevens paid me to keep my mouth shut."

"That's right. Now, let's go back to the night of Cody's disappearance," the sheriff started.

"We already talked about that. I got nothing more to say about that," Sammy declared.

"Didn't you say that you had seen Edgar out and about that night?" the sheriff asked, his face impassive.

"Yeah, I saw him that night. Like I told you before, he was driving around."

"It's not illegal to drive late at night," the sheriff said sternly. "You'd better come up with something other than that now that Edgar is dead."

"He was just a few blocks from Houston Harrison's house," Sammy said, repeating what he had said before when he'd confessed to blackmailing the wealthy banker.

The sheriff stared hard at Sammy. "Did you ever see him in Cody's car, or even near Cody's car that night?"

"Well, no, but I know he took him."

"You've told us that before, Sammy, but you must have more reason for believing it if you were able to convince Mr. Stevens to buy your silence."

Sammy squirmed, glancing nervously at Kara on his right side and the police chief on his left. Finally his face brightened, and he exclaimed, "Mr. Stevens wouldn't have agreed to pay me if it wasn't true, now would he?"

Kara realized that Sammy had made a good point. The sheriff, however, glared at Sammy. "Do you really expect me to sit here and believe a man like Edgar Stevens would spend ten thousand dollars to get you to keep your mouth shut over something as insignificant as what *you* saw, or what *you think* you saw? Sammy, your reputation for avoiding and distorting the truth is pretty widespread."

Sammy continued to shift uncomfortably in his seat. "Well," he admitted as the sheriff's eyes bored into his. "I mighta lied just a little."

"Lied!" the sheriff thundered.

"Not to you," Sammy corrected quickly. "Just to Stevens. I mighta said to him that I saw him drivin' around that night and that I seen him in the car with Cody Lind. But I really didn't. But Stevens didn't know that, so he paid up. See, that means he did it."

The sheriff finally lifted his eyes and glanced first at Chief Worthlin, then at Kara. "Makes sense," he muttered as they nodded.

Sammy brightened considerably. "I think that Ken Treman guy was helpin' him or somethin'."

"Why do you say that?" the sheriff questioned.

"Because the same night Stevens paid me, he gave Treman money too," Sammy revealed.

"Did you actually see him give Treman money?" Sheriff Hanks asked, his eyes growing cold again.

"Well, not 'zactly, but when I went in that night, Treman was holdin' a bag just like the one Stevens gave me. And Treman acted kinda mad, like it wasn't enough or somethin'," Sammy explained.

The sheriff leaned back, lifted his eyes to the ceiling, tented his fingers, and sat thoughtfully for a moment. Suddenly, he leaned forward and almost shouted. "Sammy, did Edgar Stevens pay you to kidnap Cody Lind?"

Sammy's mouth fell open and his eyes bugged out. "No! I swear, Sheriff Hanks, I didn't have nothin' to do with Cody. Nothin' at all. Maybe he paid Mr. Treman for it. Maybe he was helpin' Edgar by keepin' the boy hidden somewhere or somethin'."

"Maybe," the sheriff allowed, his voice soft again. Then in a strong voice he added, "Or maybe he paid Treman to kill you, Sammy, and get the ten thousand back he'd given you."

Sammy's face turned white, and he began to tremble. "Maybe," he squeaked. "Sheriff, you won't let nobody hurt me, will you? Can I stay in your jail for a while? You took my money, and I ain't got another penny or I would go somewhere and hide, but I can't afford it."

"Maybe," the sheriff replied after several seconds. "I might consider that if you'll help us."

"What do you want me to do?" Sammy asked eagerly.

"With Edgar dead, Cody may be somewhere starving. We've got to find him quickly. Surely you have some idea where he is being held?"

"I swear I don't," Sammy cried, looking crestfallen.

Kara believed Sammy, and apparently her boss did too, for he said, "I'll let you stay in jail, Sammy. In fact, I'm going to insist on it. I think I'll call the prosecutor about charging you with both extortion and conspiracy to murder."

"Please, Sheriff. Don't do that. I didn't have nothin' to do with killin' Cody," he blurted.

Sheriff Hanks's face twisted with sudden anger. "Who said anything about Cody being killed?"

"N-nobody," Sammy stammered.

"So help me, Sammy, you'd better come clean," the sheriff said with fire in his eyes. "Why did you say that? Why did you talk about Cody being killed?"

"I don't know. I guess I thought he might have been murdered," Sammy squeaked. "But I don't have no reason to believe it."

Sheriff Hanks stood up. "That's all, Sammy," he stated, glaring at the man with cold eyes. Then to Kara he said, "I think we'll charge him with conspiring to murder Edgar Stevens, which is what I had in mind in the first place."

"No!" Sammy cried. "I didn't do that either, I swear!"

"If you think of something, ask the jailer to let me know," the sheriff indicated. "Until further notice, you'll be locked up tight."

"That's okay with me, Sheriff," he agreed. "But I promise, I didn't kill nobody."

* * *

Something woke Kyle Lind. He lay in bed listening for several seconds, then pulled himself upright and put on his slippers. He wasn't sure what had disturbed his sleep. The closing of a door, perhaps?

Deciding it was probably one of the girls or maybe Jake getting up to use the bathroom or get a drink of water, Kyle told himself he shouldn't get all excited. With resolve, he pulled his slippers off again and climbed back into bed. Eventually, he drifted back into a dreamless sleep.

Sometime later, Kyle awoke again with a start. He was sure he'd heard a door this time. He tried to remember if he had locked the house, and he was quite sure he had. But he was wide awake now, so he decided to check. *It would be too much if someone stole in here and took another member of my family,* he thought with a sinking feeling in his stomach.

He checked all the outside doors and found them secure. He peeked into Candi's bedroom and saw his oldest daughter curled up on her side, apparently sleeping soundly. He left her room and moved silently to the younger girls' bedroom, where he confirmed that they were also sleeping soundly.

After starting back to his own room, Kyle, on an impulse, thought of Jake and hurried to the guest room where he was staying. Kyle stopped at the door and listened to the heavy breathing of his nephew. All seemed well in the house.

Kyle went back to bed, but he couldn't fall asleep. Finally, he arose, put on his clothes, tugged on some boots, grabbed a flashlight, and left the house. He wandered aimlessly through the yard and corrals, his head filled with troubled thoughts. But outside all was peaceful—the animals were sleeping and the ranch itself was enveloped in silence. He thought momentarily about the disparity between his inner feelings and his outer circumstances here on the ranch he loved. He shined the light on the spot in the bull corral fence that Jake had fixed, noting that his nephew had done a neat, thorough job. As good as he could have done himself, or even better, Kyle admitted.

Finally, he walked up the lane to the highway, moving briskly, letting the pumping of his heart ease the worries in his mind. He did love this ranch, he thought as he walked, but he would gladly give it up to regain his son. His heart ached as he thought about Cody. *Dear Lord, if Thou wilt spare his life,* he prayed, *I'll do anything Thou wilt ask of me. Anything.*

At the highway, he turned and started back again, paused, then swung around and approached the mailbox, remembering how

Jake—out for a middle-of-the-night walk like this—had found the last note from the kidnappers. Pulling the lid open, he leaned over and shined his flashlight inside. His heart dropped like a stone.

It took him several seconds to force his hand to reach in and pull out the folded paper. It took even longer to make his trembling fingers open it. Finally, with the light shining on the paper, he read the few words it contained.

"I'll do it!" he cried aloud as great sobs racked his body. "I swear, I'll do it."

* * *

Sheriff Hanks had finally made it to bed at a little after 1:00 on Tuesday morning. He slept soundly for an hour before the phone brought him upright in his bed. "I'll get it, Vince," his wife sighed.

"You stay put, dear," he said gently. "You know it's for me. Maybe it's Gil again."

"Sheriff, Jake Garrett. Get out here, fast!" the sheriff heard as soon as he lifted the receiver.

"What is it?" the sheriff asked as his stomach knotted.

"Kyle wants you, now! He just found another note, and it's serious."

"I'm on my way," the sheriff replied as he wondered how Edgar Stevens could make a ransom demand from his cold storage box in the office of the state medical examiner, where he'd been taken for an autopsy.

He couldn't, of course. So someone else had taken Cody, he realized with relief, and Cody could still be alive. Maybe they weren't beat yet. He jerked his pants on, buckled his gun belt, pulled his boots on, and left the house, still buttoning his shirt. He charged out of town.

Jake and Kyle met him in the yard, Jake holding the note and waving it in the air as the sheriff slid his car to a stop and jumped out. "Read it, Sheriff!" he ordered brusquely.

Sheriff Hanks took the note and stepped back to his car, holding it under the dome light, reading.

I'm not fooling, Kyle Lind. One-half million dollars is due me in hundred dollar bills. If it is not delivered by eight o'clock this evening, you will find Cody's body where it can't be missed. Stay by your phone for instructions on where to deliver the money. Let the sheriff read this and then tell him and his deputies to back out of it. If he so much as leaves his office after noon today, Cody dies.

The sheriff folded the note and stuffed it in his pocket with cold but steady hands. "He means it, Sheriff." Jake declared firmly. "Buster's not fooling around. You've got to back out of this and let Kyle and me take it from here."

"I can't do that, Jake," the sheriff answered.

"You will do it," Jake stated, his face suddenly dark with anger. "The life of Kyle's son is at stake. You've had your chances—plenty of them—to catch Buster. You haven't been able to do it. Now we'll take over, and that's not negotiable. Do you agree, Kyle?" he asked, looking at his uncle for support.

Kyle nodded. "That's right, Sheriff. I've already asked Jake to follow up on the preliminary arrangements he made earlier for the ransom money. It'll mean losing the ranch, but all I want is Cody back . . . alive."

"And you think that if I let you deliver the money, your boy's safety will be guaranteed?"

"You read the note," Kyle retorted.

"It said nothing about Cody's being released if you pay. All it says is what will happen if you don't," the sheriff corrected sternly.

"It may not say it, but it implies it, Sheriff," Jake pointed out. "We have no other choice. It's the only chance Cody has of staying alive."

"That's right, Vince. We thank you for all you've done, but you stay out of it until we let you know that we have the boy back."

"That's right, Sheriff," Jake added. "And if you don't—"

"If I don't, then what?" the sheriff interrupted angrily.

"We'll hold you personally responsible for the boy's death, that's what!" Jake thundered. "Now if you'll kindly leave us alone, we'll take it from here. We've got to be near the phone in case Buster calls."

"You're both convinced it's Buster, aren't you?" Sheriff Hanks questioned as he climbed into his car.

"I don't know who it is," Jake responded. "Maybe it's the missing Edgar Stevens or Gil Enders, or that disgusting Sammy Shirts. But I think it's probably Buster. But that's not important now. Just remember, you are to be in your office from noon on today, or you could foul the whole thing up and cost Cody his life. We've got to do exactly as the note directs."

"If you men say so," the sheriff said angrily as he shut the door. Then he called through the open window, "Call me if you come to your senses." At least the word about Edgar's death hadn't gotten out, and the sheriff was glad now that he'd left Kyle's missing car at the bottom of the lake. Jake and Kyle obviously knew nothing about it or the murder of the banker.

Sheriff Hanks drove directly to the office. He had to know if the new note had been written before or after the old typewriter had been found. As he suspected, it matched the earlier ones. Whoever was behind the kidnapping had written all the notes several days ago—that explained why none of the notes were dated. The kidnapper seemed to know exactly what he was doing—making allowances for time and not tying himself in advance to specific days.

The sheriff's wife called as he was putting the notes away. "Mariah Taylor wants you to call her," she informed him. "She says you know how to reach her."

Sheriff Hanks had tucked Mariah safely away at his sister's home, forty miles from Harrisville. Unless she'd called and told someone where she was, only he and Kara knew where she was staying. He dialed the number, and Mariah answered on the first ring.

"Kyle just called," she indicated.

"Kyle? How did he know how to find you?" the sheriff demanded.

"I didn't give the address where I'm staying, but he has my cell phone number. He called that, and I answered. I had to talk to him, Sheriff."

"That's fine, Mariah," the sheriff sighed after reflecting for a moment. "What did Kyle want?"

"He told me about the latest ransom note, the deadline, and the threat. He asked me to call and urge you to stay out of it while he and Jake take care of getting Cody back from his abductor."

"Is that really what you want me to do?" he asked.

"I guess so . . ." she answered flatly. But then her voice rose. "No. I don't think I really do, Sheriff. I don't feel good about it. Who's to say that the kidnapper will return Cody alive once he gets the money? Is there anything you can do without Kyle or his nephew knowing it?"

"I don't know," the sheriff replied, wondering if he should tell her what had been running through his mind or if she would just relay the information to Kyle. He decided he'd better not risk it, at least not yet.

"Please, do something," Mariah begged.

"I don't want to do anything to put Cody at greater risk," the sheriff answered emphatically.

Mariah hung up the phone moments later. The sheriff felt sorry for her, but he also knew enough not to trust anyone at this point. Saving Cody's life was his first consideration.

For the next few minutes, Sheriff Hanks wrote in his notebook. After a while he leaned back in his chair and closed his eyes to think. The next thing he knew, he saw sunlight outside his window—he had slept the remainder of the night away in his office. Surprisingly, he felt refreshed and alert. Not Jake Garrett, nor Kyle Lind, nor anyone else was going to prevent him from doing what he needed to.

Sheriff Hanks prepared some rough plans in writing. He would need the help of Kara Smith, Chief Worthlin, and Mariah Taylor, if he could be sure she wouldn't call Kyle and tip him off. He thought that he could convince her; in fact, it was imperative that he do so.

The sheriff received his first phone call that morning just after his secretary came in at eight. "Sheriff, I seen that light again," Roscoe Norman announced. "I called your house earlier, but your wife said you was gone."

Sheriff Hanks groaned. He didn't have time for Roscoe Norman and his crazy lights. Time was critical if he were to save the life of Cody Lind. He was about to tell Roscoe that his problem would have to wait, but then he recalled the boot print in the ditch. For some inexplicable reason, Cody's kidnapper had been on Roscoe's property at least once. It made absolutely no sense . . . or did it? His thoughts were cut short by Roscoe's demanding voice. "It's probably too late to do anything but come out here, Sheriff. I ain't putting up with no more of this trespassin' on my place."

"Roscoe, if you'll give me a few minutes to make some phone calls, I'll be out."

After hanging up, he looked at his latest notes, read several pages, and tried to discover what it was that gnawed at his subconscious. He failed and finally gave up, grabbing his hat and heading for the door. The phone calls could wait. There was something else he had to do.

* * *

Kara had slept well, and other than the lingering soreness, she felt much improved. It was time to get back to work, she decided. But before she could call the sheriff, Jake called.

"Hi, Kara," he began gently. "Feel better this morning?"

"As a matter of fact, I do, Jake," she anwered with a smile.

"What are your plans today?" he asked.

"I was just going to call Sheriff Hanks to tell him I'm ready to go back to work. He wanted me to take a few more hours off, but I don't need them."

"Take them," Jake urged adamantly. "Take the rest of the day off."

Disturbed by the tone of his voice, Kara demanded, "Why should I do that, Jake? I'm sore, but other than that, I feel fine. Really, I do. And, by the way, you have no authority to tell me what to do or what not to do. There's no reason I can't go to work."

"Kara," he stated sternly, "there have been new developments that you are apparently unaware of. Cody's only chance of survival hinges on you and your boss and the other deputies staying out of the case today. Completely out of it."

"We can't do that, Jake," she replied. "But what are the developments?"

Jake explained about the latest note from the kidnapper.

Stunned, Kara queried, "Are you serious, Jake? The note says the kidnapper will kill Cody if the sheriff or I—"

"Or any other cops," Jake interrupted.

"Yes, of course. None of us are to attempt to do anything," she finished.

"That's right."

"But Jake, we have to. Otherwise, Kyle will have to pay out the money, and then his ranch is gone for sure."

"That's right, but Kyle wants it that way. I argued with him, but he said that he'd rather have Cody than his ranch. At this point, I'm afraid he's right. It makes me ill to think about it, but I see no alternative. So please promise me, Kara. Say you'll leave it alone until after we get Cody back. Then you and the sheriff can go after the kidnapper for all you're worth."

"I can't promise that, Jake. I'll do whatever the sheriff says," she responded, feeling helpless.

"Kara, I'm begging you," Jake pleaded in a voice full of sadness and despair. "It's the only chance we've got—the only chance Cody has of living. You've got to stay out of it. The sheriff is planning to leave it all alone today, I'm sure. So do I have your word?"

Kara was torn between her law enforcement duties and her concern for the Lind family. In addition, she liked and admired Jake, even cared a lot for him, she admitted to herself. Finally, she sighed, "Okay, but be careful, Jake."

"You know I will, and you won't regret it," Jake answered with obvious relief. "I have to come into town. So I'll stop by and see you in a little while. In the meantime, you get some more rest."

"I will. At least, I'll try."

* * *

While Deputy Kara Smith attempted to rest, Sheriff Vince Hanks faced a scowling Roscoe Norman. "I'm afraid there may not be much I can do here, Roscoe, except look for footprints or tire tracks. If you'd have gotten hold of me right when you saw the light, I might have been able to do some good."

"I tried, but your wife said you were unavailable," Roscoe complained.

"What time did you call?" the sheriff asked.

"Just after midnight," Roscoe replied. "I thought I told you that. You must have been out all night."

The sheriff nodded, but he knew why he'd missed the call. It had come in before Jake called about the latest note, and his wife had decided it was not important enough to disturb him. He didn't blame her, since he hadn't mentioned the boot prints to her.

"You'd've caught him this time, Sheriff," Roscoe said angrily.

The sheriff had started to walk toward the ditch, but he stopped and faced the old farmer. "Him? Did you actually see someone?"

"Nope, but I seen that light kind of waving around. It was over near the highway when I first seen it."

"You mean that what you saw was someone walking down the lane and into this area here?" the sheriff queried.

Roscoe shifted uneasily from one foot to the other.

"Well, is that what you saw?" the sheriff pressed.

"It was kinda like you say, Sheriff," Roscoe answered at last.

"What do you mean by that?"

"Well, you know, he was up there by the road. But he must've come down here. They always do."

Sheriff Hanks took a deep breath, exhaled, and then spoke slowly. "Roscoe, are you telling me that what you really saw was a light up on the highway, and that you just assumed that whoever was making it had been down here or was going to come down?"

"I—I don't know for sure, Sheriff. But he turned his car lights off."

"Car lights? You saw someone standing beside his car?"

"Yeah, that's what I been trying to tell you. When I tried to call you, the guy was by his car. Then, when I got in my truck an' started down here, he got in his car and left."

"Roscoe, you saw someone stop his car beside the road with a flashlight. He never left his car, or at least he didn't leave the immediate vicinity of his car as far as you know. Is that what you're telling me?"

"Well, yeah, but if you'd've come, I'd've stayed at the house, and you'd've caught him comin' down here huntin' my rabbits," Roscoe insisted.

"Let me make sure I have this straight. You did not see a light that was like the one you saw the other times you called?"

"No, not like them. It was somebody with a car, but why would they stop right up there at the end of my lane if they wasn't goin' to kill some of my rabbits?" Roscoe shouted.

"You don't have to holler at me," the sheriff said as he stepped back to his car. "And now you've wasted my time. I've got a lot to do. I don't have time to go chasing after every motorist who stops to change a tire or walk around to wake himself up if he's getting tired, or whatever was going on."

"Where you going, Sheriff?" Roscoe demanded.

"Back to work. I have a young man to find," the sheriff declared as he slammed his car door.

Then a thought occurred to him. What if the driver of that car had left the ransom note? He quickly rolled the car window down. "Mr. Norman," he called at Roscoe, who was storming toward his truck a few yards away.

Roscoe stopped, and the sheriff asked, "What did the car look like?"

"Don't know. It left when I started my truck up at the house."

Disappointed, the sheriff questioned, "Which way did it go?"

"Toward Harrisville," Roscoe grumbled.

"Thanks," the sheriff called, and then he backed his car around and headed for town.

CHAPTER 21

A hard knock on the door brought Kara to her feet from the sofa. "Anybody home?" an angry voice called out.

"I'm here," she answered as she swung the door wide to see Jake standing on her porch, fuming.

"I went to the bank to get the money for Kyle, but they wouldn't give it to me," he declared, his eyes flashing. "Kara, why did you hold out on me?"

Taken aback, she stammered, "Hold out? What do you mean?"

"You know exactly what I mean. Edgar Stevens's body turned up. He was murdered. You found him in a lake somewhere."

Kara nodded. So he knew. It couldn't be kept quiet forever, and he had a right to know. "I followed the sheriff's orders," she explained meekly. "Does Kyle know about Stevens, too?"

"He didn't when I left the ranch a little while ago."

"Jake, why are you so upset? I thought you didn't care for Edgar. None of us really liked him."

"That's true enough. It's not only that he's been killed that has me upset. It's that you knew, and you didn't even bother to tell me. I thought you'd tell me something that important. And anyway, Stevens's death changes everything—makes things a lot worse. As long as he was just missing, the bank was more than willing to lend Kyle another half million, but now that they know he's dead, they say it may be difficult. They're keeping a tight rein on all loans until they can get things under control again at the bank."

"I'm sorry, Jake, but Mr. Stevens is a murder victim. That's a terrible thing. And his death may have nothing to do with—"

"I'm sure it doesn't have anything to do with Cody's kidnapping," Jake agreed as he followed Kara into the house and slammed the door behind them. "But it sure messes things up for us . . . for the kid."

"Why, Jake? Because of the money?"

"Yes, because of the money! Everything hinges on the money." He sounded furious. "If the bank can't come through like they promised me, it's all over for Cody."

"The sheriff and I can do something," Kara stated, wondering what that might possibly be. She didn't blame Jake for being angry— she was angry too.

"Your boss has botched this thing from the beginning," he thundered, "but maybe there is something he can do to redeem himself with Kyle. That's why I came by. I stopped by his office, but they said he was out. I think he can convince the bank to let us have the money if he'll tell them it's the only way to save Cody's life. Will you find Sheriff Hanks for me and help me talk to him?"

"I will," she answered, "if you'll promise to keep your temper with him. If you talk to him the way you just talked to me, you won't get anywhere."

Jake's face softened. "Whatever you say. I'm sorry. I feel awful. I had no right to take my frustration out on you. I'll do whatever you say. We'll save Kyle's son yet."

"Do you really think so?"

"I have to think so. Yes, if we get the money, I'm sure we'll save his life," Jake replied.

"But Kyle will lose the ranch, won't he?"

"I'm afraid so. Although that creep Stevens would never have let on, Kyle had enough collateral in the ranch to more than cover the half million dollars demanded by the kidnapper. But old Stevens had the loan with Kyle written up so that he controlled Kyle's right to sell anything and could get the ranch if the payment was even a few days late. Now, the vice president says he will give us the money on two conditions."

"One is that the sheriff must convince him that it's the only way to save Cody?" Kara guessed.

"Yes, and the other is that he sign over the ranch. And Kyle is more than willing to do that, despite the pain it must cause him. So it's up to you to convince the sheriff. Let's find that boss of yours."

* * *

Sheriff Hanks sat at home eating breakfast when Kara called. "How are you feeling this morning?" he asked her.

"Much better," she reported. "How long before you go back to the office?"

"Not long. Do you feel well enough to meet me there?"

"I'm still sore, but I can do whatever I need to. We'll meet you as soon as you get there," she indicated.

"We?" he asked curiously.

"Yes, Jake is with me."

"Then you know about the note?"

"Yes. That's what we need to talk to you about."

"All right. I'll see you shortly."

"Was that Kara?" his wife asked when he turned from the phone.

"Yes."

"How is she this morning?"

"She's feeling better," he responded glumly.

"Dear, aren't you glad?"

"Of course, I'm glad. It's just that I have a feeling she's going to be working against me now instead of with me."

"Vince, why on earth do you say that? You've told me dozens of times what a good job she's doing."

"And she always has. The problem now is her sudden friendship with Jake Garrett. He seems to have quite a bit of influence over her. They seem to be getting rather fond of one another."

"Why is that bad?"

"Because Kyle and Jake Garrett are both determined to keep me from helping until they've given up the ranch and handed over the money to the kidnapper. And that's just plain foolish."

The sheriff told Jake and Kara the same thing a few minutes later, but they wouldn't listen to his reasoning. Jake spoke very little, but Kara tearfully begged the sheriff to go to the bank and help Jake get the money. The sheriff finally agreed reluctantly. He also decided he'd have to leave his young deputy out of his plans—to prevent the money from falling into the wrong hands.

* * *

At the bank, Sheriff Hanks wasn't surprised when the new acting president insisted that the money would not be available until late in the afternoon, and that Kyle would personally have to come in to sign some papers before he would turn the cash over to the rancher.

When the sheriff left the bank, Kyle, Jake, and Kara met him outside. Jake declared, "Now remember, Sheriff, that you are to be in your office from noon on, and it's ten minutes to twelve right now. Don't think I'm not grateful . . . that Kyle and I aren't grateful for what you just did in there, but now Kyle and I have to comply with the wishes of Cody's abductor."

"You're welcome, Jake. I just hope I didn't do you both a great disservice. I'm really not at all convinced that Cody will be returned alive after the kidnapper gets his greedy hands on Kyle's money," the sheriff said bitterly.

"But Sheriff, why shouldn't Cody be turned loose? All the kidnapper wants is my money," Kyle reasoned.

"Is it?" the sheriff questioned.

"Of course it is," Kara interjected. "What else could he possibly want?"

"The freedom to spend it, for one thing," the sheriff replied soberly.

"What do you . . . oh!" Kara's hand flew to her mouth.

"Don't be ridiculous, Kara. The sheriff is just trying to alarm us," Jake assured her.

"And he just succeeded . . . in alarming me, at least. If Cody knows who's been holding him, and he almost certainly does, then there's no way he'll be turned loose. It wouldn't be safe for his kidnapper!" she exclaimed.

The sheriff nodded, watching the growing alarm in Kyle Lind's eyes. Then Jake said, "I disagree with both of you, but there isn't time to argue now. Kyle and I need to get back to the ranch. We only have Agnes and the girls watching the phone, and if Buster calls and one of them answers, that could cause a problem. And yes, I do still think it's Buster. And he won't be spending the money around here. That's why I still believe the guy will turn Cody loose."

"Kyle, are you absolutely sure you want to do this?" the sheriff queried.

Kyle looked anything but sure, yet he nodded. "Jake and I have talked it over, and we need to do what we decided earlier. I can't see any other way."

A look passed between Jake and Kara, and she remarked, "I think we better let them try first, Sheriff. Then we can go after him."

"All right! Have it your way!" Sheriff Hanks growled in frustration. "Get on your way, and I'll go to the office and begin my helpless wait." He hoped they all bought his performance.

"Thanks, Sheriff," Kyle said quietly.

"I know it goes against your grain as a lawman, but we appreciate it," Jake added with confidence, and he and his uncle went their way as the sheriff stood and watched with growing concern and determination.

"I'll wait with you at the office," Kara stated gently after Jake's car was out of sight.

"No you won't, Kara. You go on home and take the rest of the day off," the sheriff ordered in a voice she had never heard before.

"Sheriff, please. Maybe something—"

But the sheriff ignored her and walked to his car, leaving her standing on the sidewalk. She would only hinder him now. And he was angry with Kara, with Kyle, and with Jake. Yet he could not really blame any of them. He had failed them all. Maybe with the help of Mariah and the chief he could change all that. He knew he had to try.

Back in the office, he checked with his secretary. "Have there been any messages while I was out?"

"Yes, several, but nothing important except this one," she reported, handing him a note.

"Thanks, I'll be in my office."

The sheriff didn't look at the note until he was sitting comfortably behind his desk, then he held it up and read. Immediately the blood drained from his face. He read it again. Feeling weak, he lifted the phone and buzzed his secretary. "What did Gil say when he called besides what you wrote here?"

"Nothing. He just asked for you, and when I told him you were out, but that he might be able to reach you on your cell phone, he said, 'Tell the sheriff he screwed up, and that I wash my hands of the blood of Cody Lind.'"

"Was it Gil's voice?"

"Yes. I'd know his voice anywhere. He didn't even attempt to disguise it."

"And he didn't leave a number where he could be reached?"

"No. He hung up before I could ask. There was a number on the caller ID. I tried it, but it just rang and rang. I checked with the phone company. It's a pay phone in Salt Lake."

* * *

Kara felt discouraged and guilty. She couldn't blame the sheriff for his anger toward her, but what could she do? She cared for Jake and for his uncle and cousins. Jake had persuaded her that what they were doing was their only option. And yet she wavered.

Although Kara wanted to feel justified in promising Jake she'd stay out of it until they had paid the ransom money, for some reason she didn't. Jake was a good man, but so was Sheriff Hanks. And the sheriff had a vast amount experience in law enforcement. Jake, for all his concern over Kyle and Cody, simply did not understand or appreciate the danger of the situation. And there was the matter of an oath she'd taken, and loyalty to the man she worked for.

Instead of convincing herself to stand behind Jake and keep her promise to him, Kara decided to help the sheriff. But was it too late? With a trembling hand she reached for the phone.

* * *

"Sheriff, Kara Smith is on the line," Sheriff Hanks's secretary announced.

"I wonder what she wants," he grumbled.

"She didn't say, but she sounds upset," the secretary stated reprovingly. She liked Kara, and the sheriff sensed that he was subtly being accused of treating her unfairly.

"Put her on," he ordered brusquely. "Hi, Deputy," he said. "What do you need?"

"Sheriff, I'm afraid I might have been wrong. I'm sorry."

"It's a little late to be sorry now."

"I'd like to help. May I?"

"No, I'm afraid not. You're too close to the family to be objective," the sheriff sighed.

"You have my word. I won't say anything to Jake. What are you going to do?"

"Who said I was going to do anything?"

"Well . . . I just know you," she replied. "I want to help, Sheriff. Please."

Sheriff Hanks couldn't take the chance of trusting Kara at this point. He knew that for him to help Cody, Kyle and Jake must not know about the simple plan he had already put into motion. As they spoke, a tap was being placed on Kyle's phone line.

"You can help by staying home," he declared. "I'm sorry, but that's how it is, Kara. You've become too personally involved."

"All right, but I'll be here if you need me," she muttered in an emotion-choked voice.

The sheriff would have responded, but he didn't trust his own voice, which was also suddenly filled with emotion. Sometimes he hated his job. He quietly replaced the receiver and dropped his head into his hands.

* * *

Several minutes earlier, a telephone call from Sheriff Hanks had spurred Mariah Taylor into action. She dressed quickly, getting ready to leave the safe haven of his sister's house. "I need your help," he'd said. "I don't dare take a chance on leaving the office, but would you mind coming in?"

"I'll be right there," she'd promised.

"Great. Have my sister drive you to town and over to my office."

Thirty minutes later, the English teacher from Harrisville High got in the car with the sheriff's sister, and another thirty minutes after that she entered Sheriff Hanks's office.

* * *

The sheriff kept busy while he waited for some officers and Mariah to arrive. He wished Kara was there, but he didn't know if he could trust her not to tell Jake Garrett and Kyle Lind about what they discussed. And Shawn was ill again, in the hospital with appendicitis. Other deputies across the county were standing by, but the sheriff had chosen not to have any of them drive in to Harrisville. He was awaiting the arrival of Deputy Phil Simmons and Chief Ron Worthlin when Mariah walked into his office.

"Hello, Mariah," he greeted. "Thank you so much for coming down. Would you have a seat, please?"

"Thank you, Sheriff. It's nice to be sitting here as an assistant instead of a suspect," she said somberly. "And what exactly do you need me to do?"

"I mostly just need to pick your brain," he answered as he leaned back in his chair and picked up a notebook from his desk.

As the sheriff studied his notes, he became so engrossed that he nearly forgot about Mariah. Something again nibbled fiercely at the fringes of his mind—something important, he was certain, but he could not quite grasp it. Uneasiness crept over him and it startled him when Mariah asked, "Do you always chew your pen, Sheriff? I'm constantly telling my students not to do that."

He grinned sheepishly. "I only chew it when I'm confused. And I'm thoroughly confused right now. There's something I'm missing that might clear this thing up before it's too late, but I don't know what it is."

At that moment, Chief Worthlin entered with Phil. "Sorry it took me so long," the chief said.

"What can we help you with?" Phil asked, looking questioningly at Miss Taylor.

"Sit down, gentlemen," Sheriff Hanks said. After they'd both taken a seat, he went on. "Something is going to happen tonight, and I have been warned off, both by the suspect and by Kyle and his nephew. Kyle is ready to pay up. He signed his ranch and home over to the bank this morning in order to get the money for the ransom."

"Kyle's lost his ranch?" Mariah asked with wide eyes. "He actually signed it away?"

"Well, sort of," the sheriff confessed. "That's what Jake and Kyle think, but I got to the bank ahead of them and fixed it. Kyle only loses the ranch if the money is actually lost . . . taken by the abductor."

"But he plans to hand it over to the kidnapper tonight," Mariah declared earnestly. "So it will be lost to Kyle."

"Yes, he and Jake do plan that, but I hope to prevent that from happening, or at least to be in a position to recover the money quickly. If the bank doesn't have its money back within two days, they—meaning Edgar Stevens's wife and daughter—own the ranch, house and all," the sheriff explained.

The intercom interrupted Mariah as she began to speak again. Sheriff Hanks waved her to silence and picked up the phone. "Sheriff, an officer from the Salt Lake City Police Department is on line one. He wants to talk to Chief Worthlin."

"I'll put him on," the sheriff replied. But before he punched the appropriate button, he said to the others, "Salt Lake PD. Maybe they've heard something about Ken Treman. It's for you, Chief."

Indeed, the caller informed Chief Worthlin that Treman had been located. After concluding his phone conversation, the chief explained that Treman lay in a hospital with a gunshot wound to the stomach. Although in serious condition, he was lucid and had spoken briefly with a pair of detectives. He wouldn't tell them who had shot him or why, but when he learned that he was the prime suspect in Edgar Stevens's murder, he adamantly denied any involvement.

"That's a surprise," Sheriff Hanks said sarcastically. "Surely they didn't think he'd confess."

"I'm sure they didn't, but like us, they hoped. But get this: Treman told them he knows who killed Edgar—that the same person tried to kill him, but he got away. Treman insists that he can't say who shot him because he thinks that person will come after him again. Even the promise of protection wouldn't loosen his lips. So we don't know much more than we did before, but I personally doubt that Treman is the killer. The shooter must still be out there."

"And that shooter may be involved in the abduction of Cody Lind, although we don't know that for sure," the sheriff added.

"Sounds like a lovely man," Mariah commented dryly.

"So who else could have killed Edgar? And with what motive?"

"Buster Ashton, because Stevens was fouling up his plans to gain a big ransom," the sheriff suggested. But that solution didn't feel right to him. Something wasn't adding up.

"Maybe, but something is bothering me, Sheriff," Mariah said thoughtfully.

"My thoughts exactly. I mean that something's bothering me too. What is it that you're thinking?" the sheriff asked.

"Nobody in this town but me knows Buster. At least, I think that's the case."

"You're right, as far as I've been able to learn," Sheriff Hanks affirmed.

"I know what I said about Buster earlier, when I was a suspect too . . ." Mariah began and then paused.

"Go on," the sheriff urged.

"Sheriff, tell me the truth. Do you still wonder if I had something to do with it?"

"Mariah, you've proven yourself to me," the sheriff declared with conviction. "If not, you wouldn't be here right now. And I'm taking the chance that you won't say anything to Kyle until we've wrapped this thing up."

"I already promised that I wouldn't, and I meant it," she responded soberly.

"Good. Now, I agree with what I think you were about to suggest. Buster was after you—not Kyle—for money. And he got it. He knows nothing about Cody. His pressing you was simply bad timing, and it threw us on the wrong trail early on. Is that what you think?"

She nodded. "Buster's a wretched man, and if he'd known about Kyle and thought he could pull off a kidnapping like someone else has done, he'd have done it. But as much as I despise him for what he did to me, and especially to Kara, I don't think he's the one who took Cody. And I also don't think he would have had any reason to kill Edgar Stevens. For that matter, I doubt that he even knew the man."

Phil was staring at Mariah with his mouth open. The sheriff noted the old deputy's expression and stated, "She's right, Phil . . . I think. Of course, at this point I can't be certain, but I believe we need to turn our thinking to several others, and we've got to be quick about it."

"Who do you suspect?" Chief Worthlin asked.

"Right now, I think it has to be one of four people. I'll list them. Then I want you to go over everything you know with me to see if anything falls into place. But we don't have much time, because a call or other communication could come in to Kyle Lind at any minute, and when it does, we'll have to act fast."

"But how will you know? I mean, the way they have you sequestered here in your office and all?" the chief wondered.

Sheriff Hanks smiled. "I have a tap on Kyle's phone, and it's tied into the dispatch center. It took some doing this morning, but it's done. Every call that comes in or goes out on Kyle's phone is being monitored as of thirty minutes ago."

"Okay," the chief began, "and who are the four? I assume one of them is Mr. Ken Treman."

"That's right, but if he is involved in the boy's abduction, I don't believe for a minute that he acted alone. If he was involved, it would have been in helping Edgar Stevens, who is suspect number two."

"But he's dead," Phil broke in. "And somebody shot Treman."

"That's a big concern, but it also points suspiciously to Edgar Stevens," the sheriff indicated.

"Oh, no," Mariah broke in. "If it was Edgar, with or without Treman's help—and with Edgar dead and Treman in the hospital refusing to talk—who would be calling Kyle to arrange to trade Cody for the money?"

"That is exactly what I've been wondering. That's why I'm worried, and that's why we've got to do some fast thinking. If it turns out that Ken Treman is the only one who knows where Cody Lind is, we've got to force him to tell us, and we can't waste a lot of time, especially if Treman's in as bad shape as they say he is. Of course, if Edgar and Treman abducted Cody, there won't be another call coming in about the ransom unless there's another person involved with them."

"Yes, and there would have to be, for we know that neither Edgar nor Treman could have put the note in the mailbox last night," Mariah Taylor astutely pointed out.

"You're right. So let's go on for a minute. The next man still on my list is Gil Enders," the sheriff revealed.

"Yes, big time," the chief agreed.

Sheriff Hanks sighed. "I'm just sick that I was so close to having him admit it to me. But when I tried to meet him like he insisted, I was late, and he was gone. If it is Gil, he may soon be calling Kyle. There's still another suspect, though—Sammy Shirts. He claims to have blackmailed Edgar because he thought Edgar was the kidnapper, but I'm not at all sure that he wasn't involved himself in some way, and that Treman wasn't actually hired by Edgar to get rid of Sammy."

Phil, who was experienced in law enforcement but lacking some of the more essential reasoning powers, threw his hands in the air and exclaimed, "We haven't got a chance! It could be any of them."

"That's right, or a combination of some of them, but we still have a chance, Phil," the sheriff clarified sharply. He wished Kara and Shawn were here instead of Phil, but that couldn't be helped. "Listen now, all of you. I'll go through everything we have to date as quickly as I can. Feel free to interrupt, any of you, if you have a thought. We'll begin with—"

Suddenly Sheriff Hanks knew. The idea he'd been struggling to define had just come sharply into focus.

"Oh my!" he exclaimed, slamming his hand against his forehead. "I've been so blind." He picked up the phone. "I've got to make some long-distance calls," he explained, and Mariah, Phil, and Chief Worthlin all stared at him as if he had just lost his mind. "I may be wrong, but I don't think so."

"Sheriff, it's past eight," Chief Worthlin noted.

"So it is. And we haven't heard from the kidnapper. Well, we can't give up. He's probably playing with Kyle's mind. He'll still call."

CHAPTER 22

Bridget Harrison was sitting at home, reading a book to try to get her mind off Cody, when her father called her to the phone.

When she answered, a muffled voice said, "Bridget?"

Her heart began to pound. "Yes, this is Bridget."

"You don't know who I am, but there is something you can do if you want to save the life of your precious Cody," the voice stated coolly.

Flooded with emotions, Bridget wanted to scream, to cry, to faint, and to demand that the caller identify himself, but all she could do was mumble meekly, "What?"

"Call that stupid sheriff. Tell him you know who took Cody."

"But I don't," she said, and the tears she'd been fighting for the past half hour began to flow.

"But I do," the voice declared.

"Who are you?" she demanded as her courage began to rally.

"I can't say."

He didn't need to. Bridget had just figured it out. Although his voice was muffled, he had called her enough times that she knew his voice well, even disguised. "Gil, I know it's you."

There was a long period of silence on the line, and she wondered if she'd just blown it for Cody. Tears blurred her vision, but eventually the voice returned. "Okay, so you know." It was no longer muffled. "I love you, Bridget," he revealed to her shock and dismay. "And I hate that rat Cody Lind."

Gil took Cody away! Bridget thought with a sinking stomach. *It's been Gil all along.*

Gil went on. "I hate him, but not enough to let him be killed. I swear, I didn't have anything to do with what happened after he left your place that night."

"Gil, what are you talking about?" Bridget demanded as hysteria threatened.

"I . . . I was following you and Cody and—"

"Gil Enders! How dare you?" she broke in. "That's horrible."

"I know. I'm sorry, Bridget, but I love you. I couldn't help myself. Anyway, I saw who got in Cody's car while he was at the door with you."

Bridget's knees buckled, and she sank to the floor with a moan, barely managing to keep her grip on the phone. "Gil, are you telling me the truth?" she managed to say after a moment.

"I swear it, Bridget. I've tried to tell the sheriff, but he keeps screwing things up, and the guy will kill me if he finds out what I know. I think he also had something to do with Edgar Stevens disappearing. I saw him at his house, too. After that happened, I got scared and ran. But you've got to help me, Bridget. Well, I mean, you've got to help Cody."

Bridget pulled herself together. She felt that Gil was telling her the truth, but she was terrified to learn the identity of the person he had seen that horrible night—or both of those nights. "Why don't you call the sheriff again?" she suggested.

"I don't dare. This guy might be listening or watching or find out somehow. Believe me, he's smart, and he has his ways," Gil said.

"Who has his ways? Tell me!" Bridget shouted. "And I'll tell the sheriff."

"Don't say where you heard it," Gil demanded. "You've got to promise me you'll never mention my name. If you don't promise, I won't tell you."

"I don't understand, Gil," she said fearfully.

"Promise, Bridget. I mean it. It's the only chance you have of saving Cody. I know you, Bridget, and if you promise, you'll keep your promise."

"I promise, Gil," she said quietly, not knowing whether she was lying.

"Thank you. My life is in your hands, Bridget. Now I'll tell you who it was." Bridget Harrison gripped the phone tightly and tried to keep from passing out as Gil revealed the name of the kidnapper.

* * *

As Kara drove herself crazy with worry, a knock came at the door. Eight o'clock, the time mentioned in the latest ransom note, had come and gone, and she hadn't heard anything. She rushed to open the door. "Jake!" she exclaimed. "What are you doing here?"

"I can't quit thinking about you," he said softly as he drew her into his arms. "And I feel so bad for getting angry with you earlier. I'm sorry."

"But what about Kyle? He needs you right now, doesn't he?" she asked, resisting his embrace and ignoring his apology.

"I think I was driving him crazy," Jake said. "After eight o'clock came and we hadn't heard from Buster, I got even more uptight than Kyle. I think I care about Cody as much as he does, although I don't know if that's true, because I've never had a son. And I think I care more about his losing the ranch, even though it's not mine. Anyway, he suggested that I go for a drive and try to calm down. He said the call would come, just later than we thought. So I left. And the only place I wanted to go was to see you. Maybe Buster will call while I'm gone. And it's probably for the best if he does, because I'm so upset I'm afraid I'd say something to blow the whole deal for Kyle."

"Oh, I don't think you'd do that," Kara commented as she finally freed herself from Jake's arms and stepped back.

"You don't know me," Jake replied. "I can get pretty fierce when I think someone has done something they shouldn't have."

"Can't we all?" she quipped.

"I'd like to wring Buster's neck, and it's not good to feel like that. But Kyle's right. We need to just hand over the money and get the boy back. I just wish he'd call and get it over with."

Taken aback by his intensity, Kara said, "You guys have been through so much. I hope it all works out the way you plan, but I have my doubts. There is nothing to guarantee that once the money changes hands, Cody will be released." She looked up at Jake's concerned face and immediately wished she had said something to reassure him instead of add to his worry. "Here, come in and sit down," she said soothingly. "I'll make us some smoothies and you can just sit down and relax for a minute."

She turned toward the kitchen, and Jake followed her, catching her around the waist as she reached up to open the cabinet where she kept the blender. "I thought you were going to relax on the couch!" Kara exclaimed, smiling, as he turned her around to face him.

"I came over here to be with you, not to take a nap," Jake reminded her softly. "And besides, holding you is the best way for me to relax." This time Kara leaned in for a quick kiss, before squirming free again. "Okay, okay, you can help me with the smoothies."

Reluctantly he let her go, and a few minutes later they were sipping strawberry smoothies on the sofa. Neither spoke, not wanting to spoil the feeling by talking about the awful kidnapping, which was never far from their minds. When they had finished their drinks, Jake put their glasses on the coffee table and then pulled her closer to him. Kara smiled and snuggled up against his shoulder. She had never felt so safe and comfortable as she did with his strong arms around her.

"You know something, Kara?" Jake whispered into her hair.

"Hmm?" She looked up into his warm eyes.

He planted a kiss on her forehead and breathed, "I think I'm falling in love with you."

A tingle went through Kara as he pulled her in for a long, meaningful kiss.

Finally pulling away, Kara said breathlessly, "I'd better go clean up in the kitchen." She needed time to think. But when she saw the disappointed look on his face as she picked up their glasses, she quickly added, "I won't be long."

As Kara washed the glasses and the blender, she smiled to herself. She couldn't believe this was actually happening. Jake Garrett was in love with her! And she'd almost, just almost, wanted to say those three little words back to him—those three little words meant only for the man of her dreams. But they'd known each other less than two weeks! She hardly knew anything about him. Still, she felt something different with Jake than she'd felt with anyone else she'd dated. *Yes, this could be it,* she thought. She grabbed a package of cookies and headed back for the small living room.

Jake had stretched out with his head on the back of the sofa, his feet propped up on her coffee table, his eyes closed. Kara stood there for a moment, quietly studying him. He was one attractive guy, but she realized that she didn't really know him. After watching his face for several moments, she slowly studied his reclining figure, stopping at his boots. She couldn't remember seeing this particular pair before. They were brown. She'd only seen him in a pair of black leather ones, some very expensive-looking alligator-skin boots, and the sturdy ones he used on the ranch—the ones he'd worn the day he'd helped her search the old homestead.

The soles of his boots faced her across the coffee table. Suddenly, she almost dropped the cookies she was holding. "What's the matter, Kara?" Jake asked as his eyes opened.

Kara's voice cracked as she answered, "I thought you might like some cookies. I didn't mean to disturb you."

"I wasn't asleep," he replied. "Did you think I was asleep?" He smiled tiredly.

"You looked like it. You don't have to eat these." She could scarcely keep her voice under control.

His dark eyes scanned her face and his eyebrows knit together as he pulled himself erect. "No, cookies sound great—thanks." He reached out and took two of them, popping one into his mouth. "You seem upset, Kara," he said with a full mouth.

"Oh, no, I'm fine," Kara lied. "I . . . uh . . . it just seems like you should be out there with Kyle right now. I'm sure he needs you."

"Are you saying you want me to leave?" He looked genuinely confused.

Jake pulled the offending boots from her coffee table and rose to his feet. He suddenly seemed taller, more intimidating than he had before. Kara wanted him to go. She moved toward the front door and opened it, and he followed her. "You're kicking me out?" he asked in apparent disbelief. "I just told you that I'm in love with you, and you're kicking me out?"

"I'm not kicking you out," Kara protested, making a heroic effort to keep fear from her voice. "I just think you need to be with Kyle and the girls instead of me. Later we can talk about us." That last remark was her attempt to disarm him. *I hope I never see him again,* she thought.

"Okay, so I'll go. But I'll be back," he said as he stepped through the door. He stopped and faced her from her porch. "And Kara, I meant what I said. I have to admit I expected a different reaction from you, but I guess it probably came as a big surprise. I want you to know, though, I still mean it. So we'll talk about it soon, okay?" He actually smiled then, but his smile only frightened her more now.

"Okay, soon. But after we find Cody." Kara wanted Jake out of her house, and she didn't want to say anything that might make him stay for even one more minute, so she added, "Here, take the cookies. Give some to the girls and Kyle if you'd like." She held the package out to him.

"Thanks," he replied awkwardly as he took the cookies. Then he looked at her. "So I'll see you soon." He attempted another smile.

"Good," Kara said, hoping she sounded sincere. "But first, you've got to go help save your cousin."

He paused. "It'll be great when this is all over. Great for both of us." Then he was gone.

In a matter of less than two weeks, feelings of deep affection had developed in Kara's heart for Jake Garrett. And they had died in a matter of seconds.

After Jake had gone, Kara shut the door and stared blindly at it. She moved toward her bedroom, feeling like she was in a trance. She reached onto the top shelf of her closet for her pistol.

* * *

Sheriff Hanks was on the phone again. He was well aware that it was already over thirty minutes past the eight o'clock deadline imposed by the latest ransom note. He'd just talked to a police chief in Arizona but had learned nothing. Maybe he was wrong again. As the sheriff tried to think who else he might call, he was interrupted by his secretary, who had just run down the hallway. "Sheriff," she called breathlessly from his door, "there's a call on line two. You'd better take it."

The sheriff took the call. "Sheriff, it's Yvonne Harrison, Bridget's mother. Something terrible has happened! You've got to come right over."

"That would be very difficult right now," he replied. "I'm right in the middle of something. Can't we talk on the phone?"

"Well, yes, but I'm frightened, and Bridget is scared to death."

"What happened?" the sheriff asked, realizing this was no ordinary phone call. Yvonne Harrison sounded terrified.

"I'd been to the store, and when I got home, Bridget was lying on the floor," she began.

The sheriff felt his stomach knot. "Is she okay?"

"Yes, but it's terrible, Sheriff. Gil Enders called her—"

"Gil!"

"Yes. He told her that he saw who took Cody."

The sheriff froze. Before Yvonne mentioned a name, he wondered now if he had been right after all. Cody Lind was in grave danger. When Yvonne spoke again, her words confirmed the sheriff's thoughts.

The intercom buzzed again. "Sheriff, Kara's on line one. She's . . . she's almost hysterical."

"Kara!" he almost shouted as he punched the line.

"Sheriff, I saw Jake's boot! It's not a pair I've seen him wear before. I've been so blind."

"Are you okay, Kara?"

"I'm frightened."

"Where is he now?"

"He just left. It's the boot from the ditch at Roscoe's! I'm so sorry. I—"

The sheriff cut her off. "Get over here right now, Kara. No, wait. I'll send someone to meet you. Lock your door. It'll be Phil. Don't let anyone else in." He dropped the receiver in place as he said, "Phil, get over to Kara's. Watch for Jake Garrett on your way and—"

"Why would I want to do that?" Phil interrupted with a puzzled expression on his face.

"Because he's a killer!" The sheriff thundered as he rose to his feet. "Make sure she gets here safely. Mariah, will you stay with her when she gets here? I've got to run. We've all been duped badly by one of the craftiest and most cold-blooded men there is. I just pray we're not too late. Chief, can you come and give me a hand? We're going to Kyle Lind's ranch."

Sheriff Hanks bounded out the door ahead of the rest, his heart racing.

* * *

Kara walked into the office a step ahead of Phil. "Where's the sheriff?" she asked as she paused at the secretary's door.

"He and the chief went to Kyle's place," the secretary explained.

"Hello, Kara," Mariah Taylor said from behind her.

"Hi, Mariah. What are you doing here?" she asked in surprise.

"The sheriff asked me to come in," Mariah said with a shrug. "I was going to help him, but now it looks like he doesn't need me anymore."

"I wish we had time to talk, but the sheriff had to go out to the Lind place. I suppose you know that. Anyway, that's where I'm going, too," Kara stated rapidly as she headed for the door she had entered just a moment ago.

"The sheriff said I was supposed to keep an eye on you," Mariah declared. "I guess you don't—"

"Come on," Kara suggested. "You can go with me. That way you'll be obeying the sheriff's order."

"I'd like that," Mariah responded, jogging to keep up with the deputy.

Kara had brought her patrol car from the house despite Phil's insistence that he was supposed to bring her. He objected again as he saw her leaving. "You can follow us if you want," she retorted tersely as she opened her car door and hopped in.

As soon as they were on the highway, Kara put the accelerator to the floor. "You'd better hang on," she warned the schoolteacher.

"Just hurry! I'm worried about Kyle," was Mariah's response.

It was a hot evening, and Kara adjusted the air conditioning with one hand while steering with the other. "I'm sorry about everything. I guess I kind of loused things up."

"No, you didn't. I don't know what more you could have done," Mariah said soothingly.

Kara glanced at her. She seemed sincere. "Thanks. You're a good friend," Kara remarked. "But I should have listened to Sheriff Hanks. He told me not to assume things, but I did. I assumed that Jake was what he said he was. I just learned a few minutes ago that he isn't. He came to my place and he was acting strange, and he frightened me. Then I saw his boots—a pair I haven't seen him wear before. I even argued about Jake with the sheriff earlier. But, Mariah, I didn't really know Jake. And oh, how right the sheriff was."

"I'm sorry it had to happen like this," Mariah sympathized.

"So am I," Kara sighed. "The fake Jake was a great guy. Too bad he wasn't real." She experienced a surge of hot anger. "I hope I get the chance to arrest him," she growled fiercely.

"You don't really," Mariah contradicted, shaking her head. "Anyway, the sheriff has already put out a bulletin for him to be arrested wherever he's found."

"You're right, I would rather not have to face him for a while. I'm not sure I could stand it. I hope someone will pick him up. Hey, he could be back at Kyle's! Surely Jake wouldn't leave without the money, and he's still got Cody somewhere. He may win yet." As she said it, a shiver of fear rushed down her spine.

* * *

Sheriff Hanks's patrol car came to a stop in a cloud of dust. Kyle Lind's yard appeared deserted, and the only yard light, over near the barn, flickered on. The sheriff realized it would soon be dark. With the chief on his heels, he jogged up the long walk to Kyle's house. When he knocked briskly, Agnes answered the door. Her eyes were red, but she smiled as she invited, "Come on in, Sheriff. Kyle's in the kitchen, sitting by the phone."

"Hello, Kyle," the sheriff greeted as he and the police chief entered the room.

Kyle's head was in his hands, his eyes on the table below him, and he looked up slowly. Candi stepped to his side, and she spoke first. "I thought you were going to stay in your office."

"Yes, isn't that what the note told you to do? Please, Sheriff," Kyle begged, "don't make things worse. Please."

"Kyle, it's way past eight now. Things have changed."

"Not really," the rancher answered. "We still haven't had a call, but it will be coming any minute, I'm sure. You shouldn't be here."

"That's what Jake Garrett said," Sheriff Hanks remarked sarcastically.

"Yes, and he's right."

"Is he really?"

The rancher flared. "He's my nephew, Sheriff. And he's a bright young man. He'll be very upset to see you here when he gets back from town."

"Jake had to go again," Candi added. "He was here for a few minutes, but he left a little while ago. He said he wouldn't be too long. We need him here. I wish he hadn't gone."

Her chin quivered, and the sheriff reached out and lightly touched her arm as he thought about Jake. One thing he was sure of, and that was that Jake hadn't passed him as he was coming out from town. But he didn't mention that. Instead he questioned, "Candi, are you saying that he was here in the last few minutes?"

"Yes. He's really upset, but he said he had to go to town again. I don't know what he forgot. But he'll be right back. He left just a few minutes after Dr. Odell did."

"Dr. Odell?" Sheriff Hanks said.

"Yes. He came out to see how Dad was holding up," Candi explained. "Dad told him what was happening, and in a few minutes he left. I think he felt bad. We weren't very good to him, I'm afraid."

The sheriff shook his head. "We can't worry about the doctor's feelings right now. He'll get over it. Kyle, where is the money you got from the bank to pay the ransom for Cody?"

"Why do you want to know?" Kyle asked with a touch of hostility. "I'm not letting you take it, if that's what you have in mind. It goes to Buster. I want my son back."

"Buster didn't kidnap your son, Kyle," the sheriff said quietly.

"He didn't?" Candi asked in surprise.

"He didn't."

"Well, if he didn't do it, the money goes to whoever it is," Kyle insisted as he eyed the sheriff with suspicion.

"Kyle, do you have the money?" the sheriff queried sharply.

"Of course, I do."

"Where is it?" he asked in a voice that left no room for argument.

"It's in the trunk of my car, ready to go when we get the call," Kyle replied. "At least, half of it is."

"Dad! Where's the rest of it?" Candi cried.

"I took it. I thought that just in case the kidnapper didn't count it, we would at least have something to begin to rebuild with, me and you, Cody, and your little sisters," he explained, his sad, tired eyes pleading for his daughter's understanding.

Candi nodded, and the sheriff started to heave a sigh of relief but stopped himself. "Does Jake know you hid part of the money?"

"No, I decided to take it out when he was in town. I was going to tell him when he got back, but he was here for only a minute or two before he left again. He left in a hurry, so I didn't get a chance to tell him."

The sheriff stood thoughtfully for a moment before saying, "I think we should look in the trunk of your car and see if it's still there."

"Of course, it is," Kyle protested. "It hasn't been an hour since I saw it. Who would have taken it?"

"Jake," the sheriff replied evenly.

That brought Kyle to his feet in a rage. "Of all the rotten things to say, Sheriff! He's family, you know. He wouldn't—"

"Let's go see," the sheriff interrupted forcefully.

"Do you know something we don't?" Candi asked suspiciously.

"Yes, I do," Sheriff Hanks said firmly. They started through the house. "Jake visited Deputy Smith a while ago, and—"

"I think he's in love with her," Candi broke in.

"No, he's not," the sheriff replied with disgust. "He was using her, just like he's using all of you."

"Sheriff, I won't stand for it!" Kyle thundered, coming to a stop and turning to face the sheriff, his fists clenched threateningly.

The police chief stepped between them and suggested calmly, "Kyle, let's just do like the sheriff suggests."

"Dad, please," Candi begged. "Let's go look in the car."

Kyle shook his head like an angry bull, glared at the sheriff, glared at Chief Worthlin, and then led the way outside. At the car he hesitated and finally reached into his pocket for the keys. He fumbled around for a minute, then admitted, "I seem to have misplaced my keys."

"Dad, I saw them on the table in the kitchen earlier. I'll go get them," Candi offered, taking off at a run.

"Hold it," Sheriff Hanks called out. "They weren't there just now. I'm sure of it."

"Then I'll get mine," Candi called over her shoulder and continued running. She was back in a flash. "You were right, Sheriff," she said, breathing rapidly. "Dad's keys weren't there." She jammed her own key into the lock and jerked open the trunk of her father's car. "Dad!" she exclaimed. "It's gone! The money's gone!"

"It can't be!" Kyle burst out as he stepped closer. "It is," he admitted after staring blankly at the empty trunk for several seconds. He turned to the sheriff, his face ashen and his eyes suddenly hollow. "It was in an old briefcase. He . . . uh . . . Jake must have taken my keys."

"And your money. He'll be angry when he finds it's not all there," the sheriff muttered as the sound of an approaching car caught his attention.

"It's Kara," Chief Worthlin remarked.

Nothing more was said until Kara stopped her car. Mariah hopped out and ran to Kyle. He stepped back, startled. But she said, "It's okay, Kyle. The sheriff believes me."

Kyle stared and said nothing to her, addressing the sheriff instead. "So, did Jake take Cody?" he asked in almost a whisper.

"It appears that way. You see, Kyle, I got to thinking when I couldn't get things to add up. I'm just sorry I was so slow, but Jake fooled me, just like he did the rest of you."

"But he's my sister's boy," Kyle mumbled.

Mariah took Kyle's arm. "But you didn't really know much about him, only what he told you."

"That's right, Kyle," the sheriff agreed. "There must be some anger in him from something that's happened in the past."

"Like what, Sheriff?" he asked, looking at him imploringly. "He was never anything but helpful when he was visiting us."

"I honestly don't know what it could be. I was hoping you would," the sheriff declared.

"Maybe . . ." Kyle began.

"Maybe what?" Sheriff Hanks pressed.

"Maybe he thought that half of this place should have been my sister's, meaning that after her death, that half should have been his."

"That could explain it," the sheriff affirmed.

"He may not even know that his mother didn't want it. She said I should have it all, that the ranch shouldn't be broken up," Kyle explained. "And I did send her money until she was killed in a car wreck, even though she protested. But he may not have known any of that."

"Cody! What about Cody?" Candi suddenly asked in alarm.

"We don't know where he is," the sheriff sighed, turning toward her. "But we've got to do some serious thinking about—"

"Roscoe's place," Kara interrupted. "The boot print in the ditch. Remember, it matched the boot Jake was wearing today. That's what gave him away. It had a big nick in the sole, just like the print at Roscoe's. But I searched out there and—" Her face suddenly blanched. "Jake—he helped. Oh, no!"

"What do you mean, he helped you?" the sheriff replied with a gasp and then a sigh. "Well, he could have made sure you didn't look in the right place. Let's get out there, just in case Jake hasn't moved him." He didn't dare say what he was thinking—that Cody might well be dead. "Kyle, you'd better come too."

"Of course!" Kyle exclaimed with more energy than he had displayed in days.

Phil had arrived shortly behind Kara, and the sheriff turned to him. "Phil, take Agnes, Mariah, and the girls to headquarters, just in case Jake comes back looking for the rest of the money. Stay with them and make sure no one comes into the office. Kara, you watch Kyle's place from that hill over there," he ordered, pointing to the hill that overlooked the ranch from the south. "Stay out of sight, but watch for Jake. If he comes, give us a call. Don't try to arrest him by yourself."

Kara nodded even as a huge knot formed in her stomach. "I'll head over there as soon as you leave. Sheriff, I'm sorry that I let Jake help me search the old homestead, and that I didn't tell you right away."

Sheriff Hanks stated brusquely, "Kara, you went against policy, but we can't cry over it now." Then he spoke again to Kyle. "Get the rest of the money from the house. We'll take it with us."

"But we may need it," Kyle disagreed, shaking his head. "That may still be the only way we get my son back."

The sheriff didn't argue. He simply explained that the money was safer with them than in the house. Kyle listened, and then without another word he went after the quarter of a million dollars he had hidden in the house.

Mariah turned to the sheriff and said, "I'd like to go with you. After all, you asked me to help."

A weary smile creased the sheriff's face. "That was before things took such an unexpected turn. But I guess you're right—I did ask you to help." He turned to Kara and asked, "When you and Jake searched out there at Roscoe's, where did Jake look that you didn't?"

"He searched over toward that old cellar and the outhouse," she answered. "He volunteered to cover that area. Now I wonder about that flashlight he says he found."

"So do I," the sheriff stated. "Those are bright little lights. It seems like half the town must have bought one from Harry."

"I didn't," Kara said with a weak smile.

Kyle could barely see the beginnings of her smile since they were standing on the outer fringes of the area covered by the yard light. But he could tell she was trying to lighten the atmosphere oppressing all of them. "I didn't either," he said gently to let Kara know he recognized her willingness to help.

"I did," Mariah indicated, and she opened her purse and produced one. "I brought it with me. I didn't know what you were going to have me do tonight, Sheriff. But I brought it just in case it got dark. And it is."

Phil arrived with Agnes and the Lind girls and immediately headed for Harrisville with them. A moment later, Kyle rejoined Mariah and the law enforcement officers. "Let's get moving," the sheriff ordered. "And remember, Kara, don't try to arrest Jake by yourself. Call us for help if he comes back."

Kara turned and headed for the hill that the sheriff had pointed out earlier. Only a short distance from the corrals—with just one small pasture between them—the hill was surrounded by alfalfa fields. Several big cottonwood trees grew at the base of the hill, and there were quite a number of juniper trees on top of it. She could easily conceal herself there.

The sheriff, the police chief, Kyle, and Mariah got into the sheriff's car and started for the highway. A few minutes later, they arrived at the old homestead. When they had all piled out of the vehicle, Chief Worthlin spoke first. "At least Jake isn't here."

"I didn't really think he would be," Sheriff Hanks replied. "Until he discovers that half the money is gone, he'll be on the road trying to put as much distance between us and him as possible." As he looked over the quiet landscape, he asked, "Now, where is that cellar Kara was saying that Jake searched?"

Suddenly, Kyle shouted, "Look, Vince! Isn't that a light shining up from over there?"

The sheriff looked in the direction he pointed. The light was dim, but it was shining straight into the air. "A rigid light," he said in astonishment. *Just like old Roscoe claimed,* he thought, as he reached back in his car and grabbed his flashlight. "Come on!"

The others eagerly followed the sheriff as he leaped over the ditch, ran down the old stone walk, and located the cellar. The door, cracked and gray with age, lay almost horizontal over what he knew would be a stairway. With one hand, Sheriff Hanks grabbed the door and flung it to the side, wrenching it from its rusty hinges.

As his flashlight hit them, the rotting wooden steps showed distinctly where the years' accumulation of dust had been disturbed. With a prayer of hope in his heart, the sheriff started down. A spiderweb brushed his face and a rat scurried past him, up the stairs and out into the weeds.

He continued down. At the bottom of the stairs was another door, heavily insulated, but sagging on its ancient hinges. As he shoved it open, a shower of dust fell on his head. Brushing it off, he stepped through the doorway, his light shining ahead of him. The stench that assailed him was nauseating, reminding him of an overused outhouse.

Lying in the far corner was a dirty bundle of rags. They stirred. "Cody?" the sheriff called hopefully.

A faint moan accompanied a slight movement of the pile. A hand moved, and a small, very dim flashlight dropped from the hand. "He's in here!" the sheriff shouted. "And he's alive!"

Kyle bounded down the stairs, and in an instant he was cradling his son in his arms. Tears washed his face as he lifted the weak boy and backed toward the stairs. He had gone only a few feet before a chain, fastened to the boy's leg, jerked them both back.

"Put him down," the sheriff instructed as he fumbled to examine Cody's ankles. The boy was shackled with a stout pair of steel leg irons, the kind the sheriff occasionally used on his prisoners. A chain was padlocked to the leg irons, which was wrapped around a thick post that still bore the weight of the cellar's ancient beam and roof.

Using one of his own handcuff keys, it took the sheriff only a minute to unlock the leg irons. Then Kyle carried his son through the door and up the stairs. Cody's eyes were closed, and his clothes, which the sheriff had at first glance mistaken for rags, were filthy and damp. The acrid smell coming from him was almost overpowering. But his father seemed not to notice as he carried him to the patrol car and laid him gently on the backseat. The young man was thin, his flesh almost hanging from his bones. Where the irons had encircled his ankles, the skin had been rubbed raw and was obviously infected. Cody was so weak he couldn't speak other than to mumble faintly.

"It was Jake," were the only words the sheriff was able to make out.

Not until Cody was whisked away in an ambulance thirty minutes later, accompanied by Kyle and Mariah, did the sheriff venture into the cellar again. "He was lying right there," he said to Chief Worthlin as he pointed with his flashlight beam.

"I can't believe he's still alive," the chief murmured in amazement. "It's so smelly, so dark, so cold in here."

"Looks like he had a little to eat, at least for the first few days," the sheriff noted. The beam from his flashlight illuminated a pile of garbage containing wrappings from a variety of fast-food and junk food.

"And here are a couple of empty canteens," the chief pointed out.

"Even had a toilet," the sheriff ventured, directing his light toward a bucket full of a foul-smelling sludge. "I think Jake must have planned to keep Cody here just a short time, but apparently when it took longer than he'd intended, he made no effort to replenish the boy's supplies."

The sheriff picked up the small flashlight that Cody had dropped when they found him. "Shut off your light," he directed the police chief as he did the same. He then looked up. Through a small, rusty, tin chimney pipe located directly above where Cody had been lying, the sheriff could see the stars.

"Hey, is somebody down there?" a gruff voice called. Then the door burst open and a beam of light illuminated the two officers.

"Roscoe," the sheriff called.

"What are you doing on my place?" the old farmer demanded.

"Solving the mystery of your rigid light," Vince responded lightly.

"What do you mean?" Roscoe demanded.

"Cody Lind, the boy who was taken by a kidnapper over ten days ago, has been in here all along. He's still alive, but barely. He must have used this little flashlight at first, probably trying to attract attention by shining it up through this old stovepipe above me," the sheriff explained.

"That's the vent pipe," Roscoe stated, seemingly unmoved by the amazing story he had just been told. "All these old cellars have 'em."

Outside a little later, the sheriff turned to Roscoe. "We'll need to take a few photos here, you know, for evidence, and then we'll leave you alone. I think you won't have to worry about trespassers or rigid lights after this."

CHAPTER 23

Shivering as the temperature fell, Kara sat under a large juniper tree about halfway up the hill. Though it was a dark, moonless night, she could see Kyle's yard and the fields that extended to the highway nearly three-quarters of a mile away. She prayed the Lord would help them find Cody. Knowing that they needed to check the old homestead again, she prayed that if Jake had hidden Cody there, he hadn't moved him in the past few hours.

Kara's thoughts kept reverting to Jake and how foolish she'd been to fall for him when she really didn't know him. She hadn't even discussed the Church with him! She couldn't believe it now, but she'd just assumed he had the same values she did, since Kyle and his children were active Church members. Of course, now she knew he couldn't possibly have a testimony of the gospel. She'd just let herself be swept away by his good looks and masculine charm. But then she thought, *What girl wouldn't have been attracted to Jake and enjoyed his attention?* That thought, however, didn't comfort her.

Something brushed against Kara's leg and she jumped to her feet in alarm. She wondered if it was a rat—and she was deathly afraid of rats. When she realized it was just a cat, she settled down again and stroked its soft back.

Suddenly, she remembered another rat. When Jake had said there was a rat in the old cellar, she hadn't even considered going in the place, but she'd seen him shut the door after—after doing what? Looking inside? Going in himself? Come to think of it, she hadn't actually seen him open the door all the way and go in. *Maybe he didn't go in at all. Maybe he just didn't want* me *to go in.* She groaned.

Was there ever a rat at all? Grabbing her cell phone, she dialed the sheriff's cell number. When he answered, she practically whispered, "Sheriff, I know where Cody might be. The old cellar. Jake—"

"We found Cody there already," the sheriff cut in. "He's alive, and he's on his way to the hospital. I'll fill you in later. The chief and I are just talking to Roscoe. Have you seen anything of Jake?"

"No," she reported. "But I'll keep watching."

Kara shut her cell phone, put it carefully back in her pocket, and gazed over the Lind ranch. It seemed deserted and still, except for the occasional bawling of a calf, the neighing of a horse, and other normal ranch sounds. A few cars passed on the highway to the north.

Elated that Cody Lind was alive and would recover, Kara was also sad that Jake had stooped to such depravity as to kidnap his own cousin. Deep in thought, she stared at the darkness that extended beyond the hill where she sat, broken only by the single yard light between the house and barn. Suddenly, she caught a quick glimpse of a light between the highway and the house and yards. *Someone was coming through the field from the road!*

Jake!

It had to be him. He must have noticed that he had been short-changed and decided to come back for the rest of the money. Kara shook her head sadly. What a fool he was! If he'd been content with what he'd already stolen, he might have gotten away with it. After a quick call on her cell phone to alert the sheriff that Jake was approaching the house, Kara made sure the phone was on vibrate, shoved it in a pocket of her jeans, and began creeping down the hill. Still very sore from her ordeal in Mariah's car, she moved slowly to keep from stumbling. Without using her flashlight, she had only the stars to light her way.

Kara thought she heard a rock roll behind her, and she stopped, statue-like, to listen for a moment. She thought she heard something moving over the rocky hillside through the trees above her, and her heart rate quickened. But when she looked back and saw nothing, she decided it must be an animal, maybe a deer, and she moved on. Again she heard the sound behind her. It wasn't close, but in the stillness of the night sounds carried clearly and were amplified. She moved more quickly, trying to ignore whatever it was—she had to focus on Jake as he came closer to the yard. Reaching the bottom of the hill, Kara climbed carefully through the barbed-wire fence that bordered the small pasture and dashed through the short grass to the far side, where she had to crawl beneath a section of wheel line. Then she approached the next fence, where she paused, scanning the yard ahead for any sign of Jake.

Suddenly he appeared in the outer fringes of the glow cast by the yard light. He stood tall and was dressed in dark clothing, as he had been earlier that evening at her home. Her knees felt weak, and perspiration broke out on her face and palms. Telling herself to be calm, she took several deep breaths of the sweet night air.

Kara watched as Jake pointed his hand toward the big light. Even at this distance, she knew he held a gun. A split second of bright orange light erupted from the barrel, and the yard was plunged into darkness. She hadn't heard a shot, which could only mean his gun had a silencer on it. Shivering with fear, she took another deep breath and began to climb through the fence in the darkness. She snagged her jacket and felt it rip as she forced her way through. Moving even more slowly now, she crept toward the corrals.

A few moments later Kara stopped to verify Jake's location. He entered the house, using his flashlight only occasionally. She skirted the corrals and watched as Jake's flashlight lit a window from inside, and then she dashed to a big poplar tree at the edge of the yard. Although Kara carried her flashlight in one hand, she didn't dare turn it on.

While she wanted to enter the house and confront Jake, she remembered that the sheriff had ordered her not to attempt to arrest him on her own. Anyway, she knew the sheriff and Chief Worthlin were on their way. *They should be here any time now,* Kara told herself. She crossed the fence into Kyle's yard and took refuge behind the trunk of another large poplar tree. Then she waited.

After a few minutes she heard a mumbling voice as the door opened, and Jake Garrett, his flashlight in his hand, came out. He headed up the sidewalk rapidly, still murmuring to himself. Kara silently moved from behind the tree, determined to keep him in sight until the sheriff and chief arrived to back her up.

Headlights turned from the highway and onto Kyle's lane, stopping Jake in his tracks. Then he turned and began to run—straight at

Kara. Impulsively, she switched on her flashlight, blinding him momentarily. In her right hand she held her pistol. Jake stopped when she yelled at him. "It's me, Jake. Don't give me an excuse to shoot you."

He laughed—a strange, unfamiliar laugh. Kara noted the handgun in his grip. "You won't shoot me," he stated. "I'm your future."

"Your future is the rest of your life behind bars," Kara answered derisively, wondering why his voice, like his laugh, didn't sound quite right. It frightened her. *I never really knew him,* she thought.

"Now, my dear Kara," he started as he glanced back at the head-lights that were rapidly approaching, "you need only step aside so I can pass on by and make my escape."

"You know better than that, Jake. You're under arrest for murder and for kidnapping," she declared.

"Lower your pistol, my love, and step aside," he repeated. "I don't want to have to kill you."

"You're sick," Kara said.

"Lower your gun," Jake ordered. "I'll use mine if I have to. I know you won't use yours."

Kara trembled but tried to keep control of her hand on her gun. Jake's voice definitely sounded strange, strained perhaps. Maybe he was as frightened as she was, thinking that she might accidentally discharge her weapon. It seemed to be taking forever for the sheriff to make it up the long lane, even though she knew he must be driving recklessly fast. Somehow she had to stall Jake. The last thing she wanted was to have to shoot him.

"Jake, you'll never get away. The sheriff is almost here," Kara told him, her voice surprisingly strong.

"I'll bury you both," Jake said, his voice as cold as an arctic wind. "Now drop your gun. I won't tell you again." He raised his arm and aimed directly at her.

"Jake, it doesn't have to end this way," she sighed as she began to apply pressure to the trigger of her pistol. Suddenly, a flash erupted from Jake's gun, accompanied by a slight popping sound. She felt the thud of the bullet as it hit her in the center of her chest. Simultaneously, she heard the report of another gun from somewhere nearby. Kara flew backward into the poplar tree she'd hidden behind only a minute before, then bounced off it and began to fall forward. As her flashlight flew from her hand, she thought she saw Jake falling too, but she caught only a fleeting image before she hit the ground face-first.

* * *

Sheriff Hanks drove as fast as he dared—much faster than he would under normal circumstances—praying that Kara still had the kidnapper under surveillance and that they'd be able to take him into custody. He'd seen the yard light go out from the highway. "He just shot the light out," the chief had commented.

While driving up the nearly half-mile-long lane toward the darkness of Kyle's yard, the sheriff saw a beam from a flashlight and wondered what was happening. He hoped desperately that Kara wasn't trying to make the arrest by herself. His stomach began to tighten and his hands gripped the steering wheel tighter, as if that would somehow speed up the vehicle. Then he saw a flash of flame as it spouted from the barrel of a gun, followed only moments later by another flash with a distinct bang right behind it. The second shot had appeared from somewhere near the barn. Sheriff Hanks let out a wild cry, recklessly ramming the accelerator to the floor.

"Look out!" Chief Worthlin shouted as a large deer suddenly jumped directly into their path.

The sheriff jammed on his brakes, but there was no way to avoid hitting the animal. When his car struck it, the deer flew onto the hood and shattered the windshield. As he instinctively ducked to avoid the flying glass, the patrol car skidded sideways, off the road, and into the fence.

* * *

Kara was aware of someone coming toward her, and she tried to crawl away, but any kind of movement caused agonizing pain in her chest. Her flashlight was still on, but it now lay several feet away from her, and she didn't know where her pistol was. "Kara, are you all right? I'm sorry I was too slow. Oh, Kara."

She heard Jake's voice, but he didn't make sense. She thought she'd seen him fall, but now she wasn't sure. She'd heard a gunshot from somewhere near the barn, but she hadn't seen the sheriff and chief arrive.

Kara struggled to crawl faster toward her flashlight, but before she could reach it, someone's hands reached out, and strong arms turned her over and set her gently down on the grass. She struggled to get away, but the arms held her tightly. "Sit still," Jake Garrett begged. "You've been shot. You're hurt. Let me help you."

"Get away," she gasped.

"Kara, I love you," Jake cried. "Please let me help you! I can't let you die."

Her flashlight, from where it lay only a few feet away, furnished enough light to enable Kara to see an outline of the face so near her own. "Kara, it's me, Jake. You're no longer in danger. I shot whoever was threatening you. Please, quit struggling and tell me that you'll be okay."

Kara quit struggling, but her mind seemed incapable of reasoning. She was so confused. First Jake had shot her, and now he was saying he loved her and wanted her to be okay. And he was even saying he had shot whoever had shot her. And that couldn't be, for he'd shot her, and he certainly wouldn't have shot himself.

As her thoughts tumbled over each other, she heard Jake's voice again. This time it was coming from several feet away and it sounded strange, as it had just before he'd shot her. "You didn't do much damage to me," the voice from the darkness said. "Now, we have unfinished business."

Kara's head began to clear. *There are two Jakes. Only that isn't possible, so one is an imposter and a very good actor. But which one is which?* she asked herself.

The one who had been shot came closer and demanded, "Jake, tell me where the rest of the money is."

That voice, though it sounded like Jake, was strained, just as she'd thought earlier. And in that instant she knew why. It wasn't Jake's! The real Jake was holding her.

"Who are you?" Jake asked the imposter.

"I'm *you*," came the answer. "At least, some people believe I'm you, most important among them, Sheriff Hanks."

"But why?" Kara spoke up. "Why are you doing this?"

"Because Jake's dear departed mother helped Kyle get a date with Ellen. And then she wouldn't go out with me after that. Kyle stole Ellen from me. And then, to make matters worse, he did it again."

"Did what again?" Jake demanded, suddenly recognizing the voice. "Ellen is dead, Dr. Odell. You know that. You signed her death certificate."

"That I did," the voice from the darkness agreed. "And it was a sad day. I'd always hoped that someday she'd leave Kyle and come back to me. She was too young to die. I tried to save her, but I couldn't."

The doctor dropped the charade and continued in his own voice. "And if it wasn't enough that Kyle, with your mother's help, stole one woman from me, he had to go and do it again."

Kara could hardly believe what she was hearing. The evidence had pointed so clearly at Jake. She had seen him—the real Jake—wearing the kidnapper's boots. But it was very clear now that somehow the evidence had misled her. And now she and Jake were practically face to face with the real criminal. Kara was also painfully aware that her flashlight, from where it lay on the ground, was providing the only light there was. If she could somehow get to it and shut it off, she and Jake might be able to get away from Dr. Odell in the darkness before he shot them both. She struggled, and Jake let his grip on her loosen. She began to slowly edge away, counting on the darkness to keep her hidden.

As she did, Jake spoke again. "Who did he take away this time?" he queried, apparently playing for time.

"Mariah Taylor. She actually went out with me, not once, but three times. We were a perfect match, and she was beginning to like me. Then along comes Kyle, even though the dirt has hardly settled on his wife's grave, and steals her away, too. That was just too much. Now he's paid for what he did to me. But I've been shorted half my money. And you, Jake, must know where it is. Get it for me, or I'll kill your little cop girlfriend. And this time, I'll know not to shoot her where she's wearing a bulletproof vest."

Now that they knew his identity, Kara knew Odell wouldn't leave either one of them alive. But they had to buy some time. She continued to wriggle her way toward the flashlight. Suddenly, Dr. Odell fired his gun, and the bullet threw up dirt and grass directly in front of the flashlight. "That's far enough, Deputy Smith," he said. "Now, both of you get on your feet."

"I don't know where the other half of the money is," Jake finally answered. "Remember, Kyle thought you were me. He thought he was keeping me from getting all the money tonight."

"Ah, yes, that's right," Dr. Odell snarled. "But surely you know where he might have hidden it. You could help me look in the house again."

"I'll do that, if I can," Jake agreed. "But what happens if I don't find it?"

"Then you'll call Kyle, wherever he is, and tell him that you have Kara Smith, and that you'll kill her if he doesn't give the rest of the money to you," Dr. Odell instructed fiercely.

As Dr. Odell continued speaking in his own voice, Kara thought she'd never heard one more devoid of human feeling, and she was shocked. Dr. Odell—the physician, the healer—had always seemed like such a good, caring man. "Get up, both of you!" he ordered again. "And don't you try to get your gun out, Jake. I know it must be on you somewhere."

Kara then realized that Jake had told the truth—he had shot Dr. Odell, although clearly the doctor must not be seriously injured. "Move slowly as you get up," Dr. Odell directed. "I'll want the gun before the three of us go back in that house to look for Kyle's money."

Kara knew they wouldn't find the missing quarter of a million dollars, because she had seen Sheriff Hanks put it in his car. She wasn't about to share that tidbit of information with Dr. Odell, however, knowing it would ensure a bullet through each of them immediately. Time was on their side for the moment, but Kara wondered again where the sheriff and police cheif were; she knew they should have been there by now. With Jake's help, Kara rose painfully to her feet, and as soon as she had her balance she glanced up the lane. It was dark. Something must have delayed the sheriff and Chief Worthlin. She and Jake were on their own.

"Good. Now move back from the flashlight. I'll be needing it," the doctor stated with venom. "I'm not sure where mine landed when you shot me. And both of you, raise your hands. Now! No more games!"

Kara glanced at Jake. His hands shot up, and she followed suit, although she raised them gingerly because of her injuries. Her vest had done its job and the bullet had failed to penetrate, but it had still struck with such force that her whole chest throbbed.

"Now, get moving over to your right so I can pick up that light," Dr. Odell ordered.

"Where's Cody?" Jake asked. "I'm not moving an inch until you tell us where he is."

"What difference does that make?" Dr. Odell quipped unfeelingly.

"A lot," Jake replied harshly. "He's an innocent boy. You can't let him die."

"Who said he isn't already dead?" the doctor questioned with a hearty laugh.

"So help me—" Jake began angrily.

Kara spoke up, afraid that Jake might do something foolish and provoke Dr. Odell into shooting them. "It's okay, Jake. The sheriff found Cody, and he's alive. He's on his way to the hospital, but he'll be fine."

"Where was he?" Jake asked with obvious relief.

"In the old root cellar at Roscoe's place."

"Yes, so he was," Dr. Odell said. "Roscoe's son and I used to play there when I was a kid. The rats and spiders didn't bother me. Cody, though—he didn't like them. But I suppose by now he's gotten used to them. Course, he thinks it was his cousin, Jake Garrett, that put him there." He laughed—but he laughed alone.

The doctor's voice held no trace of remorse. "Enough stalling. Now move over there so I can get that flashlight, and I'm not telling you again!" he barked.

Kara began to shuffle, but Jake stood firmly, not moving an inch. She hesitated as Jake asked, "Suppose you were to shoot me, Dr. Odell. Where would that get you? The sheriff would know then that it wasn't me that took Cody or killed the banker."

"Edgar Stevens deserved to die," Dr. Odell stated without emotion. "He wouldn't lend me the money I needed to take care of some little gambling debts. And yet he paid off Sammy Shirts to keep quiet about his activities the night of Cody's abduction. Stevens knew Sammy's accusations were groundless, but he just didn't want the public attention. So he paid him ten grand but turned me down. In fact, he sent that muscleman, Ken Treman, after me to collect on previous loans. Then, what topped it off was when Stevens was about to take Kyle's ranch. And that would mean Kyle couldn't raise the money for me. And then where would I have gotten the money I needed to pay off my debts?"

With all the motives now explained, Kara knew she had to stay alive so she could testify against the doctor. And so did Jake. Despite her intense fear that Dr. Odell would kill them both at any moment, Kara felt horrible for having misjudged Jake so badly.

"I didn't care for Stevens either," Jake indicated. "But I still say that if you kill me, the sheriff will know I didn't commit your crimes."

Again the doctor laughed. "That little problem is quite easily solved. I can make it look like the two of you did each other in. Makes perfect sense."

Kara's flashlight was still on the ground, pointed in front of where she and Jake were standing, but it lay between them and the doctor. In its light, just through the yard fence, Kara thought she saw two figures. She prayed they'd be the two she needed right now.

"Dr. Odell, drop your gun or I'll shoot!" Sheriff Hanks's voice rang out with authority.

Kara didn't even have time to feel relief before Dr. Odell spun and fired. A very loud boom followed the doctor's shot. Kara knew what that meant—she'd fired shotguns many times in training. That one shot ended the nightmare of the past eleven days.

Kara fell into Jake's arms. "I'm sorry," she mumbled. "I'm so sorry."

"It's okay," he responded. "I still love you, Kara. I've been praying for you almost nonstop all night."

Kara's fondness for Jake, which had died in an instant earlier that evening, found new life. Maybe in time she would be able to share with him her feelings, as he had with her. But before she let her feelings go any further, she knew she needed to learn a lot more about him.

"Kara, I do have a question," Jake said. "Why did you suddenly want me out of your house earlier tonight? I've been thinking about that, and I still don't get it."

"Your boots, Jake. One of them matches the print from the ditch at Roscoe's. And I still don't understand why."

"Wow!" Jake exclaimed. "The doctor really did have it in for me, didn't he? He gave me these boots the other evening when I went to his house to talk to him about Kyle. He said they were a little too tight for him, and he asked me to see how they fit. They fit perfectly, so he said to go ahead and take them."

"Okay, that settles that little matter. Now, why don't you answer a question for me," Kara said. "What were you doing out here in the dark tonight, and why are you limping so badly?" She had noticed his limp as soon as she'd seen him in the light.

"That's actually two questions," he chuckled. "But I'll answer them both. When I told Kyle I was going back to town, I didn't. Instead, I drove to the highway, turned off my lights, and circled back into a field to the south. My car's parked out of sight in a little grove of trees just a few hundred feet east of the house. I got the gun that I carry in my trunk and walked back here. I was sure that Buster—who I honestly believed was the kidnapper—would eventually call Kyle, but I decided that I wasn't going to let him get away with the money and cost Kyle the ranch, and probably his son's life as well. So I sort of had a plan in my head to wait just outside the kitchen and listen, and when the call came, I'd simply follow Kyle to where he went to meet Buster. Then I'd make sure everything went all right."

"Did you really think you could pull it off and that we couldn't?" Kara asked.

"No. You see, Kara, when I drove in to see you, it was my intention to ask you to get the sheriff and do it yourselves. I'd never felt like we were doing the right thing by shutting you and the sheriff out, but Kyle had insisted. At any rate, when you were so cold to me, I got the feeling that there was something I didn't know, and it made me very hesitant to ask for your help. I mean, you more or less kicked me out of your house, so I figured that I would have to do it myself.

"So anyway, I was right outside the kitchen when I heard Kyle tell the sheriff that he'd kept half the money back. I was ready to walk in then and let the sheriff know that I was ready to support him in whatever he thought was best, but it only took a second more of eavesdropping to realize that I was the prime suspect. That explained your coldness. I really couldn't blame you. But I didn't dare take the chance then. I knew that I hadn't taken the money or kidnapped

Cody, but it was clear that you and the sheriff thought otherwise. I also knew that if I came in right then, none of you would believe me. I was as surprised as Kyle when he opened the trunk and found the money missing. I was puzzled, and yet it never did occur to me to suspect the doctor. He'd seemed so concerned about Kyle all along."

"The doctor was a good actor. He was also a good makeup artist. None of us suspected him," Kara admitted.

"So I wasn't sure what I'd do until I listened to the sheriff lay out his plans to the rest of you in the yard after Kyle had discovered that the money was gone. When you were told to go and wait on the hill, I decided to do the same. Only I got there ahead of you and climbed a little higher."

"Why did you do that?" she questioned.

"So I could protect you, if you needed it, and so I could make sure the killer, whoever he was, didn't get away if he came back looking for the rest of the ransom," Jake explained.

"Okay, now I understand something else. It was you behind me on the hill when I started down."

"That's right. I was kind of loud, even though I didn't mean to be. But I didn't dare let you know it was me. I was afraid you'd try to arrest me, and the real kidnapper would get away."

"And I decided it must have been a deer or something, so I ignored it. Good thing, huh?" Kara remarked, then breathed a heavy sigh.

"I sure didn't walk like a deer. I stumbled over a stump and sprained my ankle," Jake revealed. "I can hardly walk. I don't know how I'll ever get the doctor's boot off my left foot. Because of my clumsiness, I was almost too late to help you, but I couldn't move any faster."

Kara stepped close and kissed Jake as the sheriff looked up from where he knelt beside Dr. Odell's body. "Thanks for coming when you did, Jake," she said quietly. "You saved my life."

"A life well worth saving," Jake responded with a grin.

* * *

Later that night Sheriff Hanks and Deputy Smith returned to the sheriff's office, where they waited for the arrival of Gil Enders, who was no longer afraid for his life now that Cody had been found alive and his abductor was dead.

Kara ran her fingers through her hair, scratched her cheek, and said, "Sheriff, I haven't been able to figure out one thing. Just before you shot Dr. Odell, when you ordered him to drop his gun, you called him by name. How did you know it wasn't Jake? The light from my flashlight on the ground certainly wasn't enough for identification."

"Good question, Kara. You know, for days something had been gnawing at my mind, always interrupting my thoughts, and then disappearing again just before I could grasp it. But after Kyle had taken Cody out of that cellar and Chief Worthlin and I went back down to take photos of the scene, I finally figured out what that little annoyance was. It was a clue, of course. Pop tabs, pull tabs—you know, from soda cans. There was a pile of them by the food wrappers in that cellar."

Seeing Kara's bewildered look, the sheriff continued. "For the past couple of years, Dr. Odell has been promoting a pop can collection program in the schools to raise money for the Ronald McDonald House. I heard him give a presentation on it once. Seems to be a popular thing across the country. The cans are collected, weighed, and recycled. Then the proceeds help operate the Ronald McDonald houses. They're the homes families live in during medical crises. Well, Dr. Odell was always carrying around those little tabs from the cans, jingling them in his pocket, pouring them from one hand to the other, dropping a few here and there."

Kara nodded.

"I saw some of those tabs when I first visited with Bridget Harrison at her home. I parked my vehicle exactly where she said Cody had parked his the night he disappeared. There were a few pull tabs in the street, not in a pile, of course, but scattered around."

"But I guess I can see how that wasn't enough of a clue to really be helpful," Kara stated thoughtfully.

"You're right. But then, Kara, remember when we visited the old Norman place and found the boot print? Well, I saw some more pull tabs there, not all together in a group, but scattered here and there. I just figured it was Roscoe's mysterious rabbit hunters having a few cans—maybe beer, maybe soda. I thought it was strange they'd take the time to remove the tabs from the cans, but other than that I didn't give it much thought."

Kara saw it all coming together now. "So, when you noticed the pile in that horrible place where Cody had been kept, the evidence all made sense."

Sheriff Hanks nodded. "Exactly. I realized that soda can tabs don't really come off as easy as they did a decade or more ago, and it just triggered my memories of the other tabs I'd seen. I just wish I could have put the pieces together sooner. We were lucky to find Cody alive," he added soberly.

* * *

Gil Enders arrived at the sheriff's office a short time later. Early in his statement it became apparent that he didn't know the true identity of the abductor, and the sheriff didn't bother to tell him at first. He wanted to learn what Gil did know, if anything.

"I was scared," Gil told the sheriff. "I didn't know who this guy was when I saw him get in Cody's car that night. I was really puzzled."

"Why didn't you come forward then?" the sheriff asked.

"You know why," Gil replied with a frown. "Cody stole my girl."

"I see," the sheriff replied, but he really didn't understand.

"I kept thinking that this guy would let Cody go. Then when I saw that guy, Jake Garrett, hanging around with Cody's dad, I knew it was him that had taken Cody. When I learned that he was a cousin of Cody's, I really got curious, but I didn't figure he'd hurt Cody. That just didn't make sense, where he was family and all. It was about that time that I began to notice Sammy Shirts acting strange, so I followed him one night. I had nothing better to do, since I couldn't sleep. When I saw this Jake guy haul Mr. Stevens right out of his house, I got scared. At that point I knew he obviously didn't have the interest of Cody's family in mind. So anyway, when you came in the store to talk to Harry, I decided it was time for me to split while I was still in one piece. I figured if the guy would take the banker the way he did, he'd also get me if he knew what I'd seen. It wasn't worth the gamble, so I ran. I tried to tell you what I knew, but I couldn't get you to meet me," Gil complained.

"I tried," the sheriff sighed. "But why were you so afraid? I would have protected you."

"How was I to believe that?" Gil wondered. "I could see how your own deputy was acting around this guy, and I was afraid Deputy Smith was involved in Cody's kidnapping. And if she wasn't involved, she certainly could let something slip that would get me in trouble with Cody's cousin. No sir, I wasn't taking any chances."

"So you believe it was Jake Garrett?" Kara asked.

"Of course. I saw him enough times."

"What was he driving that night, I mean, the night he took the banker from his house?" the sheriff queried.

"Some big black car. Might have been a Cadillac," Gil reported.

"Did you see what he was driving when he came to town at other times?" Kara asked.

"Oh, yeah, it was a pretty little Mustang."

"Did you see anyone else in the black car?" the sheriff pressed.

"Nope, just the two of them. Garrett had a gun, and the banker was doing as he was told."

"Did you hear them say anything?"

"Well, yeah. Garrett told Mr. Stevens that if he didn't cooperate, he'd do to him what he did to . . . Wait a minute. Yeah, I remember now. He said he'd do what he did to some other guy. Seemed like he called him 'the Tree Man' or something like that. It didn't make any sense to me, and I forgot about it until right now. Hey, did Garrett kill someone else?"

"He tried. The guy's name was Treman," the sheriff clarified. "Now, let me tell you what really has been happening the past few days."

Gil looked stunned when he heard the full story. "So the doctor dressed up to look like Jake?" he asked in amazement.

"That's right. They were the same height and build. And he also did a pretty decent impression of his voice."

"Have you given up on Bridget Harrison?" Kara asked with concern for the girl.

"I'm afraid so. She'd never have me now."

She would never have had you before, Kara thought. Just like Ellen—and later, Mariah Taylor—wouldn't have had Dr. Odell.

EPILOGUE

Cody Lind lingered on the porch, savoring the presence of the girl that a few months ago he had feared he would never see again. The porch light reflected from her eyes, and it made her white teeth sparkle.

She grinned up at him. "You'd better go. Your dad and . . ." She hesitated. "Your dad and your stepmom will be worrying if you're late."

Cody grinned back at her. "Do I get a goodnight kiss?"

Bridget Harrison stood on her toes and planted a warm, sweet kiss on his lips. Then she opened the door and stepped into the house, closing it softly behind her. Cody stood there for a moment before turning to leave.

A click brought him back. She had opened the door a crack.

"Are you still here?" Bridget asked playfully.

"Just leaving," Cody said sheepishly to the pretty face that peeked through the slightly open door.

Bridget smiled, revealing a dimple at each corner of her mouth. Then her smile faded. "You make sure no one is in your car before you get in," she warned. "You never know who might have hidden a car out by the lake and hitchhiked in just to get you."

Her mischievous grin teased him for a brief moment. Then the door closed and Cody started down the walk.

Before getting into his car, he checked just to be sure no one was hiding in the backseat.

ABOUT THE AUTHOR

Clair M. Poulson was born and raised in Duchesne, Utah, where he spent many years enforcing the law in Duchesne County as a highway patrolman and sheriff. He also served two years in the U.S. Army Military Police Corps. As a sheriff, he was a member of the national advisory board to the FBI. For the past sixteen years, Clair has served as a justice court judge in Duchesne County. Clair and his wife, Ruth, currently help their oldest son run Al's Foodtown in Duchesne. In addition, they raise Missouri Foxtrotting Horses on what they call the Blue Rock Ranch.

Clair has always been an avid reader, but his interest in creating fiction began many years ago as he told bedtime stories to his small children. They would beg him for just one more story before going to sleep. Today, his grandchildren still enjoy his storytelling.

Clair met his wife, Ruth, while they both attended Snow College in Ephraim, Utah. They have five children and thirteen grandchildren, with more on the way.